THE
CALLIGRAPHER

THE
CALLIGRAPHER

EDWARD DOCX

FOURTH ESTATE · *London*

First published in Great Britain in 2003 by
Fourth Estate Limited
A division of HarperCollins*Publishers*
77–85 Fulham Palace Road,
London W6 8JB
www.4thestate.com

10 9 8 7 6 5 4 3 2 1

A catalogue record for this book is available from the British Library

ISBN 1-84115-543-8

Typeset by Rowland Phototypesetting Ltd,
Bury St Edmunds, Suffolk
Printed in Great Britain by
Clays Ltd, St Ives plc

To Emma

Contents

'Oh, to vex me, contraries meet in one:
Inconstancy unnaturally hath begot
A constant habit;'
John Donne

'I am thinking of aurochs and angels, the secret of
durable pigments, prophetic sonnets, the refuge of art.'
Vladimir Nabokov

'He stretched out his arms to the crystalline, radiant sky.
"I know myself," he cried, "but that is all —"'
F. Scott Fitzgerald

Titivillus the Devil

I might as well confess up front that I am in league with the Devil. It's not a big deal – a stint of social nihilism here, a stretch of marital sabotage there – and I'm afraid it goes with the job. Seek for long enough and you will find that most human pursuits have a patron saint; but, of all the arts in the world, only calligraphy has a patron demon. His name is Titivillus. And he is a malicious little bastard.

Imagine a medieval monastery – somewhere in the high Pyrenees, say, with a great arched gate and tall white stone walls. In one corner of the cloistered courtyard there is a tower. Up the spiral staircase, nearer to the light and away from the damp, is usually to be found a large, round room. This is the *scriptorium*. And here, seated on stools, bent over their desks, arranged in a horseshoe around the senior supervisor, the *armarius*, are the monks.

In their right hands they have quills, and in their left they hold their knives. They work in silence and the only sound is their breathing and the continual rasp of their nibs across vellum. Despite their elevation, the light is dim and the older brothers are squinting. But there is no question of burning a fire or even a candle because the safety of the rare and sacred manuscripts is far more important than the monks' mere earthly comfort.

Every so often, one of the brothers will raise his hand to signal the *armarius* to bring him additional quills, another pot of ink or some more skins. The knife, a treasured possession, will be used to pin down the undulating page at the point of writing as well as to sharpen the pen (hence pen-knife); but now and then, and with a bite of his lip, a monk will also have to use it to scratch out a mistake.

These mistakes are what Titivillus lives for.

He is a short, low-ranking demon, with a pot belly and a puckered, petulant face. Most of the day, he skulks about the corners of the *scriptorium*, sometimes sitting on his swag bag, other times scratching at his pointed ears or picking his nose with his stubby fingers, but he is always watching, always alert. Best of all he likes those errata that neither monks nor proof-readers notice and that survive in the new manuscript unchecked, to be reproduced by the next generation of scribes; but slips of the pen so big that the calligrapher must start the entire page again are also welcome – because these set back the Work of God.

Every night, after it has become too dark for the monks to continue and they have left the *scriptorium* for vespers, Titivillus carefully collects all the mistakes into his sack and drags them down to Hell, there to present them to the Devil so that each sin can be registered in a book – against the name of the monk responsible – to be read out on Judgement Day.

These unsatisfactory (some would say unfair) arrangements continued for more or less a thousand years – until the Renaissance flared across Europe and the calligrapher's lot began to turn from bad to worse. By the beginning of the fourteenth century, the monks found themselves being forced to work at a furious pace, on and on into the darkness in order to meet the ferocious demand for manuscript copies from the newly founded universities. Before long, sick of the blind rush, the brothers were desperately looking for ways to evade responsibility for the burgeoning number of flaws in their work and so save their ever-more imperilled souls.

Now Titivillus saw his chance.

He offered the holy scribes an eternal bargain: personal absolution from their sins in return for a secret guarantee that the number of mistakes would continue to increase dramatically. As the errors were already out of control, the monks gladly agreed.

Thus Titivillus became the patron demon of calligraphers: he kept their sins hidden and he rescued them from Hell.

Human endeavour, however, was having one of its periodic sprints, and by 1476 William Caxton (who learnt his filthy disgusting ways in Cologne) had set up his printing press in Westminster. All too soon, it looked as though Titivillus's deal was worthless.

You might have thought that such a development was pretty much the end for the ugly little runt. You might have thought that one of Lucifer's slicker lieutenants would have called Titivillus in for a personal assessment meeting and explained how, regrettably, some personnel were no longer required. But the Devil never fires his staff; he simply demotes them, drops their wages and forces them to carry on in ever-worsening conditions.

And so believe me, the pot-bellied little son of a bitch is still alive and well in twenty-first-century London, a maestro of distraction, kicking around my attic flat, sulkily intent on fucking things up just for the hell of it, whenever opportunity presents. Unfortunately for him, I don't take on much biblical work. But what can he do? There aren't that many calligraphers around these days and he has to take whatever he can get. Nevertheless, an eternal pact cannot be undone: he remains the Devil's envoy and I remain confederate. Which suits me well. For should I make the occasional mistake, should I slip a little here and there, then absolution is surely only a formality.

Surely.

PART ONE

I. Confined Love

Some man unworthy to be possessor
Of old or new love, himself being false or weak,
    Thought his pain and shame would be lesser,
If on womankind he might his anger wreak,
        And thence a law did grow,
        One should but one man know;
        But are other creatures so?

    Are sun, moon, or stars by law forbidden,
To smile where they list, or lend away their light?
    Are birds divorced, or are they chidden
If they leave their mate, or lie abroad a-night?
        Beasts do no jointures lose
        Though they new lovers choose,
        But we are made worse than those.

    Who e'er rigged fair ship to lie in harbours,
And not to seek new lands, or not to deal withal?
    Or built fair houses, set trees, and arbours,
Only to lock up, or else let them fall?
        Good is not good, unless
        A thousand it possess,
        But doth waste with greediness.

Like so many people living through this great time in human
history, I am not at all sure what is right and what is wrong.
So if I appear a little slow to grasp the moral dimensions of
what follows, I'm afraid I will have to ask you to bear with
me. Apologies. It's a difficult age.

    Actually, I do not believe I was behaving all *that* badly

when these withering atrocities first began. (And if it would now be helpful for me to admit that mine was a crime of sorts, then I feel I must also be allowed to maintain that I did not deserve the punishment.) Rather, I seem to recall that I was trying to be as careful and as sensitive and as discreet as possible; it was William who was acting like a fool.

We had finally come to a halt in the middle of 'The Desire for Order'. Lucy and Nathalie were somewhere up ahead – progressing unabashed through the room designated 'Modern Life'. I had been hoping to slip away without detection. But matters were not proceeding to plan. For the last two minutes, William had been following me through the gallery with the air of a pantomime detective: two steps behind, stopping only a slapstick fraction after me, and then raking his eyes accusingly up and down my person as if I were responsible for the summary immolation of an entire *pension* of pensioners or some such outrage.

He spoke in a vociferous whisper: 'Jasper, what – in the name of arse – are you doing?'

'Ssshh.' The artificial lights hummed. 'I am attempting to enjoy my birthday.'

'Well, why do you keep running away from us?'

'I'm not.'

'Of course you are.' His voice was becoming progressively louder. 'You are deliberately refusing to enter "Modern Life" – over there.' He pointed. 'And you keep drifting back into "the Desire for Order" – in here.' He pointed again, but this time at his feet and with a flourish. 'Don't think I haven't been watching you.'

'For Christ's sake William, if you must know –'

'I must.'

'I am trying to get off this floor altogether and back

upstairs into "Nude Action Body" without anybody noticing. So it would be very helpful if you would stop drawing attention to us and go and catch up with the girls. Why, exactly, are you following me?'

'Because you've got the booze and I think you should open it. Immediately.' He paused to draw a stiffening breath. 'And because you always look oddly attractive when you are up to something.'

'I'm not *up* to anything and I haven't got the wine: I stowed it inside Lucy's bag, which is now safely inside a cloakroom locker.' I feigned interest in the mangled wire that we were facing.

'You didn't. My God. Well, we must mount a rescue. We must spring the noble prisoner from its vile cell straightaway! The Americans put their cream sodas in those lockers – I've seen them do it – and their . . . their *bum bags*. And God only knows what's in Lucy's bag: women's products probably. And cheap Hungarian biros. You realize –'

'Will you please keep your voice *down*?' I frowned. An elderly couple wearing 'I love Houston' T-shirts seemed to be choking to death on the far side of the installation. 'Anyway, Lucy uses an ink pen.'

But William was undeterred. 'You realize that you may have ruined that great Burgundy's life. One of the most elegant vintages of the last millennium traumatized beyond recovery within minutes of your having taken possession. It's barbarous. I am holding you personally resp—'

'William, for fuck's sake. If you must talk so bloody loudly, then can you at least try to sound more like a human being from the present century? And less like a fucking ponce.' I cleared my throat. 'Besides, you're not allowed to wander around Tate Modern swigging booze. It's against the rules.'

'Balls. What rules? That's a 1990 Chambertin Clos de Bèze you've got locked up in there like a . . . like a common Chianti. Bought by me – especially for you, my dear Jasper, on this, the occasion of your twenty-ninth birthday. How could they stop us drinking it? They wouldn't dare.'

I mimicked his ridiculous manner: 'As well you know, my dear William, that bottle needs opening for at least two hours before we could even go near it. It's my wine now and I forbid you to molest it before it's had a chance to develop. Look at you, you're slathering like a paedophile.'

'Well, I think you're being very unfair. You drag your friends out to look at all this – all this bric-à-brac and mutilated genitalia and then you deny us essential refreshment. Of course I am desperate. Of course I need a drink. This isn't art, this is *wreckage*.'

I took a few steps away from him and turned to face a large canvas covered in heavy ridges of dun brown paint. William followed and did the same, tilting his head to one side in a parody of viewers of modern art the world over.

'Actually,' he said, a little less audibly, 'I was meaning the small bottle of speciality vodka that Nathalie bought you. I thought you might have stashed it in your coat or something. I only need a painkiller to get me through the next room.' Mock grievance now yielded to genuine curiosity: 'Anyway, you haven't answered my question.'

'That's because you are a complete penis, William.'

'Why are you in such a hurry to leave us? What's so special about "Nude Action Body"?' He looked sideways at me but I kept my attention on the painting. 'Is it that girl you were staring at?'

'No.'

'Yes, it is. It's that girl from upstairs.'

'No, it isn't.'

'The one you were pretending not to follow before we came down here.' He paused. 'I knew it. I knew it.'

'OK. Yes. It is.'

He gave a theatrical sigh. 'I thought you were supposed to be stopping all that. What was it you said?' He composed his face as if to deliver Hamlet's saddest soliloquy. ' "I can't go on like this, Will, I am going mad. Oh Will, save me from the quagmire of womankind. No more of this relentless sex. Oh handsome Will, I have to stop. I must stop. I will be true." '

I ignored him. 'William, I need you to buy me some time and stop fucking around. Lucy and Nathalie will be back in here looking for us any second. Go and distract them. Be nice. Be selfless. Help me.'

He ignored me. 'OK, maybe not the "handsome Will" bit – but those were more or less your words. And now look at you: you're right back to where you were a year ago. You can't leave your flat without trying to sleep with half of London. And never a moment's cease to consider what the fuck you are doing or – heaven forbid – *why*.'

I walked towards the exit on the far side of the room and considered a collection of icons made to evoke the Russian Orthodox style. The figures were blurred and distorted and appeared to recede into their frames, so that it was impossible to tell whether they were indeed hallowed saints or grotesque contorted animals or merely half-smudged lines signifying nothing.

'Look, Will, I need fifteen minutes. Will you keep an eye on the others for me – please? Don't let them leave this floor. If they look like they're moving, set off the fire alarm or something. I don't want to fuck up and have to concoct some stupid bullshit. Not tonight. It would be awful. Lucy gets so uptight. I just want everyone to have as relaxed and pleasant a dinner as possible this evening.'

'The fire alarm?'

'Yes, it stops the escalators working.'

He shook his head, but there was amusement in his eyes.

'I'm sorry, Will. But I swear to you: that girl winked at me and she is far too pretty for me to ignore. Admit it, she is. What am I supposed to do? I can't just let it go. Come *on*. Millions of men would pay to be winked at by girls like her. I have a responsibility to act. Fifteen minutes max.'

He smiled. 'Well, go on then: get on with it. But if the authorities arrest me for false alarms I shall instantly confess that you made me do it. I shall explain that you are dangerously persuasive and the worst sort of unscrupulous libertine –'

'I'm exceptionally scrupulous.'

'And I shall tell them that you are incapable of behaving in a decent manner towards friends – *or even your own girlfriend* – and that you deserve to be taught a serious lesson. See you in fifteen.'

'Thank you, William.'

'And don't forget to check for sisters.'

Now, I don't want to start blaming Cécile for the first wave of demoralizing set-backs that followed hard on the heels of this, the otherwise inauspicious evening of my twenty-ninth birthday, but as far as immediate causes of disaster go, then she has to shoulder full responsibility: *J'accuse Cécile, la fille française*. Had she not winked at me, I probably wouldn't have risked it. But what could be the purpose of such fetching Mediterranean looks as hers, if not to fetch?

All the same, the fire alarm surprised everybody.

Chaos followed fast, rushing through 'Nude Action Body'

like a messenger from the Front with news of approaching armies. From hidden antechambers and doors marked 'private' dozens of orange-clad ushers emerged and began urgently to usher; the lifts stopped; small blue lights flashed from odd places high on the walls; and (as if all this were not encouragement enough) an unnervingly measured female voice interrupted the revels every thirty seconds to spell the situation out in an exciting variety of languages. 'This is a routine emergency. Please leave the building by the nearest fire exit and follow the advice of the officials. Thank you.'

I had only just returned to the fifth floor and had taken no more than three steps into the gallery proper. But now I doubled back and stood to one side by the wide emergency exit doors at the top of the escalators, waiting for Cécile. Along with everyone else, she was sure to leave this way. There was no longer any need to seek her. And I was rather enjoying all the panic.

Parents issued taut-voiced instructions to their charges. Scandinavians strode calmly towards the emergency stairs. Italian men put their arms around Italian women. A litter of art-college day-outers roused themselves reluctantly from their beanbags. Two children came careering out of 'Staging Discord' opposite. And an American woman began to scream 'oh my God, oh my God'.

Given that Irony and Futility still seemed to be filling in for God and Beauty on the art circuit – the thought occurred to me that had I been filming the whole thing, I could perhaps have submitted the results for exhibition myself; perhaps a showing in 'History Memory Society': 'People from All Over the World Leaving in Uncertainty' (Jasper Jackson, calligrapher *and* video artist).

Of course I didn't actually know that Cécile's name was

Cécile as I fell into place three or four people behind her. (Jostle, jockey, joke and jostle all the way down six flights of unapologetically functional fire stairs.) I didn't know anything about her at all, except that she had short, choppy, boyish, black hair, a cute denim skirt cut above the knee, thin brown bare legs and unseasonable flip-flops, which flapped on every step as she went. And that she had (quite definitely) winked at me as we circled Rodin's *Kiss*.

Outside, safely asquare the paving slabs of the South Bank, I looked hastily around. The light was thickening. St Paul's across the Thames – a fat bishop boxed in and stranded flat on his back – and two bloated seagulls, making heavy weather of the homeward journey upstream. Crowds continued to eddy from the building but there was as yet no sign of William or Nathalie or Lucy's adorable light-brown bob. Still, I had to act quickly.

Cécile was standing with her back to me, looking across the river.

'Hi,' I said.

She turned and then smiled, an elbow jutting out over the railings. 'Oh, hello.'

'That was quite exciting.' I returned her smile.

'You think there is a fire?'

I looked doubtful. 'Probably terrorists or art protestors or rogue vegetarians.'

'I wonder what they save from the flames?' She bent an idle knee in my direction and swivelled her toe on the sole of her flip-flops. 'The paintings or the *objets*?'

'Good question.'

'Maybe in an emergency they have an order for what to keep – and they begin at the top and then descend until everything is burning too much.'

'Or maybe,' I said, 'they just let the bastard go until it's finished so that they can open up afterwards as a new sort of gallery: Burnt Modern. A new kind of art.'

'Perhaps that's what the protesters want – a new kind of art.' She was a born flirt.

I met her eye and moved us on. 'They evacuated the building very quickly.'

'Yes. But there are some people still coming out, I think.' She gestured. 'I like how in an emergency everybody starts to talk. As if because there is a disaster, now we can all be friends happy together.' She looked past me for a second. 'Will they let us back in, do you think?'

'I'm not sure. But I am supposed to be going to a restaurant at eight so I don't think I will be able to wait. This might take a couple of hours.' I paused. 'I should find my friends and see if they are OK.'

'Me too. I have already lost them once today – when we were on the London Eye.'

'How long are you in London for?'

'I live here.' She frowned slightly – amused disparagement.

I pretended to be embarrassed.

She relented. 'I am teaching here.'

'French?'

'Yes.' A pout masquerading as a smile.

'You have an e-mail address?'

'Yes.'

'If I write to you, do you think that you'll reply?'

'Maybe. It depends what you say.'

I found William sitting on a bench with a diesel-coated pigeon and the man who had earlier been selling the *Big Issue* outside the main entrance.

'Jasper – Ryan. Ryan – Jasper. We haven't thought of a name for this little chap yet.' He indicated the creature now pecking at a chocolate wrapper.

'Where's Lucy?' I asked, acknowledging Ryan.

'She's fetching her bag with Nat. Did you meet anyone nice' William winked exaggeratedly '– in the toilets?'

'Yes, thanks.'

William did an American accent: 'I hope you were real gentle with him.'

Ryan snorted and got up. 'See you Thursday, Will mate,' he said, 'and let's hope this new bloke knows how to deal with those fucking tambourine bastards.'

'See you later.' William raised an arm as Ryan left.

I sat down and was about to speak but William motioned me to be quiet.

'Here they come,' he said, 'they've seen us.'

Lucy and Nathalie were making their way towards the bench. William addressed the pigeon: 'You'll have to piss off now, old chap, but we'll catch up again soon, I hope. Let me know how the diet works out.'

Before we go much further, I should explain that William is one of my firmest friends from the freezing Fenland days of my tertiary education. (Philosophy, I'm afraid, man's most defiant folly.) I can still remember the pale afternoon, a week or so after we had all arrived for our first year, when we were walking back from a betting shop together and he came out to me. It was going to be very awkward, he confided, and he was at a bit of a dead end with the whole idea because – apart from his sister, who didn't count – he hadn't really met any women before now, but – how could he put this? – he was rather worried that he might *not* be homosexual and – as I seemed to be rather, well, in the know on the subject, as it were – had I any suggestions as to next steps *vis-à-vis* the ladies?

Unfortunately, several centuries in the highest ranks of government, church and army had left the men in his family quite unable to imagine women, let alone talk to them. Indeed, William suspected that he was the first male child in sixteen generations not to turn out gay. As I could imagine, this was a severe blow both to him and his lineage but he had tried it with other boys at school on several occasions and there was absolutely nothing doing. The truth of the matter was that he liked girls; and that was that. And as he was now nearing twenty, he rather felt that he should be getting on with it. Could I offer any pointers?

Naturally, things have moved on a good deal since then and these days Will is regularly trumpeted by various tedious publications as one of the most eligible men in London. He is an invaluable ally and well known on the doors of all good venues – early evening, private and exclusive as well as late night, public and squalid. I regret to say, however, that his approach remains erratic and hopelessly undisciplined. Though many women find him attractive, the execution of his actual seductions is not always the most appropriate. It is as if a strain of latent homosexuality bedevils his genes – like an over-attentive waiter at a business lunch.

All else aside, William is the most effortlessly charming man that anybody who meets him has ever met. He is also genuinely kind. And though he claims to feel terribly let down by the astonishing triviality of modern life, this is merely an intellectual arras behind which he chooses to conceal a rare species of idealism. He does not believe in God or mankind but he visits churches whenever he is abroad and runs a music charity for tramps.

On the subject of William's relationship with Nathalie . . .

Back in March, he claimed that it was purely platonic and I have to say that I think he was telling the truth. Under light questioning, he explained that it was only in this way that he could maintain the exclusivity of their intimacy since – of the few women who shared his bed from time to time – Nathalie was the only one with whom he was not having sex. They were therefore bound together by uncompromised affection and happily unable to cheat on one another. (She, too, I understood, was at complete liberty.) This approach, he confided, was an ingenious variation on the arrangement his forefathers had shared with their various wives since they had first come to prominence (under Edward II); dynastic obligations aside, they had kept sex resolutely outside of marriage, thereby removing all serious woes, threats and resentment from their lives.

A little before midnight, the birthday evening's rightful *enchaînement* having been long re-established, Lucy and I were alone at last, intimately ensconced at the corner of the largest table in La Belle Epoque, my favourite French restaurant. We were considering the last of our dessert with a certain languid desire, and feeling about as happy as two young lovers can reasonably expect to feel in a London so beleaguered by medieval licensing laws. A little drunk perhaps, a little reckless with the cross-table kissing, a little *laissez-faire* with the last of the Latour; but undeniably at ease with one another and, well, *having a good time*. The bill was paid and my friends had all left – William and Nathalie among the last to go, along with Don, another university friend, over from New York with his wife, Cal, and Pete, Don's fashion-photographer brother, who had arrived with a beautiful Senegalese woman called Angel.

If pressed, the casual observer would probably have

informed you that he was watching a boyfriend and girlfriend quietly canoodling while they awaited a final pair of espressos. If he was any good at description, this observer might have gone on to say that the woman was around twenty-eight, five-foot six or seven, slim, with dead straight, bobbed, light-brown hair, which – he might have further noticed – she had a habit of hooking behind her ears. Had he dashed over and stolen my chair while I visited the gents', he would also have been able to tell you that her face was very slightly freckled, principally across the bridge of her nose, that she had thin lips (but a nice smile), that her eyes were a beseeching shade of green and that she liked to sit straight in her chair, cross her legs and loosen her right shoe so she could balance it, swinging a little, on her extended big toe. He might have rounded the whole thing off with some remarks about how – even now – England can still turn out these roses every once in a while. But at this stage we would surely have to dispute his claims to being casual and tell him to fuck off.

It is more or less true to say that back then, Lucy and I were more or less a year into it – our relationship, that is. I'm not sure why – these things happen . . .

Actually, I *am* sure why: because I liked Lucy very much. That is to say, I still like Lucy very much. Which is to say I have *always* liked Lucy very much. Lucy is the sort of woman who makes the human race worth the running. She's not stupid or simpering, and she only laughs when something is funny. She's intelligent and she knows her history. Yes, she can be cautious, but she's quick-witted (a lawyer by profession) and she will smile when she sees she has won a point. Then she'll pass on because she's as sensitive to other people's embarrassment as quicksilver to the temperature of a room. She keeps lists of things to do. She remembers what people have said, but doesn't hold it against them. She seldom talks about her family. And she has no time for magazines or horoscopes. If you were sitting with us in some newly opened London eatery, privately wishing you had an ashtray for your cigarette, you might well find that she had discreetly nudged one to a place just by your elbow. Which is how we met.

Even so, it is with regret that I must add that Lucy is a nutcase. But I didn't know that then. That all came later.

'Close your eyes,' she said, putting her finger to my lips for good measure.

I did as I was told and lowered my voice. 'You haven't organized a –'

'Too late. It's tough. I've got you a big cake with candles and all the waiters are going to join in with "Happy Birthday to You", so you'll just have to sit still and act appreciative.'

I heard the rustle of a bag and the stocky chink of espresso cups.

'OK, open your eyes.'

A young waiter with a napkin over his shoulder hovered nearby – curious. A neatly wrapped present lay on the table.

Lucy smiled, infectiously. 'Go ahead: guess.'

I leant across and kissed her.

'Guess.'

'Earrings?'

'You wish.'

'A gold locket with a picture of Princess Diana?'

'Oh, go on, for God's sake . . . open it.'

I undid her neat wrapping and unclasped the dark velvet case: a gentleman's watch with a leather strap, three hands and Roman numerals. I held it carefully in my palm.

'So now you have no excuses.' Her eyes were full of delight. 'You can never be late again.'

I felt that tug of gladness that you get when someone you care about is happy. 'I won't be late again, I promise,' I said.

'Not ever?'

'Not for as long as the watch keeps time.'

'It has a twenty-five-year guarantee.'

'Well, that's at least twenty-five years of me being on time then.'

On the face of it 'Confined Love' is one of John Donne's more transparent poems: a man railing against the confinement of fidelity. Neither birds nor beasts are faithful, says his narrator, nor do they risk reprimand or sanctions when they lie abroad. Sun, moon and stars cast their light where they like, ships are not rigged to lie in harbours, nor houses built to be locked up . . . The metaphors are soon backed up nose to tail, honking their horns, like off-road vehicles in a downtown jam.

On the face of it, Donne, the young man about town, Master of the Revels at Lincoln's Inn, seems to be striding robustly through his lines, booting the sanctimonious aside with a ribald rhythm and easy rhyme, on his way to wherever the next assignation happens to be. But actually, that's not the point of the poem. That's not what 'Confined Love' is about at all.

2. The Prohibition

Take heed of loving me,
At least remember, I forbade it thee;

Some introductions. My name, as you may have gathered, is Jasper Jackson. I am twenty-nine years old. And I am a calligrapher.

My birthday, 9th March, falls exactly midway between Valentine's Day and April Fool's – except when there's a leap year, when it comes closer to the latter.

What else? I am an orphan. I have no recollection of the day itself but it would appear that my father, the young and dashing George Jackson, wrapped both himself and my mother, Elizabeth, around a Devon tree while trying to defeat his friends in their start-of-the-holiday motor race from Paddington to Penzance. My mother did not die straightaway but I was never taken to visit her in hospital.

From the age of four onwards (and very luckily for me), my upbringing and education was placed in the hands of Grace Jackson, my father's mother, at whose Oxford home I was staying when news of the accident arrived. In a way, therefore, my entire life can be viewed as one long, extended holiday at my grandmother's. And I am pleased to report that I can recall nothing but happiness from my

early years. Even the reprimands I remember only with
affection.

It is a hot summer afternoon. The whole town is wearing
shorts or less. My grandmother and I stand contentedly in
the grocer's queue. We are buying black cherries – a special
treat – as a prelude to our usual Saturday afternoon tea.
(Grandmother has a fondness for scones on Saturdays.) I am
holding the fruit in a brown paper bag, waiting to hand them
up to be weighed. My movements go unnoticed because I
am living at waist height (oh, happy days). I glance around.
I see a red-haired girl about my age passing by the vegetable
stands outside. One hand is holding her mother's and the
other is clutching the sticky stick of an orange iced-lollipop,
which is cocked at a dangerous angle and visibly melting as
she half-skips along.

I move without thinking. Still carrying the cherries, in a
second I am out of the shop and on to the street. I turn one
corner, then another. For the first time in my life – with
exaggerated care – I cross a main road alone. There is a cry
behind me – my grandmother. Then comes a shout – a man
from the shop running along the pavement after me. The
girl turns, wrist pivoting on her mother's arm; the ice slides
clean off and drops to the pavement. My sweetheart registers
the disaster for a long moment, then her grey eyes come
slowly up and look directly into mine. I too am visibly melting. I am five or maybe six.

But scolding was never my grandmother's strong suit.
Rather, she believed in punishment by improvement. (Perhaps this was because we had, between us, lost too many
relatives to waste time being cross with each other: my grandfather had died suddenly, while in Cairo on business just
after the Suez crisis.) So once we had returned the cherries,

there were a few serious words – 'Jasper, you cannot go anywhere by yourself until you are twelve, do you understand?' – and then it was off to the library with me for a miserable afternoon indoors. Which was a blow because I had been planning to play on my bike with Douglas Wilson from down the road.

I say miserable, but actually the library in question was beautiful, the most beautiful in Britain. Although, due to the war, Grandmother never finished her post-graduate work (something to do with medieval French), Somerville College felt that she was far too clever a scholar to lose. And when she returned from Egypt with my father still a boy and a pitiful widow's pension, they quickly made her deputy librarian. By the time I arrived on the scene, two decades later, she had become an authority on late medieval manuscripts at the glorious Bodleian, a building in which, I maintain, it is impossible to be anything but enthralled – even when, ostensibly, one is being punished.

Between the ages of four and twelve years, I must have spent more time in the Bodleian than most academics manage in their entire lives. Often during the school holidays (although rarely on Saturdays) my grandmother would sit me down at the table near the reference section that was reserved for members of staff, and bring me a book to read. 'It didn't seem to do your father any good in the long run, Jasper,' she once said, 'but at least he *knew* a few things before he died, which is all we can any of us really hope for.'

Evidently, my grandmother was following exactly the same method of combining childcare with a career that she had when bringing up my father; and, like him, I think I became something of a mascot among the librarians, many of whom used to mind me on odd days when Grandmother had to go and give a lecture somewhere or there was a serious section count going on. Indeed, over the years, just about anybody who was anyone at the university came to know me. People would stop by to say hello on their way in or out, and ask me what I was reading, and sometimes (as in the case of Professor Williams, Grandmother's friend) take me down to the canteen for lunch, and even bring me presents (which, at Christmas, I used to have to hide to avoid giving the impression that I was getting too many).

If, however, I was in need of 'improving', as was the case on the afternoon of the cherries, my grandmother would sit me down and, instead of giving me a book, place a large illuminated manuscript before me. She would then provide me with a range of sharpened pencils and some stiff paper and instruct me to copy out an entire page – 'as exactly as you can, please, Jasper, I want your letters to look just like those. No noise. No trouble. Come and find me when you have finished.'

Secretly, I loved the task, but I had to pretend otherwise in case Grandmother realized and changed my punishment to something awful like washing cars, which is what Douglas had to do when he was in trouble.

The fateful cherry-day page was in Latin of course, but I remember asking one of the Saturday assistants what it was about and he told me it was a prayer written in 1206 by a monk, who was hiding in the Sierra Norte above old Seville, asking God to deliver him from the women in his dreams.

My grandmother and I decided we should stay in Oxford until I was twelve. Then we moved to Avignon, where she had been offered a job cataloguing some of the exquisite work left behind by the scribes who lived there during the hundred years of papal occupation until 1409. I attended a *lycée* while she worked in the Livree Ceccano, the municipal library, which was housed in what had originally been one of the many sumptuous palaces built by the cardinals who came to take up expedient residence near their pontiff.

In two years her task was complete and our next destination was the German university town of Heidelberg, where she led a restoration programme, which brought some of the earliest Reformation documents back to light.

'Finally the boss, eh, Jasper – at sixty-three,' she said. 'Who says that women are held back in this clever old world of ours? And all because I bothered to learn German in the war.'

I never noticed how much money my grandmother had, which suggests she had enough, but we were by no means well off – a librarian's salary is thin, even at the best of times. Nor is restoration exactly lucrative. I seem to remember that we spent a lot of time waiting for buses and persuading one another that second-hand clothes lent a person an air of bohemian charm unavailable to those lesser folk whose imaginations could not travel beyond the high street.

In Heidelberg, as in Avignon, our flat was small, designed for one not two. However, because the old universities always own the best property, the building we shared was both characterful and well situated. We lived at the top of an old house on Plock, an oddly named medieval street, that ran parallel to the Hauptstrasse and was overlooked by the castle. I should also mention that on the ground floor was the finest delicatessen in Germany – run by my two friends, Hans and Elke. They are still there now although Hans has grown a moustache to celebrate his fiftieth birthday and Elke is refusing to allow him into the shop until he relents. My first real job – Saturdays and late-night Wednesday – was behind their counter.

As a hollow-cheeked, fourteen-year-old English boy, now

with a French accent and ever darker hair, I devoted the
next four years, with increasing success, to the twin joys of
reading and the pursuit of my pretty Rhineland classmates.

At school, I was never popular with the other boys in
the usual kinds of ways: I was not a natural team captain,
I did not draw an appreciative gang around me at the back
of the class, and I never got around to beating the shit out
of anyone. In fact, from about thirteen onwards, as far as
I was concerned, male company was a complete waste of
time. What can one boy teach another? Very little. Conkers
perhaps.

No. The only thing that ever got me thinking, got me
wondering, got my heart kicking with the sheer excitement
of life, was the girls.

The girls were everything – their opinion, their glances,
their moods; the way they walked or changed their hair;
what they said, did, wanted to become; where they lived,
how they had their bedrooms; which film stars they liked
and why; who they read, who they imagined themselves
with at night, which clothes they preferred at weekends;
what they liked boys to say, why, and how often; what they
wanted to buy; what they disliked about their brothers,
fathers, uncles, each other; what amused them, what sickened them; how they put their socks on, how they took them
off; when and how often they shaved their legs; what they
thought about school, tangerines, Goethe, their mothers,
holding hands, history, rivers, Portugal, and kissing strangers
– all of it *mattered*. I had to know. To my mind, the girls were
the point of being alive.

Two days after we arrived in Germany, I discovered
that it was possible to walk along the narrow wooden balcony outside my bedroom window, climb over the end and
swing across without too much peril on to the fire escape.

Persuading my female classmates to accompany me up those skeletal steps at night was, I think, the first serious labour set for me by that merciless taskmaster whom Donne refers to as the 'devil Love'. But I was always a good student and I studied hard.

I learned, for example, that a young lady who has just emerged, blinking, back into the forbidding glare of the real world from, say, a cinema would adamantly refuse to scale a precipitous iron stairway merely to clamber into the bedroom of an over-eager adolescent male.

'Why not?' I asked.

'Too dangerous,' claimed Agnes, an even-tempered girl with dark corkscrew hair, who sat as close to me as possible in chemistry lessons.

'No, it isn't.'

'Yes, it is.'

'I do it all the time.'

'Really?'

'No. I mean I climb up there *by myself* all the time.'

'I was joking. I know what you meant.' She smiled.

'Oh.' I clicked my tongue. 'Anyway, why not, Agnes?'

'My clothes would get covered in rust.' She ran her finger along the handrail as if to prove her point.

'Not if you took them off.'

'Jasper!'

I grinned. 'Why not then?'

'We might get found out. What if I got stuck?'

'You won't. It's dead easy – I'll help.' I made as if to start up the first step. 'Who's going to find out?'

'Your grandmother for one –'

'She's gone to bed early. Professor Williams is coming tomorrow. And her room is on the other side. Anyway she doesn't mind.'

I stood, stalled on the lowest rung. Agnes looked suspicious again: 'How do you know she doesn't mind?'

'She told me.'

Frank disbelief. 'She told you?'

'Yes.'

'When?'

'Once. Anyway, Agnes, why not – just for a bit?'

She said nothing for a moment – vacillating perhaps – then she shook her head. 'Because I have to be home by midnight or Dad comes out looking for me.' She made a pretend-serious face: 'We're Catholics.'

'What has that got to do with anything?'

'Plus he knows I am with you so he'll probably set off at quarter to.'

'And what's *that* supposed to mean?'

'He thinks that girls are in danger the minute it turns midnight.' She widened her eyes histrionically.

I took the step back down. 'OK then – it's only eleven-thirty, so I could rush you home now, get myself in his good books and bank an extra half an hour so that we can stay out until twelve-thirty next time. That way if you do suddenly turn sex-mad next Friday, you'll have someone to talk to about it.'

'Who says I am free next Friday?'

Sure enough, the next Friday but one I learnt another lesson: that the most efficient way from the cinema to my bedroom was not necessarily the most direct. Take lovely Agnes first on a walk up the crooked steps to the old *Schloss*, and wander there among the battlements; look down upon the river, see how the moonlight casts the water in silver as if it were a necklace running through the town (I was only fourteen); imagine how the sons of the city merchants would leave their beds and scale the ramparts to meet secretly with the daughters of the court – and then bring her back into town, and presto, what was previously a grotty and precarious fire escape has miraculously become *un escalier d'amour*. Seduction, I realized, was all about setting an appropriate scene – a scene into which the subject can willingly walk and there abandon her former censorious sense of self to take on a new and flattering identity. As we all know, it becomes more complicated when everyone grows up but even the most recalcitrant old hag once dreamed herself a Juliet.

Nowadays Agnes teaches chemistry in Baden Baden and has two children. She writes me the occasional letter – and I write back; but we dare not meet up in case something *happens*. Catholics.

After Heidelberg, it was back home to England – to the icy Fens, there to wow all comers with my deft grasp of the German philosophers. This was not, in any sense, fun, but if I thought my chosen subject unyielding, it was as nothing compared to the arduousness of attempting to sleep with the women. Try as I may, I can scarcely exaggerate the skill and endurance that a young man is required to develop if he wishes to navigate the freezing sea of female sexuality that surrounds a Cambridge education.

Imagine the most socially awkward, sexually confused and neurotic people in the whole world and put them all in the same place for three uneasy years: that's Cambridge University. And don't let anyone tell you different. *Talk* about sex by all means – talk about it till you're blue in the balls – but you're sick if you even think about doing it. Worse than sick: you're dangerous.

Nonetheless, I had my successes amid the crunching icebergs and the raging Arctic winds and fared better than most of my fellows, many of whom were lost for ever – buried like Captain Scott beneath the tundra or fallen, snow-blind and lust-numbed, into the ice-tombs of the Nuptial Crevasse. Having overcome such hazardous and bitter conditions, I arrived in London full of triumph and resource.

Then I really started work.

In fact, during the next seven years, I think I must have had some sort of a physical relationship with pretty much *all* the women in the city: young, old, dark, fair, married or lesbian; Asian, African, American, European, even Belgian; tall, short, thin or hefty; women so clever that they couldn't stand the claustrophobia of their own consciousness; women so thick that each new sentence was a triumph of heart-breaking effort; fast and loose, slow and tight; sexual athletes, potato sacks; witches, angels, succubae and nymphs; women who could bore you to sleep even as you entered the bedroom; women who could keep you up all night disturbing the deepest pools of your psyche; aunts, daughters, mothers and nieces; crumpets, strumpets, chicks and tarts; damsels, dames, babes and dolls; all that I desired and quite a few I didn't. And then, when I was well and truly satisfied that there was nothing more to want, I did it all again.

It was a difficult time for everyone.

There were nights I could not go out for fear of fury or beatings, or grim-faced boyfriends bent on brutal reprisals; and yet neither could I stay in for fear of a deranged and raging flatmate. (I know, I know, but it was *his* girlfriend who started it). Once, things got so bad that I had to spend a couple of nights at one of William's tramp hostels. But then I fucked the cook. (Largely because I caught sight of her using fresh coriander in the soup. It was pure lust, but sixteen stone, for Christ's sake, and forty fucking three.)

When I met Lucy, she was my way out. My best hope.

But I am getting distracted. I should explain how I became a professional calligrapher.

After I arrived in London, I did quite a few jobs, all of them monumentally senseless and too depressing to go into here. From what I could discover, the corporate arena of employment is best compared to a stinking circus, full of grovelling clowns, fawning jugglers and boot-licking buskers, all running around in circles as they frantically try to outdo one another in feats of sycophancy and obsequiousness and irrelevance. There is no ring-master and not a single thing is ever accomplished to the wider benefit of mankind.

No wonder then, that on my twenty-sixth birthday, worn out and wretched, having resigned from yet another job, I journeyed to Rome to visit my grandmother, who had finally 'retired', taking a surprisingly lucrative consultancy role at the Vatican.

Professional calligraphy was her idea.

'The truth of the matter, Jasper, is that *all* calligraphers are to some extent in league with the Devil,' Grandmother explained, carefully slicing through a truly delicious *vitello tonnato* at Il Vicolo, our favourite trattoria, on the Via del Moro, in the heart of beautiful Trastevere. 'You might want to bear that in mind before you decide to pursue it. All other arts in the world have their patron saint, only calligraphy has a patron demon.'

'Serious?'

'Yes. Look it up: St Dunstan for musicians, St Luke for artists, St Boniface for tailors – I even found a patron saint for arms dealers once – St Adrian of Nicomedia. Don't underestimate the capacity of the Roman Church for intervention. But you'll never come across the patron saint of calligraphers: they have thrown their lot in with the opposition. It's well known.'

'Not that well known.'

'Among people who read, it is well known.'

'Who read Latin manuscripts from the Middle Ages.'

'Among people who *read*.' She looked at me directly for a moment – her eyes blue and always watery; then her face cracked into the familiar lines of her smile. 'The patron devil's name is Titivillus. He crops up all over from about 1285 onwards, especially in the margin doodles. I've mentioned him to you before, I'm sure I have.'

A typical grandmother trap. If I agreed that she had indeed mentioned him, then why had I forgotten? If I shook my head and claimed that she had not, then she would probably be able to cite time and place.

'Yes, actually, now you bring it up, I do remember something you told me about the little calligraphy devil – or was it Professor Williams who explained him to me? How *is* Professor Williams, by the way?'

'He's very well, thank you.' She took a sip of her Dolcetto and tried to frown, 'Anyway, if you are going to make a living out of calligraphy, then you'll have to make a deal with the Devil.'

I shrugged. A *motorino* buzzed by – the girl on the back still fiddling with her helmet strap as her tanned knees joggled slightly with the cobbles.

Grandmother finished what was left on her plate and arranged her cutlery neatly before carefully brushing some breadcrumbs into her palm. 'Don't worry, there are lots of advantages. Guaranteed absolution from sin for one. I imagine that could come in quite handy.'

I returned to the last of my rigatoni.

She picked up her glass and settled in her chair. 'Seriously, Jasper, the main problem is that although you are very good, you have no experience of commercial art – of the art of art-for-money business. And you don't know anything about the more technical side of things, like how to prepare vellum or which pigments to use for which col—'

'How much do you get for a commission?'

'Hang on a second. Slow down.' Grandmother scowled. 'Commissions do not just fall out of the bloody sky.'

'Of course not, I mean –'

'First, I think, you'll have to go on the course at Roehampton.' She raised her finger again to stop me interrupting. 'I know you *think* you don't need to but there's a whole world of craft skills behind the art – which flight feathers are the best and why, how to cure the quills with hot sand, layout grids, organic pigments, not to mention gilding or mixing gesso . . .' She shook her head. 'You don't know any of that. And then there's the history too, and the theory behind the scripts. Also, I imagine the teachers will help you understand what's going on right now – on the commercial side of things. You might make some good gallery contacts there. And, apart from anything else, there's no harm in having a qualification that everybody can recognize.'

I nodded. 'Right. I accept I will probably have to go on the course.'

'Not probably. Definitely.'

'But surely it can't be all hand-to-mouth nightmares – trying to sell stuff at exhibitions? I thought your friends all worked on commissions. What about Susan or that man who's doing the Bible thing? Surely there must be some way of getting a salary.'

'I'm not saying that it is all hand to mouth. There *are*

commissions to be had, and good ones. Of course there are. But you should look at the facts.' She took another sip of wine, pausing to taste it. 'There are two hundred or so professionals already working in England – all ahead of you in the queue. Not to mention all the locally celebrated amateurs.'

'Mmm.'

'Of that two hundred probably fewer than fifty actually earn a living with quill and ink. Most of them are doing wedding invitations or the menus of pseudo-Bavarian restaurant chains.' She pursed her lips. 'Of that fifty I would say fewer than twenty are regularly commissioned to produce formal manuscripts and even then, most do a bit of parliamentary or legal work whenever they have to. And of that last twenty, there are fewer than half a dozen artists who can afford to keep themselves in *mozzarella di bufala*.'

I broke some bread and dipped it in the olive oil. 'OK. So how much do they get for a commission?'

'That depends.'

'On what?'

'Lots of things: on talent, of course, but also on reputation, contacts and – most of all – who their clients are.' Grandmother raised her eyebrows. 'Granted, you are considerably better than any other professional I have seen in the last few years, and certainly there cannot be many people in the world with your repertoire of hands, but that's not enough on its own. You need to get a few good clients – and for that you need to get a reputation – and for *that* we need just a little more than me saying "my grandson is a genius with a quill".'

'Perhaps I should enter the church.' I helped myself to more bread.

'No, you're too handsome for that. Besides, I didn't say I couldn't help you. Calligraphy is about the only thing in the world that I can help you with. You have the talent, Jasper, and I have the contacts. If you promise to go to Roehampton, then I will fix you up a meeting with my friend Saul – he works out of New York. America is –' Grandmother broke off. A warm breeze, that seemed to come from the Gianicolo hill, had suddenly disturbed her white hair. She adjusted her ancient sunglasses on her head. 'America is the only place to make any sort of money these days. If we are to get you to the front of that queue, you really need a big New York agent with a serious client list. Saul was a friend of your grandfather's. In fact he was your father's godfather. I think you've met him once.'

I must have looked blank.

'He started off in rare books years ago and he has hung on to that side of things, even after he moved into paintings and traditional art. He's become a bit of a dealer in his old age but he is respected and there is nothing that he cannot sell.' She finished her wine. 'He is definitely our man. In the meantime, you must begin by doing some speculative pieces – let's say three or four of the famous Shakespeare sonnets – in a few different hands – so that we have something to send him when the time comes.'

I pretended injury. 'Why didn't you suggest this when I was twenty-one? I've wasted five years labotomizing myself in offices.'

'Because you wouldn't have listened to me when you were twenty-one.'

'Yes, I would.'

'No, you wouldn't. You only listen to me when you have already decided something for yourself.' She picked up her battered clutch bag. 'Shall we go to Babington's for afternoon tea?'

'I thought you had to go back to work.'

'Oh bugger that. I am seventy-five – I can do what I like. And anyway this *is* work. I am a consultant. You are consulting me.'

I stayed in Rome all that summer courtesy of the Vatican and the remains of the money left to me by my mother. I practised and I learnt, studying more intently than ever before and seeking constant advice and criticism from Grandmother. I returned to London in September, rented a threadbare room and enrolled on the course. By December, she finally gave the all-clear (never was quality control so merciless) and we sent six Shakespeares to Saul, each done in a different hand.

Two weeks later I received notice that one of them had already been sold as a Christmas gift – for $200. While this was by no means a great deal of money, I felt that at least I was on my way.

My first real commission came the following spring (just as I was preparing for my exams): twelve 'Let me not to the marriage of true minds' at $750 a shot. That was more like it. In all they took four months to complete. But I was reasonably certain that they were well done. And Saul – to whom I spoke more and more on the telephone – was confident that if I could stand doing 'True Minds' for the rest of my life, then I would be able to survive.

I walked the exams and was one of only three to sell my work at the end-of-term exhibition. I received a second commission on the back of the first, and then a third. I became a little faster and the money got better every time. Then, in the autumn of that year, I flew to New York and met up with Saul himself – a man of such significant girth that you might journey for several seasons to encircle his waist once.

And it is Saul who saves me still. Since then, my commissions have come from the heart of art-loving America, where he is thick as thieves with that little band of insightful millionaires, who consider that the best gift they can give their satiated friends is an original manuscript copy of something beautiful. For these people, I am truly grateful. But I owe Saul the most. He was responsible for securing me my current work – the most interesting and extended job to date: thirty poems taken from the *Songs and Sonnets* of John Donne.

3. The Sun Rising

Busy old fool, unruly sun,
Why dost thou thus,
Through windows, and through curtains call on us?

'So, what is for my breakfast?'

'What would you like?'

'Something nice.'

'OK. Something nice it is.'

I rose and stepped silently into my pyjamas. Always a good way to begin the day.

'Strawberries. And coffee. Not tea.' She lifted her head from the pillow to open one eye a challenging fraction.

It was the morning of Saturday, 16 March, seven days on from my birthday, and the sun was indeed insinuating its way through the gap in my carelessly drawn curtains. Give the old fool three hours, I thought, and the brazen slice of light now lying across the chest of drawers by the window would find its way across the room to where she lay in bed. But by then, she would probably be gone.

Between you and me, I find it almost impossible to guess breakfast requirements in advance for women like Cécile. As with so many children of the ecological revolution, you would presume that she prefers fruit – cleansing, nutritious, zestful. And yet no doubt she sometimes wakes to find herself craving the immoderate satisfaction of a chocolate croissant or even, on occasion, the wanton candour of bacon and eggs. In the end, I'm afraid, I don't think there is any way round it: you just have to accept life as an uncertain business and make provision for all circumstances.

Even here there is danger. The talented amateur, for example, will stride merrily out to the shops on the eve of an assignation and buy everything his forthright imagination can conceive of – muesli, muffins, marmalade, a range of mushrooms, perhaps even some maple syrup. Thus laden, he will return to stuff his shelves, fill his fridge and generally clutter his kitchen with produce. But this will not do. Not only will his unwieldy efforts be noticed by even the most blasé of guests – as he offers her first one menu then another – but worse, the elegance and effect of seeming only to have exactly what she wants is utterly lost, drowned out in a deluge of *les petits déjeuners*.

No – the professional must take a very different approach. He will, of course, have all the same victuals as the amateur but – and here's the rub – he will have *hidden* them. All eventualities will have been provided for, and yet it will appear as though he has made provision for none. Except – magically – the right one.

Anyway, thank fuck I got the strawberries.

'It's OK if I use your toothbrush?' she called from my bathroom.

'Yes, of course. You can have a bath or a shower if you like. There are clean towels in there.'

'After, maybe.'

I listened to her moving about. She was light on her feet.

I live in this attic flat, at the top of what was once a smart stucco-fronted Georgian house on Bristol Gardens, near Warwick Avenue, London. What with all the eaves and so on, I'm afraid it's not exactly roomy: OK-ish size lounge, small studio, bedroom, *en suite* bathroom, and a so-called hall with a kitchenette at one end and the stairs down to my internal front door at the other. But at least the relative cramp prohibits dinner parties – a real mercy in these blighted days of celebrity chefs and self-assembly furniture.

When I moved in, there were two bedrooms; as I only needed one, I was able to switch things around and have my studio at the back. This arrangement ensures that I get street noise when I am asleep and not when I am working; additionally, it has the great benefit of allowing me to have my draughtsman's board by the north-facing window, which overlooks the beautiful garden below – a retreat surrounded on four sides by old buildings similar to my own and which is for the communal use of all the residents. North – because calligraphers prefer an even light.

My studio is not half as spacious as I would like but I have set it up to be as perfect a place to earn a living as possible. It contains everything I need – my reference books, magnifying glasses, knives for cutting and shaping my quills, and the quills themselves: swan for general writing, goose for colour work because it's softer and, for the finest details, crow feather. The light is not perfect because my window actually faces slightly west of north. But the finest results are always achieved in natural conditions, so, unless I am on a serious deadline, I try to avoid working with the spotlights.

'You've got a very clean place. I like it.' Cécile was now standing in the doorway to my bedroom, naked except for my toothbrush, which she had now returned to her mouth and was rather lazily employing across her teeth.

'You think?'

Out came the brush. 'Tidy and clean for a man, I mean.' She didn't seem to be using very much toothpaste. Either that or she had swallowed it.

'Thanks. Do you inspect a lot of men's flats?'

'Yes.' A quick brush. 'I have many brothers and they ask me to come over and see if their places are good for' – she raised her eyebrows – 'pulling the chicks.'

I brought down two bowls from the cupboard.

She frowned. 'But my brothers – they never actually get any chicks back. They say: "Cécile, it is a terrible nightmare, there are no chicks in Dijon."' She came over and put her chin over my shoulder. 'You really have strawberries!'

'Yes.'

'I was only making fun.'

'Too late. We're having them now. I haven't got anything else. You want cream?'

'Of course.'

'OK.'

She stood back and watched me grind the coffee beans.

Ordinarily, I would have preferred to bring my trusty Brasilia to life, firing it up in all its shimmering glory and producing some coffee we could all have been proud of. (The true espresso, I submit, is modern Italy's gift to the world – their great and most eloquent apologia. Meanwhile, here in England we seem to have traded our inheritance for a jamboree of high-street chains, peddling lukewarm coffee-flavoured milk shakes and lactescent silt.) However, not only is an espresso machine a little ostentatious, especially when still (in effect and despite the intervening night) on a first date, but also – crucially – its use results in single cups which, in turn, result in significantly shorter breakfasts-in-bed. So cafetière it had to be.

'Shall I carry something?'

'Sure.'

Cécile returned my brush to her teeth and turned on her heel with a bowl in each hand.

I have to say that I love the mornings almost as much as the nights. Best of all, you get to wake up and be the first person that day to see the true untroubled beauty of a woman's face – brow clear, hair unfussed. (*'She is all states, and all princes, I,/Nothing else is . . .'*) But almost as enjoyable, in different ways, is the awkward choreography of the bathroom sequence, the dressing, the where-are-my-earrings?, the what-do-we-say-now?', the strangely stilted wait for the minicab, or my offer to come down to the Tube. In a slightly sick way, I also look forward to the mutual hangovers (we're in this together) and most particularly that evanescent feeling of surprise that you sometimes experience after you've both been awake for a few minutes – surprise that despite all the static and interference and fundamental insecurity, which so often sabotages English heterosexual encounters, grown-up strangers still do this stuff *on a whim*.

Broadly speaking (and with all the usual disclaimers about generalizations duly assumed), there are three sorts of women in the morning: those who don't want to be seen at any cost (as they dash from duvet to duffel coat); those who don't care and stride around the place naked, daring you not to look (clothes forsaken where they fell); and those who would like to count themselves among the unabashed but can't quite bring themselves to abandon cover, their modesty clinging like their childhood. Curiously, which type a given woman will turn out to be has nothing to do with class, age or even looks – and you can never tell beforehand – but, paradoxically, you can usually rely on the exhibitionists not to cause any trouble once they have gone. (I don't know why this is: something to do with their 'fuck you – you've got my number but I don't give a shit whether you call' attitude, I guess, whereas the shy ones . . . *oh brother*).

I set down the coffee on my side of the bed, passed Cécile her bowl, offered her a spoonful of demerara sugar and then climbed back in myself.

'So what is it that you do, Jasper? You never said all the time we were at the dinner. I was listening. You are something bad? Like a tax person. Or you sell cigarettes in Africa?'

'I am a calligrapher.'

'*Un calligraphe?*'

'*Absolument.*'

She sat up further, holding her bowl out of the way and pushing pillows awkwardly behind her back with her other hand. Her dark skin made her teeth look even whiter.

'How is that?'

'It's good. I mean I enjoy it.'

'You make your living?'

'For now. Yes.'

'You have some work here?'

'Yes. I work at home.'

'Can I see after?'

'Yes, if you like.' I twisted around to pour the coffee. 'In fact, last week I started a new job for somebody – a collection of poems – and I just finished the first verse of the first one yesterday, but I'm not sure about it and –'

'Which person?'

'A big-shot American guy from Chicago. I'm not supposed to say his name. He owns loads of newspapers and television channels and I had to sign this confidentiality clause because – apparently – he's so famous and important that if anybody ever found that he had commissioned some poems then Wall Street would collapse.' Though facetiously spoken, this was true. My client was Gus Wesley – and although I couldn't conceive of any way in which my disclosure could matter, I had been religiously following Saul's advice and had told nobody who the work was for, not Will or Lucy or even Grandmother.

Cécile made a mountain under the bedclothes with her knees and set about her strawberries. 'Money makes men forget they are full of shit. He sounds like a pain in the arse to me.'

'To be fair . . .' – I felt obscurely moved to defend my client – '. . . to be fair, I think the reason he doesn't want me to tell anyone is because the poems are a present for his new girlfriend's birthday. He's already had two marriages and he gets torn apart every time his private life finds its way on to his rivals' pages. So he's keeping this hot new honey all to himself. Nobody knows about her. I guess he wants it to stay that way.'

Cécile shrugged and then scraped her spoon with her teeth. 'I don't know anything about it. I am not interested in media typhoons.'

It seemed inelegant to correct her. I ate my strawberries.

'Actually,' she turned her head, 'I meant which person – which poet? Not who the poems are for.'

'Oh sorry: the poet is John Donne.'

'Now I have heard of *him*.' She let her tongue travel across her front teeth. 'He wrote a poem about death being too proud, I think. I had to write about it for an exam when I was a student. Not easy. But he's a love poet, yes?'

'Sort of.' She had the French way of saying 'love' as though it were indeed a god. 'He writes about men and women – or he does in the collection that I am doing anyway. A lot. But I think there is a whole bunch of other stuff too. Sermons and Holy Sonnets and so on. He seems like a serious guy. I'm going to find out more about him.'

'You are very lucky, I think. Everybody else in London talks only about the prices of houses and which of their colleagues they dislike.'

'I know. Sometimes I think it would be better to be deaf.'

She smiled. 'Yes, but you love London too?'

'Yes, I do. Half the time.'

'For me, it's good to be here for a while but when I have finished my training, I am going to Martinique to teach real boys who want to know.' Keeping her eyes on me, she twisted her hand so that she could lick between her fingers where some stray sugar had settled. 'A lot of the boys here – I think they don't want to learn. A lot of boys do not have the way to become real men.'

She sunk her teeth halfway into her last strawberry and left it clamped between her lips.

After Cécile had bathed, we stood together in my studio, and considered my week's work. Although, admittedly, there were only a few lines (I was still going slowly back then, feeling my way) I could tell she was impressed. Perfectly defined, clear and elegant upon my board was the first verse of 'The Sun Rising'.

> Busy old fool, unruly sun,
>   Why dost thou thus,
> Through windows, and through curtains call on us?
> Must to thy motions lovers' seasons run?
>   Saucy pedantic wretch, go chide
>   Late schoolboys, and sour prentices,
>   Go tell court-huntsmen, that the King will ride,
>   Call country ants to harvest offices;
> Love, all alike, no season knows, nor clime,
> Nor hours, days, months, which are the rags of time.

This, as I had said to Cécile, was the first poem that I had tackled – my first hand to hand with Donne's style, my introduction to the man. (It was also one of the five poems on Wesley's must-include list; the other twenty-five I was at liberty to choose myself – one for each year of her life, I guessed.) And what a piece of work it is: rigorously intellectual and yet all the while artfully erotic; full of swagger but the speaker still the supplicant; simultaneously contemptuous and craven; relentlessly bent upon making that lover's bed the centre of the universe, while irascibly conscious of the rest of the world; the verse swathes back and forth through its paradoxical business like a wrathful snake through dewy grass. Truly Donne is the great antagonist, the undisputed master of contrariety – his antitheses reversing into his theses, his syllables crammed with oppositions, and every clause sent out to vex the next.

Of course, back in March, I saw only a fraction of what I find in *The Songs and Sonnets* these days. In truth, at that time, standing with Cécile, both of us barefoot and tasting of coffee, I admit my response was rather linear. I was distracted by my professional eye, which had been drawn to the dimensions of the gap that I had left for the first letter of the first verse, the versal – my glorious, decorated 'B', which would only be added when I had finished the rest of the poems. Now that I had completed a stanza, I was beginning to feel that I hadn't left quite enough space: the verse-to-versal proportion looked wrong. I would have to rethink and start over.

Cécile spoke up. 'So it is a poem about a man waking up and thinking: fuck-off Mr Sun, I am not interested in today, I want to stay in my bed and make love with my woman – right?'

I nodded. 'I think that's pretty much exactly what it's about, Cécile.'

Like all calligraphers, I hate mistakes with a vehemence I can hardly describe. And my abhorrence leads me to dwell with a vagrant's fixity on the reasons for my downfall – but my primary mistake was not, I think, that I misjudged Cécile. Because she was so incontestably at home in the 'Nude Action Body' department (which was, after all, where we had met), I think I could have relied upon her not to behave inartistically had she known what devastation her actions were going to cause. But, alas, she did not. No – my primary mistake was to let her stay another night. We didn't discuss it out loud. But come five, I found myself stepping out to the shops and begging Roy, my excellent local supplier and a man who looks as close as is possible to an obese version of Hitler, to let me have one of his brother's fresh salmon. It cost me more than any other human being in the history of mankind has ever paid for a single fish, but life is short and inconvenient and there is no sense protesting.

Perhaps it was the light that day – bright, sharp, enthusiastic, a real rarity – or perhaps the spirit of the poem with its heavy insistence on the altar of the lovers' bed as the only dwelling place of truth worth worshipping.

> Shine here to us, and thou art everywhere;
> This bed thy centre is, these walls, thy sphere.

Either way, I was scarcely conscious that the afternoon had given way to a wine-suffused evening. I had recruited two bottles of the crispest Sauvignon Blanc and a handful of haricots verts to go with the salmon and, at seven-thirty, we were still fooling around together in my kitchenette (already quite drunk) as I prepared the creature in lemon and tarragon before wrapping it in foil and placing it carefully in the oven.

There then followed nine truly Caligulan hours, during

which several really good things happened including, I think, Cécile finding an old cigarette-holder that William had left and an attempt at a bilingual game of pornographic forfeit Scrabble which I very happily lost.

When, finally, I fell asleep, the sun was rising.

4. Love's Exchange

> Love, any devil else but you,
> Would for a given soul give something too.

And then my entryphone buzzed.

Jesus Christ.

I squeezed my eyes shut. But the racket persisted – on and off, on and off, on and off. Cécile shifted. I turned to look at my clock: five to seven *on a Sunday morning*. I could scarcely have been asleep for more than an hour and a half.

Semi-conscious, panicking, I thrashed my way out of the wound-round sails and rucked-up rigging of my bedclothes and stumbled towards the window. I hoist up the frame and stuck out my head.

'YES! WHAT?'

There, four storeys below me, her hand raised like a peak cap to shield her eyes from the sun, Lucy stood waiting.

I confess: this was not an eventuality I had anticipated. Indeed, during the past twelve months of our relationship, I had devoted a tremendous amount of energy to preventing situations of exactly this kind.

Lucy's voice rose from the pavement below: 'Jasper? For God's sake, open the door! I've been ringing for ages!'

With my head still stuck out of the window like some early-disturbed village idiot, gaping down from his hay loft, and conscious all the while that at my back, and doubtless speculating from the cool vantage of her many pillows, Cécile was also roused, I took a moment to consider.

Lucy was moving her stuff out of her flat today. The plan was that she would store it at her mother's while she looked for somewhere to buy rather than sign down for another twelve months renting her current place. This much I knew and understood and even accepted. But my presence was not required until lunchtime, or so I had thought. And yet here she was – six hours early. What – for fuck's sake – was going on?

'Jasper? Come on. What are you doing?'

'I'll be down in a second, Luce,' I said, as loudly and as quietly as I dared. 'The electric lock is broken.' I took a deeper breath of air. 'The lock is broken . . . I can't let you in from up here. Hang on. I'll be right down.' And with that I pulled in my head, shut the window and returned my attention to the room.

Time cleared its throat and tapped its brand-new watch. If Cécile had been listening, she gave no sign. She was lying with her face turned away from me, one lithe and sculpted leg brandished across the sheets. The room smelled sweetly of her warm body. I could tell she wasn't asleep but there was a thin chance that she had heard only confusion in the conversation rather than deducing the full horror. Truth be told, I did not care what Cécile may or may not have been thinking. My main concern was to spare Lucy.

Once in my little hall, I stood, hot-breathed, arid-eyed, parch-tongued, leaning on the banisters by the entryphone, trying to wrest my mind into clarity. (My hangover, like a drunken Glaswegian in the opposite seat at the beginning of a long train ride, sweating and swearing and wanting to be friends.) My thoughts were confused and came in crimson flashes. I did the only thing I could: I went into the bathroom to empty the bubbling cauldron of needles in my bladder. After this there really was no more time. I grabbed a pair of jeans that were loitering by the bath, squeezed a measure of toothpaste into my mouth, and set off down the stairs.

Now, in the normal run of things, I am an absolute master of the old Cartesian pack drill: if 'a' is the case, then 'b' must surely follow, et cetera, et cetera. But I would be deceiving you if I were to say that I had anything quite so formal in my head as I rushed headlong down the five flights of doom that morning. My lock ruse was as far as I had ever planned ahead. All I recall thinking was 'I'll think of something' every seventh step, whereupon I would instantly forget that I had settled on this as my strategy and panic all over again on the eighth. Worse still was my anger, my rage, at having allowed such an oversight. I was furious. How could I have forgotten that she was coming in the morning? Beyond all question, this was the most shameful and disorderly fuck up in my entire career. I hated myself.

I thumbed the red master button that popped the lock and, grinning a grin calculated to convey a hopeful blend of benign insouciance and penitent disarray, I swung open the mighty front door to greet the waiting Lucy.

'What kept you?' She stepped up and hugged me tenderly.

It was enough to make you weep.

'What's wrong with your buzzer?' she asked, changing tone, leaning back and looking up, meeting my eye.

'Nothing,' I replied, in a voice as blank as a pure white page. 'It's the lock that's gone. The buzzer works fine and I can hear you through the intercom but I can't unlock this door from my flat. I have to come down. I'm not sure what's wrong. I was going to find out if it's the same for the other flats later today – when they all get up.'

'You don't exactly look ready to go,' she said, her head moving safely back towards my chest.

'No. Yes, I am. What time?'

'Now, idiot. The van has got to be back by one.'

'Now. But Lucy...' – exasperation to cover feverish brain-ransacking – '... it's not even seven o'clock yet and it's ... it's *Sunday* and –'

'Oh Jasp, you are hopeless. I'm moving today, remember?'

I blinked.

'You know – moving house – when a person takes all their things out of one place and drives them to another.'

'I know. I know.'

'Well, don't act all surprised about it then.' She rocked back on her heels. 'Oh, come on stupid, let's fix you some breakfast and then we can get on the road.' She glanced over her shoulder down the street to where a white removals van waited menacingly. 'The van will be OK over there for fifteen minutes, won't it? I saw them towing someone away when I was coming over. Is parking still all right on Sundays around here?'

'The van?'

Another change of tone, concern perhaps. 'Are you OK, Jasper? What did you get up to last night?' She broke away and put her hand up as if to take the temperature of my forehead.

I moved slightly to block the entrance and hoped that the black clouds of adversity that were scudding across my face were being interpreted as evidence of the earliness of the hour rather than the deepening crisis.

Businesslike now: 'Jesus, Jasp, come on, let's get you washed and dressed.'

'We can't,' I said, a beat too quickly.

That was it. She was about to catch the insinuating scent of betrayal wafting down the stairs behind me. I could not hug her again. I had to act.

'I'm not sure about the van,' I said. 'We had better check the parking restrictions. I think they've changed them because of the Heathrow link and the Paddington basin stuff . . . and I don't think you can park here without a permit, even on Sundays. It's because all the people coming in from the airport started leaving their cars and choking up the whole area. And now they're just – you know – towing everybody away right, left and centre. Round the clock. We'd better check.' I shook my head. 'Did we really agree seven?'

Before she could get a word in, one arm around her waist and the other holding up my jeans, we were off to get a closer look at the nearby lamp-post with the parking notice on it. Three steps away from the door and it clicked shut behind us. Locked.

We stood together, bereft in the early morning street. How I berated myself. Shut out of my own home! How I cursed. And yet how adamant I was that I would not wake my neighbours to get in. Lucy, no! At this hour of the morning? No! Even if we are let into the hall, I'm not sure I left my own front door open! And the only person who has a spare set of keys is the Roach – but he's a DJ and he doesn't get up until mid-afternoon and there's no way I am waking him up now: he's probably not even home yet! I'll sort it all out later. Then, how suddenly enthusiastic I became, how eager to be off. Hey, come on Lucy, what's the problem? I'll get a shower at your house, borrow some clothes . . . we might as well get on with it now you're here. No sense hanging about. I'm up now! And, finally, how quietly apologetic: I'm sorry I forgot, Luce, I really am. I'm such an idiot sometimes . . .

So, five past seven on a Sunday morning: I had only been awake for less than ten minutes and already I was half-dressed, grinding through the rusty gears of destiny up the hill towards St John's Wood.

It was a baneful day writhing with the horrors of which nightmares are made. And help, too, was thin on the ground. As usual, Lucy's elusive sister, Bella, with whom Lucy shared her flat (and whom I had never had the pleasure of meeting in any of my scandalously few visits) was nowhere to be seen – away on holiday again. According to Lucy, Bella also wanted to 'take the plunge' and so hadn't wished to sign another year's contract either – although, clearly, she was some way behind Lucy in the property-hunting business. 'Bloody Bella hasn't even *started* looking so God only knows what she is going to do with all her stuff when she gets back tomorrow – probably ship it over to Mr Wonderful's.' (It may have been my over-zealous imagination but I couldn't help but feel that the barb of this comment was intended as much for me as for Bella's boyfriend.) Neither, I might add, were any other of Lucy's many reported pals in evidence. In fact, the only other assistance was provided by Lucy's nice-guy landlord and would-be best friend, Graham, a merchant banker with pretensions to photography, whose daily scratchings in that latter-day Golgotha that Londoners call the City had yet to reduce his towering smugness by so much as an inch. (Hey, watch out ladies, here comes Mr Right . . . and guess what? He's single! And very nice manners. And so *tall*.)

Six foot two and boasting of some feeble drink-induced discomfort, Graham appeared shortly after eight, bringing with him – following a quick call on Lucy's mobile phone – an old Oxford shirt, a pair of jogging trousers and running shoes. Though everything was too big (I am a lean five eleven), I was grateful all the same. Graham, I sensed, liked to inhabit a sartorial Hades all of his own and his charitable offerings could have been a lot worse. Not that this excused the poverty of his mercantile soul.

While Lucy wrote labels and Graham wrapped crockery, I dutifully showered and changed before rejoining the fray, manfully ignoring the toxic Armageddon taking place inside my head.

In what was left of the kitchen, Graham was now pouring lukewarm water on heavily brutalized bags of sawdust and po-facedly serving the results up as 'cups of tea'. Lucy, meanwhile, was outlining the latest plan: as the van had to go back at one, we would have to make sure that all the remaining bits of furniture were moved first. After that, we were going to be limited to the use of Lucy's Renault for odds and ends and Graham's four-by-four LandWaster for the bigger boxes.

'But I'll have to be off to meet some of the lads around three, Lucy, I'm afraid,' Graham said, loyalties already torn so early in the morning. 'Although I can come back this p.m. if there's any more needs shifting . . . and bring a couple of the lads with me – if you want us to tackle the dining room.'

Lucy smiled. 'No, it's all right, Graham. That's very kind. But I really just want to move my desk and that big bookcase out there before you go. My dad did the bed and my sofa yesterday. And the table and all the chairs in the dining room are Bella's.'

'Well, tell her she can give me a ring tomorrow when she's home if she requires –'

'She's not getting back till very late but I'll let her know you're up for helping when she needs it.' She turned to me. 'Are you OK, Jasp?'

'Yes, I'm fine, thanks.' I smiled weakly.

Lucy put a hand on my head. 'Sorry – don't you like the tea?'

'No. Yes. It's OK. I'll be OK. Just a little . . .' I cleared my throat.

She made a face at Graham and then lowered her voice. 'Jasper is a bit of an arsehole about tea and things. Spends a lot of time on his own.'

Graham shrugged, charitably. 'Well, there's nothing wrong with being an arsehole. Plenty of people are arseholes. Just got to make the best of it is all.'

'You're right,' I nodded.

By nine, we had set to – hefting and heaving, staggering and swaying, pushing and pulling, levering in and out and round about, and pounding up and down and up and down and up and down the bastard stairs. Did ever a woman have so much stuff? And to what *end*? Rails and rails and rails of clothes and shoes innumerable; and then the mutinous fucker of a dressing table and more boxes of clothes (now neatly labelled 'keep for two years' or 'winter' or – most gallingly – 'don't keep'); and then the bookcase and another mirror, complete with a maddening brown blanket that seized every opportunity to embrace the floor. And then the desk. The bloody desk.

The only respite was during the few intermezzi of trundling back and forth across the city in the removal van, knee-deep in the cabin detritus of crisp packets, burger cartons and chocolate wrappers left behind by generous generations of amateur shit-shifters before us.

The van went back and we switched to the car. But it was nearly six by the time we were finished.

At six thirty-nine, I awoke for the second time that day. And for the second time was plunged head first, without apology or warning, into *die Scheisse*.

I suppose that I must have drifted off to the underpowered lull of the Renault as we pulled away from Lucy's mother's Fulham address for the last time; and I suppose that the sudden silence, as she turned off the ignition, must also have woken me up.

Naturally, I had long ago discarded all thought of risking a return to my own flat and had begun instead quietly to look forward to a night with Lucy at her father's Bloomsbury *pied à terre*. (I should say that Pa and Ma Lucy – David and Veronica – had been separated many times but had recently started living together again in Fulham, though Pa Lucy warily continued to maintain his bolthold of old. Thankfully, they were both in Scotland that weekend – on some sort of reconciliatory whisky-tasting tour – and so were unable to witness their daughter's boyfriend's multi-layered distress as he hobbled devotedly in and out of their garage.) Bloomsbury was not an unreasonable expectation since Lucy has been using her father's as her base these last few weeks, while various estate agents wasted her time and lied to her about the properties she saw or liked or thought she might buy. If pushed, I suppose I had anticipated that we might slip off to some resuscitative little brasserie by way of a prelude to an early night of muted caress beneath the guest-room duvet. But that was as far as I got. I was too tired to plan. I was exhausted.

Imagine, then, my horror when I opened my weary eyes, stretched, gathered my sluggish bearings and realized that Lucy had pulled up outside . . . *my own flat*. For yes, we were, it pains me to relate, right back at number 33 Bristol Gardens. Square one – in all its recalcitrant glory – belligerent and incontestable.

My single point of honour was that I did not flinch. Not a giveaway muscle did I move. In the leering face of disaster,

I merely yawned: 'Luce, I think I fell asleep.' Then I let a pulse or two pass before adding, as though it were a matter of supreme indifference: 'Oh, why've you brought us back here?'

'Pick up your keys for tomorrow,' she said. 'Everyone will be at work otherwise and you won't be able to get back in.'

I glimpsed the passing of a fleeting chance – a short solo sprint across the road, a ding on the Roach's ding-dong bell, a beckoning voice from the basement, a hasty thumbs-up to Lucy from across the street, a swift ascent, a covert collection of my own keys, a rapid verification of the general health of the premises, an expeditious gathering of clothes and then an equally pacy descent back down to the Renault, whereupon Lucy would hit the gas and we'd be off . . . But too late! Lucy's door was open and the cold air was coming in.

'It's all right,' I said, trying to hold her with my voice. 'I'll only be a second.'

'Might as well come with you,' she replied, 'you're going to have to change if you want to have dinner with me.'

It wasn't so much that I was worried that Cécile might still be hanging around smouldering. No – the sad and sour truth was that with or without the corporeal evidence of *la fille française* in person, I knew the bedroom would give the game away. Wine glasses, supper, bottles, everything on the floor, a hat, the cigarette-holder, make-up on pillows . . . oh God. Events were conspiring against me. No time to prepare or launder. No time to arrange or devise. A single uncharacteristic lapse of the memory and suddenly all etiquette had been breached and a squalid face-to-face with the loathsome banshees of moral outrage was pending.

Towards the big black front door of the old Georgian house we now trod. We stood on the steps. The Roach wasn't answering. Good news. We might not be able to get into my

flat after all. Hopefully Cécile had shut my internal front door
and – without my keys – we would be stuck in the hall. If
not, if Cécile had left my door open, my best chance was
that one of my other neighbours (contrary to all previous
form) might start such a riveting conversation that Lucy
would be rendered quite immobile for a few crucial minutes
while I slipped up the stairs and sorted things out. So next I
chose Leon, the cellist who lived directly beneath me and
the neighbour with whom I was most friendly. He kind of
owed me for listening to him practise.

'Hello, yes?' came the lugubrious voice through the
intercom.

'Leon, it's me, Jasper.'

'Hello. Are you locked out? Your door's been open all day
and –'

I interrupted him. 'Thanks,' I said, stepping back.

The lock clicked.

'Must be just mine that's broken,' I said, before Lucy
could, 'and it looks like I left my own front door open after
all, so we don't need the spares.'

My second best chance was this: as far as I could remember, I had cleared the table after dinner and neither Cécile
nor I had gone into my sitting room again. It should have
been – as the spymasters might say – 'clean'. And, perhaps,
with just a little luck and good management, I might be
able to contain Lucy in there. Everything depended on me
reaching my flat first, tactically blocking various views, and
somehow casually shepherding her out of harm's way. And
that all depended on me being in advance as we mounted the
first flight of stairs. Which is precisely what did not happen.

Somehow, as I pushed open the door, Lucy got ahead.
And once she was in front there was nothing I could do. I
couldn't very well barge past. Neither was there any point

in hustling up behind her. I could only behave as normally as possible and follow her in silent agony, praying all the while that Leon would venture out into the corridor as I had calculated that he might.

We climbed one flight, two, three, and so to the fourth floor. Ahead, my own front door was ajar. To the right, Leon's. But I still couldn't get past her.

Leon's door opened. And suddenly there he was: curly brown hair, five foot ten, auburn beard and Franz Schubert spectacles. He was carrying his cello case. He looked like he was on his way out.

'Hello Jasper,' he said, furrowing his brow.

'Er . . . Leon, this is Lucy. Lucy, this is Leon.'

Lucy stopped.

'Leon plays the cello in a quartet,' I went on, unnecessarily, 'he's very good.'

'Hello,' Lucy said, smiling.

'Jasper very kindly puts up with my practising from time to time,' Leon replied.

I edged past Lucy. 'Thanks for opening the front door,' I said, affecting a more playful manner and nodding in the direction of my flat, 'I went down this morning and didn't take my keys. Stupid. Are you off anywhere special?'

'Just a rehearsal.'

I needed to make the conversation stick. 'Hey Leon, by the way, I haven't forgotten about going to see the comedy news review thing – you know, at the Lock Theatre.' I turned to Lucy. 'Leon and I have been trying to go out for a drink ever since I moved in – we thought we'd check out this local theatre round the corner. They do this news comedy show and it's supposed to –'

'When's your next London concert?' asked Lucy, primly disregarding my ramblings.

'We're playing at the Wigmore Hall in July,' Leon nodded. 'Beethoven mostly. And a Haydn.'

'We'll have to come along.'

'You must.'

I attempted to drift gently away, feigning an incidental interest in my lock, an excuse which I intended only as a staging post before attempting a break-neck ascent of my own stairs beyond. But the conversational glue between them was not quite strong enough for me to get away with it and – having (rather ostentatiously I thought) checked for his own keys – Leon took his leave, making us promise again to come and see him play.

At least I was now in front.

I reached the top about four steps ahead of Lucy. Opposite, at the other end of the hall: my kitchenette. There were one or two bottles but nothing that I could not have drunk myself . . . over time.

She reached the top of the stairs. I moved slightly to obscure her view. (Oh, to be reduced to such knockabout farce . . .) She put down her bag on the side by the telephone immediately on her left. I stood between her and my bedroom door. She began untangling the headset wire of her mobile telephone where it had caught on something as she removed it from her bag. I glanced again towards the sink.

'What a day!' I sighed. 'You must be tired out. Why don't you sit down, Luce? I'll just get some clothes and jump in the shower.' I tried to keep the urgent tone out of my voice. I had to get into my bedroom and shut the door.

Lucy looked up and smiled. The wire dangled from her hand. 'OK,' she nodded, 'see you in a second. Don't be ages.'

Mercy! Mercy! She was preoccupied, flicking through the

functions of her phone to check for missed calls or messages. And into the sitting room she went. Could it be that from the credulous jaws of defeat, I would somehow wrest a victorious deception?

I span around and into my room.

I took a shallow breath. Such a mess. No time. I cleared the covers of all the clothes with a single sweep of my arm and bundled them into the bottom of the wardrobe. Then, leaping across the bed, I quickly remade it. Next I bent to gather all the glasses, bottles, both empty and full, intending to pile them on top of the clothes. But just as I stood, bottles clasped in either hand, the door banged open behind me.

I had time only to half-turn as Lucy rushed towards me. I saw hot tears rising in the corners of her eyes. I felt the flat of her hand against my head. It wasn't even a clean blow. It caught me awkwardly across the cheekbone. I staggered back, falling towards the bed, still holding the bottles as the sad dregs of French wine spilled on to Irish linen.

Before I could look up, Lucy had turned her back on me. She left the room without stopping even to slam the door. I listened to her running down my stairs, into the hall, past Leon's, all the way down until I heard the heavy front door swing shut. There was silence for a moment before the sound of a car starting.

She was gone.

I lay still for a while.

Then I raised myself, curious, and walked across the hall into the sitting room. There were two unopened bottles of wine on the table by the window, just next to the Scrabble board, which was still covered in a sickening collage of the filthiest words imaginable. Propped up against the bottles was a note.

Jasper,

Your keys are under your pillow. I got you the wine since we drunk all yours. Aren't I a good girl? Your girlfriend seems very boring to me – maybe you should tell her that Sundays are for lying in bed? I thought of an eight-letter word for you to put on that c in cock: how about '*connerie*' as in '*faire une*'. You get bonus points for using all your letters.

Cécile.

Part Two

5. The Indifferent

> Rob me, but bind me not, and let me go.
> Must I, who came to travel through you,
> Grow your fixed subject, because you are true?

I wasn't lying to Cécile when I said that I came to John Donne for the most part in ignorance – a few ill-informed suppositions and some half-remembered misapprehensions were all I had. I vaguely recognized the highlights: *'Death be not proud, though some have called thee/Mighty and dreadful . . .'* ('Holy Sonnet 6'); *'. . . never send to know for whom the bell tolls; it tolls for thee . . .'* ('Meditation XVII'); *'No man is an island . . .'* ('Meditation XVII'). But I had never really taken the time to read his work properly. Nor did I know much about his life, other than that he was a contemporary of Shakespeare and that he wound up as Dean of St Paul's.

However, one of the many plusses of being a calligrapher is that you get to hang around with some quality writers. And you do start to know their work quite well – more intuitively, perhaps, than the academics and certainly more intimately than the average reader. (It's letter-by-letter stuff after all.) I suppose the bond is something like that between the musician and the composer: the audience loves to listen to the piece, the professors love to analyse and deconstruct the piece, but only the musician really lives within its dynamic energy.

Seeking to fuel what was fast becoming a genuine enthusiasm, I remember that it was during my work on 'The Indifferent' – the third poem I tackled after 'The Sun Rising' and 'The Broken Heart' – that I decided I must know more. And so I duly braved the throng and journeyed down to the Charing Cross Road to purchase a good biography.

As far as I could glean, the two most important facts of Donne's life were these. First, that in 1601, aged twenty-nine, he married in secret; and second, that he betrayed his birthright as a Catholic when he took holy orders in the Anglican Church.

Ann, his wife, was the daughter of a wealthy Surrey landowner, whom Donne met while serving as secretary to the Lord Keeper. Unfortunately, Donne was not of fit rank or estate to merit the match. Worse, he found he had disastrously miscalculated when he later confessed of the deed in a letter to his father-in-law: instead of the forgiveness and reprieve he was gambling on, he was summarily dismissed and disgraced. (He was even imprisoned for a short spell.) Thereafter, his career prospects were effectively ruined. He spent the next twelve years fretting a living on the fringes of the very society in which he had looked so certain to advance himself. When finally he was ordained into the Church of England, in 1615, it was not least because he could find no other way of regaining suitable employment. Almost immediately, James I appointed him a royal chaplain.

Which brings us to religion. Donne was brought up in a devout and well-known Catholic family at a time when being a Catholic could easily mean gruesome (and often public) death – disembowelling, stringing up, that sort of thing. On his mother's side he was descended from the family of Sir

Thomas More; his uncle became head of the secret Jesuit mission to England and was caught trying to flee the country during a storm and sent to the Tower; and his younger brother was arrested for sheltering a priest and subsequently died in prison when Donne himself was only twenty-one. The twin legacies of martyrdom and ultramontane loyalty therefore framed his existence; for most days of his life, he must have been acutely conscious of the implications of his Catholicism.

These linchpins notwithstanding, I should admit (if I am to be honest) that the biographical discovery which sealed my affinity for John Donne was a matter less intense. In the course of my reading, I also came across a first-hand account of the twenty-something man, left to us by Sir Richard Baker. This report relates how on 'leaving Oxford, [Donne] lived at the Innes of Court, not dissolute, but very neat; a great visiter of Ladies, a great frequenter of Playes, a great writer of conceited verses'. Naturally enough, this description appealed: the portrait of a serial philanderer, who was '*not* dissolute, but very neat'. Here was a man, I thought.

As well as marking the beginning of my pilgrimage of discovery, and aside from the intimate punch of the poem itself, 'The Indifferent' also presented some difficult technical challenges. With 'The Sun Rising' and 'The Broken Heart', I had followed a similar textual scheme to that which I had employed for one of the earlier, single-sonnet Shakespeare commissions – a scheme derived, I happily admit, from the hand of my favourite calligrapher and personal hero, Jean Flamel, secretary to the Duc de Berry in the early fifteenth century. Now, however, with this poem, I had a problem.

Bâtarde, the hand that Saul, Wesley and I had agreed on for the Donne, is one of the most elastic scripts; and there are as many rules concerning the precise rotation and relative dimensions of the letters as there are examples of the form. These rules the good scribe will know, then disregard, then cleverly reinterpret. But even such ingenious reinterpretations are themselves to be cast aside when it comes to the lawless land of poetry. Let us ignore the vexed question of the versals; let us also forget the potential confusion of the lettering particulars (cursive or textura feet? cojoins? ligatures? serifs and hair-lines?); and let us look instead at the wider problem of layout. How, for example, does one legislate for margins, spacing or letter discretion when the lines of text are all different lengths? Good poets have good reason for fashioning their lines the way they do and it is not for the calligrapher to go barging in and breaking them up. And yet, so often the overall aesthetic effect of so much irregularity – even when written out well – is somehow to clutter and stifle, detracting from the words themselves. So rendering poetry *per se* is problem enough. However, with a manuscript collection, the whole thing is made infinitely more complicated because there will be such a diversity of lengths – two words a line here, thirteen there – all of which need to share the same script. Consider: in *The Songs and Sonnets*, Donne uses *forty-six* different stanza forms and only two of them more than once.

Put simply, my problem with 'The Indifferent' was this: some of the lines were too bloody long to fit on the fucking page.

The first verse goes as follows:

> I can love both fair and brown,
> Her whom abundance melts, and her whom want betrays,
> Her who loves loneness best, and her who masks and plays,
> Her whom the country formed, and whom the town,
> Her who believes, and her who tries,

> Her who still weeps with spongy eyes,
> And her who is dry cork, and never cries;
> I can love her, and her, and you and you,
> I can love any, so she be not true.

Executional troubles notwithstanding, you can well see why 'The Indifferent' became one of my early favourites. I like the exhaustive catalogue of that opening stanza and you can feel the speaker's familiarity breeding its contempt even as he writes – 'abundance melts', 'want betrays', 'spongy eyes', 'dry cork': knowing phrases if ever I saw them.

Of course, the speaker of the poem is not entirely to be identified with Donne himself – this is partly an exercise in posturing and the work is based on one of Ovid's *Amores*. But, between ourselves, I am not so sure that the pose is all. Although Donne is indeed playing the languid courtier, I believe his final trick is that he actually means it:

> Rob me, but bind me not, and let me go.
> Must I, who came to travel through you,
> Grow your fixed subject, because you are true?

This is not merely sport or showing off. There's a freight of cruelty travelling with that 'travel through you' – all the more so because on the surface it seems so casually delivered, a nonchalant relative clause passing time on the way to the next big verb: 'Grow'. (Calligraphers love their capital Gs.) Plus, by way of further compression, 'travel' can also be glossed as 'travail', and of course, whichever word actually appears on the page, the homophone's meaning will be bound to sound in the reader's (or listener's) mind – exactly as Donne intended. Then there's the mock (and mocking) indignation at the curse of women's faithfulness. But it's in the third verse that he delivers my favourite bit of the poem.

> Venus heard me sigh this song,
> And by love's sweetest part, variety, she swore,
> She heard not this till now; . . .

It is not enough for Donne that the goddess of love grants that variety is her most delectable aspect; he must have her *swear* upon it. Yet when you read, and indeed write, the verse as a whole, the crucial line gives the impression of being incidental to the guiding contour of the argument. However, nothing in Donne is ever *en passant* and those seemingly innocuous commas turn out to have been the means by which he has smuggled in the central credo of the entire poem: for Donne, 'variety' was what it was all about.

And so it was for me.

But how to explain this to Lucy?

The silent telephone calls began the day after the disaster and continued with increasing frequency in the week that followed. At random times of the day or night – just as I was poised to stroke the difficult stem of a 'k', or when I had at last cast myself into bed and was about to close my eyes – the spiteful persecutor would suddenly screech into life. The vicious ring would send me racing madly into the hall, where I would lunge for the receiver and quiet my tormentor until the next attack, two minutes or seven and a half hours later, at three thirty-six in the morning. Lucy never spoke but I knew it was she. She did not even bother to withhold her number.

For several days, I soldiered doggedly on, seeking to make

light of the situation, blaming myself and quietly reflecting that if I was going to make such an unholy balls-up of my affairs then relentless telephonic harassment was no more punishment than I deserved. Most trying of all was the necessity of keeping up a breezy manner in case the call turned out to be somebody else.

By the middle of the second week I could take it no more. I pulled the phone from its socket and temporarily suspended all contact with the outside world. What else was I to do? I had tried talking into the receiver. I had tried ringing the poor girl back. I had even tried to out-silence her: the two of us just sitting there on either end of the line, listening to one another's breathing, both parties bleakly determined not to hang up first as we clung on, hour after hour, into the wordless night. All to no avail.

I was aware that Lucy had not deserved my stupidity. And I knew well that only an idiot could have created such a banal mess. Indeed for a day or two, I considered going round to see her at her mother's house, but I feared this would cause more damage than it might repair. No – Lucy was clearly no longer interested in discussion. Even abject apology would sound sickeningly glib to her. As for attempting to explain that I had recently discovered that I shared something of the outlook of a hopelessly contradictory, sybaritic metaphysical poet and that I was of the strong opinion that fidelity (let alone marriage) most often resulted in a state of physical torpor closely resembling death – forget about it.

Still, something had to be done. So that Saturday, the last in March, I sat down to pen her a short letter in the hope that its burning or shredding or chewing or flushing might have a worthwhile therapeutic effect.

Choosing for the occasion my finest italic, I constructed

a devilish paragraph or two in which I painted as black a picture of myself as I thought she would believe, mixing truth and falsity so that they couldn't be distinguished. And having thus fully ceded to her the moral high ground   that most unscenic of human viewpoints – I went on to point out, in as careful and delicate a manner as I could, that she was well advised to forget all about me and get on with the rest of her life.

Even so, my letter was, I confess, a little disingenuous. Maybe I exaggerated my behaviour just a fraction too far in order that she might sense a deliberate attempt to manipulate her into detesting me, and thereby identify a perverse strain of kindness on my part. Too convoluted? Possibly. But the truth was I knew from experience that few people had the heart to destroy my letters and I was confident that in all likelihood Lucy would read it through more than once, if not keep it for ever. And perhaps, in time she would perceive my hidden intention.

Fuck it all, I thought, after I had finished. Saturday night approaches. It was time to break my self-imposed exile and embrace the coquettish world once more: collect my linen from the launderette and pick up some provisions from Roy, the fat Hitler.

Around four that same Saturday afternoon, I tentatively plugged the phone back in. And before it could ring, I set off down the stairs with my bundles.

It is a truth at least mutually acknowledged that without Roy and his son, Roy Junior, I would die. I buy pretty much everything I eat from them. (Supermarkets are no longer bearable – too many people forcing you into the audience of their domestic lives – the mothers and the fathers and the couples and the single folk, all with their look-at-us brand

decisions and mutely signalled checkout-queue superiorities
. . . That the glory of human life should have fallen so *low*.)
For the sake of convenience, Roy's Convenience Store is
closed only on Christmas Day and when it is impossible for
Roy himself to stay awake any longer. Roy Junior, a seventeen-year-old, thinner and slightly less deranged version of
Roy Senior, is the only person allowed to assist him. Of the
two, although it is sometimes irksome to be forced to listen
to what Roy Junior believes is involved in 'having it large',
the son is less alarming to deal with as he does not have his
father's sinister talent for psychological attrition, nor does
he possess the menacing note of the older man's lingering
Yorkshire accent. Indeed, it's not that much of an exagger-
ation to say that I have become friends with Roy Junior in
a neighbourly sort of a way; he delivers whatever I need,
whenever I need it, and he also helps me out (at extortionate
charge) when I require odd jobs done reliably, such as provid-
ing a private minicab service. Most important, the sheer range
and quality of the produce that the Roys stock is staggering;
and, if by some chance there's something I need which they
haven't got in, then they pride themselves on their unrivalled
ability to get hold of any ingredient large or small at less than
two hours' notice.

'And a packet of your cashew nuts,' I said.

Having offered up my basket, full of provisions, ready for
the reckoning, I stood at the smooth wooden counter with
my laundry folded over my arm.

'Right you are, Mr Jackson,' Roy Senior nodded, rotating
to reach down a packet from the extensive nut display behind
the counter.

'How's Roy?' I asked.

'He's off in Keele this week. *Organizing* things.'

'Right.'

There was a pause. Roy Senior smoothed his little moustache. Then he said: 'You know they've gone up again, don't you?' He dangled the cashews before me for a moment. 'I'm afraid they'll be five . . . er . . . sixty-nine. Er, yes: five sixty-nine.' He punched the numbers in quickly and dropped the nuts into one of his blue plastic bags.

'Why's that? Is there a shortage?'

'No shortage. No.' He began going through the other items one by one, slowly and carefully, entering the price of each item, using only the index finger of his right hand.

'Global price-fixing agreement?' I volunteered, not that interested, and wondering idly how much Brylcreem he must get through in a year.

Roy Senior stopped what he was doing. I looked up from his scrubbed-clean hands to his scrubbed-clean face. He seemed to struggle with private demons for a moment. Then he returned my glance with an expression that mingled concern with frustration: 'Actually, Mr Jackson,' he said, 'I've been putting them up every seven days for the last *fourteen* weeks. Ten pence each week.'

'Really?'

'Yes. I was going to tell you before but I didn't want to ruin my experiment.'

'Experiment?'

'Yes, my experiment, Mr Jackson,' he said, smugly. Then, taking his time, he weighed my tomatoes on the electronic scales. He rang in the cost per pound. (The price came up as £1.435 and they were thus entered on the till at £1.43; Roy is scrupulous in all things and always rounds down to the nearest penny with fruit and up with vegetables, confirmation that the English eat more vegetables than fruit, I always think, and useful verification of the status of tomatoes if ever it is needed.) He turned his attention to my single green pepper and smiled in what he obviously believed to be a superior fashion before saying: 'I have to own up, I have been using you as a guinea pig.'

'Right.'

He drew breath. 'As you know, I am a capitalist. And like the great woman herself, I am a grocer –'

I started to interrupt but he held up his hand.

'I am a grocer. A while back, I thought to myself, why not try a little experiment? Why not? OK, I thought, so what are the facts?'

'What *are* the facts?'

'One: I know that Mr Jackson buys cashew nuts every week. Two: I know that he lives very locally. Three: I know that he doesn't pay any attention to how much things cost. Witness this damson jam.' He held it up and then entered £3.99 into the till. 'So, I cogitated further and came up with an idea for an experiment in basic economics. Why don't I put the price of his cashew nuts up by exactly ten pence every week, I thought, and that way find out what their true value is – their value, that is, to you as a customer?'

He rang up the grand total and I got the impression that he was becoming more agitated. 'And I have been doing this, as I say, for *fourteen* weeks now and still nothing. Nothing, Mr Jackson. Not a thing. You haven't noticed.' His index finger came up from the till. '*I* have had to tell *you* about the cashews.'

'You mean these cashews should really be two pounds whatever it is? And I've been –'

'I can no longer stand by and watch you pay such a ridiculous price for them, Mr Jackson. The experiment is at an end. At an end. I can no longer stand by. This isn't the way the system is supposed to work. You're supposed to notice, go elsewhere, refuse to purchase. As a guinea pig, you are a failure. At five pounds and sixty-nine, you are being . . . you are being . . . you are being *fleeced*, Mr Jackson. It's daylight robbery.'

'I had no idea, I mean –'

'Listen to me.' He leant forward over the counter and lowered his voice threateningly. 'For the next few weeks I want you to buy your cashew nuts elsewhere . . . I want you to take your cashew custom away . . . I want you to . . .' He waved his arm, mortified, close to breaking down, lost for words.

'Eschew your cashews?' I said, helpfully.

'*Exactly*. Exactly. That way I can build up an unacceptable surplus and that will force me to have a half-price sale to clear stock and that will bring the price back down to more or less what it should be and *that* will get us out of this . . . this *mess*.'

A single lick of thick black hair had come loose and now looped across his shiny forehead. He thrust the blue plastic bags across the counter. I left in chastened silence, the shop bell jingling behind me as I went out.

A Renault was parked at the end of the street. The female driver was talking into a mobile phone. For a heart-splintering moment, I thought it was Lucy.

I slogged all the way back up to the Himalayan summit of number 33 and managed to crawl, breathless, teeth-gritted, sinew-strained, up the last few steps into my own hall. Instantly, the telephone began to ring – as though it had been sitting there like a pining dog, waiting for my return. I put my bags and my laundry down quite slowly by the hat-stand and then stood, eyes shut, breathing deeply, and counted to five.

I snatched up the receiver.

'LUCY, FOR CHRIST'S SAKE! PLEASE, PLEASE, *PLEASE*

STOP RINGING ME UNLESS YOU WANT TO TALK. PLEASE.
I *WILL* TALK TO YOU IF THAT IS WHAT YOU WANT. OR
WE CAN MEET UP OR I'LL COME OVER BUT FOR GOD'S
SAKE STOP CALLING ME EVERY TWO SECONDS. I
DON'T –'

'Jasper?'

'– KNOW WHAT I AM SUPPOSED TO –'

'JASPER. *JASPER!*'

It was a man's voice.

'*What?* What? Sorry, who is it?'

'What's going on?'

'William?'

'What?'

'Is that you?'

'Of course it's me. Will you stop being an arse and tell
me what is going on? What are you *doing* with your phone?
You've been out of order for a week and a half and when
you do pick the fucking thing up you start calling me Lucy.'

'Sorry, Will, sorry. Things have been a bit awkward lately.
She's gone insane. I am being harassed and silent-called.
Almost stalked.'

'Well, you'd better do something about it and quick or
else the few friends you do have will give up on you for the
worthless fucker you are.' He took a sip of something. 'So,
has the sham come to an end and everything fallen apart?'

'Yes. Totally.'

'Do you care?'

'Of course I care. I mean, I know it wasn't going to last
forever . . . But I wasn't intending . . . Oh Christ, Lucy more
or less found me in bed with that girl from the fucking Tate.
Now she's ringing me up all the time . . . I think she's in quite
a bad way. I care about that.'

'Very nice of you.' He sighed. 'Jesus, Jasper.'

'What can I do?'

'Kill yourself on television. Wrap big apology signs around your head, explaining how you are sorry for being such a low-rent human being and behaving so disgracefully all your miserable life. That should do it. Give us the nod as to when you plan to go ahead and we can all tune in and watch. I think a burning tyre around your chest, that sort of thing, or maybe –'

'And how can I help you today, William? Is there something you would like to share with the rest of the class?'

'Yes, actually. I want you to get yourself to Le Fromage by eight sharp tonight, young man. I have a little treat for you.' He hesitated. 'But – well, we can do something else if you . . .'

'I'm fine. Go ahead.'

'Really, it's OK if we need to leave it awhile. I'm only planning on a –'

'There's nothing I can do, Will. I've written a letter. It's a motherfucker; that's all.'

He clicked his tongue. 'OK. So, do you remember those two girls that we ran into last time we were there?'

'No.'

'Well, they have finally had the decency to call me back and –'

'You mean you called them.'

'Precisely. They are prepared to meet up with us tonight. And for some reason unfathomable to humankind they want you to be there.'

'Well, I'd better come along then. Refresh me as to their names?'

'Tara and Babette.'

'The Czech girls?'

'Actually, I've found out their real names. When they

aren't on the catwalk in Paris or Milan or Rangoon – they're called Sara and Annette. They have confided in me.'

'Oh God.'

Le Fromage is William's name for his club. (I have no idea what the real name is – 'Settee' perhaps?) Situated in a fashionably dismal Soho back-alley, it is silted up most days of the week with the detritus of humanity – fabulously talentless men and women, who ooze and slime through the half-light in a ceaseless search for the dwindling plankton of each other's personalities. On Saturday, even the regulars avoid the place. Only William would ever sink so low as to organize a date there.

In the event, however, there were no celebrities around to degrade the dinner and things went surprisingly well. Well enough to occasion a group expedition back to William's house for further drinks and what he insisted on billing as 'an exciting midnight party'.

But thereafter we found ourselves becalmed. And had you happened to look into the wine cellar of an old house in Highgate at around one o'clock in the morning, you would have seen two figures crouching in the claustrophobic semi-darkness: one, sandy-haired, blue-eyed, the product of thirty generations of inbreeding, cradling a bottle of fino sherry; the other holding a bottle of Sancerre. Had you also stooped to listen, you would have heard the following hushed exchange.

'You can't *make* them take all their clothes off and pour sherry on their heads, Will. I don't care if you've got to get rid of it –'

'I am not going back into that room and ... and just sitting there. It's grotesque. I want something to happen. They must be lesbians.'

'They're not lesbians, they are Czech.'

'Well, it rather turns out to be practically the same thing. What is *wrong* with women these days? Why can't they just admit they want to and get on with it? Why the need for all this senseless prevarication? Those two up there are worse than bloody English girls.'

'Get rid of them then. Tell them you're sorry but it's way past your bedtime and that you are a priest and that because it is Sunday tomorrow you have to go to work. Or you could thank them very much for their company, but say that now you are drunk you fancy going upstairs with me and so if they wouldn't mind leaving –'

'Will you stop being such a fuckpig and think of a plan? And I am *not* tight. I just refuse to let them leave after they have had so much of my wine. They are drinking their way through the fucking Loire Valley and what are you doing about it? Fuck all. Except cowering in this wine cellar like a penis.'

'I am enjoying my evening.'

'Jasper, you may laugh but I intend to sleep with one of those girls within the hour and I am holding you personally accountable if I don't. Come on. Think of a plan. I'll sit very still and let you concentrate.'

'Perhaps you could try *talking* to them instead of going on about vintage cars like a tit. Or at least listening to them. Where do they live?'

'How the bloody fuck should I know?'

'If they live in separate places we could order two cabs – but stagger them on the quiet. I'll pretend I'm near Annette – wherever that is – and share the first with her. Then you've got half an hour alone with Sara and well . . . you'll just have to see how you get on. If things take a turn for the better you can always give the driver a tenner and tell him to fuck off.'

'It's an awful plan. And I hate it. And I don't see why you should be heading into the night with the lissom Annette either.'

'Because, Will, I have asked her, and she says that she hates you.'

Annette and I kissed all the way back to Bristol Gardens, breaking off only for the speed bumps. The driver, a truly revolting human being, insisted on four million pounds for the journey and the night would brook no argument so I handed over all my earthly possessions and reluctantly offered my limbs when it became clear he was refusing to leave without a tip.

Once inside, we sat up talking about nothing and drinking tea for an hour while some local radio station played soft. Annette was funny and told me about her home near Ostrava and her first boyfriend, who was called Max and designed submarines, even though Ostrava was about as landlocked as it is possible to be in Europe. Eventually, she asked if she could borrow a T-shirt and I found the shortest one that I had and (pretending innocence and the devout intention of decency) we went to bed, whereupon, aside from being generally attentive and instantly reciprocal, I left all the big decisions up to her. Such is the modern man's lot.

Afterwards, she slept halfway down the bed with her red-brown hair spread crazily on the pillow and I remember that I lay as the light turned slowly blue, listening to her murmuring in her sleep. In Czech.

6. The Bait

> Come live with me, and be my love,
> And we will some new pleasures prove
> Of golden sand, and crystal brooks,
> With silken lines, and silver hooks.

I awoke to the acid jazz of a secular London Sunday: cars, buses, dogs barking, the air traffic, the street shouts, the stereos, the swearing, the sirens, the scaffolding clang, the Paddington clank . . . But Annette's breathing was as regular as waves and so I set my pulse by that.

Of course I knew nothing of what the day was planning to unleash and though Lucy's legacy still lingered, I am mildly ashamed to report that I was feeling quite happy to be back in my old routines. More fool I.

Though I sensed I was on safe ground with croissants, I decided against bringing breakfast into the bedroom as I guessed it wasn't really Annette's thing. Instead, when I knew she was awake, I got up and offered her a cup of tea. In a voice both businesslike and bashful, she said that yes, she'd love some tea – milk and one sugar – but that she liked it quite strong and to leave the bag in for quite a while please. I left her to get dressed in privacy and tarried in the kitchen the better to give her time and space.

In any case, making a cup of tea is not as quick or as straightforward a matter as it may at first seem. (*Au sujet de*: I must mention that my explorations in the magnificent garden world of tea came to an end two or three years ago when I at last beheld the regal splendour of Darjeeling. In my youth, I laboured on the pungent terraces of Assam – distracted, perhaps, by a certain brutal charm – until, in my middle twenties, I found myself quietly seduced by the more aromatic company offered by a passing Russian Caravan – still my favourite blend. Eventually, after further wanderings in both China and Ceylon, I pledged myself to lifelong service of the true Queen. Of course, in my Lady Darjeeling's realm there are many mansions and it took me a few months of delicate experimentation to discover which of these was to be my chosen dwelling place. In the end, I settled on Jungpana, the tea garden of all tea gardens, and thereafter I have served only the first flush from the upper slopes thereof – uniquely supplied, I should add, by the excellent Tea Flowery on *Neugasse* in Heidelberg.) No no no – making a cup of tea is by no means quick or straightforward. As with so much in life, it has become principally a matter of protracted disguise. Annette, for example, having lived in London for three years, was quite understandably more familiar with the muddy sludge of a mashed-in-the-mug teabag – that nameless mixture of grit, sand and wood chip so beloved of the curmudgeonly Britisher – and did not expect her tea to contain any trace of actual tea *leaves* at all. Consequently, my task was to arrange matters covertly by abandoning my usual methods of infusion in favour of stewing the ill-fated Jungpana to buggery before straining it from my treasured pot and into a mug, whereupon (tears gently welling) I added the required milk and sugar. In this way, I hoped she would not notice anything suspect and the unflustered mood of the morning would be preserved. I even went so far as to take a little milk myself.

My efforts to try to make everyone feel more at ease must have worked reasonably well because, after we had both gone about our separate ablutions, we enjoyed a mock-formal breakfast during which she called me Mr Jackson and I had to call her Miss Krazcek. This lasted a pleasant hour or so but then she had to leave; she was due, she said, to meet someone (her boyfriend, I guessed) for lunch. We kissed at the top of my stairs – two friends – and then she was gone.

It was one of those mornings during which the light is forever changing – as though they are testing the switches in heaven. Absolutely fucking useless for calligraphers. Especially shagged out ones. So I returned to my bed.

Not until nearly two, after a scrupulous assault on both bathroom and kitchenette, as I was crossing the hall (eating a pear as it happens), did I realize that the telephone wasn't ringing.

For a second or two, I simply stared at it. In all the excitement, I had completely forgotten about the Lucy situation. Could it be that I was saved?

Warily, I edged towards the little table.

First I checked that the receiver was properly down. (It was.)

Then I lifted it up to check that the line was connected. (It was.)

And finally, I dialled the test number to check that the ringer was sounding. (It was.)

Hallelujah!

And thank Christ for that.

I admit: I thought I was in the clear.

The city summer lay ahead: sunglasses, suntans, sexiness.

Arms not sleeves. Legs not trousers. A better life. Or so I hoped.

But pucker-faced fate had other ideas. That very same afternoon events took an unexpected turn. The ratchet wound up by Lucy and sprung by Cécile now began to unravel its ropes in directions that no sane man could ever have predicted. That same afternoon everything changed and became blind and dazed and confounded and difficult to comprehend or process or even to believe. That same afternoon I fell apart.

By three, the light had steadied and it was reasonably hot – the first really warm day of the year. (Summer and winter are the world's new superpowers, oppressing spring and autumn and running them as miniature puppet states.) I entered my studio and was soon relishing my labours. I had the window open a little and was grateful for a mild breeze. I remember that I was beginning my first draft of 'Air and Angels' and almost daring to think that I might be happy. I didn't even mind the early wasp which came buzzing by, flying into the room for a brief turn before heading back out to the garden below.

I am not sure what the time was exactly when I decided to change the sketching paper for a proper skin of parchment in order to make a start on the opening lines – *'Twice or thrice have I loved thee, / Before I knew thy face or name'* – but it was no later than four-thirty, and probably nearer to four.

Professional calligraphers are divided along ethical, artistic and financial lines as to the medium they prefer to work with. But as far as I am concerned, on a commission like this, there can be no alternative to parchment. Not only is it a joy to write upon, but it is also the nearest one can get to authenticity. Strictly speaking, vellum (made from calf skin) is what the likes of Flamel would have used, but aside from being hideously expensive (which is not to say that parchment is in any sense 'cheap'), vellum is totally unacceptable to your average American media baron, seeking to impress his latest water-and-wilted-spinach-only woman. (And yet, though parchment is made from sheepskin, somehow, perversely, it seems problem-free; perhaps the word itself carries sufficient cultural resonance to disable scruples and exonerate all involved from guilt. {Inconsistency at every turn.} Or perhaps it's just that Gus Wesley, like most people, simply doesn't realize what parchment is made of.) In any case, modern preparations tend to leave the vellum sheets too stiff, too dry or too oily; and even parchment takes a good deal of extra private preparation to revive consistency after all the chemicals they treat it with. (Skins are washed in baths of lime and water, scraped and stretched; whiting is then added to them before they are scraped again and dried under tension. Tough going by anyone's standards – dead or not.) If, as is most often the case, the skin is still a little greasy, the diligent calligrapher will first rub powdered pumice over the surface with the flat of his hand, then French chalk, then wet-and-dry paper to 'raise the nap'. And after all of that, when he has finally set the sheet upon his board, he will apply silk to the surface in a last and loving effort to ensure that it is as free from residual grain and as receptive to his ink as possible.

It was sometime around four then that I got up from my stool to fetch some parchment from the stack by the door. I remember feeling its texture between my finger and thumb as I came back across the studio. I put the parchment down on the board, loosely, without fastening it. Then I reached up for the pumice, which I keep on a shelf, above and to the left of the window. I do not know why, but as I did so I happened to glance out, down, into the garden. And there she was. There she was.

It must have been her hair that first drew my eye – shoulder-length, tousled, amber-gold, light-attracting, light-catching, light-*seducing*.

For a minute, maybe longer, I did not move. I stood, with my arm raised to the shelf, craning my head. But the half-open frame was hindering my line of sight. So, very gently, I bent to undo the catch and push open the window as far as it would go. Then I knelt on my stool and leaned out over the ledge.

Lying on her front on the grass, just beyond the chestnut tree's shade, was a sun-shot vision of a woman so divine as to call vowed men from their cloisters. Propped up on her elbows, her shoulder blades slightly raised, her head between her hands, she was wearing an aqua-blue cotton sundress. She was reading something – something too wide and spread out to be a newspaper or a magazine, a map perhaps – which she had weighted down with her sandals and a brown paper bag. Lazily, she kicked her legs behind her back. I could not see her face but her limbs were bare, sun-burnished and so perfectly in proportion to the rest of her body that even Michelangelo would have had to alter them for fear of his viewer's disbelief. She raised her head, spat, and then waited a moment before reaching into the bag again and taking out another cherry. She appeared to be having some sort of a competition with herself to see how far she could shoot the stones.

Unreservedly, I confess, I was spellbound: pure unadulterated desire. Mainline. Cardiac.

I can't tell you how long I was transfixed. But at last I became aware that my mind was slowly dissolving – not into lust, but into *fear*. Fear that this extraordinary woman might glance around and reveal her features to be in some way less exquisite than the picture I had involuntarily allowed myself to imagine. Or fear – far worse – that she might glance around and reveal herself to be every bit as beautiful as I had envisioned. Then how was I to cope? With Venus camped in my communal garden, what chance work, what chance sleep, what chance me doing any wonted thing at all?

A lunatic's vigil ensued: I couldn't leave the window; I was bound fast to my vantage point and to my fate. No escape and no reprieve. I just had to kneel there, knuckle-whitened, and wait. Each move she made was another moment of acute crisis; another moment at which reality and imagination might be rent asunder and sent howling and crippled into their separate wildernesses of despair. In anguish, I watched her fold her arms in front and rest her chin upon them, thinking that now must come the final reckoning. In agony, I watched her hand reach back over her opposite shoulder to pull up the strap of her dress where it had fallen down her arm, convinced that she would have to turn. In awe, I watched her raise her head to follow a passing butterfly, certain that the gesture would disturb the geometry of her relaxation and cause her whole body to stir and show to me my destiny. Until, at last, in no time and with no ceremony or thought for her attendant disciple, she simply turned over on to her back.

And I nearly fell from the window.

What can I say? That she was extraordinarily beautiful. It will hardly do. That she looked like the sort of woman whom men do not dare to dream of? That her brow was delectable, her nose delightful, her mouth delicious? That she had the features of an angel? That hers was a face to melt both Poles at once, to drag the dead from their tombs,

to launch a thousand ships? None of this would quite cap-
ture it, I'm afraid. Then, as now, none of this would come
close.

Ladies and gentlemen: she was a real hottie.

> If thou, to be so seen, be'st loth,
> By sun, or moon, thou darkenest both,
> And if myself have leave to see,
> I need not their light, having thee.

I saw her face for only a second or two before she lifted her
sandals, took up the map and held it aloft so as to read while
simultaneously shading herself from the sun. Then, like a
taut rope sliced, I fell back into my studio and recoiled upon
my stool. After a moment, I laid down my quill with care
and due reverence and eased my way out from behind my
board. And after that, as I say, I fell apart . . .

I shot out of the studio, stopping only to pick up the keys
from my dining table (and not daring to look out of the
window again), and set off at spectacular velocity down my
(bastard, bastard) stairs before hurling myself along the pavement towards Roy's. I tornadoed through his door and came
twisting and harrying up to the counter.

'Roy, I . . . I need the best oranges you have got. Right
now. And a single lime – about a dozen – oranges, I mean
– and I haven't got time for you to weigh them so I'll just
take them on a guesstimate and pay you tomorrow, or later,
or whenever, and you can do the usual five per cent compound interest rate payable anew at the stroke of midnight,
every midnight, or whatever it was we agreed before.'

'Whooaah. Steady Mr Jackson. Steady. Deep breaths. No
need to panic. No need to get all carried away with compound
interest.'

'Roy – where are the bloody oranges?'

'Same as always Mr Jackson – on the fruit stand outside. You passed them on the way in. Everybody does.'

I exited the shop and began feverishly to gather the better oranges.

Roy filled the doorway. 'Having another one of our little lady-related emergencies, are we, Mr Jackson? Bit early in the week for that sort of thing isn't it . . . Fond of oranges, is she?'

'Roy, seriously: is it OK if I just take these? I really can't hang around right now.'

'Be my guest. A pleasure to see them going so fast.' He chuckled.

'Thanks. And I've got a couple of limes.'

'I'll make a note.'

Back up the road I hurtled, and across, and (fumbling for my keys at the big black front door) up, up, up I raced, back up the stairs and through my door, and up some more, and into the hall and straight to the kitchenette where I washed my hands and hastily, *frantically*, began slicing, squeezing, pouring until the job was done, lime and all, into a jug and into the freezer.

Off came my clothes, my work tunic over my head, my jeans shaken leg from leg as I tore into the bedroom. I threw myself into the shower. I scalded and froze and scalded and froze my shocked and flinching body. I leapt out. I towelled myself raw. I fetched out my trusty shorts, plunged into the arms of my freshly laundered, parchment-white, short-sleeved shirt and dashed back into the hall.

Freshly squeezed orange juice with just a little lime – the ideal refreshment and a pithy passport into my lady's afternoon.

One more check. I sprinted back to the studio window.

She had gone!

Oh *fuck*!

No. Wait!

She had only moved. She had only moved! Now she was lying across the bench almost directly beneath me. My God. But for how much longer? I eyed the treacherous sky. A grey-hulled taskforce of destroyer clouds was moving in from the west.

This time I took the stairs like an Olympic pommel-horse specialist, vaulting around the banisters with a mighty swing at each turn, rucksack pressed against my shoulder. I banged out of the front door and – sandals slapping like demented seal flippers on the twelve stone stairs down to Bristol Gardens – set off, left, towards the entrance to the communal garden.

Which was locked.

Oh, for heaven's sake. Must the human condition be forever frustration and inarticulate wrath at the sheer injustice of it all?

For a long minute I stood, stalled on Formosa Street like a bewildered and long-travelled tourist blinking in the summer sun outside the Uffizi gallery – 'Closed until next year for essential restoration work.' Vast, white, twelve foot high, the unscalable double gate mocked me, the light glaring in the bright white gloss. There was nothing else for it. I would have to go all the way round to the other entrance at the opposite end of the garden. I turned the corner back the way I had come and rushed up the hill.

And so into paradise at last I came, outwardly serene, but with a heart now beating itself blue against the cage of my ribs. Along the path, through the trees, into the open, across the grass, between the chestnut boughs, just a little further, and there she was. There she was: Venus on a bench with pillow.

At fifty paces, I deliberately scrunched on the gravel path. She glanced up in my direction. I stepped on to the grass and crossed towards the middle of the lawn between us. A black cat licked a white paw.

Fresh fucking orange juice!

What oh what oh what was I thinking? What kind of an idiot brought a woman he did not know – had not met, had only seen, had only seen from a distance – unsolicited orange juice? What in the name of arse was I doing? There she was: an innocent woman, minding her own business, quietly happy, undesiring of any man's attention, trying to read, trying to enjoy the sunshine, trying to live her life. And here was I . . . What had got into me? For God's sake man, turn it around for a single moment and ask yourself what you would think if your afternoon was hijacked by some terrible penis appearing (as if from the most casual of nowheres) with a picnic flask of freshly squeezed orange juice and two – *two* – glasses in his rucksack? Come on Jackson: only imagine her later relating the episode to her friends – their faces practically maimed with uncontrollable laughter – imagine her telling the story of this hapless, hapless scrotum of a man. Orange juice. Could anything be worse? Could anything be *less* natural?

Disgusted and horribly afraid, my faculties were fleeing the scene like so many deserting conscripts. But my stolid legs were carrying me ever on.

At thirty paces, the fiasco downshifted and became a disaster: unbelievably, unceremoniously, she started to get up. First she swung around so that she was sitting normally on the bench, her exquisite knees almost touching, then she picked up the pillow and . . . simply stood up.

Twenty paces and I could only look on aghast. Suddenly *she* had started walking towards *me*. It was appalling – desperate – ruinous. The light turned grisly pale, pregnant with doom. She cut the corner across the grass. The distance decreased at double speed.

Me: 'Finished with the bench?'

Her: 'It's all yours.'

Me: 'Thanks.'

And then she was past and there was only the faint almond scent of her sun lotion, followed by the sound of her footsteps as she reached the gravel path behind me. Six steps, seven, eight. I made the bench. I sat down. I looked up. She had already disappeared.

The wood was still warm.

7. The Triple Fool

I am two fools, I know,
For loving, and for saying so
In whining poetry;

'Finished with the bench?'

Finished with the bench?

Finished with the fucking bench?

Of course she had finished with the bench, my dear Jasper, she had risen from it, removed her things and walked decisively away. Could there be any clearer evidence than this?

I told you it was bad. I told you I fell apart. I blame horoscopes. I blame faulty chakra. I blame my parents. I blame her. I blame the shock of her face up close. If she hadn't looked . . . Oh Christ, I suppose I can no longer evade my descriptive duty. I'd better get it over with. Up close, she had the pure-skinned features of a perfume model but softer, more delicate and without the strident angles of someone employed to be striking in two dimensions. The day's sun had left a faint redness across the bridge of her pretty nose and her fleeting smile, when it came, was all the more price-less for the slightest downturn at the corner of her mouth. Her lips – parted a fraction as we passed each other – were neither full nor thin but, I noticed, the lower had been lightly bitten. Her brow, like her hair, was fair. Her eyes were a captivating hazel – quick and self-possessed. Taken altogether, there was, I remember thinking, something in the lines of her face that mingled provocation with her ridiculous beauty.

And yes, I know: it depresses me too. But the point is that from that desperate moment – down there on the canvas with the head swim and the eye sting and the blood in my ears and the referee already at nine – I was always going to demand a come back fight.

First, I called William.

'Well how many times have you seen her?'

'Three,' I replied. 'The first time I was buggering about with oranges and so I sort of fucked up what I –'

'You were *what*?'

'I . . . It's not important. Then I saw her again yesterday, walking towards the Tube when I was coming home. And now – just now – she's been out in the garden behind my flat for the last forty minutes. She started sunbathing but it's clouded over and she's gone back inside. That's three times. Anyway, listen, can you come over tomorrow?'

'I'm not sure. I half promised to take Nathalie to Good-wood and –' The void of a lost voice.

'Will, you're cutting out.' Some crackle and snap. 'Can you come over? She's killing me. I can't work in my bloody studio without looking out of the window every two seconds. I can't go to my local shops in case I run into her. Or worse, in case I *don't* run into her. It's hopeless . . . I have to know who she is. And I can't just go down into the bloody garden again, not yet, I . . . You're cutting out again. Where are you? What's all that racket in the background?'

'I am in a gents' toilet – in the Crowning Glory, actually,

just off the Strand. I am on my way to a charity dinner. The sound you can hear is a spate of rather jubilant flushing emanating from some of the nearby cabins. Hang on. Let me get out of here.'

I waited. A moment of exertion and then the regular click-clack of William's leather-soled shoes reasserted itself on the London pavement.

'Right. Back on track again. I tell you, Jackson: ever since they started closing all the public conveniences, things have become very tricky. I have to carry this guidebook around in my head with details of all the pubs in London that don't mind you taking an occasional tinkle and it's changing by the –'

'*William.*'

William cleared his throat. 'Sorry, Jasper. Where were we? A certain mademoiselle has appeared in your garden and she is interfering with your pointless life? Is that it?'

'Yes. It fucking well is it. I'm certain she's moved into one of the flats opposite. There was a basement for sale that I had to talk Lucy out of making an offer on. Maybe she's moved in there. Oh God, it's a bloody nightmare.' I paused. 'Will, seriously, I'm under *siege* here. I've never had this happen on my own doorstep before. I don't know if I can cope. If I don't speak to her by the end of the week, I will have to move.'

'It's only been a few days – she might be staying with someone. She might be gone before you know it and then you can relax – get on with your work.'

'She isn't and she won't.'

'But you haven't spoken to her?'

'No. Not exactly.'

'So you don't know. And all this excitement is based purely on the physical, on how she l—'

'No . . . Yes. No. Will, honestly, she eats cherries and spits out the stones. She reads maps. She . . . This is not like when I was twenty-one. Or last weekend with Annette or whatever. This is *serious*. She's intelligent. I can tell. No joke. She came out here before with a bottle of wine and this battered red bucket, for Christ's sake. And guess what she had in the bucket? Ice. Ice – to keep the wine cool. Can you believe it?'

'Amazing.'

'Oh fuck off. Of course it's physical. That's how the human race works. Stop being so pious. The whole planet is fucking physical. Look around you, man. *She's* very physical.'

'How come you need my help all of a sudden?'

'Because I live here and I can't go around the place asking questions. It might start to look odd.'

'What questions? You don't normally need to bother asking any questions.'

'I know I know I know. But she's . . . she's a very different proposition to normal, Will. I know it's bullshit but I have a . . . I have a *feeling* about her. And I don't want to make any mistakes.' A passing siren keened in the earpiece. Suddenly embarrassed, I collected myself. 'I have to know more about her before I proceed. I have to know the right way to go about things before I can . . . go about things.'

William was finally beginning to comprehend the gravity of the situation. 'You mean single or boyfriend or married or lezzer?'

'Yes, that sort of thing. And her name and whatever else.'

'Dear, oh dear. Whatever happened to romantic spontaneity?'

'Balls to spontaneity. She's far too attractive for that sort of crap. Spontaneity is a luxury available only to people who don't care about what happens next.'

'You *have* got it bad, young Jackson. She must be the

answer that you've spent your whole life look—' he prevented me interrupting. 'OK, OK, I believe you.'

'Can you make sure you're here in the morning – before the estate agents shut? I have an idea.'

William exhaled noisily. 'I suppose I can make myself available for a few hours. I'll think of it as visiting the sick and –'

'Good.'

'– and Jasper?'

'Yes? What?'

'I'm by no means a shrink but – in case you are interested – I would say that you are once more in the unrestrained grip of Jackson's Syndrome. Be aware that by any normal reckoning you are mentally ill.'

Second, I called on Roy. I paid him for the oranges and the limes and then asked, 'Roy, will you do me a favour?'

'Certainly, Mr Jackson – what would you like? More oranges?' He became worryingly excited. 'Oh yes, and my brother Trevor is bringing a delivery of fresh fish this afternoon for the new restaurant on Shirland Road. I am positive he can be persuaded to stop off – if you fancy a quick skate. Or how about a monkfish? Anything but cashews if you follow my drift, Mr –'

'No, Roy, no thanks. No fish just now. In fact, it's nothing to do with food. I just need you to keep a look out for me.'

'Keep a look out?' Up went two Schickelgruber brows.

'Yep. And don't worry, we can come to some sort of arrangement about fees or whatever.'

He looked alarmed. 'I can't leave the shop. You know that.'

'No, no, no,' I said, hastily. 'I don't want you to. I just need you to watch out for this woman who might –'

'Let me stop you right there, Mr Jackson.' He raised a palm and smirked. 'The subject of women is one about which I can truly say – hand on heart – that I know nothing at all. Whatsoever. Nor, I might add, do I intend to waste any remaining God-given attempting to learn. There's no *sense* to it, Mr Jackson. Nothing about women adds *up*. You always end up running the business at a loss – if you follow me. No, no,' he waggled an index finger, 'it doesn't bother me to say that I have known only one woman in my entire life – and that was my wonderful wife, or I should say ex-wife, Roy's mother. And ever since she decided that she was better suited to the Spanish . . . climate . . . well, I've not involved myself with the matter, beyond the exchange of seasonal niceties, of course. So I'm afraid if it's advice you're after, you have come to the wrong man, Mr Jackson. Now Roy Junior on the other hand, I have to say, he *does* appear to know a thing or two about the ladies and I'm sure that –'

'Roy, let me stop *you* there. I appreciate what you're saying, I really do, but you've jumped the gun a bit. All I am asking is that you keep an eye out for someone – and let me know if she's with anyone when she comes in. With a bloke, I mean.'

The doorbell jingled. I swung round. Another customer passed behind me and set off towards the frozen goods at the back.

Roy lowered his voice. 'Oh – I *see*. Right you are, Mr Jackson. No problem. You just want me to – shall we say – gauge the status – partner or otherwise – of a young lady whom you have reason to believe might be a customer of mine. Well, that's easily done. I can always tell what stage a couple have reached by the level of attention they pay to their food purchases. They start off not really giving a monkey's *derrière* about what they eat – excuse the Frog –

but, gradually, their interest deepens as it begins to take over from *you know what* – until eventually, after a bit of time, they're both obsessed by ingredients.' He shook his head, sadly. 'It's when they start asking for fresh herbs you know that things have ground to a halt in the bedroom department, as it were.'

I stood back to allow the other customer access to the counter. Six hundred litres of Diet Coke, two bottles of rat-slayer wine, two litres of death-bastard vodka, four tubs of ice-cream, chocolate sauce, chocolate sauce, a box of choc-olates, some chocolate slabs and four more tubs of chocolate ice-cream. She was around twenty-two and wearing her make-up to look as though she wasn't wearing any make-up.

She shrugged ruefully. 'We're having a girls' night in.'

I nodded thoughtfully. 'I'm impressed.'

She mistook my tone for sarcasm and shook her head – *men!* – as she helped Roy wedge things into his too-flimsy blue plastic bags. I held open the door for her and returned to the counter.

Roy leant forward, conspiratorially. 'So what does she look like, then, this young lady I've to keep an eye out for?'

'She's in her middle twenties, I think, Roy, five foot seven or eight, slim, blondeish hair – cut sort of expensively scruffy, just on the shoulder. You'll know her: she's extremely pretty and she's –'

'Got a great set of pins.'

It was my turn to look alarmed. 'I was going to say she's caught the sun. But yes. Yes, now you come to mention it, Roy, she has a great set of pins . . .'

Roy nodded sagely. 'Oh, just because I don't get involved doesn't mean I'm not an armchair enthusiast, Mr Jackson. No – no. In fact, I know exactly the woman you mean. And what's more, I wouldn't be lying to you if I said I saw her yesterday. Didn't come in here, mind, but she had her lunch over the road. Wears shorts and nice blue dresses and such – yes?'

'Yes! That's her! She was at Danilo's? Yesterday?'

'Yes. Seen her a few times now you mention it. But she was there yesterday sure enough for a couple of hours. I thought she was waiting for someone. Kept on looking around.'

Third, I went to see Carla.

For a short street, Formosa offers a number of dining options: an Italian café, an Italian delicatessen and an Italian bistro. Not exactly a dramatically contrasting range of world cuisine, you might argue, and hardly the cheek-by-jowl array of ethnic diversity that London is supposedly famous for. But nonetheless, over the last couple of years, believe me, I have come to savour their fine distinctions.

Danilo's, the bistro, is a second home of sorts. I am very good friends with the owners: Danny himself, and his wife, Carla, the Madonna of Little Venice, whom I adore and for whom I would do anything. Dark-haired, late forties, high cheekbones, disdain about her mouth, but with boundless compassion in her eyes – the mother I never had.

'Hello, Carla.'

'Hello, Jasper. How are you today?'

'OK.'

She was sitting behind the till, smoking her mid-morning cigarette and reading a magazine. There weren't any customers but from the kitchens came the sporadic clatter of pans – Cesare, the big-nosed, dwarfish chef, ugly brother to the long-suffering head waiter, Roberto. I asked Carla for an espresso. She locked the barrel in place and smiled, her cigarette lolling in the corner of her mouth.

I waited until the coffee was ready then located the most casual tone of voice I could manage: 'Carla – do you remember a girl who was in here yesterday, having lunch? With . . . sort of . . . sort of light-coloured hair?'

'Oh yes. Of course.' She pulled a peculiarly Italian expression – half appreciation, half contempt. 'She is very good. I serve her and I said to Roberto last night, he would have enjoyed doing the day shift yesterday because there is someone coming in who is very beautiful. She stayed for one hour and a half. Was waiting for somebody, I think. You know her?'

'Not exactly.' I hesitated for a moment. 'Carla, listen, if she comes in again – on her own – for lunch. Will you call me?'

'By the telephone?'

'Yes.' I drained my espresso in one.

She laughed. 'You are so stupid.'

'Will you though?'

'Yes, of course, if you want . . . you are trying to meet up with her?'

'Yes.'

She tutted. 'Danny tells me that when Roberto was ill before Christmas and you were helping us for that terrible Saturday, you had a girlfriend come in afterwards. She talked to Danny a long time. A nice English girl – Lucy, I think, yes? What happened to her?'

I shrugged. 'It was never serious.'

'It was not?'

'No. Not specifically.'

'And this new woman you want me to look for?'

I smiled, pretending to be cool. 'She is serious.'

'Oh – you know that for a fact?'

'I know.'

'You don't know. You never even speak with her.' She smiled but only with her eyes. 'I think maybe you would like it to be serious, yes? Maybe now you have no serious you want serious. Maybe you are tired of *ragazze*.'

'Here, I'll give you my number again – just in case.' I wrote on the top of her receipts pad. 'Keep it by the telephone. And, please, Carla, don't forget.'

'I won't. I will put on the shelf so I do not lose it.' She looked down at what I had written. 'How's it going, your big work?'

'It isn't.'

'*La bella donna?*'

'I can see her from where I sit. She comes into my garden – more or less naked.'

'Oh . . . then you must change where you work. Move into a different room.'

I sighed. 'That means carrying everything out of my studio, Carla, my board and my inks and my quills and –'

'The more beautiful a woman is, the more trouble that she will be, Jasper. That's how it is. This is life. God prefers that beauty is problems.'

8. Love's Diet

To what a cumbersome unwieldiness
And burdenous corpulence my love had grown,
   But that I did, to make it less,
   And keep it in proportion,
Give it a diet, made it feed upon
That which love worst endures, discretion.

Back at my board all hope of fluency was gone. But I was toughing it out. For the time being I had a new regime. I cherished grey skies but – come the first sign of the sun – I changed into my Venus surveillance mode. After every single word, I would get up and kneel upon my stool, lean out of the window and check the garden surreptitiously. Then, at the end of a line, I would allow myself a much more thorough reconnaissance: either I would go next door into the sitting room in order to change the angles and scan quadrant by quadrant (while leaning out on to the ledge, ostensibly to clip back my voracious mint plant, plead with the basil or tend to the permanently disadvantaged tarragon); or I would draw the blinds in the studio, stand upon the stool (the better to allow myself the necessary height) and peer through carefully contrived chinks in order to perform the same function or perhaps (even better) catch a glimpse of her coming outside and therefore establish in which of the opposite flats she was living.

To give you some idea of how this arrangement worked, the execution of lines two and three from 'Love's Diet', which

followed hard upon the heels of 'Air and Angels', went something like this: *'And'* (check) *'burdenous'* (check) *'corpulence'*
(check) *'my love'* (check – OK, so sometimes I let certain
inseparable words through security together) *'had'* (check)
'grown' (quills down, into the sitting room, lean out on to
the ledge and check check check). Back into the studio. *'But'*
(check) *'that'* (check) *'I'* (check) *'did,'* (longer check as befits
a comma). And so on.

Actually, it wasn't as trying as it might appear. For one
thing, I began to live the rhythms of the verse's punctuation
– the semi-quaver's rest of a comma, the quaver's semi-colon,
the crotchety full stop – and for another, ever desperate
to get to the end of the next line, I found to my surprise
that I wrote a little faster. Which was not an unwelcome
development.

Incidentally, you have to hand it to 'Love's Diet'. For a
poem inspired by a bad pun, it is extraordinarily impressive.
Just look at those phrases: *'cumbersome unwieldiness'* and
'burdenous corpulence' – the words themselves sagging and
ungainly on the line. (What other poet would dare to have
such off-putting and heavyweight bouncers on the doors of
a love poem?) And yet see how Donne controls and restrains
them even as he allows them to welter: he begins line one
in perfect iambic pentameter, lets line two bust out an extra
syllable and then yanks the metrical belt tight again (*'make
it less'*) the better to keep the verse itself in proportion. And
all this rhythm control carefully managed to bring that last
and most important word to us at its optimum weight, *'discretion'*.

Discretion: that which love worst endures.

There was no sign of her on that Friday and the weather
was still overcast when William came round early that

Saturday as requested. As an agent of espionage, he excelled himself. We had a brief 'debrief brunch' back at Danilo's, where he filled me in on the 'key learnings' garnered from his investigations. (Around this time William was spending a lot of time with many clever and very talented people from the exhilarating cut and thrust of the business world and his vocabulary was so much the subtler and more elegant for it.)

It transpired that the hog-breathed butt-child of an estate agent – opposite and just a few doors up from me on Bristol Gardens (the notorious ringleader of the dangerous 'we have lots of great bargains in the area, Lucy,' terror network) – had indeed handled the recent sales of two properties with direct access to the communal garden. As well as the one situated across from me that he had tried to push in Lucy's direction – Blomfield Road, number sixty one – there was another, up at the top end, on Clifton Villas.

William had found it relatively straightforward to elicit the information we needed by pretending that he himself was looking for a garden-access flat in my quadrangle, but of course he felt it impolitic to further enquire about the looks – sexy or otherwise – of the purchasers. However thus apprised, it was a short walk round to said addresses and an easy buzz on the buzzers of the respective Flat fives with 'a package for Flat two but there's no one answering, can you do the door so that I can put it inside?'

Clifton Villas was a close call. The occupants of the basement – a young family – came out of their flat just as William came through the main front door. But Blomfield Road was more illuminating. Nobody was around. And the post was still all over the floor. The occupant of the basement was known to various speculative credit card and utility companies as Ms. M.I. Belmont, Miss Madeleine Belmont, plain

Miss Belmont and, to one particularly zealous champion of the door-to-door 'executive rewards' club, as Miss M. Belmonté.

After 'brunch', I tried to talk Will into staking out the garden with me but he refused, saying that I was in need of help (which was no help at all) and that he had to leave for Goodwood to test drive a new old Maserati.

Looking back, I realize now that it must have been around this time that he and Nathalie started entertaining the beast with two backs. Certainly, I noticed a definite change: Will was becoming ever so slightly dutiful – a tell-tale sign that there has been more than one congress. (Try as they might, men cannot in their heart of hearts quite shake off the idea that sex is a massive favour, a singular gift from women, which it is forever their obligation somehow to repay. I daresay there's some half-arsed anthropological reason for all this, but after a couple of promising rethinks in the sixties and seventies, the chicks, I notice, seem to be tacitly promoting the whole duty regime again – and with renewed enthusiasm.)

I returned to HQ alone. Mentally, I flicked on the bare electric bulbs, shut the door, rolled out the maps and considered my dispositions.

Madeleine Belmont.

I knew her name and where she lived. But that was all. I knew nothing about her circumstances.

There were three options: either she was married, or she had a boyfriend, or she was single.

What about a husband? Well, it was a possibility, I had to admit, but I hadn't seen a ring during the ghastly bench incident, and Will's mail research militated against it. Unlikely.

Single? Obviously, the chances of that were so anorexic that I just could not permit myself even to consider them. As any young man will tell you, *all* good-looking girls have boyfriends or are married (to idiots) and to assume anything else would be something akin to betting against gravity. Indeed, so joyous, rare and unlikely an outcome was her being single that I actually preferred to proceed as though it were entirely impossible – thereby secretly allowing myself the minute chance of a blissful surprise in the event that things turned out that way.

No – all things considered, the only intelligent manner in which to advance my campaign was to assume a boyfriend scenario – at least until I saw or heard clear evidence of something else. Beyond that, the crucial question was: how close were they? I hadn't *seen* him – but that didn't necessarily mean that they didn't live together. He might, after all, simply be away. Or he might have been indoors the whole time, purposefully grappling with recalcitrant bathroom units. Or perhaps they maintained separate homes, taking it in turns to stay over and sooner or later I would run into him on Formosa Street, newspaper under arm, milk in hand, heading back for a late morning of coffee and croissants over the blandishments of the Review section . . .

In any case, whatever the exact nature of her circumstances, an operational model premised on a boyfriend was the one I was most used to dealing with and no cause for concern. Quite the reverse: though invariably repulsive in person, I have always found the concept of a serving boyfriend rather reassuring. This is because of the Great Boyfriend Paradox, which goes something like this: boyfriends are to be welcomed because they make everything *less*, not more complicated, since their presence allows the professional to bow out of the action at any time, leaving the subject no worse off than before – probably happier; boy-friends are also to be welcomed because, by virtue of their incumbency, they are duty-bound (that word again) to enact and take care of all the most tedious and quotidian aspects of the relationship thereby setting the *arriviste* off to best advantage; and finally, boyfriends are to be welcomed because they are the single most obvious indicator that the subject does not yet want a husband and is therefore – in some slight way – *amenable*.

There is another possibility of course: that the woman does not view her adult life in terms of marriage – we have, after all, moved on from the world so brilliantly satirized by the great Jane Austen. Against this can (and should) be said that even today there are very few women (or men) under forty who actually think like that. Below the waterline they are all of them harbouring the intention to put to sea in that beautiful pea-green boat; and further, that even if a given woman is flat out, no-shit, adamantly single, then, assuming she's not a lesbian, the likelihood is that she will still want to meet new and interesting men, if only because (again, like men) most women can only take so much of their own sex.

I took a deep breath and tapped my imaginary baton across imaginary contours. There were a few more logistical necessities to be taken care of. One: if I was going to give this woman the undivided attention I felt she deserved, then I had to close off and secure all other fronts – once the engagement began, there could be no distractions. And two: I needed to wrest back control of absolutely everything in the world, starting with my mind and including the weather. As to the first: well, Lucy was gone; and neither Cécile nor Annette would contact me unless I contacted her first – easily not done; which left only . . . Selina.

You are quite right: I haven't mentioned Selina before. But before everyone starts rolling their eyes, and getting all shirty and well-if-that's-your-attitude, there is (actually) a very good reason for my keeping quiet. Because – apart from her being married and the whole deal between us being about discretion – I only ever saw Selina when she called me (actually). And usually for fewer than three hours around lunchtime. Besides which, she hadn't telephoned since before my birthday, so there was no need to bring her up until now. Be fair.

I have to say that I didn't really want to go through with it though. Unilateral endings are always tough for a guy, even if the woman in question has a husband and two kids. *Especially* when she already has a husband and two kids. Getting started – sure – for that there's nobody better than your average man, but when it comes to a one-sided decision to clear the decks once and for all, then you really need to be strong like a woman. You must be unequivocal in your own mind that you want to sever relations completely – no ifs, no buts, no seeing-how-it-goes. You need to be prepared to deny every possible future from every possible angle: 'No, I mean it; I don't want to carry on any more; It's not right; It can't work; I've thought about it and it can *never* work; There are no reasons, it's how I feel; I don't think we should see each other for a few years; Actually, I don't think we should see each other ever again . . .' Plus you also have to be sure within yourself that when the amorous ghosts of nostalgia come calling (on lonely autumn amber-hued evenings) you will not succumb to their solicitation. In other words, you need to be not only hard and cruel as frozen nails but (and you have to love this twisted chick-trick) hard and cruel to be soft and kind *in the long run*, hard and cruel because you have looked deeper and further into the future and one day your now-tearful partner will be grateful for your selflessness. Only in this way – by adopting a woman's steely beaked, iron-nerved, brass-balled attitude can you be absolutely sure of killing the relationship thing dead.

What you cannot do is enter into the conversation secretly thinking that maybe there is a way (after all) that the two of you could carry on sleeping together from time to time on an *ad hoc*, carnal-necessity basis. What you cannot do is call back and be nice a few days later, with a view to calling back three days after that and saying: 'How about we get together just this once for old times' sake?' Such approaches – though beloved of men the world over – are entirely useless when it comes to shutting things down. Ending a relationship is just like giving up smoking: if you're quitting, you're quitting; the books are all bullshit and cutting down doesn't work.

Solemnly mindful of all this, I emerged at Sloane Square and set off beneath skies of sodden sugar for my rendezvous with some sadness in my heart.

Selina works in advertising and therefore has no taste whatsoever. (Except in her choice of lovers of course . . .) And her chosen spot for our lunchtime appointments was always the same: Felix G's, a well-established restaurant on the King's Road, famous for both the architectural barbarity of its façade and the uncompromising vulgarity of its many scrotal clientele within. (Behind a front of polished steel and tinted glass, their faces stretched taut by the surgeon's knife, coarsening female refugees from bad and bygone decades sip luncheon champagne and talk about their alimony payments while permatanned men scour the rules of conversation to find new ways to brag.) This time, however, it was I who had suggested the venue. And I have to acknowledge that as we waited in the mirrored portals of reception, my many reflections and I were filled with an almost rueful affection for Felix and his oleaginous staff.

Eventually, the maître d' found it within his bounty to divulge the news that Selina had already arrived and that she had changed our table and was now sitting upstairs in the far corner. I made my way up.

She was wearing sunglasses pushed up on to her head. Beside her, in a sort of ultra-modern high chair, was a runtish child with frazzled ginger hair that looked as though it were singed nightly by some strange breed of aliens with plans of their own. He grinned at me and then put his finger in his ear. I judged his age to be somewhere between one and two. I sat down.

'Who is this?' I asked.

Ginger picked up an olive on a stick and held it up for me, dangling it loosely between his thumb and finger.

'Patrick.' Selina prised the sharpened stick from his clutch and ate the olive herself.

'Very handsome,' I said.

'I'm on a four-day week so he comes everywhere with me on Mondays.' She shrugged, as if to say, I am sorry but you did break the rules: you called me, which isn't allowed, and I *am* a mother, you know. 'Do you want a drink, JJ?'

'What are you on?'

'Mineral water. With lemon. I have to drive later.'

'I'll have a Bloody Mary then.'

The waiter came towards us like a tanker spill reaching the beach. Ginger took the opportunity to grab a fist full of olives and chuck them on the floor. Selina asked for my drink and another juice for her objectionable charge.

She restrained Ginger. 'So, why did you call me?'

'I'm sorry. Was it OK?'

'Yes, it's fine on my mobile. Just please don't do it too often.'

'I won't.'

'You look well.'

'You too.'

We talked about nothing for a while. In truth, Selina looked tired. Her hair was pretending otherwise – all highlights and cut like some ideal distillation of the latest Hollywood thirty-something trend – but there were faint lines around her eyes. And yet I could not help but suspect that in a way Selina quite liked the hassled sexiness of her appearance: pressured, hemmed-in, mother, boss, colleague, wife, board director, daughter. Deep down, she knew that weary-but-flirtatious, young-mother-of-two, come-and-get-me-if-you-dare was her strongest suit. No doubt she worried a little about being thirty-six and the extra weight that her children had left behind (which she didn't need to lose because in fact she looked all the better for it) but also deep down she knew that she had exactly the life she had dreamed of. Deep down she had probably anticipated a lover ever since she was old enough to imagine a husband.

I had to cut this out. Loose thoughts the native hue of resolution dull. I'd be in a bloody hotel if I wasn't careful – Patrick or not. I made a decision. 'Listen Selina, I don't want to have lunch.'

She knotted her brow. 'You don't?'

'No, I came to see you because I wanted to say that –' I looked at Ginger. How much do one-year-olds understand? 'That we have to stop. Our thing.'

She made a scornful expression. The drinks arrived. We waited awkwardly while the waiter waited too. Selina addressed him with her professional woman's voice. 'Nothing just yet. Can you give us ten minutes?'

I took a sip of my Bloody Mary. Disappointment. Can nobody in the world make anything properly any more?

'I thought you liked seeing me . . .'

'I do,' I said. 'Very much.'

'So I don't understand.' She lifted the child from his high chair.

'I don't know how long it has been, Selina, but –'

'Three years,' she cut in. 'On and off.'

I removed the dismal celery from my glass. 'And I've always looked forward to seeing you. Honestly. Really.'

She could tell I wasn't lying. 'Well, what's the problem? I'm hardly asking for commitment.' She jogged Ginger on her knee as if subconsciously to underline her point.

'I know that.'

'And I presume it's nothing religious.' She smiled.

I smiled in return. 'If it were to do with my religion I'd be asking to see you more.'

'But you want us . . . not to. Any more.'

'Yes.'

She took a deeper breath. 'Fine. Your decision.' A moment of wounded pride and then she changed tack, evincing concern – an older woman's power ploy. 'Are you OK? Has something happened?'

Ginger opened wide, stuck out his tongue and let it drool.

I hated myself for even thinking what I said next. 'Yes. In a way. Something *has* happened. I am seeing someone . . . quite seriously . . . and I don't want to be unfaithful . . . to her.' Oh God, such premature and jinx-inviting lies. But they did the trick.

'Oh, I *see*. You should have said. And has she stolen all of you?'

I nodded.

'I didn't think it would ever happen. I thought you of all

people were a safe bet.' She was still being flirtatious but only for the sake of the routine. The fight was gone. All that was left was for her to try to patronize the younger woman, whom, of course, neither of us had ever met. 'I suppose she's very clever and beautiful.'

'Yes, she is.'

I was depressed all the way home. Renunciation is a miserable business. Especially in the cities. Especially in London, where daily life is served out so cold and raw among so many strangers. It's Hollywood's eternally adolescent all-or-nothing men and women fables that do all the damage of course. Though most of us somehow remember that bullets and car crashes kill in real life, we take the romance myth to heart, we forget to suspend our disbelief. But the disappearing truth is that a man can like a woman in a certain kind of a way – on a certain afternoon perhaps, or in the evening over dinner every once in a while. And a woman can like a man the same: now and then, from time to time, in some specific setting, in some specific role. There don't have to be promises about eternity or improbable undertakings of a responsibility beyond the moment – just the powerful then and there of a friendship, tacitly attended by desire. And it may not quite be love and it may not be for ever, but the two of them still like one another and it still counts.

It was a son of a bitch about Selina.

But it had to be done.

When I got back to my flat, I checked the weather and then cheered myself up with Bach's ridiculous Concerto for Four Harpsichords.

The forecast was for a heatwave. Several days of uncommonly hot sun followed by biblical downpours. I went into my studio and looked out of the window. There was no sign of her. Carla had not called over the weekend. There was no word from Roy. I appraised the work on my board. 'Love's Diet' was not quite finished. I read the first verse again and arrived once more at that word 'discretion'.

Very well, I thought, let me become the master's pupil: a period of temperance and withdrawal and self-control, far away from the windows of temptation and desire. I changed into my calligraphy tunic and then began slowly to move my board, my inks and all my quills out of the studio and into my bedroom. Let Venus have the garden awhile.

Part Three

9. The Damp

Poor victories; but if you dare be brave,
    And pleasure in your conquest have,
First kill th'enormous giant, your Disdain,
And let th'enchantress Honour, next be slain,
    And like a Goth and Vandal rise,
    Deface records, and histories
Of your own arts and triumphs over men,
And without such advantage kill me then.

The rain fell in the last of my dreams. When I awoke the air was cooler. I lay for a moment and listened to the heavy patter until, curious to see for myself, I rose and crossed to the window. Water was pouring from the sky, splashing thickly on the roofs of the houses opposite, coursing down their tiled valleys, welling up in the guttering. I hoisted up the frame and put out my head.

My five days in the droughty wilderness were over. Having disconnected the phone again, I had done nothing but work since my lunch with Selina. And not once – through all the scorching sunny hours – had I approached the garden-facing windows.

Now I made for the hall and tentatively entered my studio. The room seemed forlorn without my board or stool. Grateful for the rain, I released the blind and took a long look into the garden. Water was pooling in shallow muddy puddles around the empty bench.

I do not wish to mislead you: beyond returning to my proper place of work, I had as yet no fixed plans. Venus would appear soon enough, I imagined, or Carla would call and I would find her at Danilo's. Either way, I felt that my quarantine had done me much good. Some sorely needed cool had returned and I was prepared to bide my time. That scuffed old law: pursue a woman purposefully but never with impatience.

I took tea in the bath with Donne. At that time, as I recall, I was just starting 'The Apparition': '*When by thy scorn, O murderess, I am dead . . .*' But, rather naively and on account of the pissing rain, I decided to read 'The Damp' instead. I had noticed that both works – very oddly – used the narrator's death as their point of departure. Which coincidence further confirmed me in what I had begun to suspect: that *The Songs and Sonnets* were best approached as a collection of cross-commentating poems – much as one might listen to a theme and variations in music. Donne's theme is Love itself (the opening aria to which the piece must always return), while the variations range from purest union and equality between the sexes to undisguised contempt; from one of his poems entitled 'Song' ('*Sweetest love, I do not go, / For weariness of thee . . .*') to the other of the same name ('*And swear / No where / Lives a woman true, and fair . . .*'). Each variation makes perfect sense alone, of course, but it is only as a collection that the tones achieve full resonance.

At first sight, I thought that 'The Damp' looked particularly flippant. And in a way I was right: it is a work of amusement and play. These days, though, I consider it to be an exquisitely calibrated *tour de force* – not least because Donne somehow manages to move from a man's cold corpse (laid upon a mortician's slab and being cut open for forensic examination) to the intimation of a woman's naked body (likewise laid out, but on her bed and very much alive) and all in twenty-four short lines.

The title refers to something like poisonous mist or fog that arises in the first verse during one of Donne's most memorable 'scenes'. (Fuck all to do with rain, but I wasn't to know.) The dead lover is to be dissected in order to satisfy the curiosity of his friends, who cannot understand what has killed him. The physicians go ahead and dismember the cadaver, considering each body part in turn until eventually they find a picture of the lover's tormentress in his heart. This picture releases a *sudden damp of love*, which threatens to work its lethal charm on the senses of those gathered at the autopsy, so turning the single murder of the poet into a general massacre.

Such macabre melodramatics are characteristic: Donne can be a real horror-merchant when he wants to be and (as so often with the genre) there is a sick, kitschy humour lurking around the mortuary. Certainly, the intellectual urge to push love from something intoxicating to something just plain toxic is – I have come to realize – typical of his idiosyncratic artistic intelligence. However, intellectual ingenuity aside, what struck me most of all was the tone of the second verse.

> Deface records, and histories
> Of your own arts and triumphs over men,
> And without such advantage kill me then.

Not only is the poem one of those that deal explicitly with the notion of an ongoing battle between men and women, but also, on this occasion, Donne has granted himself a worthy opponent. Her presence is keenly felt throughout, partly because of the direct address with which he begins and partly because of the manner of Donne's writing, which assumes a fellow gamester, implacable but intelligent in her opposition. Women conquer too; and despite the erotically charged, nudge-nudge ending, there's an unusual tang of parity in the air.

Leon telephoned around three, just after I had finished moving my gear back into the studio.

'Hello Jasper,' he began, morosely. 'It's Leon – from downstairs.' Despite my having lived above him for two years, Leon always introduced himself in this way. 'How are you?'

'OK,' I said, 'and you?'

'Oh, struggling on with it all.' There was a pause while he swam the vast and slate-blue lakes of his inner melancholia to bring to me his request. 'Listen Jasper – can I ask a serious favour?'

With much apology and several semibreves' worth of rests, he explained that he needed to practise for a couple of hours and that he hated to disturb me and realized that it was wholly unfair but could I not play any music on my stereo either – at least until this evening?

As on previous occasions, I happily agreed and we were both about to hang up when the idea suddenly struck me.

'Leon?'

The phone came very slowly back up to his ear: 'Yes?'

'Are you around this evening – later on, after you've finished? I mean, what are you doing?'

'Yes. Nothing. Just finishing. That's as far as I have thought ahead. The finish. And then . . .'

'Well, Leon, this is our chance! Why don't we go to *The Review* – at the Lock Theatre, above the pub? You never know, it might cheer you up. A change of scene, comedy, laughter, you might even enjoy yourself . . .'

He cleared his throat. 'OK. Why not? Tonight, I suppose,

is as good a time as any. When is it on? Do they have a show on Sundays?'

'Yeah, I'm sure they do. It's at eight-thirty, I think. I'll book tickets and knock on your door at – say eight?'

Around four that afternoon, when I broke off from my work to call the Lock Theatre, I got a pre-recorded message, apologizing for itself and then giving the impression that the box office would be staffed to capacity if only I would telephone again anytime after five. This I duly did, but was then treated to ten long minutes of uninterrupted ringing. (Stranded in the hall – muffled Shostakovich in one ear and dring-dring in the other.) When I tried a third time, I got another pre-recorded message, saying sorry again but that the box office shut at six-thirty and thereafter tickets had to be 'purchased and collected in person'. So at something like six-thirty-five and feeling somewhat at a loss, I was on the brink of calling Leon to convey the uninspiring news when I realized that I might as well do as they suggested. Bastards.

Five minutes later, I stood leaning against the open front door and struggled to unwrap, unfasten, unlock, unleash my wretched umbrella. The rain was still coming down in great swollen drops, drumming lazily on the roofs of the parked cars. And the air smelled even more lush than it had earlier in the day. I set off, gingerly splashing down the stairs and on to the pavement.

The road really was awash: there were little v-shaped eddies around all the lamp-posts and parking restriction poles; and several of the grids were backed up as though the sewers themselves were already full. A car sluiced by in four dirty fountains of spray.

At the corner of Bristol Gardens and Clifton Villas the wind gusted, snatching at the umbrella and bending the rain underneath before I could tug it down again. If anything, conditions were worsening. For a stride or two I considered retreat but kept on, heartened by the sight of an old woman whipping along the opposite pavement in sou'wester and wellington boots. By the time I reached Blomfield Road, I was fighting my way through the beginnings of a monsoon. Hanging tight to the handle, I hurried along the road parallel to the canal until I came to the bridge. I turned sharp right and hastened over.

I must have been looking down at the canal itself – pock-marked, brown and turbid – because when I raised the edge of the umbrella a fraction to check my way ahead she was already close upon me.

Half-walking, half-running, staying on her toes and dart-ing this way and that to avoid the worst of the puddles and with one hand holding a sodden newspaper above her head in a futile attempt to protect herself, she looked as though she had spent the last three days swimming in from some desperate shipwreck. I had no time to contrive anything, no time – thank God – to think. We were about to pass and I acted on instinct. She slowed to go around me. I lifted my umbrella high enough so that she could see my face. She looked at me in genuine surprise and hesitated for a second. I handed her the umbrella's stem and said: 'Take it, I'm only going over there', gesturing towards The Lock. She clasped it in her hand and thumbed her wet hair off her cheek.

I said, 'Don't worry, you can give it back to me whenever', and turned to go. There was nothing more she could do except shout 'Thanks', which I only just heard over my shoul-der because already I was dashing towards the theatre door and her voice was being drowned out by the rain.

10. Negative Love

> If that be simply perfectest
> Which can by no way be expressed
>   But negatives, my love is so.
>   To all, which all love, I say no.
> If any who decipher best,
>   What we know not, ourselves, can know,
> Let him teach me that nothing; this
> As yet my ease, and comfort is,
> Though I speed not, I cannot miss.

The next day the downpour stopped, gradually giving place to a flotilla of clouds and, by Tuesday, a steady dispersing sun and a good afternoon light. I was at my board, still working away on 'The Apparition', when she appeared. She walked across the grass to her favourite spot, laid out a rug, removed her T-shirt and sat down. And I . . .

Oh well *I* allowed myself a nonchalant minute or two to appreciate the scene and then returned directly to my work, pausing only to consider the pleasing shape of the word 'solicitation'.

With almost insulting insouciance I finished another entire line – *'Then shall my ghost come to thy bed'* – before rising from my stool and checking to see if she was still there. After which I passed calmly into the hall where I picked up the phone and piped a call down to the Roach in his basement burrow, asking if six-fifteen was a convenient time to drop by and pick up the music that I had lent him. Then I took a leisurely shower and put on a linen shirt.

Diaghilev himself could not have choreographed it better.

'Hello,' I began, as I sauntered by. 'It's going to be a beautiful evening, isn't it?'

She twisted round, caught by surprise. 'Oh, hello again. Yes, it is – and it's still quite warm too.' She sat up. She was wearing her blue dress again.

I kept my eyes fixed on hers.

Now she smiled. 'Hey, thanks for –'

'No. Not at all.' I interrupted with a reciprocal smile. 'It was too late anyway. You were pretty soaked.'

'I know, I know.' She made a rueful face. 'Complete disaster. I suddenly got it into my head that it would be really romantic to go jogging in the rain. God knows why. I thought it was stopping. But it started absolutely pissing down on the way back – just when I was totally knackered and I'd settled for the walking briskly thing. Serves me right. First run in three years.'

'Bad timing.' I nodded sagely. 'Probably the wettest five days since records began; everything else these days seems to be the worst it has ever been since records began.'

She laughed. 'If you hang on a second I'll just go get –'

Again, I stopped her. 'No – seriously – don't get up now. You can drop it off anytime – I only live over there on Bristol Gardens – number thirty-three – top flat. Or I'll see you here sometime, I'm sure. Anyway, enjoy the sun. I'm running late.'

'OK. Right.' She blinked – twice. 'Thanks.'

She turned back to her book and I carried casually on my way towards the little gate that separated the Roach's overgrown patio from the garden.

I peered in through the windows. He was standing behind his record decks with his back to the sheer cliff face of black speakers and seemed to be sort of shuffling on the spot while holding one of the headphones against his left ear. For no reason that I could divine, he also appeared to be wearing a bobble hat.

OK, a two-minute exchange – nothing more than that, I admit. But enough, I felt, judging the texture of the encounter as a whole; enough for me to feel confident that our next meeting would be very soon and with considerably less embarrassment than our first. For though men may feel the need to march back and forth beneath the proverbial window – roses clenched in jaw, mandolins at the ready – women are slightly more subtle when it comes to signalling their interest. A woman can give herself away in the flickering of an eyelid. Or two.

Oh, of *course* I realized that there were many questions unanswered, a thousand tedious impedimentia to be overcome. Perhaps she was on the brink of marriage to some snake-hipped Hollywood director, famous for his irresistible good looks and near-Periclean eloquence; or perhaps, after long reflection, she had decided to join the dwindling community of some island nunnery, cut off from the rest of humanity by that grim chastity belt otherwise known as the Irish Sea; or then again, perhaps she was locked into some epic fifteen-year affair with her childhood sweetheart, an adorable baby with whom she had shared a Bank Holiday paddling pool, now grown to be a great Achilles of a man, striding hither and thither among the aid workers of Africa; or maybe she was intent on a life of predatory afternoons in provincial dyke bars. But balls to it all, I thought. For a happy while elation ruled. And I was underway. There would come a time when she ditched the director, fled the convent, cast off her childhood crushes or grew bored of boots and battered biker-jacketed weekends in Brighton.

You think I read too much into our little garden *rencontre*? Why then, oh sceptical jury, did Miss Madeleine Belmont skip so sweetly up the steps of number thirty-three Bristol Gardens and buzz the buzzer of Flat six, the residence of Jasper Jackson, calligrapher and gentleman, *the very next day*?

Suspecting telecom salesmen or worse (and fully expecting to be out), I entered my bedroom, tea in hand, and softly slid up the window. From above, I could see only the tangle of blonde. But there was no doubt. It was she all right: standing by the intercom and waiting for me as though there could be nothing more natural in all the world for a girl to be doing on a Wednesday morning than delivering a man an umbrella. I pulled my head in quickly and drained my cup. The water coughed in the pipes.

The best thing about a good trick is that as long as you keep changing your audience, you can do it as many times as you like. I went into the hall and picked up the entryphone.

'Hello?'

'Hi, it's me,' came the voice, 'I was on my way out and I've . . . brought your umbrella round.'

'Oh, it's *you*. Hi. Er . . . hang on a second – I'll come down – I'm afraid the lock's broken and I can't open the door from up here.'

A swift but contemplative moment to dismiss the idea of taking a quill with me – held casually in the hand as though mid-sonnet (which was not, after all, that far from the truth) – and down I went. I opened the door and smiled my warmest smile – a Tuscan sun shimmering across a valley of ripening vines that whisper to one another of forthcoming Montepulciano. Or so I like to think.

'Hey thanks . . . I'm sorry I don't know your name,' I lied, taking the umbrella.

'Madeleine,' she said.

'Right, well, thanks . . . Madeleine.' I offered her a light-hearted hand to shake, which she took with faint amusement. 'I hope you didn't make a special journey.' I was standing with my heel against the open door behind me.

'No, I'm just around the other side – on Blomfield Road – and I was on my way over to buy some stuff for lunch from the grocery store, so it's kind of on the way.'

'From Roy's?' I grinned.

'Roy's?'

'Oh, he's the guy who owns the shop over there – fat guy with a Charlie Chaplin moustache. You must have seen him. He'll get you anything you want if you give him enough time. But watch him on the prices – he does these weird economic experiments on his regulars.'

She nodded. 'Right. I only just moved in – more or less. And I'm still getting to know the locals.'

Curiously, there was an anticipatory quality to her voice – as though she had thrown a conversational bone. I stalled slightly. My instincts twitched. I just couldn't believe that this was going to be so facile as a let-me-show-you-around operation? Not possible. Not with a woman like her. Too easy. Acting on some unconscious principle of distrust, I stepped around the opportunity. 'Right. Well, it's a great part of London – sort of immune from the usual classification of inhabitants syndrome.'

She frowned for a second then the corners of her mouth rose. 'That's pretty much the only reason I chose it.'

'Ah . . . now you see, *that* is the problem,' I said, deliberately taking her at face value. 'More and more people are choosing to live in the Warwick Avenue environs because they see it as a haven for the type of person who can't face the possibility that they might be a type of person.'

'Mmm.' She narrowed her eyes slightly. 'I hadn't realized.'

I was aware that I was talking even more crap than usual. But all of a sudden, I had become convinced that she was expecting me to ask her out   then and there – and that (worse) she was actually deriving some private amusement from betting with herself how long it would be before I (the Typically Pedestrian Male) would think it appropriate to drop the line. (Not that I was certain she would say yes. Quite the reverse: I feared she might be quietly looking forward to saying no.) But I wasn't going to oblige her so easily. Above all else, I was determined to take no risks until I knew intimately the lie of the relationship hinterland. Instead, rather than chance so early a refusal, I decided that I would have to be vague – fudge the invitation, make it clear but non-specific.

'Anyway, I guess I'd better get back to the grindstone.' I moved back half a step.

'Sure.' If she was surprised, she did not betray it.

I nodded. 'Well – if you're ever at a loose end, I'm usually at Danilo's most lunchtimes, so drop by if you feel like it.'

'OK, I will.' She smiled. She was already down the steps and on the pavement.

I closed the door in the manner of one who has already forgotten his visitor and is much preoccupied with urgent business within.

Not great. A bit stilted. Not exactly cool. Could have done better. A little out of sorts. And for the first time in a long time: *nervous*. All of this I concede . . . But on the positive side there was an affirmative ring to that 'OK, I will' of hers. So not to worry, I reflected, over an uncharacteristically early gin sling, I had made the right decision – a matter of instinct.

Why not jump straight in? You may well ask. Because . . .

because I felt it far too risky. As Donne says: '. . . *this* / *As yet my ease, and comfort is* / *Though I speed not, I cannot miss.*' No doubt the well-meaning amateur (egged on by that canting old harlot otherwise known as conventional wisdom) may feel that honesty is the best policy. Nothing ventured, nothing gained, he muses to himself as he decisively switches off the television; faint heart never won fair maiden. If she says 'yes', all well and good, take it from there; if she says 'no', then nothing was ever going to happen anyway, so nothing has been lost. But such a thin and binary world is sadly denied the professional. Once you cannot live with the outcome 'no', once you accept the burden of believing that 'yes' is always possible if only the question is well crafted and well timed, once you *care* about the seducee, then the premature rebuke has to be avoided at all costs. Instead, you must min-imize the danger by moving with meticulous attention until you have understood both her situation and her sensibilities well enough to frame your appeal in such a way that she will find churlish to resist. A woman with a steady boyfriend, for example, will usually baulk at a straight proposal. But she might well say 'yes' to a carefree invitation which, she can tell herself, does not directly threaten or compromise her relationship . . .

But Jesus Christ the waiting was tough. Inevitably, 'most lunchtimes' now meant 'every lunchtime', since I could not afford to miss the one on which she chose to drop by. Carla, with whom I still had my standing arrangement and whom I could have trusted to be my sentinel, had been on holi-day (back to beautiful Roma to see her sister) since the heat-wave. This left me in the hands of Roberto, who, though never unfriendly or rude, nonetheless served me with the air of someone who wanted everyone to know that he was working two shifts a day. (Aren't we all, bud?) Two *weeks* passed. And truth be told, I was feeling neither 'ease' nor 'comfort'. The drawing board loomed.

On the first Wednesday in May, I had almost decided that enough was enough, that I would have to change my plan. I was seated on the pavement beneath overcast skies, eating yet another salad. (Venus must not come upon me mid-spaghetti or carving into veal.) I was also, I noticed, losing weight – at something like a quarter of a stone a week. Idly, I calculated that Madeleine had only to spurn me for another forty-three or so weeks and I would have entirely dis-appeared. No great loss to humanity, I recognized, but a bitter blow to me personally.

Inside, Roberto had his hands full with a group of over-coiffured mothers and their equally demanding infants. I meanwhile tortured myself with boyfriends. The whole ugly question lurked like an incontinent dingo on the high street of my intentions. More than anything else, not knowing this vital piece of information was holding me back, cramping my style. And still no news from Roy. More and more my feeling was that she lived alone. But the fact was, I couldn't believe – didn't dare to – that she did not have some kind of a partner somewhere. Fine if so, and amazing if not, but obviously the two possibilities required entirely different approaches and I could not move forward safely until I knew one way or the fucking other.

I have explained that I have no problems with boyfriends as a concept. But I should also say that in person, they disgust me. For the most part they are repulsive creatures: lazy, stupid, impatient, incapable of listening, complacent, insensi-tive, unappreciative, woodenly duplicitous, simpering or smug. Aside from the one or two times a year when they are seized by the sentimental need to ham it up on some

God-awful holiday somewhere – doubtless spurred on by a sunset and a bottle of New World *méthode champenoise* – they spend most of their pallid lives sprawled on their backs snoring or furtively beating off whenever they get time to themselves. In my nightmares I see legions of them, like heavy bum-cracked builders crammed into ill-fitting military uniforms – rank upon rank and file after file of boyfriends, stretching away across the monochrome of a vast parade ground, with their thuggish banners of red and black boredom, their pennants of tenure, their flags of loyalty fluttering in a steely breeze. Meanwhile, Herr Fidelity, that brutish dictator, looks down from the grey castle walls and surveys his rallied power with a functional nod.

At ten to two there was still no sign of her. I ordered another coffee. Roberto obliged. I watched and I waited. I waited and I watched. The traffic continued to fidget around the Warwick Road roundabout. I couldn't do this for another week. It was ridiculous. I flipped up my paper. For one thing, I was reading too many soul-stripping reports on what passes for contemporary British politics. (A never-ending performance given by a sixth-form cover band who can't really play but employ a wide repertoire of jejune guitar poses in a desperate effort to distract from their deficiencies.) I turned the page. I learned about the world's most obese man, who had been craned out of his bedroom so that he could appear on television. His wife – yes, *his wife* – said that she wanted to present her own cookery show. I looked up: a dun-grey day, the sky the colour of the newsprint and smirched and grubby too. An errant seagull settled heavily on a television aerial.

'Hi,' she said. 'Can I get you a coffee or do you need to get back to the grindstone?'

This time it was I who was caught by surprise.

'No, not at all,' I said, recovering fast and cheerily ignoring both the mischievous note of sarcasm and the close fit of her hipster jeans, 'I don't usually go back to work until . . . er . . . two thirty. Yeah, please: have a seat.' I stood and pulled out a chair. 'I'll go and see if I can find Roberto . . . er . . . he's the waiter. What would you like? What can I get you?'

'Espresso.' She smiled, put down her bags and began to sit down.

'OK. Hang on a sec.'

We were back in business! At long last. Out of nowhere. And there was no way of avoiding it: she was *intravenously* sexy. As quietly as they had appeared, my anxieties now vanished and my mind drew itself up to its full height. An inexcusable delay . . . but she had kept her word. Something was going on. Unless she was being nice. But who is nice these days? What's nice? Who the fuck has time for *nice*?

Inside, poor Roberto was busy servicing the mother and baby workshop – lots of screaming, spoon-feeding, dropped toys and women showing off to one another over the racket and the mess. (Come on, ladies, give us all a break: you're not the first women on planet Earth to have children.) I caught his eye and pointed towards the coffee machine. He frowned, then guessed what I was after and nodded his head very slightly before turning his attention back to the lucrative world of cutchy-coo. I locked in a fresh barrel of coffee then hastily heated the thick little cups under the milk steamer to bring them to an acceptable temperature. I needed information. But above all, I told myself, my single duty was to secure another meeting. And this time it must have a date and a time attached. A date.

'Here you go,' I said.

'Thanks.'

I sat down, blocked her beauty from registering in my

consciousness, forced myself to relax and ran a quick mental scan for something natural and straightforward.

'So,' I began, 'what have you been up to this morning?'

'Oh, nothing much. Actually, I have just been to a bath-room store on the Edgware Road to price up stuff for when my builders have finished. It's all a bit of a nightmare at the moment.' She wrinkled her nose. 'I just want to – you know – get it over. But there's so much needs fixing up.' There was a very slight twang to her accent, hardly discernible and I couldn't place it.

'How long do you think it will take?'

'I don't know. I figure it will be at least another couple of months before the major stuff is done and then I want to paint it and all that. And the frame of the patio door is rotten too – or so the builders say. So that may have to get done. And the kitchen – oh Jesus – I've just bought a new kitchen, which has all got to be sorted out and fitted in.' She took a sip of her coffee. Her shirt was sleeveless and her sun-burnt arms, I saw, were completely bare – no jewellery, no watch and no rings. Definitely no rings. 'Anyway, it's boring. How about you?'

'This morning? Oh, I've just been working.'

'You work round here?'

'Yes. At home.'

'What do you do?'

'I'm a calligrapher.'

'Really?' She arched her pretty brow.

'Yes.' I nodded. 'Really.'

'How does *that* work?'

'Well, it's lots of sitting around and trying not to smudge.'

She grinned. 'I had no idea that calligraphers were still going. I thought you guys were kind of finished what with the invention of printing and computers and all of that.'

'No. Far from it. Actually there are thousands of us in England – all over the world in fact – working diligently away at our boards. We're a thriving community. Mostly amateurs but there are more professionals than you might think. You won't meet many of us but we're out there.'

'You do it for a living?'

'Yes. Millionaires commission me to transcribe poetry.' I was going to add something about agents and exhibitions but, as ever, I was wary of talking too long (and to no purpose) about myself. 'How about you?'

'You mean what do I *do*?' She took out a packet of foreign-looking cigarettes from her bag. 'I'm a travel writer.'

'Now that sounds more like a life.'

'Very few complaints.' She lit her cigarette with a match, blinking a little against the acridity as she waved it out.

I waited, thinking she was going to continue but she sat back and said nothing. So I asked another question: 'And is it hard getting the jobs or do you get offered work?'

'I've been at it for six years now – so it's a bit easier, I suppose. Sometimes I just go somewhere on a trip – pre-arranged or not – and then try to sell it. Other times I get rung up and told to do this or that and –' she shrugged '– off I go. You build a name slowly. The work comes in. It's fun.'

'Sounds pretty good. Wish I could swap.'

She smiled. 'Everyone says that. It is one of the best jobs in the world. But there are quite a few drawbacks people don't realize.'

'Really? I can't think of any.'

'Well, you know,' she explained, 'there's a lot of research and tramping around or sitting on smelly buses, heading for places which are always shut and miles away from wherever. And then there's getting the right information out of locals, who don't speak any language you might know and then double-checking everything and finding out that you've been told a load of crap and then starting again. And although you get paid OK by the newspapers, it's actually pretty hard – physically – to do more than two or three trips in any month, so compared to other freelance work where you can knock out, say, five pieces a week if you want to, you make much less money. Plus it kind of screws up your home life.'

'Right,' I nodded, 'I see what you mean. I hadn't thought of all that.' This was interesting territory. I took a sip of my espresso, hoping to distract a little from the probing nature of the question: 'So you have to be away from home all the time?'

'Used to be a lot.' She flicked her wrist to deter a wasp from her cup. 'More or less all the time in fact. But right now I'm starting a sort of sabbatical.'

I must have looked inquisitive.

'Well, actually . . .' – genuine modesty here – 'I recently sold my first book, so I'm taking a bit of time out and only doing the pieces – the articles – that I want to do, which is how come I took the chance to buy somewhere to live and all that. Plus my old flatmate wanted to get somewhere of her own too, and you know . . .' She waved her hand to suggest lots of reasons and then let her eyes find mine for a second. 'So I'm settling down for a bit anyway. Getting on the real estate ladder. Seems like as good a time as any.'

It was an American inflection in her voice, I thought. 'What's the book about or don't you want to talk about it?'

'Oh, it's just this women's guide to the Middle East kind of thing. Syria and Jordan and Lebanon.'

'Palmyra and Krak des Chevaliers and all that?'

'Mainly, yes . . . you know Syria?' There was a whisper of challenge in the question. I felt her hazel eyes on me again – coolly sceptical – and I realized that I would have to be

careful with my lies, careful not to underestimate her percep-
tiveness. 'I've been,' I said, which was true. 'Palmyra was
the best thing – just stuck out there in the desert and so
unfenced off with people clambering all over the ruins if they
wanted to.'

'Bit like Shepherd's Bush.'

I grinned.

She drained her coffee. I sensed that our interview was
coming to an end. I needed to make a suggestion quickly.
The eternal problem with espressos is that they don't last
very long. Perhaps another coffee now? Too forced. I was
just about to suggest, lightly, a light-hearted Friday meeting
for a light lunch when she gave me a much better opportunity. Reaching over to gather her bags, she said, 'The weird
thing is that I don't feel like I even know London that well.
I mean, I've lived here officially for eight years or whatever
– since I finished college – but I've never really explored.
You know what I mean? When you're in town and you see
all the tourists, sometimes you have to remind yourself what
it is that they are looking at.'

I nodded.

She bent to hook her heels back into her sandals and
went on: 'The other day I was thinking, hang on a minute,
I haven't been up the London Eye or down to the Tate
Modern or, you know, out to Greenwich – not to mention
all the hidden-away things that I probably haven't even
heard of. I know more about Amman than I do about
London. Like when I moved in, I was amazed to find that
there were these barge trips down the canals right off my
own doorstep more or less. I've no idea where they go or
what you get to see on them, but all day I see these tourists
arriving and . . . well, you know, they are getting more out
of my street than I am.'

'Do you want to go – on Sunday?'

'Where?'

'On the barge trip?'

'*This* Sunday?'

An ambush. I stayed with it. 'Yes. Why not? It might be fun. Or maybe you're doing something already . . .'

'No.' She looked at me for a moment and then her face broke into an *insanely* attractive smile. 'No. I'm not doing anything on Sunday. Not in the day anyway – I don't think.'

'Well, OK then, if –'

'Hey yeah. That would be interesting. Why not? A canal boat trip. And it's right outside my door. I gotta go sooner or later. Perfect. Let's do it.'

With things taking such a joyous turn for the better, 'Negative Love' looks a little . . . well, negative of me. Something more upbeat would seem to be required at this stage in my account. But the point is this. As St Thomas Aquinas tells us (and as John Donne well knew), it is quite impossible to say what God is, only what He is not. The most perfect thing is describable only in negatives because we have neither the language nor the imagination to comprehend the inconceivable divine. In 'Negative Love', therefore, Donne has Love dethrone God as the supreme omnipotent power of the universe – a force which can only be described by saying what it is not, a being no greater than which can be imagined.

> If that be simply perfectest
> Which can by no way be expressed
> But negatives, my love is so.

In other words, my love is something *very* positive indeed. Really fucking cool in fact.

And yet and yet – such emboldening philosophies aside
– we cannot evade the bold type of the title's facetious declaration – 'Negative Love'; even as Love is God, it is also a bad
joke.

11. Air and Angels

Twice or thrice had I loved thee,
Before I knew thy face or name;
So in a voice, so in a shapeless flame,
Angels affect us oft, and worshipped be;

'I can tell you exactly the man you want to speak to, Jazz mate,' said Roy Junior, leaning forward slightly over the shop counter in a manner disturbingly reminiscent of his father. 'You want to speak to Desmond Parks – Insanity Dez to the likes of you and me. He's the original geezer – the man who started the barge trips up.'

'Right. *The* Desmond of "Desmond's Canal Boat Trips"?'

'That's him. He knows everything there is to know about the canals.'

'Great.'

'Because, like I say, he's the one that set the trips up and such. For the love of it: that's why it's called "Desmond's Barge Trips".'

'Got you.'

'Because it was his idea.'

'Right.'

'Still lives on his barge, mind. *And* he probably has a stake in half the moorings up there. Got to respect him for that. If you want a berth in Little Venice, the chances are you will end up talking to Insanity. But he can't run the tours himself because he's got the Fucker.'

'The Fucker?'

Roy Junior grinned. 'Yeah – that's right: he's got the Fucker. Real tragedy.'

'The Fucker?'

'It's a disease.' He whirled his index finger near his temple. 'Of the mind.'

'Oh, I see.'

'Hence *Insanity* Dez.'

'Makes sense.'

I must have appeared doubtful because Roy Junior was mildly affronted. 'It's a real disease of the mind, mind.'

'What – the Fucker?'

'The Fucker is only what *he* calls it – it's his little joke. He says that if he called it by its proper name – Clorette's Syndrome or whatever – then he would end up saying that he had "Fucking Clorette's Syndrome" every time the subject came up. Which, given the way he talks, would be quite a fucking lot. Pardon the Frog. But this way, he says, if he just calls it "the Fucker", he gets the swearing in straight off and saves himself the breath *and* he has a little bit of a joke at the expense of the Fucker itself – if you follow me.'

'Right. I do.'

Roy Junior lifted his hands to his face and rubbed both cheeks with his fingers as though relishing the evidence of his first stubble. 'Course, the danger is that he starts saying that he's got the *fuckin'* Fucker. And that wouldn't be funny. Because then he wouldn't be saving himself any trouble at all.'

'No.'

'In fact, I asked him once when I was in the Bertram. "Insanity," I says, "you know the Fucker? What would happen if you started calling it the fuckin' Fucker? Or the *fuckin'* fuckin' Fucker? Imagine that. I mean, where's it going to end, mate?" He looked like he was going to give me a slap.'

'Christ.'

'But you know what he says to me?'

'No.'

'"Roy," he says, "fuck off."' Roy Junior snorted. 'And I tell you, the whole of the Bertram pissed their pants laughing at that one.'

I was about to return us to the point when a customer came in. I looked behind me anxiously. For an awkward moment, I thought it might be Madeleine. I didn't want her to see me back out-and-about only half an hour after we had parted company. But thankfully, the intruder was a youngish man – innocent if slightly unappealing overspill from the launderette next door.

We waited for him to approach the counter. Forty Silk Cut Fresh Airs, a packet of frozen cauliflower cheese grills, two frozen pizzas, two six-packs of beer, two maxi-bags of 'gourmet' crisps (sea salt *with* balsamic vinegar – whatever happened to 'and'?), a bottle of death-bastard vodka, a bottle of fuck-face whisky, cigarette papers, cola, four cartons of microwave chips, two speciality Czech beers and onion rings.

'Lads' night in,' he smirked ruefully, then added in a Deep South drawl: 'Gamin' time, whoa yeah! Bring it on, boy.'

'Cool.' I nodded.

Roy Junior waited until the guy was safely out of the shop and then carried on where he had left off. 'Anyway, because of the Fucker, Insanity had to cut his old cow in, even though he is the one who knows all the info and the history and such. She doesn't even live with him on the canal any more. Got her own place down Westbourne Park.

So now they split it: he drives the barges – low profile at the back – plus he keeps the boats running sweet and looking lovely, while she handles the people side of the business and does the microphone. They hate each other but it's made them both a lot – and I mean *a lot* – of serious wedge.' He tapped the side of his nose.

'I can imagine.'

'Makes me laugh, though, thinking about Insanity running the tours on his own with the Fucker: all the little kiddies and the grannies and the mummies and daddies sailing up and down the canal with him shouting into the mike: "Ladies and fucking Gentlemen, we are now approaching Little fucking Venice, and over on the left – that's a fuckin' park, and over on the right – that's a fuckin' bridge –"'

I dived in. 'So where does . . . Dez live?'

'*Insanity*, Jazz mate. He gets upset if you don't call him his proper name. You know – he's got a bit of a reputation for stuff.'

'Right. Insanity.'

'Like I said, on one of the barges.'

'Any idea which one?'

'I think it's called the *Dirty Duck* but don't quote me on that. The thing is, you don't want to just go knocking on his door, Jazz mate. Not out of the blue.'

'Well, what's the best way to get half an hour of his time?'

'In the Bertram.'

'Oh Christ, Roy, you know me. I can't hang around the bloody Bertram for the rest of the week hoping to meet him. Anyway, how would I know what he looked like?'

Roy Junior resumed his father's manner. 'Well . . . for a small consideration . . . I suppose I could let you know when he was in . . . and maybe introduce you . . . if you really think it's worth your while, that is.'

'Tenner, Roy.'
'Plus drinks?'
'Done.'

Following our inaugural *tête-à-tête* at Danilo's and having
accompanied Madeleine – oh how the cherubim danced and
seraphim sung – to the corner of Bristol Gardens and so
returned to the lofty lair of my *garçonnière*, the reason I was
so swiftly out pounding the pavements of Formosa Street
was, of course, to lay in my provisions. The barging trip was
scheduled for Sunday, so there wasn't as much time as I
would have liked and I wanted to allow Roy maximum
opportunity to gather my requirements – principally: real
fresh *wild* Scottish salmon, real fresh horseradish root, real
fresh dill and some decent, recent walnuts. My plan was
to supplement our barge's stately progress with a small but
exquisite picnic: two or three of my special fine-cut sandwiches each and a bottle of Sancerre. Discreetly carried in a
straw bag, easily introduced, nothing too dramatic, nothing
too distracting – but a simple, delicious, propitious accompaniment to the main theme of the afternoon: polite enquiry.

Clearly, we two were now on a new footing. Madeleine
and I were no longer strangers. We were – acquaintances.
Acquaintances with each other's phone numbers! And we
were going . . . on a date. Our first date. Whether or not she
realized it. Now – as a matter of some urgency – I had to
discover what the bloody fucking boyfriend situation was.
Because if – and still I could not really believe this – if the
coast was clear, then I had to move quickly and decisively,
though gracefully of course. If, conversely, the coast was
congested, then I needed to know as much as possible about
who he was and, most importantly, how she felt about him.

How did I get her number?

Quite simple. On the way home, as we were walking down Formosa, I started slightly as though suddenly struck by a thought.

'I had better give you my telephone number,' I said, 'just in case you can't make it.'

'Oh yes. Right.'

I told her my number. She programmed it into her mobile phone – the only entry under 'J', I noticed.

'And what's yours,' I went on, 'in case I fall desperately ill?'

She told me hers. I committed it to memory.

You will note how I softened the intrusiveness of the moment by offering mine first – as though she were far more busy and important than I and much more likely to have to cancel – while, at the same time, giving her no room to refuse the return request. You will also note that she never asked my name.

As I say, the reason I went straight back down to Roy's was to place my urgent order. The idea of asking about Desmond's stately boat trips only occurred to me while Roy Junior was writing down the details (on my insistence, since he is not always as reliable as Senior). As much as anything, I was, I suppose, just articulating out loud the parameters of my own internal dilemmas. Broadly speaking (and as with many such rendezvous), there were two options: either go and research as much as possible about the barge, the route et cetera; or do nothing at all except turn up and meet her on the day. In principle, I am against the first method – the way of the talented amateur – because it necessarily destroys the novelty, the shared feeling of discovery, the common experience . . . all of which contribute to the establishment of a conducive sense of complicity. The second method, however, leaves just a little bit too much to that treacherous little fuckpig: chance. Normally, this wouldn't matter. I could have trusted my wits to get me through, but with Madeleine I just couldn't bring myself to risk it. What if (I could not help but think) the route took us past a series of architectural masterworks about which only a blind and heavily sedated Philistine would know nothing? *She* may well have been abroad for the last decade or whatever, but I was supposed to live here. So when I asked Roy Junior whether or not he knew anyone, I was really only fishing for an alternative approach – a way of finding out any necessary information without jeopardizing the experience. Insanity Dez, however, was much more than I ever could have ever hoped for.

'Listen, son, you look like a bit of a fucking prick to me,' Insanity drawled, his crooked finger tapping the side of his pint of London Pride by way of emphasizing the accusation. 'But because you're a mate of young Roy over there and because you're buying the Pride tonight, I'm not going to hold it against you and I'll tell you whatever the fuck it is you fucking want to know.'

'Thanks. Appreciate it.' I nodded, realizing that it was going to be impossible to work out when Insanity was suffering from the Fucker and when he was just being rude. He was fifty or thereabouts: stocky, tattooed, bald from forehead to sunburnt crown, but with a frizzy ring of brown hair that circled around the back of his head from ear to ear and signed off with a pair of feverish red sideburns that raged in a frenzy of disgruntlement down either cheek.

We were side by side, tight-trousered and hunched over like a pair of turtles on two unsteady stools, in the maroon penumbra of the Bertram's back bar. This was the very bottom of the Paddington basin. Here, even the air was torpid, heavy with sediment, thickened with sludge. The pub dog, Duncan, most eloquently embodied all the Bertram stood for: acute hearing, sensitive teeth, a matted coat, and permanently on the lookout for a get-rich-even-quicker scheme, he lolled between the tables with a lopsided grin and an air of having suffered long through the stupidity of all those beyond the immediate range of his yellowing eye. Like everyone else, he had a lot more ready cash than he ever let on, he was shit-scared of the missus and he was steadily putting on weight.

Over the Tannoy, the music asserted itself softly: 'My heart . . . is like a yoyo string . . .' Uneasily, we waited for the song to finish. '. . . I'm tied to you right or wrong.'

'So,' said Insanity, taking a loud gulp of his Pride as the repeat to fade did just that. 'What the fuck do you want to know?'

I swilled my beer around the glass. 'So . . . I was just wondering if there was anything of particular interest on the canal route – you know – that your boats take.'

'Fucking too right there is.'

'Oh, great. So –'

'Why the fuck do you want to know?'

I hadn't anticipated this. 'Well – I'm thinking of going on a trip next week and I wanted to know what to look out for. And I heard – I mean Roy said – that you were the man.'

He ignored the woeful attempt at flattery. 'So why the fuck don't you just go on the trip and *find out* what to look out for? It's fucking cheaper than standing me and Roy fuck-ing beers all night.'

'Right. I suppose because I wanted to know in advance what was coming up . . . so I could, sort of, be ready for it.'

'You want me to tell you what to look out for on the fucking trip so that when the fucking guide tells you what

to look out for you will know what the fuck to look out for.'
Insanity grimaced. 'You *are* a fucking prick.'

From the corner table came the brisk and carefree click
of Roy Junior's newly outed dominoes.

'Well, you know, I just thought that if I knew what was
on the trip, I could maybe do some background reading and
get more out of it.' The words sounded awful even as I was
saying them. Who the fuck does 'background reading'?

He shook his head and selected what I guessed was his
favourite tone of voice – confidential in tenor, while somehow of broadcast volume: 'Listen, son, if I fucking tell you
everything I know about the fucking Grand Union Canal –
or the Regent's for that matter – then you're not going to
get anything *more* out of my fucking boat trip; you are going
to get *less*. Because anything my fucking missus has got to
say on that fucking boat will seem like Peter and fucking
Jane by comparison to what I know. And all you will get is
depressed and disa-fucking-ppointed.' He was now openly
derisory. 'For fuck's sake. If you really want to get the most
out of Desmond's Canal Boat trips, then my advice is just to
fucking go on one of them like everybody fucking else.'

'Insanity, listen. I need to impress a fucking bird.'

And with these magic words, the mighty gates to the
citadel of knowledge swung open before me and I hobbled
gratefully inside.

For the next hour or so my guide proved himself as eloquent
and as knowledgeable as had been promised. Even the Fucker
seemed to trouble him less as he waxed about John Nash's
original designs for the Regency canal villas or traced with
his hand the route to Limehouse. Two pints of Pride later
and immeasurably better informed, I was ready to leave:
'. . . and it's OK to take sandwiches and a bottle?'

'No problem, mate,' Insanity affirmed. 'Not strictly fucking supposed to because of the fucking restaurant on the quay where the boats leave from. They like to do the nosh for special occasions and such. But if my fucking missus kicks up – just tell her I said. I'll be there to sort her out if there's any trouble. Fucking cow.'

'Thanks for that.' I nodded.

'No fucking problem, Jazz mate, anytime. Fucking pleasure to have an interested fucking audience for once.'

'One more?'

'Don't mind if I do.'

I slipped forward off the stool and bought both Insanity and Roy Junior another drink.

'Nothing for yourself?'

'No. Sadly not.'

'Oh?'

'I'm on the job tonight,' I winked. 'Bit on the fucking side.'

'Nice.'

'Fucking nice.'

He smirked. 'You'd better fuck off then.'

I tactfully negotiated the length of the back bar over to the far side where – beneath a cupreous and nicotine-stained ceiling and against a tile and flock-paper mural of subtle algae brown and emboldened mustard yellow – Roy Junior was trying to cheat back the money he had already lost at dominoes. Seemingly glad of the distraction, he stood carefully to take the offered pint, swayed a second, nodded, stuck out his tongue, winked slowly, swayed some more . . . and then, like a detonated tower block, sagging at the knees with his arms flailing weakly by his side, he crumpled from the waist, summarily upending the table as he fell. The immediate aftermath of his disintegration seemed to happen in slow motion:

there was the sound of splintering wood, a sudden sundering of joinery and glue, crisps and beer mats flew like so many oddly weighted Frisbees, bottles toppled over and over again, then bounced across the carpet; glasses thudded to the ground, mobile phones slapped against tiles, dominoes hurled themselves suicidally into the void; walls, floor, shoes, shirts, trousers and (in a couple of cases) hair became instantly sodden as vast floods of Pride sprayed and splattered and surged and sluiced in all directions; a fistful of glowing cigarettes cartwheeled through the air; some of Roy's friends dived one way, others jerked the other, one smashed his shin against the newly protruding table leg, one lost his balance as his hand slipped on the freshly-doused wall; a wet ten-pound note was rent in two by a thrashing boot that dug desperately for purchase in the oozing bog. For a second nobody moved. A fine rain of cigarette ash settled gently on the devastation. Then Duncan lolloped into view and lowered his head to lap up a few pints and help himself to the nuts.

Oh, Grand Union Canal – blossom-strewn Danube of my blameless dreams. How I ache for thee! Thy languid pools where nymphs do bathe; thy bowery banks where naiads bask; thy sweet waters where at dusk the unicorn and aurochs sup. Oh, Grand Union Canal, my cradling Tigris and Euphrates both, my shimmering dove-sung Jordan, my glorious queen-kissed Nile! Hie me swift to thy hopeful bosom . . .

At 16.25 hours on a cloudless Sunday afternoon, the first in May, I swung cheerily on to Blomfield Road and – straw bag in hand – sashayed towards the rudely magnificent entrance of Desmond's Canal Boat Trips. A line of front-garden saplings bowed like loyal pages as I passed and here and there the branches of the trees curtsied like ladies in waiting. Beneath a lapis lazuli sky, with all around the sounds of summer tuning up, I could not help but anticipate that the afternoon would become a glowing success.

I was close upon the entrance when Madeleine appeared – coming out. 'Hello,' I said, friendly and cheerful as the gentle air.

'Hi,' she replied.

I must have been beaming or something because she looked at me quizzically for a second before steering us out of the momentary awkwardness: 'Hey, isn't it a beautiful day? And hot too. Guess what: I just asked them and they said that it's OK to bring a bottle so I'm going to get a couple of glasses from my flat and something out of the fridge. Hang on, I'll be two seconds.'

'OK. I'll wait here.'

She hastened across the road. She looked . . . I don't know . . . heart-dissolving. She was wearing a white shirt unbuttoned two down at the neck and an above-the-knee cotton skirt with her leather-thonged sandals. But it wasn't just the clothes. It was her manner: unregarding of herself, in no doubt, seemingly heedless of the quagmire of degeneration that squelched all about her and yet impetuously, sharply, riskily alive – assuming, requiring, betting heavily upon the very best from the day and its many grubby personnel. (Always, whenever she wished, Madeleine could become that girl in the frayed straw hat, certain to coax down the chivalrous instinct somewhere languishing in the dusty attic of even a bad man's better nature.)

I waited for her in the restaurant on the wharf, idly looking at the menus and wondering to what extent the seafood theme was offered as an ironic commentary on British canal culture. There was no sign of Insanity, but a fifty-year-old woman, whom I took to be his 'missus', was bustling a gaudily clad family on to the boat. I thought I might as well pay

for our tickets and crossed over to the counter just in time
to beat a pandemonium of intrepid Japanese tourists. I was
collecting my change when a familiar voice whispered in
my ear.

'Hey Jazz, I've reserved the best fucking seats up at the
fucking front for you, mate.' Pause. Then, in an even quieter
hiss, 'She's a fucking dream by the way. Makes me want to
fucking buy a bunch of fucking flowers spur of the fucking
moment or something.'

Before I could say thanks, he was gone.

'You Desmond's friends?' asked the bustling woman,
officiously.

'I'm not sure. I think so.'

'Well, the chairs up at the front are yours if you want
them – otherwise you can sit at the back with me.'

I explained that I was waiting for somebody and she said
not to worry, they wouldn't leave without such a fine looking
young lady and that she would send her through. So I
climbed across the first boat – *Desmond No. 2* – moored in
tight against the bank, and jumped lightly down into *Desmond
No. 1*. Behind me, someone shouted: 'When he puts his foot
down he can get her up to four miles an hour.' I caught sight
of Insanity himself – blue-peaked sailor's cap and striped
shirt, lurking like the ghost of Captain Ahab at the back.

The narrowboat was indeed narrow – more or less four
chairs wide, with a solid roof supported on poles, but with
sides and front wide open to the fresh air. I walked carefully
towards the bow – past families, pensioners, more tourists,
a school outing, a young couple with their baby and a trio
of bikers steadfastly leathered up despite the sun. The last
two chairs – side by side in the rounded prow – had a piece
of A4 paper on them saying 'Reserved'. I picked it up and
folded it into my back pocket. (A close shave *vis-à-vis* giving

away my preparations: in such ways do the gods like to piss on mankind's little party.) Two chubby ducks waddled smartly along the towpath, took to the cloudy water in the way only ducks can and set off at full tilt towards the opposite bank on a sudden and unknowable errand.

'Job done,' she said, holding aloft a bottle of white wine, as she excused her way past the bikers. 'Hey, excellent: do we get to sit at the front?' She stepped past me. 'Thanks for sorting the tickets.'

'No problem.'

At the back, Insanity turned the key and the engine started up – a regular, comforting, low-register chug.

'It's pretty low in the water, isn't it?' she said, as we sat down.

I nodded: 'If you stick your hand over the side there's only about six inches clearance.' I was going to add a footnote about how, when the canals were privately owned, the tolls were paid according to the weight of cargo, which, in turn, was measured by how deep in the water the boat was sitting. But mercifully, the announcer's voice came over the speakers: 'Ladies and gentlemen, hello – my name is Daphne and your skipper today is Desmond. Although the canal is only five foot deep and we travel at only three miles an hour, I am required to inform you that life rings are to be found on the roof. Also, please could I ask you to keep legs, arms and fingers *inside* the boat as we have been known to bump into things now and then and we don't want you losing any limbs.' The microphone clicked off and Daphne herself came down to the front, climbed on to the empty chair behind us and administered a firm push off with her foot.

Carefully, Madeleine placed two glasses – a whisky tumbler and a flute – down on the interior ledge beside her seat. She pulled out a small penknife attached to her keyring and selected the corkscrew function. Holding it up as though it were a magic symbol, she looked at me with mock solemnity. 'Shall we start drinking straight away?'

'I think that would be a great idea,' I affirmed. 'In fact, I was going to say, but you dashed off – I brought a bottle as well, just on the off chance. So we've got two.'

'Oh good. I noticed your basket thing. There's nothing better than drinking in the afternoon. Especially when it's sunny. Shall we start with yours or mine?'

'I think we should get started with yours while it's still cold and have mine on the way back.'

'OK. Here – you hold the glasses for a moment.'

She passed them over and I did as ordered. I couldn't help but notice that there was not a trace of nervousness in her voice. In the company of a virtual stranger, she was totally relaxed. She bent over, slipped her feet from her sandals, jammed the bottle between her insteps, twisted in the corkscrew and heaved out the cork. She grinned: 'Now we're sorted.'

'Pour away.'

Glasses charged and bottle stowed, Madeleine insisted that we clink. Then she settled back, lifting her legs so that she could put her feet up on the ledge in front of her.

'So – any ideas which way we go?'

'Up there,' I indicated straight ahead, 'just a little way and then left at Browning's pool into the Regent's Canal.'

'Browning's pool?' She turned her head enquiringly.

'Yeah, it's the sort of mini-lake-kind-of-pond-area – you can see it from the bridge when you go towards Paddington.'

'Oh right, yeah. Near that little memorial garden place.'

'That's it. Robert Browning used to have a house up there. In fact, he's the one who first came up with the name "Little Venice". Because it reminded him of –'

'Venice.'

'Yes.' I cleared my throat. Already I felt I knew too much. Why, oh why did I do this to myself? 'He used to have a summerhouse on the tiny island and sit there with Elizabeth, his wife,' I added weakly. 'And write his poems.'

The speakers clicked and the announcer's voice came on: 'The area we are now entering is called Browning's pool, after Robert Browning, the poet, who used to have a summerhouse on the little island you can see to your left . . .'

I drank some more wine and then frowned for no reason.

'You seem to know rather a lot.' She extended a lower lip to blow a stray strand of hair from her forehead. 'Have you been anxiously reading local guides or something?'

Ouch, I thought. Ouch.

'I've been doing nothing else for weeks now. I get up at six and cycle furiously to the British Library where I pore over canal-related history books until dusk every day. Then I go to Grand Union night schools Sunday and Tuesdays. All so I can impress newcomers to the area.'

'Oh . . . I see. Well you're not doing badly in your studies. You sound like you might be able to do some official tour-guiding if you stick at it. Something to fall back on anyway – if the calligraphy fucks up or your hands get cut off or whatever.' She nodded thoughtfully and produced another soft pack of unfamiliar imported cigarettes from her breast pocket. 'Want one? They're delicious. Pure nutritional goodness. I picked them up at a camel station in Tajikistan.'

I found it impossible to tell if she was joking. She gave no hint either way. 'No thanks,' I declined. 'Not yet – later though – maybe.'

'Fair enough.' She tapped one out for herself and lit it with a lighter. 'And do all newcomers get the chance to go out on a barge trip so that they can be suitably induced and impressed? I have to say, I think it's very community-minded of you.'

'Well, I prefer to concentrate on old men, actually. It's the least I can do. They move into the area and they just look so . . . so *lost*.'

She smiled.

We continued to talk our way down the Regent's Canal, through the dankness of the Maida Hill tunnel, past the Widewater turning pool where the barges used to deliver their cargoes to the old coal power station and where a couple of men were hunkered silently over their motionless rods. After a while, with the London sun still bright and self-confident, we found ourselves drifting along the back of Regent's Park proper, the gardens of Grove House to our left and the elegant John Nash villas to our right . . . Her sense of humour, I freely admit, was a little disconcerting: as dry as the desert in the grip of a two-hundred-year drought. In fact, her self-assurance in general was having a curiously powerful effect: somehow unnerving me *and* making me more relaxed both at the same time. Perhaps, I thought, it was something to do with her having travelled so much.

That said, everything was going well – almost too well. Certainly too well for me to rend the mood asunder with blundering, pitiful arsehole questions like, 'Do you have a boyfriend?' or 'Can I just butt in to establish whether or not you are single at the moment?' or 'Am I right in thinking that you are not going out with somebody – probably a man; or is it that you *are* seeing someone – probably a man – as we speak? And if so, how long has this been going on and what – if you don't mind me asking – are your long-term expectations?' No way. I just couldn't. Not with her so close and real. So I put it off. All the way past the aviary and the zoo and the floating Chinese restaurant and right up until we were safely docked in Camden. We talked and joked and began to get a little less sober and I put it off.

'But I don't really *want* to go to Australia. I really don't. I mean, take a look around . . .' I gestured vaguely as if to prove the point. 'There's no *need* for me to go to Australia. Australia is coming here.'

Having wandered through the Australian throng at Camden Market, and having decided against buying any aromatherapy products or ethnic rugs off the ever-cheery Australian vendors, we had settled for interim drinks prior to the return voyage. And so we were now sitting in what could only be described as an Australian theme pub, listening to what sounded suspiciously like Australian rock music, having just been served by two genial Australian bartenders who, when Madeleine had attempted to order the drinks, had taken it upon themselves to enact an impromptu (but oh so amusing) piece of comic mini-theatre – one elbowing the other aside to serve her first, while the other then ducked between his legs to pop up in front of the first, who in turn clapped his hand over his rival's mouth and dragged him out of the way et cetera ad nauseam et cetera. Very funny, the Aussies.

I took a tentative sip of my glass of Australian wine. 'I mean, there are millions and millions of Australians in London – everywhere you go. In fact, London is more or less *the same as Australia*. Admittedly without the kangaroos or the didgeridoos, thank God – but still – all over the city – today, now, as we speak – people are preparing for barbecues. Even my Cypriot friends on the Edgware Road have started asking me if I "want a few tinnies, mate" to take home with my olives.' I sighed. 'Oh, we made a brave effort to isolate them, to dump them on the other side of the world, but we have to face facts: it hasn't worked. They are all coming back – one by one – *to have their revenge*. In fact, Australia must be practically deserted.'

She laughed. 'I still think you should go.'

'But I'm European. I don't like marsupials. I like history, literature, music, the dynastic struggles of inbred monarchies. That kind of thing.'

'Well, you are missing out. Because it is a beautiful place.' She exhaled a blue arc of cigarette smoke. 'Have you ever been diving?'

'No . . . I haven't.'

'Didn't think so.'

'What do you mean by that?'

'You don't look like a diver.'

'What do divers look like?'

'They're slightly sort of . . . you know, cooler.'

'Slightly *cooler*?' I pretended not to be hurt.

'A diver wouldn't have a picnic basket.'

'I borrowed it . . .'

'Really?'

'Off a professional diver friend of mine who lives upstairs. It was one of many possible choices. He has a comprehensive picnic basket selection.'

She smirked. 'All I am saying is that maybe you should start getting out more. Go see Australia. Go see the Great Barrier Reef, because you really don't know what you are talking about. Come on: you have to see stuff like that. Think about it: it used to take months to get round the world, not to mention, only a hundred years ago, the diseases, the disasters, all the dangers, human and natural – I mean fuck, just getting to Scotland used to be an epic struggle. But now it's a few hours, a few hundred dollars and you can be anywhere. How can you not love that? How can you not take advantage of that? You're just being parochial and – you know – small-minded. What's the phrase? A life without exploration is not worth living.' She shrugged. 'Something like that. In any case, you never know, it might broaden your horizons.'

Ouch again. 'You are talking about the place. I am talking about the people,' I said.

'We can talk about the people if you like.' She made a thoughtful face. '*I*, for example, am an Australian. Born and bred.'

Ouch ouch *ouch*.

She let me live with myself all the way back to the barge before she put me out of my misery.

'Shall we have our sandwiches now?' she asked.

'How did you know that I'd brought sandwiches?'

'I looked in your picnic bag when you went to get the bottles of water,' she smiled, apologetically and not sorry at all.

'OK. Definitely. Let's get stuck in. And I'll open my bottle too. Although I am a bit worried that it might not be cool enough . . .'

Unnervingly, she put her finger and thumb lightly to my jaw and turned my head to look at her. 'Hey, I'm not Australian by the way. That was a joke. You don't have to feel bad.'

'A joke?'

'Yes.' Now she was really laughing.

I must have looked startled or something. But it was her touch, more than her amusement or what she had said, that had caught me off guard.

Her eyes softened. 'You really mustn't take everything so seriously.'

I had absolutely no idea what to say so I opened the wine with unnecessary professionalism and poured it into the two glasses, which I had taken care to have rinsed in the pub.

Soon enough we were chugging homeward, Little Sydney dropping away astern, the welcoming old world salve of Little Venice ahead. The evening was falling, soft and balmy over the city, and we sat in contented silence, enjoying our sandwiches. I was left alone for a few minutes to recover my equilibrium and gather my thoughts. At some point, Madeleine lit a meditative cigarette and shifted in her seat so that – very slightly – she could lean against me.

Meanwhile, in my head – which I freely own is not the most reasonable of places – the problem to which I was still seeking an elegant solution persisted. Somehow or other – and soon – I had to know. And yet . . . if a woman refuses to volunteer the information, the boyfriend question is virtually impossible to ask without being crass. The signals? There were no signals. Or maybe there were too many. She was flirting. But all women flirt. *Especially* the unavailable ones. Intellectually, I admit I was lost. I was zugzwanged. But we were passing the aviary and I made the decision to find out one way or another before the Maida Hill tunnel.

'I'll have one of those cigarettes now – if that's OK,' I said.

'Sure.' She sat up slightly. 'I feel very lazy. I had no idea that London could be so . . . pleasant.'

'Regent's Park is underrated,' I said, taking both cigarette and the offered lighter as she settled back down. 'Although I can't understand who would want to go and visit the zoo any more – I was under the impression that zoos were pretty much calling it a day. And you would have thought that keeping birds in giant nets wasn't exactly all the rage anymore. But it seems there are still a few thousand diehards who need their fix of lethargic penguin and mangy giraffe. Are these really from Tajikistan?'

'No, they're from Damascus.'

'Oh.' I inhaled. 'Well, they're fucking strong.'

'Not really – these are actually made with special, selected tobacco.' She held her cigarette at arm's length and examined it. 'The best quality you can get in Syria. And not available in the shops either. I have a Turkish friend, an interpreter, who gets them for me when I am out there – Mario. Although that's not really his name. Or at least, it's not what the Syrian women call him.'

The alcohol was working its impish magic. Gently, I sat up to reach down for the rest of the wine. 'How are you doing?'

'Let's finish it.' She released her almost empty flute from where she had trapped it between her legs, dropped her feet down from the side of the boat and sat up again.

Our heads were almost touching. 'And what do most people call you?' I asked, carefully draining the last of the bottle into first one glass then the other.

She looked up at me sharply, a surprising tautness in her face, her eyes making themselves directly intimate with mine.

I drowned the urge to kiss her. 'I mean, does everyone call you Madeleine or Maddy or Mad or something else?'

'Oh . . . I get you.' She paused. 'Most people call me Maddy, I suppose. But I like my full name too. What do most people call you?'

'At school I was called Jacques.' I explained: 'I went to school abroad and my surname is Jackson. But these days it's pretty much Jasper – even with girlfriends.'

'Have you got a girlfriend at the moment?'

I put down the empty bottle. 'No. Not at the moment. I

was going out with somebody but we . . . she sort of left me. That was a few months ago. And you?'

'Oh,' she frowned. 'My boyfriends call me John or Frank or sometimes Bradley.'

I laughed. 'Which is it at the moment?'

'I don't have a boyfriend at the moment.'

A young guy cycling down the towpath ahead of his family pulled up his front wheel and held the stunt all the way into the darkness of the tunnel.

12. The Dream ('Image of her . . .')

So, if I dream I have you, I have you,
For, all our joys are but fantastical.

A fanfare of heavenly trumpets. Oh yes, sometimes things just fall into a man's lap, and all he can do is wish he believed in a God unto whom he might give thanks. The coast, it seemed, was unguarded. The boats must not only now be beached, they must also be burnt.

Taking a serious girl out to dinner for the first time is not easy. Men throughout the world will throng the witness stand to attest to the manifold horrors and catastrophes their efforts have unintentionally occasioned. And no doubt there are millions of women who could outdo these testimonies with gruesome tales of agonies suffered and atrocities endured.

As far as one can tell, there are some four or five basic approaches adopted by our mutual friend, the regular guy. Although these depend upon the health of his wallet and the impression that he wants to make, they can nonetheless be outlined according to the type of regular guy he believes himself to be.

The first is what I call the Clapham method: our hero (an arts graduate in his late twenties, who likes to keep in the

Zeitgeist) flicks through his *Time Out* for some newly hailed East End gastro-pub before making the call from his office during a handy gap between status meetings. On the appointed day at the appointed hour, he turns up to await his willing counterpart, who duly arrives ten minutes late, whereupon, after some initial awkwardness, they get stuck into amicable conversation and seared tuna loins (never reflecting for a moment whether or not the great fish can – strictly speaking – be said to have any such body part). The second approach is that adopted by the Money Boys – the groomed-up, buttoned-down, switched-on jerkers-off, who have been stupid enough to make themselves a lot of money (the City, drugs, information technology, consultancy et cetera). The Money prefers to sweep the night off its feet with a round of badly made cocktails and a hot-shit visit to a fiendishly over-priced, chrome-décor arse-pit of a hotel restaurant bar, where, after much consideration, they wash down their medium rare steak *et frites* with lashings of Château Baron Rothschild (because it's a wine that somehow sounds like wealth). The third method is that of the poor, honest, open-palmed actor or television researcher or struggling section-2-journalist-would-be-*film-noir*-director. In this case our man may even get a bus to the rendezvous in order to feed a misplaced sense of metropolitan guile that he derives from knowing the timetable and routes. He and his date chow down over a rustic *faux*-Lebanese, after which they splash out, she giggling, he wriggling, on homemade ice-cream (which isn't homemade) before agreeing to catch the latest Danish reality-flick the next Sunday afternoon. Last, and by all means least, we have the hateful West London trustafarian crowd – the sallow-faced and unwanted progeny of the last generation's *arrivistes*. Sensationally unintelligent, dressed down to the nines, and with their boredom worn like a badge of courage, these would-be men drag their tarted-down little vixens out to Ladbroke Grove for apathetically ordered whatever-the-fuck with the veneer of ethnic authenticity on the street outside and similarly pointless friends within easy beckoning distance and the unspoken promise of a line of bad cocaine in a toilet somewhere if things go well.

All of which leaves us – you and me both – crying quietly into our hands with shame and despair. But by such roads does the regular guy – in his many guises – like to travel. The world is full of fuckers and there's nothing we can do. Idealism, as you will have noticed, has died a short but tragic death. Don Quixote rode in vain and Karl Marx is long forgotten, muttering the truth into his beard like a mad tramp lying on a broken box on the pavement outside King's Cross station. We live in the age of the Lowest Common Denominator. And boy oh boy is it low.

I do it like this.

At eleven-thirty, I put down my quill and I call Carla at Danilo's.

'Hello, Carla,' I say. 'It's me, Jasper. Did you have a nice holiday?'

'Yes. Very nice, thank you. I see my sister's children and we go to see Roma play for the first time – I think we shall win this year. It's amazing in the big stadium. And the sun is always out. I hate to come back to London now. I say to Danny, we must open a new restaurant back there and finish here. But he says that everybody in Italy knows how to cook so what would be our difference?' She sighs. 'And the money is much less. Anyway, how have you been?'

'Good.'

'I haven't been here to see about the girl but –' a smile

tinkles through her voice 'but Roberto tells me you don't need me to say if she was here any more. You have been with her having coffee – everybody knows. Are you coming here for lunch together today?'

'No, not today,' I tell her. 'But I was wondering whether you could call Bruno for me? I need a special favour for next Tuesday?'

'Yes, sure. For your friends . . . or for two people?'

'For two.'

The sound of another smile. 'OK. No problem. Do I see you tomorrow?'

'Yes, you do. Thanks, Carla.'

Carla then calls Bruno. (And let us note in passing how Carla's instinctive Italian grasp of life's subtleties leads her naturally to separate the category 'friends' from 'girlfriends', be they potential or otherwise.) I go back to work and complete another couple of lines.

At four-thirty, I break and call La Casetta – by some distance the best Italian restaurant in London. The telephone is answered by Bruno.

'Hello, Bruno, it's Jasper here, how are you doing?'

'Very well.'

'And business?'

'Is very good now again. But the bastards upstairs are still complaining about the noise so I have to still have my problem with them. Oh, why me I say . . .'

The conversation continues in this direction for about three minutes while Bruno reprises the difficulties he has been having with his neighbours and their noise complaints until, at the right moment, I move us on.

'Listen,' I say, 'I need a special favour next Tuesday.'

'Oh yes, Carla said you were coming to see us.'

'Is it OK to have the table?'

'Sure it is OK. Sure. I will change things around if there is a problem. Don't worry.'

'And Bruno, you will take care of the fat men?'

'And Jasper, I will take care of the fat men.'

Why all this? Because I am not family to Bruno and Carla – they are cousins and Bruno will never ever say 'no' to Carla however busy he might be. And because it indicates to Bruno how seriously I am taking the evening and thus ensures that he will guarantee me not only my favourite table but also – crucially – *who sits at the other tables near me*. Which is to say: no fat men.

Making sure that you have a certain table at the best Italian restaurant in London is only half the job. In order to be certain of everybody's comfort – mine, the other men dining and most of all Madeleine's – the best thing is to segregate: business women, elderly friends, lesbians and so on near me; staring, lechery-prone fat men far away. And make no mistake, the fatter they are, the more they stare.

How come I get such special treatment at La Casetta? The menus . . . the menus, of course. All forty-four of them, hand written in exquisite *Littera Gothica Textualis Rotunda Italiana* – much to the delectation of both Augusto, the generous proprietor, and that great uninformed tribe of the palate-dead, otherwise known as restaurant reviewers. An enjoyable job, sent my way through Carla and completed entirely gratis along with a promise of twice-yearly revisions in return for free dining every so often. Not such a dumb game this calligraphy business, after all.

Next, at quarter to five I call the Roys. Roy Junior answers.

'All right, Roy?'

'Total.'

'Listen, how much for Tuesday eleven-thirty until one?'

A sharp intake of breath, then: 'We-e-ell . . . I'm supposed to be in Keele Tuesday. Got things going on. You know what I'm saying?'

'Again? On a Tuesday?'

'Busy man.'

'Couldn't you drive up afterwards. I mean – I reckon I'll probably be back before midnight.'

'Not really, Jazz mate. They need me – you know – to sort things early.'

'Shit. I really needed you. It's very serious.'

'Forty. That's my final offer, Jazz mate.'

'Can't do it for twenty?'

'Split?'

'Done. Thirty it is.'

There is a pause while he reconsiders what he has let himself in for, then he says: 'But twenty more for every extra hour after one – yeah?'

'Right. It won't be that late.'

'Sorted.'

I am about to hang up but then I add, 'Roy?'

'That's my name – don't wear it out.'

'This is an important job so I need 100 per cent from you. Just like we did last time.'

'With that Lucy girl with the perky tits?'

'That's right.'

'Jazz, mate, don't you worry about a thing.'

As you may have guessed, following the barge trip, I simply came right out with it and asked her if she would like to have dinner later in the week. No strings. No presumptions. Just – would she like to have dinner? Casual as a cat's stretch.

Routine. An almost nothing question as we stepped back on to the quay at Warwick Avenue.

And she said 'no'.

And my heart stopped beating.

And she watched with a smile as time and space shrivelled, blushing, into the dusty earth.

And I promised to fashion a new god in her image and put lambs to the sword by the million if only she would speak some little kindness to me before I turned the bloody blade upon myself.

And finally she broke the silence and explained that she had agreed to do a special job for *The Times* in Philadelphia and that she would be away in America all week – sorry. But how about the Tuesday following?

And I managed to pull my disintegrating self together and said that I would call her next Monday to confirm and arrange a place to meet and a restaurant – if that was OK with her?

And she said 'sure' and 'thanks for such an unexpectedly nice day'.

And I went home and spent the night in a deep parody of sleep.

I take the Tube whenever I am going out to meet someone with whom I expect to have a decent conversation. I find that the speculations set off by the presence of so many strangers, none of whom I actually have to talk to, somehow stimulate my mind and serve to make me slightly more receptive, slightly more implicated. Indeed, I always think travelling on the London Underground is something akin to the experience I imagine some of the Victorian anthropologists used to have when they visited their lunatic asylums – similarly beset by institutional shades of green and black, prey to strange winds and distant groaning, beloved of scurrying mice and shuffling men, a place where time itself is routinely stretched or shrunk or lost, a place of too much light or too much dark, of grime-choked air and inexplicable hum, of hot breath and break-neck rattle, of private tremors and mad convulsing . . . That Tuesday evening, my fellow loons and I scorched and banged along the Bakerloo together, trying not to stare or collapse or chew off our own gums. At Piccadilly Circus, fighting our way through the throngs of asylum-seekers coming the other way, those of us still strong enough to walk managed to get off. We broke ground to find ourselves freshly amazed at the weather – gusts of wind, darker skies, the promise of a storm and nothing like the hazy, late afternoon we had so recently left behind above the more northerly reaches of the line. Obviously the West End had signed up to an entirely different weather system provider – more channels presumably.

Once alone, I knifed my way up Shaftesbury Avenue, splitting the bloats of American tourists, rolling like hot-dogs on the sidewalk between restaurants, slicing through the mobs of Asian teenage tough-guys, idling between arcades with their fake-black accents and low-slung jeans, past the cash-dispenser camps of the homeless, all chattering into their mobile phones, around the football fans down from Sunderland for the weekend to teach London a lesson in how to have a night out and already off-their-faces-and-falling-down-drunk, through the Marks and Spencer masses, milling around the musicals, swinging left up Wardour Street where the thirty-something media crowd sport soft-leather satchels the better to advertise their creative credentials, and finally into Soho proper and Old Compton Street, where the gay battalions troop their colours and aimless men pedal birthday girls around in big yellow rickshaws.

I saw her the moment I walked into the bar. She was wearing a white suit – long, loose mannish trousers and fitted jacket with a single button. She looked like a creature from Yves Saint Laurent's dreams. And she was sitting in *my* favourite chair on the far side, a spot which gave her a complete view of the room and, in particular, the door through which I had just entered. She had seen me too and now she stood up. Heads turned. Conversations stalled. There was nothing else to do but go straight on over.

'Hello Jasper, how nice to see you again.' She smiled and I thought for a minute she was going to offer me her hand to shake. 'I got here way earlier than I thought. How are you? What will you have?'

'Hi. Fine. Good.' I was flustered. 'You look lovely and suntanned – it must have been very hot in America. It's been chaotic here. Did you manage to get some sleep yesterday?'

'Yes, thanks. I think I've beaten the jet-lag for now.'

I eyed her glass with some trepidation. 'Er – what are you on? I'll have whatever you are drinking.'

'Believe it or not, today I am drinking Pernod. It's not particularly nice but I like the way it changes colour in the glass. And it sort of reminds me of St Tropez – not that I have ever been there. I think I was reading about it in the paper yesterday.'

'OK. I'll get them.'

'No. I have a card behind the bar and I have to spend more than fifteen pounds so please –'

'Oh right . . . well, I'll have one of those. Will that do it?'

'Probably not, but we have plenty of time.' She stood up and gestured in the exaggerated manner of an air hostess: 'Please, have a seat.'

I did as I was told.

The Ear Bar: frayed, louche, indifferent; rattan chairs,

leather sofas, dark wood tables and cream-coloured walls –
owned by a Frenchman; my favourite pre-dinner rendezvous
and so called because the two lights which were supposed
to close the loops of the 'B' of 'Bar' had fallen off long ago
and had never been replaced . . . The Ear Bar was no stranger
to the stray, off-duty hip-swing of the London sex symbol
wandered in to escape the harrowing boredom of the Soho
clubs or the relentlessly cynical appraisal of the street, but
even so . . . As she walked across the room, it took maximum energy and concentration from everybody to wrench
themselves away from watching her and back into their
conversations, their drinks, their lives.

I, meanwhile, took advantage of the brief remaining me-
time to hypnotize myself into believing that she was just
another girl and this was just another dinner. Quietly promising them indulgence to come, I shut down my senses.

She turned from the bar and came back towards me. I
ignored the new hairstyle (sort of slicked-down somehow
and lending extra emphasis to the lines of her cheekbones),
I ignored the clear forehead, I ignored those hazel eyes of
hers, I even ignored the walk . . . Who cares, I said to myself?
Not me. Not tonight. No sir. Shake your booty some place
else, lady. I'm here to listen and learn. And that's it. Don't
you *dare* try any funny business.

By the time she had sat down with the drinks, I was ready
for her. 'So, how was America?' I enquired.

'Interesting – as always.' Leaning forward, she poured the
water into the Pernod and watched delightedly as the liquid
in the glasses clouded a sickly yellow.

'Where were you?'

'I was in Philadelphia.' She handed me my drink. 'Writing
about gourmet getaways.'

'Oh yeah, you said. Why Philadelphia?'

She sat back and I didn't notice her cross her legs. 'Because they like to think of themselves as the gourmet capital of the States, a sort of food-lovers' mecca. Obviously, it's mainly an attempt to boost tourism. But there is some truth in it. Anyway, one of the publicists flew a whole bunch of journalists out there to go see for ourselves. I guess they reckon there's enough people in the UK market to make it worth their while. Though I can't think who they are.' She shook her head.

I was going to say something about real food and Europe. But I held back, mindful of the last time I set about the New World. 'So was the food good?'

'No idea. I never really got a chance to eat much.'

'Right.'

She lit a cigarette and waved out the match. 'No, it was a bit weird actually. I left the main group on the second day and ended up skipping the restaurant tour because I found a better story which I can use to hang the whole piece on.'

I relaxed another three notches. We were picking up more or less where we had left off on the barge and there was no doubt about it: in some half-cynical, half-respectful, half-amused way we were getting along as if we'd known each other a long time.

She continued, 'Basically, it turns out that the mayor of the city has just lost three stone and is feeling really hot about his new shape. And now he wants everyone in Philly to go on a diet because he says they are all too fat.'

'Are they?'

'Yes. Way. So he's spearheading this civic slimming-down initiative. He says that the city has got to lose 76,000 tonnes between them – or something like that – I can't remember the figures. But it breaks down to be an average of one and a half stone each.'

'Wow.'

She smiled. 'And so everyone is sort of locked into this kind of diet war. There are all these factions: fat and proud; fat and guilty; fat and happy; fat and miserable; fat and friendly; fat and angry and so on. Plus all the health freaks and the libertarians and the environmentalists and the food lobbies and the farming interest. And they're all fighting like itchy ferrets in a bag. In fact, the whole city is up in arms. I spent less than two days researching it and I got enough good quotes to fill an entire Sunday newspaper.'

'Jesus.' I had another go at the Pernod.

'It's obscene. The whole thing is obscene.'

'I read philosophy,' I said ruefully, in answer to her question, as Bruno personally refilled our glasses with the last of the sumptuous Barolo and discreetly insinuated the dessert menu on to the table. The hours had passed unnoticed and we were both a little wine-loosened. 'Almost entirely useless . . . well, not completely. It teaches you how to think, I suppose. How to argue – sort of – in a remote kind of a way. But you get left with this terrible legacy of – I don't know – of –'

'Existential misgiving?' She was teasing me.

'Yes,' I nodded, ignoring her gentle ridicule. 'And the other problem is that you become clinically incapable of taking anything at face value; it heightens – or deepens – your sense of how other people think – or rather what belief systems they have. And how inconsistent and unthought-through they are.'

'Does that surprise you?'

'No. But it sort of offends me. I can't help feeling that if you believe in such and such a thing then you have also to take a logical position on related or ancillary matters, but there's so little coherence around. Nobody seems to notice that the positions they are taking are mutually untenable – worse than that, ridiculous.'

She reached into her bag for her cigarettes. 'Like jogging to an anti-capitalist march in orphan-stitched running shoes.'

'Exactly.' I was taken aback yet again by how quickly she anticipated me. 'Or discounting God out of hand but conscientiously arguing the case for *feng shui*. There's no rigour of thought. It's all kind of mix'n'match and unconnected. As though the waters of ignorance are rising, leaving only unconnected, isolated islands of people who actually know anything about anything. I mean, I don't care which way you go – Virgin births or *feng shui* – and I freely admit that it's all equally implausible but I get disappointed when I see that people haven't really understood the implications of the stance they've taken.' I was conscious of rambling and not for the first time in the evening, and perhaps a little too clumsily, I attempted to get us back on to her: 'Anyway, what about you?'

She sparked a match. 'What about me?'

'What did you do?'

'At college?' She let go her first drag without inhaling.

'Yes,' I shrugged, 'at college.'

'I majored in South American literature.' She made an earnest face. 'But I have a résumé in my bag. I thought we could go through it together over coffee. I presume you have yours with you?'

'Of course, and very nicely written it is too.' She smiled and I took a sip of wine. 'You majored?'

'Yes. I was at university in the States.'

I thought she was going to say something more but instead she did her trick of simply looking at me and carrying on smoking. So I persevered. 'Did you grow up there? You hardly have any accent.'

'No – I grew up all over. My father works for the Foreign Office. He's been in France for a while now but he was posted around the world when I was little. I went to school wherever he was sent. Every time he moved, I moved. Mostly annoying diplomats' kids schools. But fun in some ways. Then he put me into an English boarding school which was . . . what it was.'

'And your mother? What does she do?'

'Nothing. My mother died when I was a baby.' Almost as an afterthought, she asked: 'Yours?'

'Both of mine died when I was four years old. I can't even remember them. I was brought up by my grandmother, which I think was probably better for me. I'm afraid I don't think much of the last generation.'

'Baby-boomers suck.'

How did it go in there? How did it go in the alcove of La Casetta, our little Italian cottage, with its whitewashed walls and a single candle and a bay tree growing in a terracotta pot in the fireplace? What did I learn? A great deal. Over *zuppa di fave* (for her) and *caponata* (for me) I discovered that she was the same age as I and that she spoke fluent Spanish; over *ravioli grandi ripieni di cozze e coda di rospo con salsa di pomodori freschi san marzano* (large parcels of pasta for her – heavenly tomatoes) and *agnolini ripieni di selvaggina con salsa al tartufo* (small parcels of pasta for me – truffle nirvana), I learnt that her favourite sort of music was jazz – but not big band, which 'she absolutely hated' – and that her special favourite was Oscar Peterson, about whom she was fanatically well-informed (or perhaps it was just that I knew nothing at all), and, oh yes, also anything at all featuring Nina

Simone, Ella Fitzgerald, Billie Holiday or Ann Peebles, especially in this last case a song called 'Tear Your Playhouse Down' or something. Over *scaloppina di vitello* (was there ever a girl so nakedly carnivorous?) and *branzino in padella* (I felt I had to have fish by way of contrast), I found out that she had very nearly been married to a much older man when she was only nineteen and living in Buenos Aires on a year out, and that if it hadn't been for her sister she would almost certainly have gone through with it, turned down her place at Yale and fucked her life up and 'probably have had twelve children by now and be some kinda trailer trash'.

As for what she told me about her parents, I left it there. And I really don't think the subject came up more than once or twice in all our time together. For my part, the exchange of family information was never a rite to which I attached the customary importance. One thing that I did notice, though, was that Madeleine was continually using my own tricks against me. More or less every time that I tried to get her to talk about herself, she would either resort to facetiousness or switch the subject back to me.

'Whom do you usually hang around with when you're back in London?' I asked, dropping back into my chair after a trip to the bathroom, and immediately regretting the relative accusative pronoun. 'Where do you normally go? Do you still keep in touch with friends from college in America?'.

'I didn't really have any. I was very alone.' She made a pained face.

I nodded sarcastically. 'I suppose it's because you went to school in lots of places as a young child and you never really learnt how to form enduring friendships?'

'That's it.' She smiled.

'And travel journalists being away all the time, I imagine

that they don't much congregate in Fleet Street or West-minster like the other hacks.'

'No,' she shook her head. 'You're right. I am tragically isolated. I have no friends. Most girls don't. Deep down, we're all consumed by a carefully calibrated rivalry that prevents us from forming truly meaningful relationships with one another. So most evenings I sit alone in the mess of my new flat, reading self-esteem manuals and staring tearfully into the middle distance with a bottle of wine listening to "All By Myself".'

'Well, if it gets tough you could pay me to call you at certain times when you think it might cheer you up or look good or whatever.'

'That's very kind of you, Jasper.' She picked up the dessert menu. 'That really was delicious food. And this looks seri-ously beautiful.'

'Yes,' I replied evenly. I had no idea whether she was referring to the writing or whether she meant the desserts themselves.

'But I am going to pass, I think. I just want coffee.' She looked up. 'You?'

'I'm not much of a desserts guy.'

She fingered out another cigarette. 'You know, one of the saddest things about being a woman is that we starve our-selves insane so that we can look nice – partly to piss our friends off, sure, but also so that men like us and –' I tried to interrupt but she prevented me. 'Yes, we do. Of course we do. And it works. Men *do* like us when we're thin. We starve ourselves insane and guess what our reward is? Guess what happens when everything works out and we get our much-prized man?'

'What?'

'He takes us out to dinner.'

I laughed.

'It's a farce. A woman's life turns out to be one long diet with the sole aim of being taken out to dinners she dare not eat.'

One of the waiters came over. I ordered a couple of espressos and stole another of her cigarettes. She offered me her book of matches (from the Village Vanguard, a jazz club in New York) and we sat in silence for a while, smoking. Then, seemingly without premeditation, she asked: 'So what's your favourite letter then, Jasper?'

I had to conceal my astonishment. Nobody – not William, not Lucy, not Saul – had ever put that question to me before. Only my grandmother, when I was much younger – six or seven maybe – playing on the floor of our sitting room in Oxford, practising the alphabet with felt-tip pens.

'X,' I said, exhaling, 'the letter X.'

'That's rather predictable, isn't it?'

'Why do you say that?'

'Because it's the most glamorous letter.' And then, with a stage sigh and in a deliberately breathy voice: 'The letter of love and anonymity.'

I shook my head. This was my turf. 'I don't agree. The most glamorous letter is definitely Q. Both in terms of its shape – in particular the wonderful potential of the descender – the tail – and in terms of its refusal to stand the presence of any other character but U beside it. What other letter would dare such arrogance? There's a catwalk quality to Q – pure untouchable glamour. Certainly more so than X.'

'OK, fair enough – so why X?'

'Well, of course there *is* the love and anonymity thing. But actually the reason is because it is the only letter which requires a counter stroke.'

'How do you mean?'

'If you imagine that the basic and most fluid line of the quill is from bottom left to top right – and the quicker the scribe works the more he wants to stay in this pattern. OK? And then think about the alphabet . . .'

'Mmm.'

'The only letter which consistently demands a stroke running against this flow is X. Discounting non-integral dots and crosses, every other letter can be negotiated. But you have to come back for the X – even when you are in full flow, as it were.'

She nodded slowly. 'It must be weird thinking about letters all the time.'

'It is – a bit.' I considered for a moment. 'The nearest I think most people get to it is playing Scrabble. You know how it is when you pick a letter out of the bag: you have an individual relationship with that letter. You think, oh great, a P, or, oh fuck, another A – you no longer think about words as the basic unit but rather letters instead. You look forward to Xs and Qs and so on and you start to think of the alphabet as twenty-six characters, each with their own personality. In fact, now I come to think of it, "characters" is a much better word than letters. It's no coincidence the Chinese are the best calligraphers – they understand the difference.'

The coffee came – hot and strong and perfectly made.

Roy Junior was outside, six doors up, baseball cap pulled down low, seated impassively at the wheel of his father's slightly shabby Mercedes. It wasn't quite midnight and the London night was still charging around the place like a coke addict. We were both relaxed – still not drunk exactly but at our ease. All the same, I wanted to avoid any awkwardness during those first few post-dinner seconds outside the restaurant, so often the bane of first-time, night-time, man–woman get-togethers. What to do? The questions proliferate. Suggest another drink? If so, where? And to what end? Hail a cab for her? And hope she asks you to climb in too? Come right out with it? Your place or mine? Or confirm a future meeting and bow out with good grace? Thank her for her charming company and leave her to make her own way home as she does every other night of her life? Attempt a kiss? . . . The pavement panics of the amateur.

I had, of course, predetermined that I would suggest a cab home (for once there was no geographical excuse not to) unless she was specific in her request to go on, in which case I knew exactly where we would go – as did Roy. My only other duty was to secure a third date, which I intended doing during the ride home. And after that job was done, my plan was to fly off chastely to my perch – unless, again, she was clearly of a different mind, in which case . . .

But, in the event, she drained the situation of any potential ungainliness by pre-emptively suggesting we go home before I had time to say anything. Whereupon, after some reflections on the *staggering* price of black cabs in London, I beckoned Roy Junior over with an apposite remark about us being lucky to get a mini-cab so quickly, and we set off.

Somewhere in between all the looming lights and the madcap traffic cavorting around Marble Arch, she said, 'Hey, you know I was talking about jazz before?'

And I said, 'Yes.'

And she said, 'Well, there's this band on at the Shepherd's Bush Empire in a few weeks. They play kind of jazz funk but the paper says they are really good. Do you want to come and see them with me if I find out what night they are on?'

And I said, 'Yes, I'd really like to.'

And she said, 'Cool, that's a date.'

Ten smoothly driven minutes later, as Roy drew up outside number 61 Blomfield Road, Madeleine reached across and placed her hand over mine.

'Hey, thanks for a nice evening. You sure you're OK getting this?'

'Yep. Sure.'

'OK – well, listen: call me soon.'

'I will. We'll sort something out for next week maybe.'

'OK – yeah – definitely.' She hesitated for a second. 'Bye. See you later.'

'Bye.'

She stepped out and I watched her fumble a moment with the lock. Then she disappeared into the darkness of the hall beyond and the green front door of her building swung shut.

There were a few seconds of silence, as Roy Junior turned around slowly and removed his cap. He gave a low whistle. 'Fuck me, Jazz mate. Fuck *me*.'

I sat back and sighed, exhausted from the effort of not thinking about her in that way. 'I know, Roy, I know.'

'Jazz mate, I admit it. Man to man. I'm totally jealous. I thought that Lucy girl was quality but fucking *hell* . . .'

'You haven't had to look at her all night, Roy. I tell you – it's killing me.' I ran a hand through my hair. 'You better drive around the corner. Or she might get the impression we are hanging around unnecessarily.'

He looked at me in the rear view. 'I know you get through the birds, Jazz, and respect, mate. And I know you know what you're doing but bloody hell . . . you've got to be happy with that.'

'You think I should have tried to go in with her? I never know how hard to push it?'

'No mate. First date. Let it wait.' He pulled way from the kerb.

'You think? (What I was doing asking Roy Junior for advice, I have no idea, but it was an emotional time for everybody.)

'Jazz – she just asked you out, didn't she? Call me soon? Tickets for two? Birds don't bother bothering unless they're bothered – if you know what I mean.'

'Yes. I do.'

'So it's in the bag. Chill. It will happen.'

'You're right.'

'But I'm telling you: when it does, Jazz mate, throw in the towel. That's my advice. Pack it in and settle down. Don't let her out of your sight. Because you have got to be happy with that result.'

13. Song

> Go, and catch a falling star,
>   Get with child a mandrake root,
> Tell me, where all the past years are,
>   Or who cleft the Devil's foot,
> Teach me to hear the mermaids singing,
>   Or to keep off envy's stinging,
>   And find
>   What wind
> Serves to advance an honest mind.

'I am a complete arsehole. Seriously, ladies and gentlemen, I am. My mother hates me and so does my dad. I have no friends – only people who are physically too weak to force me to leave their company. When I walk down the street, lamp-posts mutter "piss off" under their breath . . .'

Barge, dinner, comedy club: welcome to date three. In the brawny parlance of the great unwashed: a crunch match. The time: a little after ten-thirty on a Friday in late May. The place: a cosy, smoky, low-ceilinged basement of the Frobisher, a grand old pub in kick-ass Belsize Park, London's least amusing *arrondissement*. Just arrived on stage, the last act and the man to whom we, the fee-paying public, are now excitedly listening: Vernon Turn On and His Amazing Cod Piece!

'. . . They say an apple a day keeps the doctor away. Well, why not just tell him to fuck off? If you keep giving him things he's bound to keep on coming back for more . . . No, but seriously: everyone is still getting married, aren't they? Twenty years ago we all thought that was it: game over for marriage. "What's the point?" we all said. But tell me this:

what does everyone still want? Black, white, rich or poor –
what do all the little boys and girls want in their heart of
hearts? To get married. And not just that – they want the
whole shebang: churches, priests, confetti and a beautiful
white dress . . . Oh *doesn't* she look pretty? Who's doing the
flowers? Honeymoon in the Seychelles. Flat in Balham . . . I
know, sir, I know – there's no need to look so disgusted . . .
No, but seriously: I don't understand why we have to give
gifts at weddings – I really don't. The special couple – they're
the lucky ones. Not the rest of us single losers. If you ask
me, the whole thing is all the wrong way round. If two people
have somehow managed to find love and happiness and
mutual fulfilment and regular consenting sex then the least
they can do is *buy their poor lonely bastard guests a fucking
toaster each*!'

Someone – presumably his promoter – shouted from the
back: 'Way to go, Vern!'

I realize that there are those who might maintain that my
choice of venue from which to launch the final *coup* was far
too *déclassé* and that therefore I got exactly what I deserved.
It is not for nothing (mutter the octogenarians) that so many
of the best comedy clubs are below stairs. A concert hall in
Vienna – yes, or St Petersburg for the ballet, or perhaps the
gentle inevitability of the Venetian gondola – are not these
more fitting preludes to the great act of consummation?

To which I would respond: sadly not. We live in times of
high farce and low comedy; our art galleries and our parlia-
ments bulge with excrement alike and the protest of our
radical youth is confined to a cappuccino taken without chocolate sprinklings. These days, more often than not, the path
that leads most directly to the bedroom door is to be found
amid an evening of cordial merriment, an evening of tavern

warmth and intimacy, of careworn jeans and faithful old jackets, of the world as a topsy-turvy place ... Regrettably, I'm afraid, modern seduction is not so much about songs or sonnets; rather it is about laughter and forgetting. Plus, after all the buggering about over dinner, the chicks usually prefer it if you can at least pretend that you're normal on the next outing.

After a very enjoyable London evening walk – Abbey Road and the quasi-sylvan pleasures of St John's Wood – we had taken our seats in the corner: close enough to observe the nuances of the comics' expressions but at sufficient remove to prevent unnecessary involvement. Behind us, a row of four: two couples who (to judge from what they mistakenly believed to be a conversation) were clinically obsessed with the exact learning abilities of each other's children. And in front: a five-strong wedge of fifty-something women out for a good night – each of them privately hoping to be picked on by the compère so that they could 'give as good as they got'. With the exception of some precocious seventeen-year-old girls – sacrificial virgins no doubt and local to the area – the rest of the milling audience consisted of men and women in their late twenties and thirties: London's red-eyed wage slaves come to seek balm for the trauma of their chains.

The room was smoky and close – wooden floors, white-washed ceilings, a collection of cobbled-together chairs, benches and stools, arranged in neat rows, all of which were duly shuffled around as people arrived. At the back was a smallish bar, equipped with all the basics but clearly unused apart from on comedy nights. But what really gave the place its flavour was the posters plastered all over the walls: men popping bemusedly out of manholes; women coolly lighting cigarettes the wrong way round; men with ironic, starry glints coming from their teeth; women with their tongues stuck out and polka-dot head scarves; some comics shot from above so that their feet looked tiny and their heads looked amusingly large; others dressed in wacky clothes with wry moustaches – 'Dominic Cake-Mouth as Gunter the Bavarian!', 'Denny Mauve in The McMauve Monologues! (You Won't Enjoy a Better Night Out!)', 'Phil Hill! More spontaneous than combustion', 'Wankers in Space!'

The first half had gone quite well. Not funny exactly – but not not funny either. Things got underway with a guy with a truncheon. Then came a woman with a bicycle and the statutory gags about menstruation, chocolate and how men can't do more than one thing at a time. (How about lying and cheating, sister? Right on.) After which there was an admittedly amusing man-and-woman double act, who had honed a series of scripted spoof interviews – police, job, television and so on. And finally, to introduce the interval, an adroit master of ceremonies took the stage. Throughout, I had proudly supped on my pint of London Pride while Madeleine had likewise slummed it with vodka and tonic. She was in those low-waisted jeans of hers, a tight T-shirt and a short denim jacket that didn't match and didn't care.

'OK, ladies and . . . gentlemen,' said the compère, coming to the end of his patter, 'this is a game of two halves and we are now at half-time. And half-time means three things: one – I am available for sex in the back room over there if any of you ladies feel the need; two – you can all go and get fresh drinks; and three – those of you who have not wet your pants laughing can now go to the toilet. That means you too, sir.'

'What did you think?' I asked Madeleine, as everyone started to head for the bar.

'The girl was OK. Pretty funny. And I thought the interview sketches were a laugh, especially when they started to mix them all up.' She smiled and then lifted her hand to my face to remove a stray lash that was in the corner of my eye making me blink. 'Gone,' she said.

'You want another vodka and tonic?' I asked.

'Get me two – I ran out halfway through. How many acts are there in the second half?'

'Two. Andy Shandy, The Gentleman Dandy! And Vernon Turn On and His Amazing Cod Piece!'

She grinned.

All the time I was at the bar and all the way back to our seats – 'excuse me, coming through' – and all the time waiting for Madeleine to come back from the toilet, I was comfortable and relaxed and – yes – *certain*. As certain as I had been about anything in a long while.

Something else had started to happen as well. From the very beginning I had been banishing any thoughts of Madeleine undressed to the backstage of my mind, lest their riotous appearance distract me from the intricate demands of what was actually happening between us at any given moment. But now I was finding myself fixing more and more on the shape of her naked body, hovering like an angel in my mind's coulisse – for which hubristic temerity and presumption, the gods rightly rewarded me with a thunderbolt.

Madeleine returns from the ladies. I hand her one of her drinks. We talk for a while. Then, just as the interval is coming to an end, she looks at me as if suddenly making up her mind and says: 'Jasper, can I ask you something?'

'Yes . . . sure.'

'There's a man I really like. But I'm not sure how he feels about me. And you're into all that men and women stuff and I just wanted to get your opinion . . . on what you think he thinks of me. You know, if he likes me too. We've only seen each other a couple of times but it's getting kinda funny with him.' (A fool, an arrogant fool, even now I think she's talking about *me*.) She continues: 'I'm not sure whether he thinks of me in that way. Anyway, if I organize a dinner party, will you come and check him out? I'd just like to see what you think. He's a nice guy. He's called Phil.'

'Anyway,' said Vernon, winding up for the night, 'even though I am a tosser and everybody hates me, at least I am not nasty with it. My little brother, on the other hand, he's a real bastard. When we were small and our parents used to try to abandon us in the woods, I would say to him, "Did you remember to drop the stones, Melvyn?" And for years he would say, "Yes, Vernon, I did." Then one day I noticed that he wasn't dropping the stones any more and I fell back from our parents to where Melvyn was lagging behind and whispered, "Melvyn, what are you doing? Where are the stones? How shall we find our way back?" And Melvyn just looked at me with his little piggy eyes – he has piggy eyes – and said, "I got bored of the stones so I'm dropping bread, Vern." And I said, "But Melvyn – look, the birds are eating the bread and the trail is disappearing and we will be lost for ever in the woods and cold and hungry and alone." And you know what he says, the little bastard? He says, "Hey, Vern, relax. I poisoned the bread. We can follow the trail of dead birds."'

Vernon Turn On held up a wet and shiny silver slab of dead cod, winked and left the stage.

The following is rather resentful. But then there are some occasions in life when a man feels resentful. There's nothing more to say about it: verse two from 'Song':

If thou be'est born to strange sights,
   Things invisible to see,
Ride ten thousand days and nights,
   Till age snow white hairs on thee,
Thou, when thou return'st, wilt tell me
All strange wonders that befell thee,
      And swear
      Nowhere
Lives a woman true, and fair.

14. Love's Alchemy

Some that have deeper digged love's mine than I,
Say, where his centric happiness doth lie:
         I have loved, and got, and told,
But should I love, get, tell, till I were old,
I should not find that hidden mystery;
         Oh, 'tis imposture all:
And as no chemic yet the elixir got,
         But glorifies his pregnant pot,
         If by the way to him befall
Some odoriferous thing, or medicinal,
      So, lovers dream a rich and long delight,
      But get a winter-seeming summer's night.

Actually, 'Song' turns out to be just a warm-up. 'Love's Alchemy' on the other hand, now *that's* what I call the real thing. Balls to resentment. Bollocks to rancour. How about some bitterness and disgust? Rhythm like a nail gun: '*I have loved, and got, and told / But should I love, get, tell . . .*' Love as a treasureless mine. Women as treasureless mines. Slag heaps, shafts, vanishing seams. Men like blind miners tunnelling on though all rumours of fulfilment have been discredited. Or men like alchemists, grubbing around foul-smelling pots in the dark, kidding themselves that sooner or later they might just find the philosopher's stone. And all you get is a winter-seeming (i.e. bastard cold) summer's (i.e. far too short) night. If you're lucky, pal.

Deep breath.

You will, by now, have come to appreciate that I am a fair man – a man quite willing to see the good in everything and everyone. When, during the course of this account,

persons or events have presented themselves in such a way
as to invite instant derision, you will have noted how I have
courteously held back and, with a shrug of the shoulders,
pressed on politely, ever reflective that it takes all sorts. 'In
all mankind is my joy,' sings Bach's choir and I am happy
to hum along. But even St Jasper the Tolerant has his limits.
Even I find myself in the border towns of despair every once
in a while. Even I must flick my cigarette towards the rolling
tumbleweed, hunch down to take up the sun-bleached stick
and drag it purposefully through the desert sand . . .

. . . And so to the dinner party of all dinner parties. I
arrived at Madeleine's (what else could I do?) at around
seven-thirty-five, five minutes late but early enough, I
hoped, to seize a few sacred minutes alone with her, during
which I might be able to cobble together some private rap-
port, the better to drive a wedge between her and her gallant
suitor before he arrived.

Having been buzzed inside, I went quickly down the stairs
to Madeleine's front door where I ventured a conspiratorial
rap and listened for her step. She greeted me bare-armed in
an apron with *Chat Noir* written across the front.

'Hello, Jasper,' she smiled, effusively offering me one
cheek and then the other. 'Watch out: I've got cider and
honey all over my hands! Come on in.'

Unnecessarily, I stooped a little as I entered.

'The others are already here,' she said in a slightly lowered
voice.

Fuckpigs, I thought. I had guessed they would take seven-
thirty to mean eight. Like all decent Europeans do.

'Come through. What's this?'

'I bought you something good,' I said.

'What is it?'

'A Gigondas '98. We should open it right away.' I followed

her down the short corridor: stripped plaster walls in mid-repair on either side, electric wires dangling here and there, and on the left an open door through which I caught sight of an upturned packing case and an old-fashioned alarm clock beside a double mattress lying on the floor. An assassin's bedroom if ever I saw one.

'Is it lamb?'

'It is, it is,' she said over her shoulder as she went through the door at the end of the hallway. The flat opened out at the back where she had the whole width of the building. She had a generous living space. There was a portable television, which squatted on another upturned wooden box by the patio doors, a single easy chair covered in a brown blanket, a decorator's wall-papering board pushed against the near wall, a pile of paints and a huge stack of boxes shrouded in old sheets. This area gave way to a sort of dining zone with a carefully laid candle-lit wooden table, beyond which, over against the far wall, I saw her newly appointed open-plan kitchen area in all its terracotta glory. Two people were sitting at the table. They looked over.

'Rache, Phil – this is Jasper.'

'Hello,' I nodded, very politely. 'Sorry that I am a little late.'

'Oh don't worry, I've only just got here' – this from Rachel, with a sort of game-show-contestant wave.

'And I came over early to give Maddy a hand anyway' – this from Phil, standing to offer me his hand.

'Jasper, I'm afraid we've all got to sit at the table tonight because . . . well, there's nowhere else really. My chair is the one nearest to the oven' – this from Maddy (*Maddy!*) as she bent to take a bottle of white wine out of the fridge. 'What would you like? You can have a glass of Phil's delicious white or I can fix you a vodka and tonic or something if you prefer to get started that way?'

'The white wine sounds great.' With a cheerful face to screen my writhing soul, I took my appointed seat – opposite Rachel, I noted – and prepared myself for Calvary.

'Sorry about the mess,' Madeleine said, in her not very apologetic way, as she handed me a glass, 'but everything seems to take ages.'

'Well, you know I've offered to lend a hand at the week-end,' beamed Phil. 'Whack on some tunes, get it done, have some fun.'

I glanced at Madeleine. She was leaning back against the sink, wiping her hands on a tea towel with a hey-why-not? expression on her face. Underneath her apron, she was wear-ing a man's white vest.

Rachel joined in. 'You are *so* brave, though, Mad, doing it all. I never dared to touch a *thing* when I found my place. I had to get all these men to come in and do everything. Even then it turned out to be an absolute *nightmare*. Just about everything that could go wrong did and it took *for ever* and I couldn't cope with any of them after a week. Except for the two painters: they were absolute *lambs*.'

'Oh, I'm only doing the easy bits – the decorating. All the serious stuff, like putting in the shower and the bathroom and all this –' Mad (*Mad!*) indicated the kitchen area '– is being done by the professionals. Plumbing, tiling and gas are way beyond me.'

I took a tentative sip of my wine: a muddy Pinot Grigio from the reed-riddled fields of some reclaimed Italian marsh.

Rachel pressed on. 'But it's coming along, though, Mad. I mean, on the phone I thought you were inviting me to an absolute *bombsite*. And even though you are such a sweet-heart I thought that there was no way that it was going to be so nice. And the patio is just *perfect*.'

'Yes, well,' Madeleine laughed politely but quite without

sarcasm, 'apart from the patio doors, which are rotten, and all the rewiring and replastering and putting the fireplace back together, and buying some furniture and the bathroom . . . I suppose it's almost finished. But you're very kind, Rache. And I'm glad that I have finally got some people round because it reminds me that progress *is* being made.'

Clearly, I had walked into a trap. This was atrocious. Dinner parties make me ill with boredom at the best of times but when there are only four people present and two of them will never say anything interesting in their entire lives, and the hostess is insanely attractive and all you want to do is be alone with her, but instead she is contriving to set you up with the other woman while she eggs on the other man, oh then, truly, you know you are lying at the bottom of a pit, impaled on the rusty spikes of life's pitiless sense of humour. But there was no hope of rescue. If Madeleine (or Maddy, or Mad) had the hots for another, then – whatever my feelings for him or for her – my duty was clear: I must not cause an unseemly disturbance or let my wretchedness poison the air; I would serve her best by passing quietly away. I must lie where I had fallen and courteously wait for death. That was all there was left for me to do. But how cruel of her to treat me thus . . . how cruel.

'What's this we are listening to?' I asked, addressing Madeleine as she threw what looked like rocket leaves on to her salad.

'This is the Oscar Peterson Trio – and this song is "You Look Good to Me" – the live version from Chicago. Or, hang on, is this the New Orleans recording? I'm not sure. What number does it say on the machine behind you, Phil?'

'Erm . . . Hang on . . . Track six.'

I hate the word track.

'Yes, I thought so – it's Chicago.'

'Well, it certainly *smells* good to me,' offered Rachel.

'It's going to be ready pretty soon, actually,' said Madeleine. 'I've misjudged everything and made it all too quickly. Do you ever mix with jazz, Phil?'

'No – we use a lot of jazz funk but not much of the older stuff, which is what you mean. It's kind of bad to synch in – you would end up laying it over the top.'

'Shame – it's the best.'

Weakly, I took another sip. 'Are you a DJ?'

Phil laughed. 'No way. I just gig sometimes at this bar near Old Street. I've got a full-time day job.'

'Can I lend a hand, Maddy?' Rachel asked. 'I *so* feel guilty about just sitting here and watching? And it does smell *outrageous*.'

'You could slice up that loaf of bread over there – that would be great.' Madeleine was concentrating on the food. 'And then we are done.'

'What do you do by day?' I asked Phil, very nicely.

'I am a sort of special adviser – for the Government.'

I placed my glass quietly on the table. 'Right. On what? I mean, on what do you advise?'

'Europe.'

'Sounds very front-line. And interesting. Have you spent a lot of time there?'

'Where?'

'In Europe – France, Germany –'

He smirked. 'I get over to Brussels a lot and some of the other summits. But you know how it is with working – never seems like there's enough holidays. Last couple of summers I did Mauritius and Thailand. But I'm planning to go to Italy with the gang this summer. I need to rack up some quality EU time. Oh yeah, and of course I've done the Eurostar minibreak thing in Paris. Which is a laugh. How about you?'

'I lived there for ten years.'

'Where?'

'In Europe – France, Germany, Italy a bit –'

'Lived there?'

'Yes. I went to school in Germany – and France.' I shrugged in a very friendly way. 'But it must be great to be part of the decision-making process.'

'It is, man. We have our bad days but I'm glad I'm part of . . . the project. I think we're still making a difference . . . where it counts.'

'Right.' The air seemed to be collapsing, giving way at last to a vast universe of anti-matter. For the first time in my life, I needed an inhaler. 'Excuse me just a second.' Dizzily, I stood. 'Madeleine –,' I stressed all three of her syllables, 'would it be OK if I poured the red into some glasses, I mean, if we're getting near to the food being ready?' In Italian, I thought, it would be four: *Maddalena*.

The food at least was good. Madeleine judged her salads well – just the right amount of each ingredient so that all flavours were able to participate without fear of being bullied into corners by rocket leaves or trampled underfoot by marauding goat's cheese; and an understated dressing that supported rather than deluged. All the same, I couldn't help but observe, Madeleine was one of those people who sifted her plate, rejecting baby-gem lettuce leaves here, teasing tomatoes out of the way there, so as to get a free run at what she clearly most enjoyed: forkfuls of feta and olives. And yet, given that this was the taste she herself evidently hankered after, there were surprisingly few olives around: her ability to suppress her own cravings in order to play to the palates of her guests was telling – most people just prepare food the way they themselves like to eat it.

The lamb, too, was cooked to within range of perfection, though had we been alone and had the moment presented itself, I might have tentatively floated the idea of rosemary spears – a method of piercing meat that is to be roasted with metal kebab skewers and then packing the holes with said herb, rather than relying upon the pouting caprice of an unbaptized *bouquet garni*. Honey and cider performed reliably as ever and I was almost sprung from my death-trap by the surprise appearance of a troupe of parsnips that arrived at the last minute to the zesty tune of a lemon juice march. But my cheer was short-lived and by the time the ice-cream hove into view even my staunch and secret ally, the Gigondas, was all but exhausted.

Rachel said something like: 'I don't understand how to take advantage of the equity in my property.'

Phil said something like: 'Everyone loves the creative guys in an advertising agency – they're so anarchic – but me I prefer the planners. They're the ones with the real ideas.'

Rachel said something like: 'I am *definitely* voting for Danny – he's got an amazing voice and he's such a nice guy. You can *so* tell.'

Phil said something like: 'If you're going to move to New York, then it has to be Brooklyn.'

And time passed like a wounded slug hauling itself across a runway to die.

A while later, I was at the sink with my back to them, having firmly insisted that I would wash up despite protests of varying sincerity from the others. Rachel was expounding her views on horoscopes: 'Just because you can't *prove* something to be true or argue about it or whatever doesn't mean it isn't true – I mean, there are heaps of things which we do on gut feel, aren't there? Even at work. And maybe the way we feel *is* – you know – governed by other things that we don't know about – things that are nothing to do with us. Of course, I'm not saying that I *totally* believe everything – but there *are* different tides caused by the moon and where we are in relation to the other planets and they *do* find out how things are interconnected all the time. It's a bit like when Sam – my ex – when Sam and me went to Barcelona last year before – you know – we had total relationship *melt*down – and we got to this hotel in a really horrible mood and I said that it just felt wrong and then Sam moved this desk away from the window and suddenly everything sort of fitted back together – between us as well, I mean – and it suddenly felt like we were *meant* to be there. That's when I started getting into *feng shui*. Actually, Mad, you might want to think about that for in here . . .'

I was doing a very thorough job, taking care to wash each piece of cutlery separately. If nothing else, Madeleine would have the cleanest knives in the world. I was desperately grateful for the break. I imagined myself in the 1870s as some bearded Fellow of the Royal Society, an eminent anthropologist touring the New World, exhibiting a happily babbling Rachel and a relaxed but thoughtful Phil to eager and astonished lecture halls. They were my two prize specimens – beyond all previous discoveries – of human ignorance, and they were making me a fortune. My thesis: that they represented some strange genetic projection and that if we did not amend our ways, then by the beginning of the twenty-first century, all twenty- and thirty-something people would become like them.

'And now, Ladies and Gentlemen,' I would declaim with a flourish, having ushered off the Talking Monkey and the Boy with Two Heads, 'we come to the sum and substance of this evening's lecture, the apogee – if you will.' (I cough.)

'Some few years ago, it was my grave privilege to discover, languishing in the London slums of Fulham Broadway and Clerkenwell respectively, two people, seemingly in their late twenties, whom, in the interests of science, I felt must be brought before the world that we may further our knowledge through observation and examination, and that we may see what horrors we are already breeding for the future, even as we go about our lives unknowingly.' (Anticipatory rustling.) 'I need hardly say that their legend has been growing ever since their discovery and I know that many of you will already be acquainted with their names from the pages of our better scientific and anthropological journals . . .' (A low buzz of affirmation) '. . . Ladies and gentlemen, without further circumlocution, it is my great pleasure to introduce to you all Miss Rachel Forsythe and Mr Philip Felton . . .'

There is general applause, which gradually gives way to murmurs of trepidation and sighs of wonder as my assistants wheel on Philip and Rachel, parking them at their places at the dinner-party table which is set downstage and slightly to one side. Once in their positions, the two specimens start talking quietly, sometimes addressing one another, sometimes turning to make some remark to the two well-dressed dummies that make up the four.

Now I stride forward on the stage and, punctuating my address with waves of a great stick, I let fly.

'Ladies and Gentlemen, let us consider first the case of Miss Rachel Forsythe. Be in no doubt of the fine education she has received; imagine, if you will, the long line of teachers who have so bravely attempted to inculcate her with learning; witness, too, the constant access she has always enjoyed to the science, culture and endeavour of our times; observe her natural status in the world – the opportunities she has had to travel, to work, to rest herself in some of the most beautiful places on earth; note the social energy that craves combustion all around her. And yet . . .' – here I would pause dramatically, – '. . . and yet witness, ladies and gentlemen, how little – how extraordinarily *little* she has managed to understand.' (The auditorium gasps in collective horror; Rachel does not pause from her chatter.) 'Come! Ladies! Gentlemen! Marvel at the paucity of her contribution to life's great discussion! Wonder at her failure to apprehend the woven structures of power and influence that rise on every side! Look on aghast as joy and suffering alike go soaring by! Laugh to listen to her account of human relations! Weep to witness what she offers as insight! Gape as she prizes horoscopes over history, as she seizes sentiment from the flames of emotion and clutches to her bosom a sheaf of charred parlour fads! Gawp at her blank naivety as she walks, head down, beneath the architecture of ideas that support her world! Gasp to find her over-dressed and half-asleep in the great concert hall of existence, while around her very ears the choir sings of the glory of God! *Herr Gott, dich loben wir!*'

The audience is on its feet, hands spontaneously, wildly clapping.

'But Ladies . . . Ladies, Gentlemen, please . . . no . . . no . . .' (I hold up my palms and bid them sit) '. . . let me say that she is as nothing . . . *as nothing*, I say . . . as nothing . . . when compared to Mr Philip Felton!'

Some feel for the back of their chairs thinking to sit down again. Others continue to stand, necks craning towards the stage.

'Here is a man, I say to you, here is a man quite deluded. In his mind, you can be sure he thinks himself important, influential, thoughtful, amusing, capable . . . yes, even *talented*. In his mind, he considers himself a worthy gentleman for a lady. He cuts a dash with the latest fashions . . .' (titters)

'. . . his hair is arranged in the latest styles, his shoes are smart but carefully informal. His reading, though light, is always *au courant*, his music the same. Yes, in his mind, he is a reliable friend, a teller of jokes, a man who might hold his head up among his peers and feel a certain pride when he returns to his hometown. He is successful, worthwhile, illustrious, a fellow of ideas and wise counsel – Ladies and Gentlemen – in his mind Mr Philip Felton thinks that he is an adviser . . . *to the Government of Great Britain*.' (Laughter now.) 'ON THE SUBJECT OF EUROPE!'

There are howls, hoots, near hysterics. I, too, cannot resist a smile of my own.

'But ask him, please ask him, has he read a single paragraph written in a language other than his own? Would he recognize great Goethe or Dante or Molière if one or all came calling at his bachelor's rooms in Clerkenwell bearing a little *parmigiano* for his over-boiled fettuccine? I'm afraid not. But perhaps – I hear you charitably demur – perhaps his ascribed European acumen has its locus in music – clever Vivaldi, holy Monteverdi, beautiful Mozart, heart-broken Beethoven, glorious Bach? Again, no – he does not recognize the strains you hum, ladies and gentlemen. Does he rather love Europe's painting then – Raphael, Da Vinci, Vermeer, Rubens, Gainsborough? No, he does not. The battle of ideas? Maybe philosophy is the sustenance that has nurtured him on the long road to his present high pass of responsibility; maybe it is Europe's lengthy conversation with itself that animates him when he is alone at night, wrestling with the future of nations? No, ladies and gentlemen, he does not know the philosophers. Well, does he at least have a feel for the history – the wars, the delicate alliances, the conceited kings, the iron queens? No, alas, he comprehends none of this. What about the course of the great rivers – the Rhine, the Danube, the Loire? No. Or the architecture – the *palazzi*, the castles, the cathedrals? No. The wine? No. The food . . . (At least *surely* the food, you cry?) No. No, no, no and no again.' (Stunned silence.)

'Ladies and Gentlemen, though this man talks and walks and has the semblance of life about him, nonetheless I tell you: his palate is dulled, his ears are deaf, his eyes are blind, his heart is closed, and his soul is dead. And the platform on which he builds his special advice for Europe, his special advice *about the greatest continent man has ever known* . . . his platform is made of nothing more than a fondness for the froth of *faux*-Italian coffee and the fizz of *faux*-French wine.

'Ladies and Gentlemen, we are in grave danger: even as we are stalled and stranded by our horror here tonight, we are delivering the future into the hands of people such as these.'

As one the audience rises, there is a hesitation at first, but slowly the applause starts and –

'How are you getting on, Jasper?' Madeleine was at my elbow.

I cleared my throat. 'Almost done.'

'Leave the rest and come and sit down. I've got one more bottle, which we might as well finish, and a tiny bit of cheese.'

And with that those twin jailers cheese and biscuits came swaggering and belching into our midst and I knew that there could be no gracious exit until they had been overcome.

I really don't know how I made it through the rest of the evening. Somehow I struggled on through the swampy undergrowth of the conversation – thoughts and feelings held in a rucksack high above my head to save them from the mire – laughing here, joking there. But truly the danger was pressing in on every side: Phil trying to enlist me as his laddish sidekick; Rachel, whose myriad insecurities were rising to the surface as she got more and more drunk (like litter emerging from a flooded drain) and who was becoming more and more earnest in her efforts to deny them, pressing me with questions, to which anything even approaching truthful answers would have caused her to have an instant mental breakdown; and Madeleine herself liable at any moment to make some private signal inviting me to take note of Phil's comments or gestures so that I might add them to my calculations of her chances with him. *Her* chances with *him*.

As I saw it (from the bottom of my tear-swamped pit) the big question was this: if this was life, how the living fuck did someone like Madeleine stand it? Intelligent, attractive, absurdly well-travelled, nobody's fool – how did she fit in? How did she cope? Perhaps, I reflected, the problems were all mine. Perhaps I needed to do as William suggested and get myself to a shrink. Perhaps my adult life had been one long psychological condition – I was ready to admit as much. But surely, I thought, surely I was not alone in the world: surely, so-called advertising planners *are* the most fraudulent people alive; surely the price of property *is* the least interesting subject available to humanity; and surely, surely, surely viewer-vote-in television talent shows are utterly inexcusable life-insulting excrement. Surely, out there somewhere, all but forgotten, the truth *is* still standing, on a lonely mountainside perhaps, cragged and tall in the mist?

Eventually the end came – and with it what I mistook at the time for a thin strand of hope.

Phil was talking to me. 'That's a bit harsh, mate. Just because someone doesn't share your taste in music you kill him.'

But Madeleine answered for me. 'Jasper's a bit anti-relativistic when it comes to the arts but I've got him on a programme to widen his horizons – oh yes, that reminds me: you remember that band I told you about? At the Empire in Shepherd's Bush. It's actually *this* Thursday. Can you still make it, Jasper?'

'Yes. I think so. I mean –'

'I've got a lunch that day but we could meet there or something.' She smiled her killer's smile in Phil's direction. 'And hey, who knows? Maybe pretty soon you'll be coming with me to one of Phil's nights in Old Street.'

And he grinned back. 'Are you gonna come down next weekend, Mad?'

'Sure,' she said.

I broke in: 'What are they called again?'

'Who?' Madeleine turned.

'The guys at Shepherd's Bush.'

'Oh . . . they're called Groove Catharsis.'

Rachel sat up drunkenly: 'Boys are *so* much more competitive than girls. Don't you think?'

I left them together when Rachel's minicab arrived. For a while, I lingered in the street, choking on exhaust fumes and stillborn dreams as the car pulled away. Then I walked home. The night was black and cold.

15. The Message

Send home my long strayed eyes to me,
Which (oh) too long have dwelt on thee,
Yet since there they have learned such ill,
Such forced fashions,
And false passions,
That they be
Made by thee
Fit for no good sight, keep them still.

I stand alone on the grim grim grass of Shepherd's Bush Green and wait for London's oily night to smother me in its slick. Nearly ten o'clock and still the light won't call it a day – hanging on, determined to stick around as long as possible as if to make some kind of a point.

Dead ahead, outside the fading Empire, the ticket touts have long ago knocked off and the three or four that remain talk among themselves in leather jackets halfway up the entrance stairs. Outside the burger bar, the young tramps hold hands and pray for money; and someone switches on the whirling blue light above the door to the minicab office.

I sit back down on my grimy bench. Here is no place to be waiting. Resentment is running things in this part of town, taking over, spreading out, claiming both elbow rests, demanding justice. Even the sign by the bin warns 'Don't feed the pigeons because it encourages the rats' as if to suggest a degree of bitterness on the part of other residents about anyone getting any sort of encouragement about anything. The bin itself is on its last legs, pleading for urgent rescue before it chokes to death on cold kebab and rigid potato and bright red copies of 'The Daily Gutter Sludge' – 'Match the Botty to the Totty'.

On the top decks of buses, which burp clockwise around my sentry post, gangs of youths point me out to other rival gangs of youths and they bury their differences and laugh. I am, I realize, thrice encircled: dog dirt, diesel dust, and an unbroken ring of fast-food joints: Shepherd's Bush Green.

At least the pigeons don't give a shit. At least the pigeons haven't noticed. Listen, pal, we've got three hundredweight of kebab to process here before we hand over to the vermin for the night shift and – yeah – we appreciate you've been stood up and that's tough, but we are *seriously* fucking busy right now so can you get out of the way or at least move your foot, for Christ's sake? Jesus. Thank you.

And believe me, on Shepherd's Bush Green there is a lot of shit to give. Tonnes of the stuff. Hillocks. Mountains. Ranges. So much so that I cannot believe that it is 100 per cent locally sourced. There just can't *be* that many dogs in W12. They must be radioing for back-up. Pets from all over the country must be jetting themselves in around the clock to keep the place covered in shit.

Ten-thirty and now she's two hours late. In another fifteen minutes Groove Catharsis will have finished their set and the audience will be coming out. It's far too late to call her, of course. But I wish it would rain or the wind would get up or something.

> Send home my harmless heart again,
> Which no unworthy thought could stain,
> But if it be taught by thine
>   To make jestings
>   Of protestings,
>   And cross both
>   Word and oath,
> Keep it, for then 'tis none of mine.

A sleepless night listening to the ghost of a summer storm go stealing through the city.

> Yet send me back my heart and eyes,
> That I may know, and see thy lies,
> And may laugh and joy, when thou
>   Art in anguish
>   And dost languish
>   For some one
>   That will none,
> Or prove as false as thou art now.

And so to Friday morning. An envelope on the doormat of number 33 Bristol Gardens, handwritten and addressed to me. Suspiciously, I open it.

> Jasper,
>
> So so so sorry. Tried to call but you were out – obviously. And don't have your mobile. (Have you got one?) Got stuck at Casualty with a friend. Broken arm. Nothing serious. Give me a ring. Sorry, sorry and sorry again,
>
> M.

Her handwriting is hideous, especially her Ys and her Gs and her thin, serpentine S.

16. The Apparition

When by thy scorn, O murderess, I am dead,
And that thou think'st thee free
From all solicitation from me,
Then shall my ghost come to thy bed,
And thee, feigned vestal, in worse arms shall see;
Then thy sick taper will begin to wink,
And he, whose thou art then, being tired before,
Will, if thou stir, or pinch to wake him, think
    Thou call'st for more,
And in false sleep will from thee shrink,
And then poor aspen wretch, neglected thou
Bathed in a cold quicksilver sweat wilt lie
    A verier ghost than I; . . .

One of the most striking differences between the human mind and a computer is that the human mind has no 'delete' facility. Once you have an image on your hard drive, that's it. Until you die.

I didn't call her. I waited until the moon was in the garden then I climbed from my garret and stole across the grass barefoot to lay at her window a wreath of freshly cut tears.

Just kidding.

I went out and got absolutely fucking arseholed with Don's big brother, Pete.

Don, who had last been in the country around the time of my birthday, was, as I mentioned then, a fellow student of philosophy now living in New York (but not Brooklyn). Pete, his older brother (who was also at my birthday dinner), had quickly become a good friend after he first came up to visit Don at college ten years ago. We saw each other infrequently but he and I had travelled abroad together several times and the day after the Shepherd's Bush fiasco, he was the man I called. I had an extra reason: six years ago, much to everyone's delight, Pete had 'given it all up' to become a fashion photographer. (Must have been tough.) And he therefore knew and was adored by lots of seriously attractive women . . .

Of course, I used to do quite well with seriously attractive women. But that was long ago when I was cool. The night after Shepherd's Bush, I couldn't have talked a hooker into giving me a hand-job with two million, cash, up front. That Friday: forget about it.

Oh sure, I tried it on with the Vanessas and the Tessas, the Pollys and the Hollys, and even a Giselle. But did they want to know? Not a chance. I might as well have been a long-haul live-calves trucker with the whole deck: body odour, halitosis, dandruff, acne, athlete's foot, nasal hair and ungovernable wind. That Friday I slept with the dawn traffic and the drizzle and bits of yesterday's paper.

Obviously, I was superhumanly drunk, which probably means I was extremely rude, which probably didn't help. And obviously I took all the drugs that I could physically get into my body, including (I seem to remember) some weird, light brown-coloured cocaine that might just have been cinnamon. And obviously, I was suicidal.

The full details simply are not available. There are a few picture grabs and some unsatisfactory amateur footage but no proper coverage of the night's events. It seems I left Pete at whatever nightclub we were in quite early (or it could have been quite late) with a plan to say hello to an Argentinian I knew (or maybe I didn't) who often hung around one of the secret drinking dens at the back of Tottenham Court Road, dancing salsa with her pals. But I'm not sure I made it. I have a frame of me offering a cup of coffee – still in its saucer – to a woman through a taxi window. Then some blurry husband shit happened. I was definitely in Dick's for a while, telling people to fuck off while they still had a chance. Which puts me still in Soho after three. And I do remember a woman with dark hair (but it may well have been a man). Did we kiss? Who knows? I don't *think* so. (I have good tranny-resistor functionality when I'm sober but you can't be sure of anything when you're running on backup power sources and everything is continually crashing.) If she was a woman, I wish her well and apologize if I went straight to tongues. If she was a man, well then the fucker should have known what was coming.

After that – who knows? I have some more shaky snap-shots of a man who looks like me soldiering through Soho in the dead-of-the-morning dark (when even the refuse men refuse to share a joke and the all-night tramps start to shake their heads as if to say that you'd really better pull yourself together, bud, get a hold of your life and tell it who's boss) but I am also pretty sure that I decided to catch some sleep beside the Marylebone Road – so I may have quit town much earlier (or later) than I thought.

In any case, it was a complete waste of time. The very first image that came into my head when I awoke was . . . Madeleine. Full screen. Close up. Undeleted.

Four o'clock on a Saturday afternoon. And the phone was ringing.

'Jasper?'

'Will.'

'Hi, it's me – Will.'

'I know.'

'What are you doing?'

'I am trying not to die before the world has a chance to forgive me.'

'Problems?'

'Uh.'

'What's happening with *you know who*?'

'Toilet.'

'Toilet?'

'The whole thing is in the toilet.'

'Christ. That bad?'

'Best friend syndrome.'

'Oh God – *no*.'

'I think.' A desert wind blew mournfully across the line. Then my hangover screamed, angry that my attention had wandered. 'What do you *want*, William? I have been out all night and I really *have* to go back to bed. Please, is there a point on the horizon?'

'I want a nice farmhouse in the country where we can settle down together. You could paint your manuscripts – or whatever it is that you do – and I could tend orchids and keep my bees and write wry letters to the newspapers and all our friends would be secretly jealous and –'

'For Christ's sake, I am very seriously ill. And I haven't done any work for days so will you please fuck *off*.' I almost hung up. I should have hung up. In the next life, I shall insist on better friends.

'Well, how about a party in Notting Hill to make you feel better?'

My heart sank – as hearts so often do.

'You can tell me your shit and we'll think of a plan,' he added.

I could barely speak. 'I feel too ill. Honestly, Will. I was out last night with Pete.'

He continued, cajoling: 'Wall to wall with devastatingly

attractive women and all of them calling me on the hour, every hour, to say that only you – only you personally – can really make them feel better. We could meet beforehand for a drink if you like. Catch up on the latest gossip from our Yoga classes.'

'Oh Will, you know how much I hate Notting Hill.'

And so it was that at seven-thirty on a Saturday evening, clean-shaven, though still feeling jaded, faded, weak and deeply weary, I stepped out on to Bristol Gardens once again and set my course for Warwick Avenue, there to find myself a cab from the rank.

I slammed the door shut.

'Notting Hill, please,' I said. 'By the Tube.'

'You wanna get out and be sick?'

'No,' I replied, mildly alarmed at the speed of the question. 'No really, I'm fine. Just a little queasy – I've got a big hang-over still. From yesterday.'

'Right.' We pitched into the traffic. There was a moment's silence then two pale eyes appeared in the rearview mirror, stagnant pools in the wet limestone of a face. 'Because if you wanna be sick, mate, then you've gotta get out of the cab, right? Because I'm not bloody clearing it up.'

'OK, OK. Honestly, I am not going to be sick.'

We swilled around the Paddington basin a couple of times and then surged over the canal bridge towards the station itself, the black hackney sluicing through the traffic lanes like a blood clot in search of the heart.

No doubt about it, I wasn't looking my best. And the monster, though loathsome, nonetheless had a point. I was not feeling well. The sleep deprivation, the poisons, the relentless behavioural adaptation – it all exacts a toll. And now and then I *do* get car-sick, especially when I am already feeling ill before the journey begins. And especially when I get the hideous drivers ... the sproutings, the dandruff-speckled collar.

'Good day? Bad day?' I asked, as matter of fact as I could manage.

'What's that?'

I raised my voice: 'I was just asking: has it been a good day or a bad day?'

'Shit. All day. All week.'

'Oh.' The taxi banked left as we coursed into another traffic stream and I rolled sideways across the back seat, the nausea rolling through me in noxious waves. 'What do you put it down to?'

'What's that?' He lifted his hand to cup a grisly ear.

I raised my voice again. 'What do you put it down to? I mean, why is business slow at the moment?'

'Don't know, mate. Time of the month. Heh heh.'

I left it there for the time being and focused my faltering mind on the splendid views. We were cleaving our way through the various cars, buses, trucks and vans that swirl ever faster about Paddington station itself, as if looking for some plughole into which to pour themselves and so be gone forever. We came to a stop at the junction with Praed Street and the light changed suddenly as the sun slipped out from behind a cloud, so that for a moment it was possible to see the air itself, grimy as a mechanic's cloth, before the eye readjusted and transparency was restored. Gathered on the corner by the lights, smashed and raw like some final del-egation of lunatics picnicking between bedlams, the London drunks gnashed and swore at the stationary vehicles. The buses belched by in the bus lane. All around, life staggered on like some grim-faced marathon runner bearing news of defeat.

Periodically, the creature glanced up at the mirror. He was watching me. But I didn't care. I was holding my head in my hands, massaging the temples with my thumbs. Or clasping my stomach. Or clutching my knees.

Will civilization ever find the words, the phrases, the stomach to describe the true nature of taxi drivers? Where do they come from, these creatures of the swamp, these strange deformed mutants, sent out into the world to sap mankind of its will to live? I assume that their evil masters must kidnap them young: 'Hey, you, kid? – hate your fellow man? – baseless sense of grievance and injustice? – boy oh boy, have we got just the job for you! – get right in line – don't worry about a thing – everything's gonna be taken care of – you're gonna be a cab driver. Whoa yeah. Sorted.' And with that first cruel deception these ugly fledglings are whisked away to some distant marshland camp, cut off from the rest of the world, where they are caged in the semi-darkness with only steering wheels and rearview mirrors for solace until, little by little, they lose all hope, all heart, all soul . . . And then begins their long, slow tutelage in the ways of the ancient fellowship.

Even so, I'll wager that some of them don't make it. Because it's not just a mental or spiritual thing – there's the physical side to be taken into consideration too. The state-of-mind stuff is demanding but it can be taught: any would-be taxi driver has got to hate *driving*, that's obvious; and certainly he's also going to have to hate traffic; and, yes, he's going to have to hate the city in which he works; and of course he's really going to have to hate the people who live there, his passengers in particular. Such basics are taken for granted – or can be easily worked upon, given time. But beyond the straightforward character-building stuff, what the taxi masters are really looking for is someone who is also physically repulsive *from the back*. Someone who is instantly, biologically, repugnant when looked at from the rear. Aaahhh ... now that's special, that's flair. Because to look unusually revolting from behind takes real talent. There's no bald forehead, no stomach, no piggy eyes, no moustache, no loose, sagging lower lips to fall back on. None of that. It's all got to happen in a fairly small and little-considered area of the body which is almost impossible to cultivate. And not everyone is born with the right gifts: the roll of fat squatting at the bottom of the back of the skull; the pock-marked neck with that hard-to-fake, melted-then-set-again look, like solidified lava; or the grey-brown, grease-caked hair.

'So what's your line of work?' he asked, his voice somehow a perfect blend of pre-emptive sarcasm and aggrieved indignation.

'I am a calligrapher.'

The brakes squealed and I was thrown forward, almost to the floor.

'Right. That's it. Out. Get out of my bloody cab.'

'What?'

'Out.'

Three seconds of bruised anger from me: '*What*?'

'You heard. This is not an ambulance, mate, and I'm not cleaning up after you. You can spew your guts elsewhere.'

In other centuries, I might have slit him open with my sword and fed his still-pulsing heart to the eager rats, but instead, I climbed out, feeling for the pavement with my foot. For a second, I thought he was going to do the unthinkable and just pull off without getting his fare. But oh no: he waited, staring dead ahead, his jowls quivering to the vibrations of the idling engine. I could not face so miserable a fight.

'And how much will that be?' I enquired.

'Eight sixty.'

'Please, have ten . . . No, I insist, keep the change. It was an excellent ride. I thoroughly enjoyed myself. You're quite a driver.'

'Fuck off.'

Spat out by the Hyde Park railings beneath the thinning cerulean. Hardly the fate of the ancient heroes, I know. But do not forget that this particular Saturday was my very lowest ebb. Even so, I probably should have turned straight for home there and then. Faced up to things, maybe. Fallen into a deep and regenerative sleep. Forged some new and better self in the cleansing fires of self-denial. But I did not. Instead, I stood for a moment and watched the pigeons tick-tocking about their business like fat privy councillors pretending pressing errands. I was going to be late. I took a deep breath and hurried down the Bayswater Road towards Notting Hill.

Of the many centres of self-delusion around the world, the ludicrous area of Notting Hill can confidently assert its position as number one. Not only is there an impressive depth to the claim – in the very core of their souls, the inhabitants firmly believe that they are in some way chosen – but there is also real breadth insofar as the curious self-satisfaction which goes with residency affects all types of person, from banker to artisan. Of course there are notorious and well-attested districts of self-deception all over Europe – Paris, Rome, Barcelona, Berlin, even my beloved Heidelberg – and it is true these are well stocked with a significant range of pomposity and pretension. But nowhere else is there quite such a formidable discrepancy between the opinion that the residents have of themselves and that which the visitor must inevitably form.

In the normal run of things, a low-slung evening sun will wash even the bleakest of cityscapes with a lush ochre light, which will lend a building, however dismal, a softening and sympathetic splendour of sorts. Not so Notting Hill. Even in the very best atmospheric conditions, as you approach the epicentre of the farce – a miserable, traffic-vexed little junction – you become increasingly aware that you are walking along one of the shabbiest, least inspiring and most consistently unappealing thoroughfares in the modern world. Distended with estate agents and bloated with burger bars, architecturally tedious and commercially humdrum, Notting Hill, you soon discover, is just one more tiresome trunk road that has come into money.

I say farce but perhaps I mean burlesque. In a farce, the emphasis falls on the preposterousness of plot rather than the ridiculousness of the characters. Whereas, in a burlesque, the audience is invited to laugh and cry at the fakery and self-deceit of the people themselves . . . the white guys trying to be black, the black guys pretending to be white, the rich pretending to be poor, the poor pretending to be rich, the old pretending to be young, and the young pretending to be old. Notting Hill. Don't even go there.

William and I had agreed to share a pre-party drink in one of the pubs on Campden Hill Road – a dark, autumnal place, full of awkward wooden cubicles and undercover fund managers eating gourmet sausages.

He turned just as I came up to the bar: 'Jasper – at last. My God, you look awful. Have you just been sick? Are you OK?'

'Mutiny,' I croaked, melodramatically.

'Here, I've got you some sherry. It's bleak stuff but the best they had. You'd better drink it down in one – you need to regain your equilibrium. Then we can get you a drink.'

'Thanks.' I eyed the chalice suspiciously for a moment and then drank deeply.

William ordered himself a vodka straight (one ice cube) followed by two vodka tonics. When the bar tender had turned his back, he leaned over and whispered in confidential tones: 'I'm afraid the party may turn out to be a horror show ... please don't look at me like that ... it seems to have broadened out since I last spoke to Stephanie – whose birthday it is, by the way, in case you run into her. The whole of London now seems to be coming. But anyway it will take your mind off the other business and we can always cab ourselves to Le Fromage if we really hate it. Or whisk you to hospital.' He clicked his tongue. 'I have been hatching the beginnings of a failsafe plan, by the way, about the other business, I mean. How is the other business?'

'It's hopeless –'

'No, no, no.' He held up his hand. 'I will not permit you to talk in such tones. And you cannot allow yourself to think in that way. In years to come you will look back on this evening of lachrymose woe and laugh the gay laughter of someone looking back gaily on an evening of lachrymose woe.'

'It's hopeless,' I rasped, 'she likes me – *as a friend.*'

'So you said.' He exhaled a deep breath to indicate that he understood afresh the gravity of the pronouncement.

Best-friend syndrome: that terrible canker of the male heart, which leaves its victims sallow-browed and slowly wasting away until all power of speech is lost and all that remains is hallucinations and a withered, febrile lust.

William rubbed his hands slowly as though attempting cheer after a recent bereavement. 'It is my birthday soon.'

'No, it isn't.'

'I know it isn't, actually. But it *will* be.' He accepted his change and, in a single draught, drained his straight before setting the empty tumbler down slowly on the bar. A woman with a matching handbag and scarf in garish checks ordered a glass of white wine. William swallowed hard and shook his head. 'Please, I know things look bad at this stage but worry not, young Jasper: William Lacey has everything under tightest reign and all will be well in the best of all possible worlds.' He raised a fist halfway and pressed on further back into the picaresque. 'We two knight-errants must huddle our steeds together in times of maidenly revolt and we must prepare ourselves for the trials ahead – *courage, mon chevalier*, the ways of ancient chivalry wi—'

'William, will you please try and talk normally? Everyone is starting to think you are a tool.'

He made a hurt face. 'I was only trying to cheer you up.'

'I'm sorry.' I meant it.

'That's quite all right.' He sipped his other drink and looked at me with only half-exaggerated concern. 'Do you want to talk about your . . . difficulties now or shall we wait until later?'

'Later. I feel awful.'

'OK, then I suggest you drink your vodka and tonic – it will do you good – and then I think we had better try a Laphroiag and see if we can't get you looking a little less ghostly.'

I took a sip.

He smoothed a non-existent moustache. 'One thing, though, old man: can you tell me – briefly – and just so that I can factor the information into my devilish plan: is there someone else – Madeleine-wise?'

'Yes.'

'Name?'

'Phil.'

'*Phil*?'

'I know.'

'A penis?'

'Out and out.'

'How bad?'

'A complete arsehole of the worst sort.'

'Are you just saying that? Would other – more regular – people like him?'

'Probably. But that doesn't change it.'

'Handsome?'

'Not really. Looks like a sort of . . . well, yes, I suppose, good-looking in a tiresome nice-guy, sandy-haired Austra-lian-soap-star sort of a way.'

'I see. Goatee?'

'Of course.'

'Job?'

'Some kind of Government special adviser. On Europe.'
William winced.

I nodded. 'Although, needless to say, deep down he's an ignorant capitalist pig with deeply conservative instincts twitching through every nerve in his body.'

William tutted. 'Well, we can't all be straightforwardly anti-social, hypocritical, medievalist Marxists hell-bent on debauchery, Jasper. Some of us have contradictions to cope with.'

'Fuck off.'

'Has she . . . are they . . . do you . . . ?'

'I don't know, Will, I don't know. I left before I could –'

'OK. Well. It doesn't really matter. I'm sure he has very little in the trouser department – advisers rarely do. All we need to manage is to get you alone with her in a neutral environment and then let you work your sinister magic.'

'It's not like that any more. I've fucked it up.'

'Ah, but as you used to say to me, "There is always a way." And I just know you will find it, given more quality time with her. You always do. I believe in you absolutely. Does she drink?'

'Like a bitchy alcoholic.'

'Then we have nothing to worry about.' He put his arm around my shoulders. 'A picnic, I think. Yes: a picnic. Consider it repayment for all your clever intercessions on my behalf over the years.'

'Will, you are not going to solve anything by holding a picnic.'

'Oh, but I think I am.'

Having been greeted at the door by Stephanie, we were somehow stalled in the hall for a moment or two as she returned to answer a second knock. The party was well underway: the bass boom of anti-music coming from somewhere like the basement, the alto drone of human chatter, even the odd falsetto-filled helium balloon, with its ribbon tail trailing from the ceiling.

'That's *him*,' I whispered.

'Who is who?' William frowned.

'Over there.'

'Over where?'

'On the stairs.'

'I can see the stairs, Jasper, actually, but I still have no idea to whom you are referring. I'm afraid you'll –'

'Phil. He's here.'

'*Our* Phil?'

I grimaced. 'Yes.'

'Well, we must say hello.'

Phil was indeed standing halfway up the staircase amid a group of people, who were also leaning against the banisters or the opposite wall or sitting down on the stairs themselves. Judging by the unanimity with which they had misinterpreted the prevailing fashions, I guessed that they all belonged to the political scene: junior researchers, special advisers, secretaries, lobbyists, image consultants, bag carriers. As a group, they were, of course, revoltingly ugly, but it was only when the eye picked out an individual that the real wretchedness struck home – each person a living embodiment of some hitherto unimagined contortion of the human physique.

'Let's not,' I said in a low voice, soberly mindful that the conversation of such creatures when collected together – even if casually overheard – can send a grown man shrieking into the night in paroxysms of despair. 'Let's go and find some women. There must be some women we can talk to. I need to relax. I can't face Phil just yet. Not until I have worked out what to say. I'm too ill for this.'

William shrugged. 'Okey-dokey. All the same, I think I may corner him myself later on, if you don't mind. Gather some intelligence et cetera. He seems like a very pleasant young man to me. He's certainly the best looking of his peers.'

'Oh fuck off.' I sucked my teeth. 'Shit! Will, maybe *she's* here too. With him, I mean. I have to –'

'Jasper, mate!' came the voice from the stairs. 'What are you doing here? How's it going?'

William hissed under his breath: 'Too late. He's seen you. And now he *wants* you.'

There was no time to do anything but turn and pretend surprise. 'Oh, hello Phil, I didn't notice you there.'

Phil addressed me from the banisters. 'Hang on a sec, mate. I'm coming down. I've got to get a drink.' He began to make his way past people on the stairs.

A sick fascination for the man Madeleine favoured was

forming in some dissident part of my mind. Perversion by any other name.

Phil came towards us. 'Have you lads only just got here?'

'Yes, we've just arrived,' William said. 'I'm afraid I don't get to London all that much and I made Jasper come and visit my aunt so we're a little on the late side. But it looks like it's going to be a terrific party. It's just a pity we don't know anyone.'

I turned a sickened face to William – but already he was impervious, intent on his twisted entertainment.

'No worries. I'm Phil by the way.' He offered his hand – a firm, certain, regular guy's handshake.

(What is there to be so certain about?)

'*Very* pleased to meet you. My name is William. William Lacey.' William tendered his, deliberately limp.

Phil was momentarily wrong-footed. He turned to me: 'Good time at Mad's?'

'Yes, I . . .'

Phil seemed to realise that I could not finish the sentence. 'I really enjoyed it,' he said helpfully. 'Lovely food. And Mad's a star. I was trying to persuade her to come out and she said –'

'Oh, I get it.' William had now slipped completely into his favourite persona: searingly thick but well-meaning, over-compensating, second son of a high-ranking army officer. Or something like that. 'You must be the politics chap. Jasper told me all about you. *Very* interesting. In charge of the anti-capitalism protests, I understand. Must be odd coming from the left and having to –'

I stepped in. 'Phil is Europe, Will, not . . . whatever. Phil, where are the drinks, any ideas?'

'Yep. In the kitchen. Follow me.'

Aside from all my other problems, I was also cross with

William for interrupting. I urgently needed to know what Madeleine had said about coming out. Very urgently indeed. As soon as non-embarrassingly possible in fact.

In the kitchen a long room, poking out at the back of the house in which the serried ridges of bottle tops congested every spare surface not taken up by plates of half-consumed, unappetizing appetizers, which likewise clogged up the tables or teetered suicidally on shelves – in the kitchen, everyone was bald. For a moment it appeared as though we had surprised a cue ball convention. Of the dozen or so men on view, all but one or two had either shaved back to the scalp *à la mode* or they were so naturally depleted that such measures were unnecessary. For the most part, they were standing in circles, propped up against cupboards or leaning with their backs to the wall. Here and there a woman could be seen among them – tragic minarets of beauty among the bulbous domes. The most recalcitrant cluster – a dense knot of three fairly tall pug-faced individuals – was gathered around the fridge, as if guarding the main gate to the drinks supply. By the looks of things, they were attempting multilaterally to seduce a red-haired girl who had fallen into their midst.

Phil grinned his irresistible grin. 'Dave, Steve, Mike and . . .'

'Angie,' the girl smiled.

Another grin. Phil had great teeth, I noticed. 'Dave, Steve, Mike, Angie this is Jasper and –'

'William! *Very* pleased to meet you all.' The three tensed invisibly, nervous eggs waiting to learn the size of the intended omelette. But William was only just beginning. 'Is everyone in politics? I am in pork myself. Well, pigs, I should say. Bacon actually. Just up for the weekend. Glad to get away from all the muck, to be honest. Which is not to say this isn't a *boom* time for pigs – not at all – what with all the dead sheep and burning cows . . .'

This was William's unusual route through parties that bored him: to tell as many different people as possible as many different lies as he could conceive. As far as I can tell, his guiding principles are philosophical (or even artistic) rather than social: a sort of live-performance sabotage act. In particular, he enjoys baiting men who have shaved their heads. The reasons for this were once explained to me: because we are no longer called upon to wrestle lions, a man's physical strength is not of immediate consequence, but his social standing – in particular his charm – so William believes – *is* still somehow obscurely connected to his locks. Thus, having lost their hair, the bald battalions of modern Britain are consequently denied (or are denying themselves) the correlative subtleties of charisma and wit. Instead, they take up those weapons in the male armoury more befitting of their glabrous state: candour, bluntness, directness, scepticism. They adopt for themselves the role of social demystifiers. In this way – according to William – they aim to make a virtue of both their bald heads and their bald conversation, regarding themselves as a fifth army of emotional soothsayers, truth-tellers, honest-Joes. And it is this propensity to consider themselves in some way more honest than their fellows that William finds most specifically irritating, and which therefore attracts him when he is in the mood for subversion.

As the beers were matily handed out, Mike (or was it Dave?) answered William's question at last: 'I write for a magazine.'

William lifted his bottle a fraction in a gesture of understated cheers. 'And you guys?'

'Television,' they said.

William's face suffused with excitement. 'Oh right – the *media*!'

I could wait no longer. I turned casually to Phil and, quietly but at immeasurable personal cost, asked him, 'so what did Madeleine say?'

'About what?'

'About coming down here tonight.'

Cool and semi-detached, he prised the top off his bottle. 'Oh right. She said she might come down later. She's visiting her sister or something but she reckoned she would be free after that.'

'Nice one.' I swallowed. 'How long have you known her?'

'Not that long actually – I met her at a party at the Polish Club. Something to do with them trying to hurry up EU membership or something. She'd written this piece on why Krakow is the new Prague. So they'd sent her an invite too. I picked her out. Chatted her up. You know the routine.'

I nodded dismally.

By midnight, after an excruciating hour upstairs with the society magazine crowd, the Praetorian Guard of Notting Hill's tedium, I was desperate. I realized that I could no longer live without him. Anxiety was now billowing through my soul like smoke from a disaster site. I needed strong leadership. I found myself clambering down through the house, desperately seeking Phil. Oh how I wanted to be with him again. *When* was she coming, wise Philip? Had she already arrived? Should I stay? What should I say? Show me how you do it, Phil. Oh, show me how you do it. I want to be a regular guy too. Let's be buddies. Me. You. Pals.

The party had broken out of the cage of its earlier self-restraint at last, and although it was not yet roaming wild, bottles were being broken and glasses smashed on polished wooden floors. The money boys had arrived and with them came serious cocaine and the cocaine hags. The political stairs were beginning to get slippery with sycophancy. The cue balls were becoming more and more aggressively ordinary. And someone said that in the basement there were DJs. But I hastened through, oblivious, Jasper the Meek in search of Philip the Great.

I reached the sitting room: a long knocked-through space, running from front to back of the house with the usual arched divide describing where the intervening wall had once been. A little quieter, it was three-quarters full of people: some sitting on the floor, gathered around ashtrays (much as I imagine primitive societies once gathered around fires), others standing in huddles or seated with cigarette papers at the dining table or perched on the arms of chairs in a half-circle that centred on the dried flowers in the unused grate.

Any sign of Phil? My eyes came to rest on a tall woman in the far corner, standing by the window at the back of the room. I recognized her vaguely – a fashion writer for one of the papers, one of William's friends. She was wearing glasses. She was talking to a short man, who was also wearing glasses. He in turn was in the process of giving Phil a CD. And Phil was ripping open a black Velcro shoulder bag and taking out a small case in which were contained . . . his glasses.

Suddenly, I realised the horror: everyone in the room was wearing glasses. My God. What was happening? The whole of young London must abruptly have gone blind. (It must have been all the wanking.) Poor bastards. And just imagine the panic when they realized they had all been struck down together, like so many myxomatosic bats. As one, they must have made their way down to the eye boutiques to get themselves tested. Oh, the tragedy of it all. Led by the arm back into the quasi-clinical light of the marble and emerald consultancy room, minding how they went because everything was definitely a little bit hazy now that they had come to see their visual deficiency more clearly, they must have all gone through the same shocked and saddened procedure, trying on the various gauges and shapes by Giorgio or Giovanni or Giancarlo, until (still as one) they must have realized (with aching hearts) that the only way out of their terrible plight was to look as much as possible . . . like Buddy Holly. An anxious week of Brailling back and forth from the office while waiting for the fitting of lens to frame, then pow! – cool but *formidably* intellectual.

'Oh, hi again, Phil,' I said.

'Hello Jasper mate, how you doing?' He was reading the CD cover with forensic care. 'Catherine – Jasper; Jasper – Alex.'

Ignoring my arrival, Alex spoke, 'it's right at the bottom of the credit list – PF: that's gotta be your man. Come on, you gigged with him, right?'

'Not too bad,' I said, feebly, in answer to Phil.

'You're right, Alex, it says PF.' Phil grinned. 'Check this out.' He handed the CD to Catherine.

I spoke up. 'Hey, er, Phil . . . I'm just about to go because . . . I'm catching a flight early tomorrow. Did Madeleine show up yet? I was just gonna say hi before I left. Thank her for the other night.'

He looked at me – a suggestion of amusement causing his brow to knit. 'She hasn't messaged me back, so I dunno.' His glasses weren't the usual Buddy's like Alex and Catherine's; instead they made him look more like an architect in a car advertisement.

I was at a loss. Chilean Merlot was melting through my veins, dissolving my innards. I feared my heart might drop into my pelvis like a grand piano crashing through weakened floors in a fire. 'What's the CD?'

Phil was digging in his pocket for a mobile phone. 'Oh . . . it's just some tunes that a mate of ours slung together.'

I hate the word tunes.

Alex broke in: 'Come on, Phil. It's fucking number four in the charts. It's the bollocks, mate. The new Moby.' He turned to me. 'And Phil here is a contributing name.'

'You should be on royalties, Phil.' Catherine smiled and handed back the CD.

'I wish.' Phil rubbed his chin ruefully.

Catherine turned to Alex and asked something about gyms.

Phil put the CD away in his one-strap rucksack.

And finally, at long last, the vile-faced truth troll tore through the remaining skein of my own pitiful self-delusions. I had no option but to face it: Phil was actually a perfectly nice bloke. Phil was OK. Phil was *all right*. I may not wear glasses that I don't need or have a goatee, but nonetheless – I was the loser, not Phil. Madeleine was right to love him. How could I ever have thought otherwise? Of course she was. Somewhere, way back, I had miscalculated life's most fundamental equation, and my whole life since had been fatally unbalanced. The rest of the world had known this about me all along. But somehow it had taken Phil to make me see it for myself. I was a loser – a lifelong loser, busy devouring existence with pointless critique. All that was left now was to watch and imitate and cover up the best I could.

'Nice phone,' I more or less wept, 'where did you get it?'

'Yeah, it's cool.' Phil thumbed through the screens. 'Definitely no messages.' He looked up. 'You all right, mate?'

I nodded.

'How d'you get on with Rachel the other night?'

'I fucked her until her nose bled.'

Phil's eyes widened with concern.

My voice was nothing more than a whisper of a croak. 'And you?'

'Good.' He smiled. He couldn't help himself. 'I stayed over.'

William was smoking a cigarette alone on the front lawn. 'What are you *doing*, Jasper – coming out of the basement windows. Have you upset some poor young man?'

I looked around nervously. 'I am going home, Will; I feel awful. I've got everything wrong in my whole life.'

'Really? In that case, I think home is a good idea. But please try and sleep. I have –'

'You didn't see her, did you? She hasn't come in? I didn't want to run into her; I had to break out. I thought she . . . Phil said she might be coming.'

'No, I didn't notice her arriving. But then I have no idea what she looks like.' William blew a smoke ring. 'You really had better go to bed, Jasper, apart from anything else you are arseholed.'

'You would have known her if you saw her.'

'I wasn't looking at the door. Anyway, I don't think she'll come. As I was saying, I have spoken with Philip – don't worry, I was the soul of discretion – and nothing is as bad as you feared.' He stopped me interrupting. 'They barely know one another. Only met thrice. He's slept at her flat but I don't think Dr Jiggovitz has put in an appearance yet. I can't be sure . . . but the emotional swagger isn't there.' He smiled. 'So I believe we are still very much in the contest. I have invited Philip on our little picnic by the way' – again William held up his hand to stop me saying anything – 'and tomorrow you must invite her.'

I was too tired and drunk to go any further down the various cul-de-sacs of his folly with him. 'Are you coming home? What are you doing?'

'No. I am just having a breather. Then I am going back into that party to inflict suffering and enjoy myself.'

'Phil is a nice bloke,' I said. 'And don't you forget it.'

I staggered off to find myself a taxi.

17. The Good Morrow

I wonder by my troth, what thou, and I
Did, till we lov'd?

Lying on his back, somewhere to my left, Don spoke for every-one: 'Will, I have to say that that was probably the best picnic that I have ever eaten – or am ever likely to eat – in my whole life.' He clicked his tongue. 'Worth flying back to London for. I think it even beats your nineteenth birthday extravaganza.'

'Mmm – that goes double,' said Cal, Don's wife. 'We can go home happy now.'

'It was really nice, Will,' added Sam, Nathalie's sister.

'Yeah. Cheers, Will.' Phil spoke as he reached for the newspaper.

I was about to add my own thanks but William put an end to the chorus of gratitude. 'Think nothing of it,' he said, 'it was a pleasure. Not every day a fellow gets the chance to eat outdoors for three hours on the trot in England without rain stopping play. I'm just glad the weather held and that you were all free at such short notice. There's nothing worse than staging an impromptu picnic only to discover that you will be dining alone. In the rain.' Now he too lay flat, resting his head on Nathalie's lap. 'And there is one more thing to come. What time is it anyone?'

Phil answered. 'Just gone five-thirty.'

'And still so bloody hot. This heat is ridiculous. Well, I think a period of recumbent reflection is very much required all round. And then we must have my birthday champagne.'

He reached for a pillow, which he placed beneath the small of his back.

Nathalie was stroking his hair. 'How come I didn't get invited to your nineteenth?'

'For the simple reason that I hadn't met you when I was nineteen,' William replied.

'Yes you had.'

'Had I?'

'Yes.'

Of the people gathered, only Don and I knew that William's birthday was actually in September. I eased into the conversation: 'There were no women at William's nineteenth. William was still trying to be gay in those days so as not to let his family down. Isn't that right, Will? It was before you came out and admitted you were straight, wasn't it?'

'Yes, I think so. An awkward time in my life.'

'Well I for one am very glad that you have turned out to be such a star,' murmured Sam on the threshold of sleep.

A dog panted past, racing down the hill in search of something lost.

'What happens if we all pass out and someone comes and steals the cool boxes?' asked Cal.

'We'll have to appoint a guard.' Will raised his head a fraction. 'Nathalie?'

'No chance.'

Madeleine spoke up. 'I feel wide awake. I'll watch the hampers.'

'Thank you, Madeleine,' said William. 'That is very kind of you.'

I lay back, listening to the breeze shuffle through the trees. The general mood of gratitude and contentment was more than apposite: William had conducted us through the picnic afternoon like a beneficent *Kapellmeister*. Had I not been concentrating on other things, I too would have been rendered senseless by the fineness of the food. But for me the tricky part of the afternoon's operation had yet to begin and I had no intention of going to sleep in the meantime.

It was Saturday, June 15th, seven days after the party in Notting Hill, and we were already approaching the longest day of the year. Earlier, William had given Madeleine and me a lift, arriving with Nathalie and Sam in some ridiculous old Jaguar that his father had just bought. His strict instructions had been that he would pick us up *together* at my flat at twelve twenty-seven. These orders I had duly passed on to Madeleine. Phil, meanwhile, had been playing football all morning so I had volunteered to meet up with him (again, William's idea) at Hampstead Tube. Don and Cal had come under their own steam and were waiting with the others in the north car park when we caught up with them.

Madeleine and I had spoken the Sunday after the party. And no, you are very wrong, I did not call her: *she* called me.

I was very much more together: inconsolably depressed, of course, but steeled and set for one last visit to life's threadbare roulette table.

She, on the other hand, was almost gushing: 'Hello Jasper – it's me, Madeleine. Listen, I am so so so sorry about the concert. Oh God. It was a complete fuck-up. A friend of mine broke her arm jumping on to a bus on Oxford Street and I had to get her to Casualty and we were there until nine o'clock. I am so sorry. I tried to ring you but there was no answer and I don't have a mobile number for you. By the time I could have got down to Shepherd's Bush, it would have been too late. I really can't apologize enough. I called yesterday too but you must have been out. How long were you waiting?'

'Oh, I gave you until nine and then I guessed something had happened. So I went out with Will instead. It's no problem. In fact, I was going to call you today to see if everything was OK.'

'Yes, I'm fine.'

'Well, it's my fault for not having a mobile phone.'

'I'm glad you didn't wait too long. How embarrassing.'

Of course, as we now lay, so many inflexible yards apart on Hampstead Heath, I was conscious once again of the fact that I had no idea whether or not she was bullshitting. On balance, I thought not; there was not enough conviction in her voice when she made the actual excuse; most liars lie too hard, whereas the truth tends to speak for itself.

So I reasoned, as the clouds inched across the sky, sometimes merging, sometimes breaking apart, like young countries borne upon the currents of continental drift. Though nobody felt like sitting up to verify that it was still there, London lay spread beneath us, sprawling, mauling, falling away in all directions: the cobalt dome of the west, the river, the Eye, the neverending slough of the south and the towering east, glinting with avarice in the summer light.

Forty-five minutes passed before William raised himself from Nathalie's lap and started to go through his hampers. I sat up. Sam was fast asleep. Don and Cal were dozing. Phil was lying on his side, still reading the paper and drinking one of the bottles of beer he had bought. Nathalie was on her back, wearing her sunglasses. Madeleine had moved. I looked around for her. She was sitting a little way off, beyond the trees, so as to remain in the full ambit of the still-burning sun. She was leaning forward, smoking and reading a magazine. Her hair looked much lighter in the glare.

'Where's the little cool box?' William asked softly, speaking as much to himself as anyone else. He checked the baskets one after the other and then opened up both the big hampers again and rummaged through them.

'What does it look like?' said Cal, now roused.

'It's blue. Quite small.' William cast his gaze around over all the bags and hampers and packages.

'Help yourselves to beers, by the way,' said Phil, still leaning on his elbow, addressing me in particular but meaning everybody.

'No, I'm all right, thanks,' I said. 'I'll save myself for William's encore.'

'I can't see it,' said Cal.

'It's not here.' William frowned. 'Unless it's under one of the blankets or something.'

'What are you looking for?' asked Madeleine as she came back towards us.

William appeared puzzled. 'A little blue cool box. It has two bottles of champagne in it.'

Madeleine spoke. 'Well, I've been watching and nobody could have stolen it.'

Nathalie sat up and pushed her sunglasses back on to her head. 'Maybe you left it in the car. Didn't you put it on the back seat because the boot was full?'

'Did I?' William asked.

'I can't remember. You might.'

'The car was packed with stuff. Do you really think I left it in the back?'

Nathalie shrugged. 'You might have done. I really don't know.'

'I suppose.' William hesitated. 'Well, someone could nip back and check. Madeleine, you seem the most awake – would you mind?'

Madeleine smiled. 'Not at all. I quite fancy some exercise. And I'll do anything for champagne.'

'Do you remember which way it is?' William asked.

Cal sat down.

Phil flipped a page.

'No, not exactly.'

'Have you got a phone? It's in the north-west car park . . . just up that way and –'

'I'm useless with the compass, I'm afraid. I'm a travel journalist.' Madeleine placed her hand to the back of her head and winced apologetically. 'And I left my phone at home today. Is it right on that path under those trees or –'

'You'd better go with her, Jasper,' William looked over, 'or can't you face the walk? Nathalie, maybe you –'

'I'll go,' I said, quietly. 'I don't mind.'

Phil looked up.

William took out his keys. 'Two sets for the same car on one bunch. Stupid really. But my father likes to keep them all in one place.' He teased off one ring and chucked it to me. 'Don't drink it on the way back.'

Oh believe me, Hampstead Heath is a maze, a labyrinth, a jungle. In all honesty, for those unfamiliar with the criss-crossing paths, the proliferating ponds, the disorientating number of seemingly separate hills, the identical wooded vales, the constant forks and double-backs and junctions and confluences, the random railings, the bridges, it is impossible *not* to get lost. Indeed, I doubt if even the grizzled veterans of the Gents' know where they are half the time. As for the joggers, they are not running to keep fit, oh no, they are running because they are lost, because they are desperate to find a way out, back and forth, back and forth, ever more nervous, more panicky . . . What I am trying to say is that *it could have happened to anyone*. Especially two people deep in conversation and not paying particular attention to where they were going.

Oh sure, we found our way *back* to the car all right – in no more than twenty-five minutes, I would guess. And the cool box was there – no doubt about it – waiting patiently in the well in front of the rear seats. We set off on the return journey just fine too, following (I swear) exactly the same path along which we had just come. So it must have been in the trees, at one of the tricky five-way intersections, that we made our mistake.

'Down here,' I said, lifting the cooler slightly to indicate the direction I meant. 'Christ, it is still so hot. You wouldn't think England could get so hot.'

'It's lovely.' Madeleine moved ahead to allow a young family with a child buggy to pass. She had twisted her hair up in a clip and there was a faint sheen of perspiration on the back of her neck. 'It always gets me how everybody is so surprised by the weather in this country. You know, twice a year, every year, everybody is like "Oh my God! It's snow-ing! Who would have thought it could get so *cold*, and in the winter too! *Snow*!" or "Oh my God it is so hot and *sunny* today – would you believe it? In June of all months? Phewwee!!"' She turned to wait for me and we carried on side by side through the trees until we came to another divergence where we stopped. 'This doesn't look right,' she said.

'No, it doesn't. I think we should go back up there because we must have been quite high up to have had that view.'

We set off again up a small hill.

By the time we found our old spot, almost an hour and a half later, they were gone. Not a sign of any of them. I was confused. Madeleine didn't have a watch but she guessed it must be half-sevenish. She sat down with her back to the tree near where Don and Cal had been lying earlier.

'Looks like they all fucked off and left us.' She took out a cigarette and lit up. 'Now what are we going to do?'

'Shit. I guess we took longer than we thought. Have you got your phone?' This was a question to which I already knew the answer, of course.

'No, I didn't bring it out. It's charging back at my flat.'

'Well, I'll leave this here with you and go and have a look around – in case they just moved over to the next field or something. I'm certain this is where they were.' I put the cool box down and walked back towards the path.

When I came back, Madeleine had a note. 'This was on the ground,' she said.

> J and M –
>
> No idea where you two have got to ... Sam and I need to get back into town this evening so we've set off for the car. W furious with you – thinks you planned to steal his booze. Phil says can M give him a call later on about tomorrow. D and C are coming out with us tonight if you also want to join ... We'll probably see you on the way back to the car – in which case you won't read this.
>
> Nathalie.

Needless to say, we did not encounter any of them again. And it must have been getting towards nine-thirty by the time we stepped off the forty-nine bus outside Warwick Avenue Tube station – just the two of us.

The sun had not yet left the sky but had dropped behind the buildings, and the clouds were busy changing into their evening colours, pink and peach.

A car hesitated and Madeleine ran across the road ahead of me, then stopped in front of the church to light a cigarette. I waited for it to pass and walked across towards her. Above her knees, and despite her tan, her skin looked slightly burnt where the rays had taken advantage of her habit of sitting cross-legged with her summer dress bunched up in her lap.

I suffered a moment of acute weakness. I was tempted to come right out and be honest, to say what was in my mind, to chance it all on the instant. 'All this could be yours,' whispers the Devil when we are at our most starved and thirsty, perched high on a rocky ledge in the wasteland of our minds. But in my other, wiser ear, faintly I heard the generic platitudes of her reply: 'Oh Jasper, that's so nice of you to say, really, but I don't want to ruin us being friends and I don't think it would be right – and, anyway, I'm already seeing someone but hey, look, I don't want you to think that I don't like you very much because I do, *as a friend . . .*'

So I held back.

Nonetheless, without being explicit, I was now determined to push my luck as far as it would go.

'Do you want to go home and see if you can find Phil's number,' I asked. 'Or can I interest you in a bottle of whatever is inside this bloody box?'

Holding her cigarette high, she rubbed her wrist against her forehead. 'He's grown up enough to take care of himself. Let's drink – if you don't think William would mind.'

'He hasn't got a say.'

We swung around the corner on to Formosa Street and from there to Bristol Gardens. My arm ached for her waist.

'This is a very nice flat,' she said, standing with her back to the sink and watching me punch a number into my phone.

'You think? I just wish I had a proper kitchen. I even hate "kitchenette" as a word.'

'I like the feel of it. Living in the eaves. All the nice wood. But it must be a pain in the ass coming up all those steps every time. Is it OK if I smoke?'

'Sure . . . Oh fuck, he's on voice mail.' I had dialled William's work number. The last thing I wanted to do was talk to him. I waited for him to finish inviting me to leave a message. 'William, it's me. I don't know where the fuck you are or where everyone disappeared to, but anyway: I am back at my flat and I'm going to drink your wine. Sorry. Speak soon.' I hung up. 'There's an ashtray on the table in the other room. Go on through. I'm going to open this cool box and see what we have inside.'

She smiled and stood upright. 'Do I get to stay for the whole bottle?'

'If you are nice and well behaved and don't make any adverse comments about my taste in music or whatever, then yes, I may allow you to.'

'That's very kind of you, Jasper.' She lit her cigarette and went in search of the ashtray.

Jesus Christ! Truly, I thought, caprice is a many-headed monster. Perhaps William was right about Phil not having slept with her after all. Or perhaps Madeleine was just enjoying playing everybody along. All *right* then, so be it: she could drink the wine and go and take her body with her; or she could drink the wine and stay. But, I said to myself, you'd better be on your guard, Miss Belmont, because now you're at my house and I've done this before, and many more times than you.

I slid two clean champagne flutes from the cupboard and held them to the light to check for any traces of washing residue. They were immaculate. I placed them on the side where she had left her cigarette pack.

Her voice came through from the other room. 'You have a lovely view of the garden from up here.'

Carefully, I removed the champagne from the cool box. It was a 1982 Cristal. You have to hand it to William, he knows how to help a man out. It was still sufficiently chilled.

'Hey!' She shouted. 'You can almost see into my flat. There's my patio.'

Carrying the bottle and both flutes, I went into the sitting room. 'You know I'm quite pleased that we don't have to share this with the others.'

She turned and smiled – sexily, I thought – not provocatively exactly, not seductively either, and certainly not tantalizingly or suggestively, but right on the true note of the word – sexily. A difficult pitch to hit and rarely done. And different to anything I had seen from her before.

'Can I put some music on?'

I nodded. 'Yes. Have a look. Choose anything you like.'

She crossed to my wall of shelves while I set down the glasses and took my customary wait-and-see seat on my single wing chair. (Let her have the sofa, I thought. If she wanted to do anything about it, she could get up and do something about it.) I watched her as she knelt down in front of my discs and ran her finger along the line a little unnecessarily, a little theatrically, a little nervously? She sat back on her heels but the soles of her sandals stayed flat against the floor and I saw that the bottoms of her feet were covered in dust from the heath and scratched from where I guessed she had been walking barefoot in the garden.

She twisted her head round. 'It's all Bach,' she said, looking somewhere between nonplussed and disappointed.

'No, it isn't.' I grasped the bottle and clenching the cork in my fist began to coax it out. 'Try down at the bottom.'

'Oh good, Ella Fitzgerald,' she said, kneeling up again and fiddling with the stereo. 'Thank Christ for that.'

The music started. She stood and surveyed the other shelves. 'Have you read any of these books?' she asked.

'No. Not a single one. I can't read. I prefer TV.'

'Mmm. So I guessed. You're a bit too dumb to have read anything much. Which is a shame really because you are a very nice man otherwise.'

'Thank you.' With feigned concentration, I poured the wine and then topped up the glasses where the champagne bubbles had retreated. 'Well, if you know any basic sort of easy starter books for beginners then I'm very willing to try again. Have to be something without too many long words, though, and very easy to follow, because I can't really be doing with anything – you know – *clever*.'

'No,' she said. 'I can see that. I'll try to find something for you. But in the meantime you must promise not to worry.' Now she came over. 'Lots of men are very slow and they get on OK.'

We chinked glasses, she swivelled the bottle in order to read the label and then sat down on the sofa – not straight but with her legs curled under her so that her knees were pointing at me. She held her glass in one hand and with the other she rubbed her bare shin. Outside, the light was beginning to fade.

She sucked in her lips. 'This is gorgeous. But I do feel guilty drinking it.'

'Don't. Seriously, William doesn't mind. We'll save him the other bottle.'

'Where do you think they went?'

Our ease in one another's company was almost restored to pre-comedy-night levels. And we were talking about other people, always a good sign. 'I guess they thought we weren't coming back or that we had got lost. They must have returned to the car with the stuff. We must have missed them when we were buggering about. William will probably have waited for a while to see if we turned up and then driven everyone back into town, I suppose.'

'How would he have got in, though? You locked it.'

'He has spare keys. His father buys and sells vintage cars for a hobby and William is always driving them up and down the country to deliveries or auctions or just for the hell of it.'

Ella Fitzgerald was on to 'We Can't Go On This Way'. I leant forward and picked up the bottle. She reached her arm out so that I could top her up and then raised the glass quickly to her lips to catch some of the bubbles before they vanished. 'How long have you known William?' she asked.

'He's a friend from college. So I guess that makes it something like ten years.'

'Were you friends straightaway?'

'Pretty much.'

'How did you meet him?'

'You really want to know?'

She frowned. 'Yes. Or I wouldn't ask.'

'I met him on the first day. I think it was actually the very first day. I'd just put my pathetic couple of boxes away in my room and was wandering about, feeling a bit dislocated, and looking for something to do when I came across him in the porters' lodge, trying to stack all these crates of wine on to a trolley by himself.'

'I love the idea of a porters' lodge.'

I sat back in my chair. 'It was quite funny. Everybody else was bustling about with their families, stopping on the pavement outside in estate cars and clogging up the gate as they unloaded kettles and notebooks and toasters and things, but William was on his own with no one to help. He didn't seem to have any possessions at all apart from all these wooden boxes of wine. And every time he managed to pile them up out of other people's way, this bastard delivery man would dump another load right in front of the porters' desk, so that nobody could move in or out. Then all the porters started getting officious, talking about fire regulations, until William was just running around in a real state, apologizing madly to everyone.'

'I can imagine him doing that.' Madeleine smiled. 'Go on.'

'So I gave him a hand because . . . well, I suppose I was on my own too.' I took another sip. 'My grandmother was still in Heidelberg then and I had come up on my own the day before – I used to go by train because it was the cheapest way – change at Frankfurt, Paris, overnight ferry to Dover, London, Cambridge and what a journey *that* was every term.'

'Where did he put it all?'

'What?'

'The wine.'

'Oh – he kept it in his room. We trolleyed it all there – about a dozen trips' worth – and we built this massive stack. He had already moved all his furniture into the corridor to make way for it. All he had was his bed. When we finished, I said something about it being a shame that porters didn't port any more and he thought that was very funny and opened up a bottle and we sat down and shared it and he said that I must come round any time and help myself.'

'Christ. You two must have been paralytic for the entire three years.'

'In actual fact, most of the stuff wasn't really for drinking – although obviously that didn't stop us. The real reason he had to keep it all with him, or so he told me, was because every time his parents went away – which was a lot – his older brother would have another "coming out" party at their house and William couldn't trust him to stop his friends gulping their way through William's share of the cellar, which, obviously, was some kind of long-term investment or something – worth a lot of money anyway. So he did the only thing he could think of and brought it with him.'

'What a life.'

'I know.'

'You're lucky he puts up with you.' She grinned. 'He must be very generous. Today was a banquet. There can't be many people who serve fresh oysters at picnics.'

'He is very kind.'

'What's his job? Or doesn't he work?'

'Oh yes, he works. I suppose . . . I suppose you'd say he is a tramp orchestra impresario.'

'What? Like a music thing – what do you mean?'

'He runs this . . . he's basically in charge of a theatre production company.'

'Explain.'

'OK. Well, going right back to when we left college he decided to be a communist for a while – quite literally, living in a commune somewhere in Bethnal Green – I know, I know, but there's actually a long tradition of it among people like him. Anyway, he paid for about a dozen people to do what they liked for two years. But he got fucked off with all the *nouveau* homeless, as he called them, who kept showing up. He said that he preferred proper tramps. So he set up this hostel for some of his bona fide tramp mates – men and women over thirty-five – drunks, drug addicts, all that. And somehow or other, he managed to start up this joke orchestra with a group of them who were quite good musicians. They got a student conductor from somewhere and it became slightly more serious. William opened up two more hostels and a few more people became involved. Then one day, a couple of years ago, the whole orchestra appeared on local television. Boom! And after that it just grew and grew. Now they're huge. Big money too.'

'Really? Wow. What kind of music is it – I mean, violins and clarinets and stuff?'

'No, no. Not really clarinets. Although – actually – yes, some violins. Mainly it's bin lids and penny whistles and stuff you can find in the street. But they perform serious long pieces now – you know, with movements – and critics go to all the shows. A lot of rhythm-driven dance-type stuff too. I thought it was just bums-aid bullshit when Will told me about it but, I have to admit, they sound pretty good and they're very, very popular – for lots of reasons. They get involved in all kinds of events – the fiestas in Spain, and loads of things in the States, plus Notting Hill Carnival and Glastonbury and all that circuit back here. The music world loves them. The Government loves them. William exploits the situation to fund more hostels.'

'You know, I think I've heard of them.' She frowned. 'Or maybe I saw one of their adverts on the Tube. I didn't realize they were anything to do with William.'

'No reason why you should.'

She sipped her wine. 'How about you; do you play anything?'

'Nope. You?'

She pouted. 'For many years I was an internationally cele-brated concert pianist but I gave it up because my Japanese-owned record company kept insisting that I take all my clothes off for the album covers.'

'Understandable.'

'In what sense exactly?'

'I meant that it is understandable that you should have given it up if you were coming under such unfair pressure.'

She smiled and glanced towards the table by the window.

I pre-empted her: 'I think you left your cigarettes in the kitchen.'

'Oh right.'

I was going to get up and find them for her but she unfolded herself too quickly and, without putting her sandals back on, she went to fetch them.

In another ten minutes it would be dark, I thought.

Her voice came over my shoulder. 'So aren't you going to show me round?'

Enough. I had made up my mind. I rose to my feet.

At the very last, though, I think it was John Donne who seduced her. To him at least must go the credit for that final, irrevocable strike. Disregarding the trifling hindrance of the four hundred intervening years, he put aside his hungry rest-less mind and won her at his first attempt with the easy charm and skill of a genuine master.

I was moving fast, it's true. In another ten minutes, in the bedroom, no doubt, I would have beaten him to it. But he was always ahead of me: the great professional showing how it's done.

'Is this where you work?' She looked around in the semi-darkness.

'Yes.' I flicked on the sidelight.

'My God. I didn't realize you actually used quills. And all these paints and inks – and gold stuff.'

'It's gold leaf – for gilding.'

She glanced sideways to where I was standing in the doorway with my glass of wine and then advanced towards the window. 'This is your easel?'

'Yes, sort of. It's a draftsman's board.'

'What are you working on at the moment. Can I see?'

'Sure.' I walked over and carefully turned my board around so that she could look at it.

And I swear I swear I swear it was complete coincidence that 'The Good Morrow' was on there. Inwardly, I flinched. I wanted to make some remark to deflect from what I knew she was about to read – or at least to lessen the awkwardness. But, in the moment, my desire to let her see my work overcame my embarrassment about the poem itself and I lifted back the covering sheet.

'Jesus, Jasper.' She was truly shocked. 'I had no idea. It's beautiful. Really beautiful.'

> I wonder by my troth, what thou, and I
>> Did, till we loved? were we not weaned till then,
> But sucked on country pleasures, childishly?
>> Or snorted we in the seven sleepers' den?
> 'Twas so; but this, all pleasures fancies be.
>> If ever any beauty I did see,
> Which I desired, and got, 'twas but a dream of thee.
>
> And now good morrow to our waking souls,
>> Which watch not one another out of fear;
> For love, all love of –

'It's an aubade,' I said.

'What does that mean?'

'That it is a poem written for the dawn.'

Probably I kissed her to prevent her reading any further. I could not bear the self-consciousness of us both standing there in silence moving down the lines.

She met my lips with hers.

But all credit to Donne, she read him through to the end before she made love to me.

Part Four

18. The Dream

> Dear love, for nothing less than thee
> Would I have broke this happy dream,
>   It was a theme
> For reason, much too strong for fantasy,
> Therefore thou waked'st me wisely; yet
> My dream thou brok'st not, but continued'st it,
> Thou art so true, that thoughts of thee suffice,
> To make dreams truths, and fables histories;
> Enter these arms, for since thou thought'st it best,
> Not to dream all my dream, let's act the rest.

Welcome to the new me!

Cancel all that stuff about me being weird and normal life getting me down. That was terrible crap. I think I must have been mad or something. Jackson's syndrome – it's a killer – it screws with your sense of perspective, it messes with your *mind* . . .

Amazing what a woman can do for a man!

Truly staggering. But there you go, you never know how it's going to feel until it happens. And when it happens . . . oh boy. I am just sorry for all those people who might never meet that special person. Imagine that. Poor lambs.

And guess what?

Despite everything, it turns out that I too am a Regular Guy. That's right. After all that fucking around back there it turns out that J. Jackson Esq., notorious gainsayer and epicurean, actually wants in on the whole package – all that modern life has to offer: girlfriendpluscarwithcoolsoundsystemdesignerglassesbaseballcapsundaysupplementsbrunchon bankholidaysdinnerpartiespromotionwifepregnancyawareness classeskidsbiggerhousegoodschoolsprofessionalrecogni-

tionneighbourhoodwatchareapensiongrandchildrensecond
honeymoonnicequietdeath.

I know, I know. This all came as a big shock to me too.
But everything was different now. No more did the calligrapher sup with artists or the disaffected; get thee hence dis-
senter, rebel and subversive; away atheist, anarchist and
protester; hie me fast to the chubby bosom of convention.
Never again shall the breathtaking banality of western liberal
capitalism steal away my will to live. Nope. Pass me the
paper: let's see what's going on in this little old world of
ours.

What was going on? Me, Her, It. That was what was going
on. And no mistake. Twenty-four seven. Me, Her, It – and
mainly It. What can I say? It was long, It was short, It was
slow, It was fast; It was sensitive and caring, It was impolite
and carnal; It was deviant, It was straight, It was dressed up,
It was dressed down; It was planned, It was impromptu; It
was action-packed, It was lazy; It was addictive, It was manic,
It was obsessive; It was compulsive; It was abusive; It was
riveting. And It got in the way of everything else. But who
really gives a shit about everything else? You don't. I don't.
Nobody does. When it comes right down to it, everything
else can go fuck itself.

Yep. For several weeks following, I freely admit that getting out of bed became a problem for me. It wasn't so much
that I was having trouble waking up. No, the problem was
that whenever I became conscious, I became conscious of
her.

There I lay, just another guy, cast up from the deep of
dreams upon the rocky shores of wakefulness – a yawn,
a stretch, an opened eye and *Jesus Christ*: there she was. –
Undeniably beside me in all her beautiful actuality.

> Thou art so true, that thoughts of thee suffice,
> To make dreams truths ...

Hand on bruised but still beating heart, I'm not sure 'happiness' came into it all that much in the beginning. (And anyway, as adjectives go, 'happy' is surely one of those most often employed retrospectively – unlike, say, 'angry' or 'upset'.) Looking back, however, one thing I can say – and with some assurance – is that there were very few (if any) early signs of Madeleine's true nature.

OK, right, so there *were* the violent sexual assaults. In particular, Madeleine liked to attack me at four-thirty in the morning as I struggled, half asleep, back from the blindness of the bathroom's bluish light, a man at his most vulnerable, weak, dry, lost. At such times, I was made painfully aware that what I was about to receive was not so much the physical expression of affection and mutual respect but an all-out punishment beating. And yet a man can take a lot of that sort of punishment before he starts complaining – or even realizes he's being punished.

No, there were not, I submit, any obvious indications. We were excited, engrossed, absorbed. We behaved as all new lovers behave. We ignored our friends. We didn't get out much. We didn't really care that we didn't. Because we enjoyed one another's company. And in these besotted circumstances, I could hardly have been expected to guess mendacity from a few moments of misgiving.

Three weeks after Hampstead Heath, on a long Friday at the start of July, we woke up at precisely the same moment: seven-thirty. We had been asleep since going to bed at four, earlier that afternoon. We stared deep into one another's eyes (see the swirling colours and the faraway stars) and found ourselves (no words were needed) to be in profound spiritual agreement: tomorrow we needed – badly – to *do* something. Anything. Leave the flat, for example.

I made some serious coffee and then, businesslike, we sat up together in bed and drew up a valiant list of bracing and useful Saturday-like things to do: I was going to purchase my first mobile phone; Madeleine was going to buy a proper double bed for her flat; I was going to write a letter to my grandmother; Madeleine was going to go through her boxes and file all her old articles; and we were both intending to spend the evening together at the Globe Theatre watching *Cymbeline* (because neither of us had ever been or knew anything about the play).

But when Saturday morning arrived (late, of course), instead of setting about our allotted tasks with the vim that the Christian world has come to expect, we found ourselves struggling against a strange zone of extra-strong gravity that refused to loosen us from its grip.

At ten-thirty, I did actually make it into my trousers but then committed the (foolishly naïve) error of taking Madeleine her coffee in the bath and attempting to read to her while she lay with the saucer balanced delicately on her chest taking prim little sips whenever I looked up.

Around twelve I rose again and had another go (and even optimistically readied a pair of shoes for active duty) but within seconds I had to rush barefoot to her aid because she said that her back hurt, and even though it was meant more as a report than a request I couldn't stand idly by and refuse her the relief my dutiful palms might provide.

The final effort – some time after three – was hardly much more convincing: she vanished into the sitting room while I went through the clothes on the back of the chair, bravely looking for my shirt and shouting back to her that her music must be in there somewhere until, a minute later, she appeared in the doorway pronouncing that if I had lost her *Birth of The Cool* then she was going to rip my head off and why didn't I have anything she could listen to – at which juncture I realized that *she* had my shirt on and I noticed that the white tails fell exactly midway between hip and pretty knee. And that was it.

Thereafter, we abandoned any plan to escape the flat as an ambition too far. The shiftless afternoon deliquesced slowly into yet another early evening. At seven o'clock I was still in bed, reading an introduction to a new old edition of Donne's poems that I had bought – 'It may be inferred that whether his affairs were few and protracted, or – as seems more likely – many and short-lived, it is obvious that he knew women of various characters, from the shallowest to the most sensitive . . .' (What an odd tone these old critics strike and how easily they slide from 'inference' to what was 'obvious'.) Madeleine, meanwhile, was sitting at my writing desk by the window, leaning back in my chair with one leg crooked up in front of her, chin resting on knee, painting her toes and making the room smell of nail varnish despite the open window. The *largo ma non tanto* from Bach's concerto for two violins was playing. Miles Davis remained safely uncontactable where I had hidden him.

After a while, she asked: 'Do you like my toes?'

'Let's see.'

She swung around in the chair and flaunted an irrefusable leg in my direction.

'Yes,' I said, 'I like your toes. What colour are they?'

'Pink. Idiot. Can't you tell?'

'Yeah. I just thought that colour might have a special name – you know, look-at-me-cerise or dramatically-different-damask or something.'

'No.' She scowled as if to dismiss the office jerk. 'It's just called party pink.'

'Well, they look great. Really . . . partyish.'

She nodded to herself as if satisfied and then got up and prowled across the bottom of the bed, keeping her toes up behind her so as to let the varnish dry. 'So, now that you have trapped me here all day, what are you going to make me for my dinner? Or am I to starve?'

'What do you want?'

'Anything at all; but *not* something which takes ages.'

'OK, that's quite specific. How about I nip down to see Roy and –'

'Actually, you know what I really want?' Now she came right up to me, a smile of certainty in her eyes. 'I want a pizza.'

I put down my book. 'You mean go out to Danilo's or something?'

'No – order one in and watch a movie. It feels too nice to go out. I think we should just – you know – curl up here and stay awake all night watching movies.'

'Is there something good on?'

'No. I mean we should get a film from the store.'

'A video?'

'Yeah. I could send you out and you could ring me and tell me what's new and I'll choose. Otherwise you're bound to come back with something that is totally unwatchable. I am too weak to traipse all the way there myself or I'd come with you.'

'I still don't have a phone. If you remember, we didn't really do any of our jobs today.'

'You can take mine. I have to be in charge of choosing.'

'And I don't have a video recorder.'

She collapsed on to her back and rolled her eyes in despair. 'Jesus Jasper, what the fuck are you on?'

'I know.' I grimaced. 'I did try to buy one a couple of months back but the guy in the shop said there was no point because visual technology was moving so fast that the minute I got it home, it would be out of date. I asked him what he recommended I do about it, and he said that my only real option was to sit tight and wait for the next Dark Ages, when he expected that home entertainment facilities would all slow down for a few centuries and I could buy something without fear of it being rendered instantly obsolete by progress.'

She sighed. 'You're such a freak-boy.'

'Sorry.'

'OK, so, there's a DVD player at mine – still in its box. So I guess I'll go get it.'

Galvanized, she swung herself off the bed and began looking for her clothes. 'You'd better remember to take some ID with you to the video store because you're going to have to join. And they're funny about it these days.' She hopped one leg into her jeans. 'Oh yeah, and I want a meat feast pizza with extra corn. You have a pizza delivery number, right?'

'Of course.' I looked suitably insulted and put my faith in the recycling bin downstairs.

Talk about becoming a Regular Guy! I loved it. You would have loved it too. My conversion was swift and zealous and the resultant life-change rich and fulfilling. And what a relief. No more unnecessary thinking for one thing. Nothing beyond the here and now – films, food, magazines. Plan for holidays and the kids, of course, and pay the mortgage; but no more thinking about the future in the sense of *whither humanity*? No more despair at the awful harrowing misery and death that our sordid and grotesque religions visit on the millions they have enslaved. No tearful reveries at the sheer loneliness of Planet Earth putting a brave face on things out on the edge of oblivion, with only a pair of over-washed and thinning Y-fronts otherwise known as the ozone layer to protect its modesty. No tongue-biting horror at the sheer implausibility of a species, that cannot last a single minute without oxygen, taking on an entire universe that specializes in very large scale not having any. None of that. Oh no no no . . .

Instead, there I was, parked up on a Saturday night next to my girlfriend – yes, I think by July we could call Madeleine that – parked up with my girlfriend (girlfriend!) in front of the television, DVD (dvd!) spinning patiently through the latest thriller (chicks kicking ass, which is all they seem to do these days; hey sisters, no more getting laid, we wanna kick butt instead, right? damn right), parked up with a pizza spread before us, Diet Cokes effervescing at our elbows, no worries and no fear of interruption. Unbelievable. There I was, hanging out on the sofa beside my girlfriend (now wearing a T-shirt and a pair of my boxer shorts) as she gently encouraged reluctant toppings from the squelchy trenches of their deep-pan battlefield and guzzled depth charges of drink between satisfied mouthfuls. There I was, indifferent to the plaintive lament of the brutalized tomatoes (as they keened for the balm of fresh basil), unheeding of the film's many and relentless savageries against art and humanity, deaf to the mournful entreaty of a spurned Chablis (half-full and getting warmer by the second). There I was, impassive in the face of the world's least convincing actors visiting torture, mutilation and assault on their already mentally retarded script. There I was, popping back into the kitchen to reheat the garlic bread. There I was, wielding paper napkins. There I was, curling up. There I was cuddling. There I was when the phone rang.

Oh, all right then. Perhaps there *were* signs. Perhaps I

did succumb too easily to that soft benighting of the mind otherwise known as affection. Perhaps, after all, there were moments when I found her behaviour just a little unnerving, just a little strange; perhaps there were actions, gestures, expressions in which we can now see (as we gaze more deeply into life's ever-widening rearview mirror) the fleeting glimpse of something false. But if we must pay due homage to Madeleine's skill in the arts of sustained deception, we must also admire her talent for spontaneous guile. Because when – as I now see – the risks and traps lay all about her feet like so many landmines in the battle sand, she simply danced on, ever more assuredly the dervish.

Ring ring went the phone. Ring ring ring.

Though I had nothing in particular to fear, I confess my blood pumped a little harder through the narrow gateways of my heart. A late-night call is always alarming. My cool, however, did not abandon me: I asked the question in my best approximation of a not-unduly-worried-but-nevertheless-curious young man whose mother (if he had one) might suddenly call him out of the blue at three minutes past eleven, or, failing that, whose many and varied friends occasionally ráng up on the spur of the moment when they needed to convey the particulars of some great personal enterprise: 'Who, I wonder, could that be?'

Madeleine was now lying more or less on top of me; she twisted her head. 'Probably one of your ex-girlfriends ringing up to tell you that, despite everything, they still hate you.'

'Not unlikely.' I eased myself out from under her.

'Shall I pause?' she asked.

'No – it's OK – just let me know what happens,' I said, already heading for the hall. 'I'm sure I'll be able to pick it up.'

Madeleine hit 'Pause'.

I lifted the phone.

Breathing. Very quiet – but breathing nonetheless. A woman's lips hovering like uneasy butterflies above the receiver's trap.

My brain scrambled from the smoky comfort of the officers' mess, desperate to get airborne.

'Will,' I said, 'Will? Will, is that you? I can't hear you . . . no . . . where are you? Yes . . . it's very *noisy* . . . no I'm just, er, hanging out with Madeleine. With Madeleine. We're having a pizza. Can't hear you . . . Will? You're cutting out. Will? William? Are you still there? For fuck's sake.' I hung up.

Did my deceit pass unnoticed? I thought so – extemporaneous invention was, after all, my *métier* too.

'Gone,' I said, not quite to myself.

Madeleine was leaning in the doorway – Venus in boxer shorts. For half a second her expression was neither intimate nor inviting but keenly inquisitive. Intrusive.

Then her hands were on me.

'Will?' she asked.

'Yes.'

'Drunk?'

'Yes.'

We fought. We fell. We fumbled. She pulled the phone wire from the socket and told me to present my wrists.

'Jazz mate – you're eating too much fucking fish.' Roy Junior was standing in the kitchenette, chewing gum and grimacing while scratching his back with his left arm, as if attempting to remove a splinter from between his shoulder blades.

'You think so?' I regarded the two sea bass which lay

resplendent on the wooden slab of my chopping board like gifts from guilty Neptune.

'I know so, mate. First it was the salmon. Then you had the lemon sole. Then the mussels – not strictly fish granted – and now these bastards.' Roy stood up straight. It was the first time he had been inside my flat, and he was determined to make the most of it.

'It's a phase, Roy, just like the mushroom thing last year. Be over before you know it.' I felt oddly compelled to light a cigarette but resisted for the sake of the fish.

'Well, I'll tell you something, mate: my uncle Trevor is loving you. You're buying more of his stuff than the new restaurant, which is – I have to say – going the way of everything else new on the Harrow Road – down the fucking shitter.'

'Shame.'

He shook his head in the manner of dismayed locals the world over. 'Have you been down the Harrow Road lately, Jazz mate?'

'No.'

'Have you seen the fucking state of it?'

'Not for a –'

'It's a wank hole is what it is. Pardon the Frog.' He curled his lip. 'The small business man makes the effort to boost the local economy, to put some pride back into the place, to get things going . . . but he might as well not fucking bother. What's the point? You might as well wipe your arse with fifty-pound notes, Jazz.' He sighed. 'I tell you: I was down there last night at ten to one – ten to one on a fucking Friday night, mind you – and what happens? I'm offered four blowjobs, three ounces and a couple of wraps – all in the time it takes me to get to the front of the queue at MFC.'

I shook my head.

Roy looked truly disgusted. 'I've got my own dealer, mind, and I'm getting plenty of action thank you very much, but even if I wasn't – which I always will be . . . Even if I wasn't, I wouldn't go down there and take a handjob off one of those filthy fucking tramps, never mind anything romantic.'

'MFC?'

He nodded. 'Maine Fried Chicken. New. Where Utah Fried Chicken was before.'

'Maine Fried Chicken?'

'Yeah.'

'As in Maine with an "e"?'

'Fuck knows.' He frowned.

'Maine is in the far north of America,' I said.

'And? Yes? Your point, Jazz?'

'I thought fried chicken was a southern thing – like Kentucky or Tennessee or Louisiana. You know: southern fried chicken. Maine is all about seafood and . . . lobsters.'

He exhaled sardonically through narrowed nostrils. 'Right. I'll tell Span and Baz next time I'm in. "Sorry lads – you're serving the wrong shit: should be Maine Fried Lobsters. There's a bloke up in Warwick Avenue says so. Better fuck the chicken and go lobster."' He gave a schoolboy's sarcastic grin before affecting a more philosophical air. 'Anyway – listen to you – you're obsessed, Jazz. I think this seafood thing is your new bird, mate. I think she's making you soft. You're not buying as much meat; you're not going out late; and the old man says you waited to hear what song was on the radio the other day before you left the shop. Chris de Bastard Burgh – apparently. What's happening?'

'Hard to say.'

Roy lowered his voice and suddenly looked seventeen again. 'She's not here now, is she?'

'No. She's gone to her place.'

He nodded.

I reached out my wallet and handed over a ten-pound note.

'Nice one.' He took out his own thick wad of notes from his breast pocket and slipped the money into their midst. 'Nice place, mate, by the way. Proper shag palace. Probably get somewhere very similar myself next year; mind if I have a quick wander?'

I had no real time to decide on an answer to this question since he was already disappearing into my studio. I shot another glance at the bass. Curious how the empty eyes of dead fish can beseech a person so.

Roy's voice came through the door: 'Very nice, Jazz. Very. Fucking. Nice. I had no idea. Thought it was just – you know – a bit of ink, a bit of pen, a bit of paper, a bit of a swirl, nothing special. But this is . . . fucking magic.'

My buzzer hummed. I walked over, pressed the button without lifting the receiver, and then followed Roy Junior into the studio.

He looked up. 'No offence, Jazz mate. But this is really fucking nice. Respect.

'Thanks.'

'How much for one of these?'

'You're looking at two grand right there, Roy.'

'Fucking bastard.'

We stood together staring at 'The Legacy'. Roy found a scholarly tone somewhere in his portfolio. 'No offence, mate, but mind if I say something?'

'Shoot.'

'What the fuck does it say?'

'What does it say?' Mentally inserting the missing blank versals, I read the poem out loud:

When I died last, and, dear, I die
   As often as from thee I go,
   Though it be an hour ago,
And lovers' hours be full eternity,
I can remember yet, that I
   Something did say, and something did bestow;
Though I be dead, which sent me, I should be
Mine own executor and legacy.

I heard me say, Tell her anon,
   That my self, that is you, not I,
   Did kill me, and when I felt me die,
I bid me send my heart, when I was gone;
But I alas could there find none,
   When I had ripped me, and searched where hearts
     should lie;
It killed me again that I who still was true,
In life, in my last will should cozen you.

Yet I found something like a heart,
   But colours it, and corners had,
   It was not good, it was not bad,
It was entire to none, and few had part.
As good as could be made by art
   It seemed, and therefore for our losses sad,
I meant to send this heart instead of mine,
But oh, no man could hold it, for 'twas thine.

Roy nodded slowly. 'No, mate, I can read what it says –
just about – I mean, what does it *say*?'

'You mean what does it *mean*?'

'Yeah. What does it mean?'

'Well,' I paused, 'there's this guy telling this woman about how he dies every time he leaves her – also, by the way shoots his load –'

'What? Spunks himself?'

'Yeah . . . but that's sort of a secondary thing. Forget that. Forget about the orgasm stuff.' I took a brisk break. 'So, anyway, there's this guy telling this woman about how he dies every time he leaves her; then he remembers that the last time this shit happened –'

'The last time he spunked off or the last time he died?'

'Both. But mainly the last time he died. Obviously, Roy, this guy is pretty fucked up.'

'Obviously.'

'But anyway . . . the last time this guy left this woman and died – because every time he leaves her he dies – the last version of his dead self made a promise to make sure that he became his *own* executioner (and executor) next time – rather than let her keep killing him – okay? – but, of course, now the present dead self realizes that he has failed in this promise because it really is still *her* fault that both the selves are dead again. The woman, by the way, is also referred to as 'my self' because the speaking self reckons that the two lovers – man and woman – have become one – and so he is she and she is he, my self is her self – which is kind of the point . . . although maybe there's a wanking gag somewhere in there too . . . And, anyway, then one of the dead selves starts getting the fear because he goes to check up on the actual real dead self and finds out that the main dead self hasn't got a heart, which is a real bastard because this heart – his heart – is what he promised to leave to the woman who killed him as his legacy to her – right? – but now it looks as though this heart – his heart – has been stolen (by her: as in 'she stole my heart') and replaced by this other dodgy heart, which he decides to send anyway, because there's fuck all else he can do in this situation – except that the dodgy heart is sort of too slippery and impossible for any man to get a hold of – because – of course – it actually turns out to have been her heart all along – which, tellingly, he has been harbouring unwittingly in his breast – except harbouring it wittingly too because, after all, he is the guy who constructed the poem in the first place knowing full well that he was heading for this heart-switch pay off – although there's also an issue here about the speaker of the poem becoming confused with Donne himself – and another issue about which of the dead selves is actually talking because it's unclear where the speech marks should close – if indeed you are going to open them after that "say" at the start of the second verse – but the bottom line, Roy, is that, dead or alive, everyone's heart gets fucked up.' I sucked my teeth. 'That's pretty much it.'

Roy considered further, his thumb coaxing the faintest beginnings of what might one day be a goatee. He drew a deep breath. 'No offence, mate, but that really is absolute fucking bollocks.'

'I probably didn't explain –'

'No. I'm following you Jazz – and I appreciate you have to stick up for the geezer. I'm not saying what *you* were saying is bollocks. I'm saying the actual thing itself – the poem – is absolute fucking bollocks.'

'You may have a point there, Roy. I'm not going to –'

'I mean,' he opened his palms – a reasonable man, 'I know you can get a long way up your own arse – we all can, Jazz, mate, that's humanity's condition – but even so that poem there is a pure 100 per cent bollocks.'

'They're not all that bad.' Madeleine was laughing. 'Some of them are beautiful.'

We both swung round.

I smiled. 'Hi. Madeleine, hi . . . er, this is Roy: he works in the shop and he's just brought the fish for tonight and –'

'I know – we've met.' Madeleine was wearing her work shirt and scruffy painting jeans – in which, of course, she looked like a million freshly laundered dollars. 'How's the gardening going, Roy?'

Roy blushed, a rare and comprehensive crimson. 'Great, actually, cheers.' He turned away to glance out of the window as if to confirm the news. 'Sorting it out.'

Madeleine winked at me.

'Anyway,' Roy kept his back to us, 'I'm due in Keele in a couple of hours. Got stuff going on.' He half-turned. 'So, er, nice one.'

Madeleine fingered a button on her shirt and said (rather breathily, I thought): 'Well, I'm going to take a shower.' She disappeared into my bedroom.

I let Roy out.

'Gardening?' I asked him quietly on the stairs.

'Yes, mate.' Roy winked.

Everybody was winking.

From late July onwards, because her flat was without hot water for a few days and then without electricity and then without any water at all, and because there was paint and plaster and pipes and piles of paper everywhere, and because there were grinning gangs of workmen forever queuing to beat off surreptitiously in her bedroom, Madeleine spent more and more time at mine. I wouldn't say she had moved in permanently. Not quite – sometimes she went out in the evening and slept back at hers; and, after our first fortnight lying around, she was out most weekdays at the British Library, writing her book; plus she spent one long weekend staying at her father's flat ('he hardly ever uses his London place, so it's nice and quiet and I could really do with getting my head down and finishing this chapter on Aleppo before it finishes me'). But, if pressed, I daresay the casual observer (having forgiven us for telling him to fuck off) would probably have said that we were, to all intents and purposes, living together.

Most of the time that we were not working (me in the studio, she tapping at her laptop in the other room) we sat in the garden – enchanted still – or hung out, watching the tennis, drinking, talking, preparing food, checking out films, making cocktails, playing cards, generally fooling around. I suppose those few weeks felt a little like the kind of summer that everybody remembers from childhood – seemingly endless, unworryingly aimless, lived in, rather than lived through. I even started liking Miles Davis.

And no, I didn't really think about it going wrong. Of course not – nobody worries about the end in the beginning. (Not even God – clearly.) There's too much going on and too much to find out. So I just relaxed and enjoyed her company and, yes, I suppose, my feelings gathered strength all the while. We never had any crass conversations about whether or not we were 'going out' or 'dating exclusively' (as they say in American sitcoms, the poor bastards). Naturally, I assumed that she wasn't seeing any more of Phil or anyone else. And she didn't need to ask me since – quite obviously – there weren't any female callers to my flat, either in person or by telephone. That one last, random, forlorn phone call proved to be poor Lucy's last.

I think I had only one other significant appointment during that entire month: lunch with Gus Wesley. My celebrated client had flown into London on business – to buy a few digital television channels apparently. That same Friday that

Madeleine went to her father's place to sort out Aleppo, I set off to the Savoy, expecting at least three courses of impassioned and intimate Donne-related artist–benefactor chit-chat and mutual reassurance. But our catch-up session turned out to be non-exclusive: he had invited me to some newspaper awards ceremony: lots of ageing journalists, admiring each other over chicken chasseur. I was given only a few hurried minutes of table-time with the great man himself.

'How you doing, Jasper – on schedule?'

'Yes. Absolutely.'

'That's the main thing. Don't be late – whatever. And when you're done – you're coming to see me and we'll go someplace we can goddamn talk.'

At least the lunch reminded me of the world beyond Bristol Gardens, and by the end of July, Madeleine and I began to get out more – initially only as far as our local, the Wellington, an old pub as yet unafflicted by the mania for the distressed ephemera of *faux* authenticity so beloved of the 'gastro-pub' marketeers and the misbegotten polenta-tendency for whom they cater. But it was a start.

The summer sun was sinking like a burning ship into the west. We were outside, sitting opposite one another across the trestle table: Madeleine in her shorts, a sleeveless vest and sunglasses and me in a T-shirt, jeans and my Roman sandals. A warm wind was ruffling through the sycamore trees. It was still hot enough for the ice in Madeleine's gin and tonic to be perceptibly shrinking. And whenever I picked up my beer, the wood felt sticky where someone had spilt a drink in the afternoon. I was reading one of Madeleine's travel articles: 'Souked Up. Madeleine Belmont is converted on the road to Damascus.'

'Does Guy Wesley still own this paper?' I asked. I already

knew the answer to this question. But for some reason I was suddenly feeling the urge to tell her about my client. I suppose it was something to do with sharing a confidence – sharing a confidence with her and only her. Something to do with formally affirming our intimacy.

She didn't look up from her book. 'Yes, I think he does. I mean, I know he does.'

'Ever met him?'

'No.'

'I wonder what he's like?'

Now she raised her head. 'The media caricature – Mr Dumb-it-Down Hardass – is probably bullshit.'

'Yeah,' I said, 'being a press baron, he's bound to get a bad press. Poor guy. I bet he spends all his private time weeping for the fate of humanity while list—'

'I'm sure he's a human being as well.'

I couldn't see her eyes behind her sunglasses but her tone was short. I decided against it. Saul's warnings came back to me. Madeleine, after all, was a journalist. It wasn't worth risking. I'd only be showing off. I'd tell her all about the commission when the work was finished. So I said nothing more. I let the subject go and returned to her article – just as she had returned to her book.

Among the many library shots of Syrian splendour, there was a single picture of Madeleine herself, seated in the middle of what I took to be a market store. She was wearing a burka though with the head-dress cast back, trying on a western-style shoe, her foot resting in the rough palm of the hunched and kneeling assistant as he fastened the strap around her ankle. Her robe was drawn up so that her shin almost touched his concentrating brow. But she was looking away, sticking out her tongue at a cat.

Some minutes passed. I tried to read other pieces but it

was useless. All pages lead back to the picture and the picture lead only to the person. I cleared my throat and addressed her across the table.

'Madeleine?'

She looked up from her book again and replied with mock formality: 'Yes, Jasper.'

'How would you feel about – when it's a bit darker – maybe going into the garden?'

'What for?' She grasped the point with her usual alacrity. 'Oh, right. You mean – to make out?'

'Exactly.'

'Sure.' She made her whatever-you-say face. 'Is there anything that you would like me to wear or is this a straightforward location assignment?'

I took a sip of my London Pride. 'Your blue dress.'

'You mean the one I was wearing when you first started spying on me.' She peered over her glasses.

'That's the one'

'OK. Anything else?'

'Can we start on the bench?'

'Sure we can, Jasper.' She paused for a second and then she said: 'Have to watch out for Roy, though.'

'What do you mean?'

'He's started hanging around the garden with a camcorder, hoping to catch sight of me naked through the windows.'

'You serious?' As usual, I couldn't tell if she was joking.

'Yeah. I pretty much caught him. He was on my patio. I went out the front and came round the other way.' She cackled. 'I couldn't believe it: he was just standing there with the thing trained directly into my flat. He told me he was the gardener, filming for a "before and after" project thing for the council. He's not a very good liar.' She shook her head. 'But the poor guy looked so – you know – so *caught*. I almost invited him in. He's only a kid. It would make his year. And I kind of like him, even though he's a pervert.'

'Oh, so *that's* what that was all about. I thought you were having an affair with him.'

'Give me a little credit. I'm very choosy about who I have my affairs with.' She took off her shades. 'Anyway – like – if I were: you wouldn't know about it.'

'No.' I took another sip of my Pride and helped myself to one of her cigarettes. 'Does it offend you, though?'

She likewise fingered a cigarette from the pack. 'What?'

'That kind of – that side of maleness.'

'You mean the grossness?'

'Yes.'

'Grossness – yes, that offends me; but men's obsession with women's bodies – no.' She took the light I was offering. 'The real truth about all that – you know – men gawping stuff is that it depends where the attention is coming from. If the guy is a stinking bum with an attitude problem who's breathing beer in your face while you're tired and trying to get home then, yes, it's deeply offensive. But if it's someone like, I don't know, let's use the cliché – if it's some good-looking movie star you meet by accident and he's obviously got the hots for you, then no, absolutely not. His desire is not offensive at all.' She exhaled the smoke through her nose. 'Really, it all depends on who – what kind of man – is doing the wanting. But the wanting in itself is not offensive. Not to me anyway.'

She waved her cigarette near a wasp which was buzzing around the rim of her glass. 'Actually, straight women who go on about how they dislike men objectifying them are mostly hypocrites who talk a lot of horseshit. Every woman deep down likes to be a little objectified now and then. As long as it's by the right man. When it is, well – nobody is ever gonna admit this – but it's kind of reassuring in a weird way. As long as he doesn't turn out to be incapable of any other mode of behaviour.'

I nodded.

'So, no, male behaviour does not offend me. Not as a general rule. Certain men do. Others don't. I figure it's the same for you with women.'

'Yes. It is. Sort of. Although I kind of have a soft spot for all women all the time.' I coughed as the acrid smoke filled my lungs.

She smiled. 'Secret filming, though – now that's a *whole* different issue.' She killed her remaining gin. 'Hey, I'm going to pop home. I need to get some clothes and shit. Prepare me something amazing for a midnight feast.'

'OK.'

'I'll meet you at eleven sharp in the garden.' She winked, replaced her sunglasses and got up to leave.

At first, 'The Dream' looks like Donne's most lyrical poem of rapture, but by the third verse doubt has once again slipped into the bedroom: (in)constancy, (in)fidelity, (un)truth. In the final lines, he asks of his lover: is this how she 'deal'st' with him (deal'st – a mean and mercantile word lying low amidst the finery)? Does she leave him to return? If not, he will die. And this time, mainly, I think, he means die for real, not ejaculate:

> Perchance as torches which must ready be,
> Men light and put out, so thou deal'st with me,
> Thou cam'st to kindle, goest to come; then I
> Will dream that hope again, but else would die.

But I didn't really notice that lurking anxiety the first time I read it. I was too busy with all the 'Dear love, for nothing less than thee' stuff. I was too busy with 'The Dream'.

19. Love's Growth

I scarce believe my love to be so pure
As I had thought it was,
Because it doth endure
Vicissitude . . .

I do not wish to give the impression that Madeleine was in any way touched by the supple fingers of psychosis. Far from it. She was as lucid and as sane and as on-the-money as Dorothy Parker two drinks in on a good Friday night. But, to flirt for a moment with Dr Freud, humanity's most sophisticated and intelligent pervert, I would say that her personality, her belief system and certainly her family history would make for a fascinating study. What, for instance, would the bearded but ever-twinkling Sigmund have deduced from our trip to Tate Modern?

Yep, back there again. Her suggestion, *bien entendu*, and offered at the time (atop one of those tourist buses while eating smokily delicious smoked salmon sandwiches) as part of our 'getting to know London' programme.

Poor fool that I am, my initial anxieties on receipt of the proposal centred not on any thought that the ghosts of Lucy or Cécile might return to haunt the galleries, but rather on an idiotic uncertainty as to how much or how little I should know. Though some of the exhibitions were bound to be new, I realized, many were likely to be exactly the same as they had been in March and I was therefore in a good position – should I so wish – to appear more than casually abreast of the currents of modern art. On the other hand, memories of the barging excursion still lingered . . . and for some reason I no longer felt the need to be such a berk. Instead, as we swung into Trafalgar Square, I decided to tell her the truth: that I had last visited on my birthday with 'some friends'.

To which declaration, her next question was, I suppose, inevitable.

To which enquiry, my explanation naturally followed. 'I went with William and Nathalie and my then girlfriend.'

To which clarification she then smiled, perhaps mal-evolently, inclined her face towards mine and exclaimed: '"Then" girlfriend! It was only four months ago or whatever, Jasper. No need for the emphasis. Not unless you're feeling bad about me, or her, or something else? Are you feeling bad? What was her name?'

'Lucy.'

'Well, one day you can tell me all about her.'

Now we were sitting together in the wide café on the top floor of Tate Modern. Having elected to go self-service (rather than wait patiently for the next millennia to pass), I had just come back to our table, bearing a thinnish and inexpressive Darjeeling for myself and a dark and syrupy espresso for Madeleine. She was preoccupied, reading her exhibition guide. I sat down quietly and set about encouraging my emaciated tea out of the dank and suffocating prison of its bag.

Outside, the summer evening was swaying home like a belly dancer returning to her scarlet caravan upriver. For a while I watched the London skyline basking. Then I turned to my fellow gallery-goers but seeing nothing there of interest or beauty, I soon settled my gaze on Madeleine's face and began trying to read her thoughts as they flickered across her features. The imp of a frown pestered her brow and a faint line declared itself on her forehead.

'Some of these titles are fucked up,' she muttered, as much to herself as to me.

'It's a cheap trick modern artists use,' I offered, 'the play between work and title – aggressive dissonance, coy irony or clunky literalism – it's a way of creating the impression of depth or extra meaning.'

She looked up impatiently – yes, we all know that, Jasper, thank you – and then carried on reading.

More and more in her company, I noticed, I was saying directly what I was thinking – being, for want of a better word, 'honest'. I transferred my attention to her lips and began a brief debate with myself about whether the best relationships were built on emotional transparency, the trading of confessions, or a certain selective blindness, the trading of forgiveness. But just as I progressed this thought far enough to give it an alliterative title – 'The Cowardice of Confession and the Courage of Conspiracy' – Madeleine gave up with the guide.

'It sucks.' She flipped back over a previous page. 'I mean, check this, Jasper: "Fatherhood #15: The Forest", "Rancid TV Dinner: September 10th", "To God, Whoever She Is". Are they asshole titles or what?'

'Is that the Macy Blake stuff?'

'Yeah.' She reached out a cigarette. 'Macy Blake,' – Madeleine did a cat whistle – 'she looks pretty hot in her picture.' She held up the artist's portrait. 'Would you – if you had the chance?'

'You know me: if it looks good, I'll sleep with it. Is she American?'

Madeleine grinned. 'Yeah, she is.' Without heed to the fact that the café was non-smoking, she lit up. 'You know – it's hard to know whether or not we're supposed to admire this kind of woman. Obviously she is full of shit – hence her titles and hence her work. But then so are all the men in here; and at least she's making everybody look at her shit instead of more men's shit and . . . Christ, is that a good thing? I'm lost on what's good for women in art. Anyway, it says here she was born in Boston, which makes me suspicious . . .'

She began to read what I presumed was the artist's biography. I watched her eyes following the lines. Then, without paying any real attention to what she was doing, she reached up and accidentally poured salt into her espresso instead of sugar. This in itself was understandable: the post-modern salt-cellar had a little silver pipe coming out of the top and looked like one of those sugar shakers you get at cheap cafés and coffee bars. I was about to stop her drinking but – I don't know why – I was sort of transfixed by the moment and I found myself just staring as she bought the cup to her lips to sip . . . *and didn't even flinch*. She simply drained the whole espresso and swallowed. There was no visible sign that she tasted anything untoward – no spitting, no wincing, no 'Yuck', not a muscle did she move. It was deeply, unnervingly disturbing.

She looked up calmly and repeated one of the titles as if to herself. 'Mmm. So. "To God, Whoever She Is".' Then she said: 'How about you, Jasper, do you believe in God?'

A fruitcake's question if ever there was one.

'No,' I said, presumably looking aghast, 'not exactly. Why do you ask?'

'Not exactly. What does that mean?'

'Are you really asking me?'

'Sure. I'm really asking you. Why do you always say that? And what's up?'

'You just drank that coffee with salt in it.'

'I know. Why didn't you tell me I had put salt in it? You were staring at me.'

'Because . . .' this was a little tricky, 'I wanted to see how you would react, I suppose.'

'Well, now you know.' She flicked her ash in her saucer. 'So: do you believe in God?'

'If you're asking . . .'

'I *am* asking. That's why I'm asking.'

'Sorry,' I shrugged. 'It's the English distrust of big questions; it's in my blood.' More truth-telling, I thought: once you start, you just can't stop – it's worse than bloody lying.

She waited for me to continue.

'Well, obviously, I think God is just a figment of the human imagination. But I also think he's the single most important and galvanizing figment. A figment without which we're lost. A figment without which all that is left to us is a kind of virtuoso triviality at best, or, at worst, and much more likely, a miserable descent into the furnace of unbridled greed, vulgarity and unenlightened selfishness – hell by any other name. I think that every other human generation, or at least their various high priests, understood the need for this figment. And I think that our own problem is that we do not. In killing God we have destroyed human kind's most impressive, life-affirming and imaginative creation. We have, if you like, given ourselves a collective lobotomy. Which is why pre-lobotomy art – Bach and da Vinci for example – is so much better, intrinsically, than most of the post-lobotomy stuff you might find in here.' I sat back in my chair and finished my tea. 'There. How about that?'

'Very fluent.'

'I've honed it a fair bit over the years. How about you? Since we're on the subject.'

'God bores me. But I'm happy to pay up and go see the Macy Blake cod feminist bullshit collection before we go. Do you want to? I feel I should. It might be fun.'

I had the same idea – but whether before or after her, I will never know. To the committed sensualist (I like to maintain) every location is a potential backdrop to the act of love. New scenery. New acoustics. New blocking. And, no offence to Ms Blake, as Roy Junior would say, but 'Fatherhood #15: The Forest' was surely made – was surely installed – to furnish Tate Modern with an appropriate space for private public intercourse. There could have been no other reason for its creation, nor for the curators to show it. Looked at from a certain standpoint, the whole work was one giant sexual gauntlet. (Not that there was anything wrong in that: after all planet Earth is surely just one big huge giant sexual gauntlet.)

The forest occupied one end of a large room. It consisted of thirty or forty tall wooden statues, the majority of which were about the thickness of a garden tree trunk and between eight and fifteen feet high. They were arranged to appear randomly spaced but were suspended or supported at crazy angles – so that the impression of the viewer was that he was looking at a branch- and foliage-free forest in the twisted aftermath of an earthquake. The statues were all of men – grotesque and distorted, stretched and without discernible limbs – but definitely male in their faces, their gnarled genitalia and, presumably, their fatherhood. The whole was roped off by an apologetic strand of thin white string.

'What do you think?' Madeleine asked.

I noticed that she was holding my hand. 'I don't know. But then I haven't got a father.'

'No. I mean what do you think?'

'We can only get caught.' I said this a little quickly and had to glance sideways to check that Madeleine was indeed suggesting what I had thought she was suggesting.

She was. Her eyes laughed. 'And then we say that we, too, are making a statement. Which is no less true than anything else.'

A genuine soulmate.

We were over the white string and between the most obvious gap in the statues in a second. But two steps inside and already the way was blocked; hurriedly but carefully, we squeezed right and left and then ducked down and half-crawled. The installation went back much further than I expected. And it was darker within than I had imagined – the taller statues seeming to lean more precariously now that we were directly beneath them.

'They fucked this up,' Madeleine whispered, 'you're meant to be inside here to get any sense of being in a forest. It doesn't work if you're looking at it from the outside.'

'If one of these wood-men falls, we're going to get hurt,' I breathed. 'Crushed by Fatherhood #15.'

Madeleine found the back wall. We edged sideways a few steps until we had reached a spot that wasn't visible from the gallery beyond.

She slipped out of her shoes, bent to take off her tights, balled them in her fist and stuffed them into the inside pocket of my jacket. Then, eyes wide open, she took my face in one hand – thumb to my jaw and fingers on my cheek – and brought it close to hers.

From beyond the statues, I heard someone speaking: 'Je les ai vus, il y avait un homme et une femme, ils ont disparu.'

Though we had spoken on the telephone, I hadn't seen William for nearly two months. So one evening, a few days after the Tate Modern, when Madeleine had gone off somewhere to see her sister, I found myself at a loose end and decided to put a call his way. But the great man wasn't at home and his mobile was switched off. On the offchance, I tried Le Fromage.

'I'm not entirely sure that Mr Lacey is here, sir; can I perhaps . . . take a mess-arge?' Though seldom over thirty-five, Fromage employees have somehow acquired the knack of sounding like fifty-something actors, reprising their roles as twenty-something desk clerks in seventy-year-old Noël Coward plays.

'Yes, please,' I replied. 'Could you ask him to phone Mr Jackson? I should be on his acceptable-call list – Jasper Jackson. Tell him that I am at home and that it is very urgent.'

'Oh . . .' The voice came down a register or two: straight Soho camp. '. . . Is that Jasper?'

'Yes.'

'Hello Jasper – it's Eric.'

'Oh hello, Eric. How are you?'

'Good. More or less. Still off the cigarettes. Which is an absolute miracle. But piling on the pounds.'

'Swimming?'

'No. Stopped it.' He sighed. 'Can't jog because of my knees, can't swim because of the chlorine and you can forget about bicycle wear in my state. I think I am just destined to be one of those people who relies on their personality.'

'How about dancing?'

'What? You mean disco?'

'Ballroom, disco, salsa, whatever. It's the perfect way to stay trim, plus you meet people, plus everybody fancies someone who can really dance. Imagine how cool you would

look at weddings. The men will be falling over themselves
to get at you.'

'Now, Jasper, you know that is not such a bad idea at all.
I think they have classes just by the Elephant; I've seen them
advertised at the Tube. I wonder how much it costs? I might
enrol tomorrow.'

'Great.' I let a polite beat go by. 'Is William there at all?'

'Yes – actually he's upstairs with some friends. I'll go up
and fetch him and make sure he calls you back.'

'That would be great. Thanks.'

'Bye for now.'

I hung up.

Some four minutes later – just as I was halfway through
prising six recalcitrant ice cubes from the permafrost of their
tray – the telephone shrilled.

'Jackson, this better be very fucking urgent. I am right in
the middle of a seriously interesting rubber and it's very bad
form to leave the table at this stage.'

'Sorry, Will,' I said. 'I didn't know they let you play cards
at Le Fromage? Isn't it against the law or the rules or
something?'

'It is and they don't. But they make an exception for
bridge as long as you pretend that it is not for money.'

'Right. Er . . . listen, Will, can you hang on just a second?
I was on the verge of fixing myself a drink and . . .'

'Oh, for Christ's *sake*, Jasper.'

'Well presumably you chose to leave the table at this
moment in the game so it can't be that inconvenient.'

A pause. Then the inveterate boozer within overcame all
rival personae and he asked with a stealthy curiosity: 'What
are you having?'

'Long Island Iced Tea.'

'Go on then. Get on with it then. And don't worry about

me. I'll just hang around here and flirt with Eric. It's not as though you rang me first or anything.'

'Two seconds.' I placed the receiver on the side and went back over to finish making the drink. Half a minute later I was back. I made sure to chink the ice within audible range of the mouthpiece before taking a slightly melodramatic sip, followed by a similar swallow. I then exhaled the irritating and contented sigh of a man in a happy relationship who, finding himself alone for the first time in a while, decides to contact his long-lost friends. 'So, William, my dear fellow, what are you doing tonight?'

'I've told you. I'm playing bridge, you penis.'

'With whom?'

'Well, there are two chaps wearing grotesque suits whom I met the other night and who claim to write soap operas – your guess is as good as mine – and Donald is here – returned from New York especially to be my excellent partner. We are about to fleece them for six hundred pounds, depending on Donald's performance in four hearts.'

'Don is back?'

'Of course he's back. He's been back for three days, which you would know if you made the effort to get off your ignorant arse and see your friends once in a while.'

I ignored William's attack and took another, more meditative sip. 'What have you got?'

'What have I got what?'

'In your hand.'

'Right now: Eric.' He sighed. 'Actually, I've got fuck-all. Not a thing – a two, two fives and some other shrapnel, an embarrassment of eights, a queen, the pointless knave of diamonds and a ten. But my cards have been terrible all night. Not that this is necessarily bad. I play rather well as dummy and I do have four hearts.' William cleared his throat.

'Look, anyway, what do you want, Jasper? I've really got to get back to the table. Is there anything that you have to say for yourself or can I go now?'

'Actually yes: can I come down?'

'Of course you can, old chap. We would all be delighted to see you. Cards will be finished after this game, I suspect, so we can all sit round and chit-chat about our new Pilates instructors or whatever else is on your mind. Be nice to see you. By the way, does this sudden re-establishment of communications mean that you are now prepared to come out again?'

'I haven't not been.'

'Balls. Because if so and speaking of which – would you and your new best friend like to come to the Lawn Tennis Association Ball next weekend? I have tickets. I daresay the whole thing will once again be packed to the rafters with depressing wankers but such is England. And I know it will be a little weird going with *partners* this year but I think it's important that we all show willing: you, me, Madeleine, Nathalie. Embrace the facts – however unlikely.'

'That's quite some invitation, Will.'

'Consider. I shall see you shortly.'

Forty tiresome minutes of nerve-mincing London travel later and I was at the reception desk.

'Hello, Eric,' I volunteered, sprightly but still a little harried, 'I made it.'

Eric grinned and pouted and grinned again – his face suddenly unable to settle on its most attractive tableau. 'Hello, Jasper. Hang on a tick, I am on a call. Please sign the register.' He pressed a button on the desk phone. 'Oh I think that would be very popular, Mr Gimbel, sir, I really do.'

Eric swivelled around the guest book before rather stagily

leaning over to watch me compose my signature. With his hand over the receiver, he whispered: 'I do love watching you write. It's so *exhilarating*.'

I handed back the pen.

'Thank you, Mr Gimbel. I know it's not easy. I know it can be very difficult. So many people seemingly determined to do the wrong thing. But I will do my best to make certain that everybody understands. Goodbye.' Eric pressed another button to terminate the call. 'It's been a such a long time no-see, Jasper. What's been going on? Have you been away or is it . . . love?' He performed a miniature swoon.

'After William, there can be no love, Eric, only memories and the endless grey afternoons.'

He laughed and then widened his eyes – a good approximation of Marilyn Monroe. 'Is he wonderful?'

'Yes. Just don't try to marry him. Or he'll stop the sex immediately.'

The main bar was fairly quiet: two older guys in black and grey, drinking mineral water with the air of men who want to draw attention to their abstemiousness – the better to hint at just how wild it gets when they really cut loose; and a cluster of girls trying too hard in their fake tans and *faux* Buddy Holly glasses, knotted around some reptilian creature whom I probably should have recognized. But no sign of William or Don. I climbed the back stairs to the third floor and checked the smaller rooms. More detritus. I found them at last, sequestered in a quiet alcove around the corner from the high gallery bar.

William stood, polite as ever. 'Hello Jasper, glad you unearthed us and very good of you to make it. Have a seat. I'm afraid you've just missed Robbie and Wes, our two show-biz pals, they had to go and catch up on their Eclogues, I'm afraid. There's some kind of television awards ceremony tomorrow and Virgil versus Homer is all they talk about at these TV industry bashes.'

'Hi Don,' I said, ignoring William, who seemed to be feeling more than customarily insane – or happy, or something. 'How are you?' I sat down. 'I thought you were in New York for the rest of the year.'

'Flying visit. Extended mini-break. They're very popular at the moment. Especially with the lasses. It's Cal's mother's wedding tomorrow afternoon.' He raised his eyes to heaven. 'Number three.'

William was still standing. 'So . . . drinks?' He looked around enquiringly. 'No, please Donald, stay right where you are – I'll go. Makes sense since I'm the only member and therefore the only one who will get served. How about a swift round of Long Island Ice Teas?'

'For fuck's sake, William, just get me a beer.' Don was smiling. 'Thank Christ you have come, Jasper, I've had to put up with him all night.'

'I'll have one too,' I said.

'A beer?'

'Yes.'

'Mmmm.' William disappeared.

'D'you win?'

'Fucked them totally.'

'Good cards?'

'Some.' Don bit his lip. 'But mainly just had to compensate for fuckface's hapless bidding and then make sure that he was dummy whenever we played.'

'Is he really terrible?'

'Shit. Treats every hand as if he's learning a whole new game. But he does have a kind of inner modesty, which can make for pleasant surprises when he turns over his cards.'

William returned, whistling in the manner of a newly

prosperous protagonist in an Ealing comedy. 'I have placed my share of the winnings behind the bar – my account is therefore bulging with credit – so I have decided that we're having a celebration.'

'What is there to celebrate?' This from Don.

'Ah-ha, goodly Donald, know you this: young Jasper here has had some luck with Madeleine – she of the golden hair and lithe bronze limbs last gazed upon by your green and envious eyes on Hampstead Heath before our skulduggery with the keys began.'

Don turned to me and raised his eyebrows just as the barman arrived with three bottles of beer and three glasses of something else.

William continued: 'Thank you so much, Otto. It is never the wrong time of day for sherry, I always say.' William took up his glass and offered one to Don. I took mine from the tray. William sat down. 'We must therefore raise a toast to celebrate the astonishing achievement of Jasper's almost two whole months of monogamy.' He fixed me with a stern stare. 'I presume you haven't . . .'

I was quite offended. I shook my head.

Otto retreated.

'You got off with her?' Don asked.

'Yes. Later that day in fact. Finally. Which reminds me, Will, I owe you a bottle of –'

'Forget it.'

'Nice one,' Don smiled.

'She came back. After the picnic,' I added.

'Well, it was a pretty major effort from Will. You had to hope that something was going to happen. About bloody time too, after all the messing about.' Don looked at me with mild concern in his eye. 'Will tells me that you were losing your way a bit earlier in the year.'

'Sort of.'

'And you are managing to hold it together now?'

'Yeah.' There was a general drinking pause.

'So, come on then,' Don urged. 'What's she like? What's it like? Are you –'

'She's a little weird sometimes but I like her.' I shifted uncomfortably. Why, I wondered, did I always find this sort of thing embarrassing? 'You know – it's good. We get on. She seems to be living with me.'

'Living with you?' Don was genuinely taken aback.

William made a face like a dating-show host who specialized in innuendo. 'She's living with him.'

'Yes, her new flat is being sorted out – it's taking for ever – so she just sort of moved in for a while . . . But she's only round the other side of the block anyway – which is how we met – so it's not that much difference.'

William again: 'She's moved in.'

Don took another more forceful sip of his sherry. 'So, she's over all the time? Fucking hell, Jasper, I didn't think that was your scene at all. You really stopped shagging around?'

'Yes. Neither did I. But it's not heavy or anything . . . anyway, she's away a fair bit – she's a travel writer and so –'

William: 'A travel writer.'

'So it's not too bad. I mean, I get my own space.'

'He gets his own space.' William finished his sherry.

'William, will you please fuck off?' I said.

William grinned. 'I'm telling you, Donald, it's terrible. Jasper hasn't been out for *weeks* – they're holed up in there like a pair of randy rabbits. Hatching plans against the rest of us, I'll bet, when they're not mating. He doesn't phone, he doesn't write, he doesn't even text . . .'

'I will never text. There is no such thing as *text*.'

Don was also grinning. 'How's that going – nearly finished?'

'More than three-quarters done. Christ knows what happens when I come to the end of this commission, though.' I grimaced. 'May starve to death unless my agent can find me some more American millionaires.'

'Well, I'm very jealous.' Don swirled his glass. 'If I wasn't already happily married I'd be begging you to introduce me to her sisters. If they look anything like her then fucking hell.'

'She's only got the one. I've not met her. So I can't help you there.'

William spoke more evenly: 'So, what do you mean she's weird? She seemed perfectly normal to me. On *the single occasion* I actually met her, actually.'

'She's just weird.'

'Go on.' William was curious.

'Well, she's sort of . . . I don't know . . . angry a lot but amused and affectionate at the same time. Not angry like cross or irascible or bitter – but maybe angry within.'

'Angry within.' William raised his brows.

'I'm sorry – I'm sounding like a self-help manual. I mean, she's kind of deliberately antagonistic about stuff and at the same time – in a weird way – deliberately acceding. Anti and pro. Erm . . . I mean she's –'

'Very nice and very horrible,' Don said.

'Yes. Thank you, Don.'

'Well – that's women.' Don shook his head. 'Issues.'

'I don't know, Don. Moods may swing but they don't coalesce – or rather coexist. She sort of hates a thing – like, say, a song or a book or me or whatever – but at the same time she sort of celebrates it. It's perverse.'

'You mean, she hates men and she loves men?' William's

perception was somehow both glib and profound. 'And she loves hating them and hates loving them?'

'Something like that.'

'Family?' William asked.

'What the fuck has that got to do with anything?' I replied, a little testily.

William sighed. 'Because there are only two ways of living: either your every breath is a conscious rejection of your parents' life and opinions or it is a subconscious repetition. The key to all human understanding is simply to work out which course your subject is following.'

'Not true in the case of orphans.' I finished my sherry.

'No. Point. Unfortunately, orphans are irreparably fucked up and their revenge is indiscriminate.' William eyed Don's as yet untouched beer. 'But, in general: women are trying to sleep with replacement fathers, which is their least attractive characteristic; and men are trying to sleep with replacement mothers, which is their most.'

'I thought,' Don ventured, 'that you believed all men to be secretly gay.'

'You mean, polymorphous perversity and all that. Well, perhaps I do,' William said. 'Perhaps they are.'

'In which case, surely we are all trying to sleep with our fathers?'

'Another good point. However, life is not mathematics and equations do not always balance, Donald.'

'Actually, life probably *is* mathematics.' Don clicked his tongue. 'It is just that we are as yet unable to understand it thus.'

'No.' William shook his head. 'I have new clarity on this. Life is actually a series of unrecoverable errors that one day combine to freeze your screen. Then, I'm afraid, whatever you do and whoever you are, some ill-favoured stranger with halitosis will come trudging into your life and turn off the power – and everything, I'm afraid, is always lost.'

'Thanks for that, William.' I took a deep swig of beer. 'Madeleine's father is some kind of diplomat. Maybe he's in the same line as you, Don, I'm not sure. His name is Belmont. He works in Paris, I think. So I presume that's the French bureau or whatever you guys call it. You might run into him at an ambassador's luncheon. Her mother is long dead. One sister, as I say.'

William, who had been behaving with more than his usual oddness ever since I arrived, now started forward. 'I have to break in here and say that I think we are now having what is known in certain circles as a lads' discussion about women. Birds, if you like. As you both know, I cannot tolerate clichés in any shape or form, so may I therefore suggest that we all refer to our respective partners – wives, girlfriends and so on – as "he"?' He held up his hand. 'In this way we can avoid sounding too hackneyed and – you will be amazed to discover – we will all be able to be far more candid with one another.'

'It is hard to say which of you two has the more severe problems.' Don shook his head sadly and switched, at long last, to his beer.

'I shall begin.' William cleared his throat. 'I am thinking of sleeping with Nathalie, but I am worried that if I do, I will have to marry him. However, this may not be a problem as I think I want to marry him. There, I've said it.'

20. The Legacy

Yet I found something like a heart,
  But colours it, and corners had,
  It was not good, it was not bad,
It was entire to none, and few had part.

Mozart was in the midst of telling yet another of his brilliant jokes when the racket erupted: first the entryphone, then a horn, then the entryphone again, and finally a car alarm. So much noise and so unannounced. I scowled at the bathroom mirror. I had been happily knotting my bow-tie, aiming for that elusive nexus between too large and droopy and too small and tight. And despite several hours spent remonstrating with a delivery company whose mesmerizing lack of clarity on the telephone was matched only by their blank refusal to deliver anything anywhere to anyone, I had managed to sustain reasonably good spirits all day thus far. But the din plunged me summarily into annoyance. I raised my voice at my reflection: 'For Christ's sake, Madeleine, tell them we're coming.'

'We're coming,' came the deliberately feeble response from the bedroom.

I looked past my mirrored shoulder. Her bare legs were lying motionless on the bed and the provocative waft of bazaar-bought cigarettes was now drifting into the bathroom.

'OK Cleopatra,' I said loudly, though still mostly talking

to myself, 'please don't trouble yourself. You stay right there: I'll tell your slaves to wait until you feel like moving.'

With one hand holding the penultimate loop of the tie in place, I backed into the bedroom and stepped smartly over to the open window to look out. The hot afternoon sun flared in the glass of the opposite panes but the summer air was as lifeless as an old dog in the afternoon. Below, in the middle of the road, at the wheel of an open-top touring car (which from my elevation looked more like a sort of glorious, gleaming, cream-coloured boat), sat a man wearing a dinner suit and what looked very much like a pair of fawn-coloured driving gloves. I leaned further out: 'WILLIAM?'

Clearly he had heard me, but he chose not to look up, revving the engine instead – a deep and well-oiled burble – and then making a protracted and elaborate show of adjusting the rearview mirror. Exasperated, I turned my attention to Nathalie, who was still standing by the front door.

She waved up: 'HI JASPER, WE'RE HERE.'

'So it seems. WILL YOU TELL HERR VON RICHTHOFEN THAT WE WILL BE DOWN IN A MINUTE?'

'OK, I'LL WAIT IN THE CAR. HURRY UP.'

I turned back to the room. Madeleine was still propped up on the bed in her knickers – knees up so as to rest her book. The thought occurred that I had surrounded myself with fanatical egotists. She looked up and let her face form one of her favourite counterfeit expressions – penitent heroine beseeches leading man with more serious matters on his mind.

'I'm so sorry, Jasper,' she said, 'I really wanted to move but it is so hot and I haven't finished this delicious wine you gave me or this lovely cigarette and I need you to help me put my dress on and I didn't want the neighbours to see me . . .' – cigarette in one hand, wine glass in the other, she made a theatrical gesture of alarmed modesty – '. . . like *this*.'

I sighed. 'Well, I'm afraid we need to get a move on. Our felucca awaits.'

'If you pass me my dress, I will put it on.' She smiled and said: 'I'm completely ready – honestly. I was waiting for you.' She drained her glass. 'You do look like an idiot, holding your bow-tie like that.'

She stood with her back to me; I let go of my tie and helped her into her dress – a backless, black ball gown. She turned and posed ironically, hand on hip.

'Madeleine, please promise me: don't say anything about William and Nathalie getting married unless they bring the subject up. I don't know what stage they are at.'

'I think it's very sweet.'

'It is very sweet – but don't say anything. Seriously, I wouldn't forgive you.'

'I won't. Don't worry.'

Six minutes later, we were on the pavement, staring with unconcealed awe at the car.

'Hello, Madeleine – you look delightful,' said William, springing up to open the door for her with a childish beam on his face. 'Perhaps tonight you will meet a man worthy of you and rid yourself of –' he lowered his voice and he pulled a face of acute distaste '– you know who.'

'Good evening, William,' I said, sarcastically.

He pretended surprise. 'Oh, hello Jasper: I was rather hoping you would be taken suddenly ill or something so that I could have the girls to myself.' He tutted. 'But never mind – seeing as you are here – you must sit in the front with me: if a thing is worth doing, it is worth doing well: boys up front, girls in the back.'

I looked at Nathalie to check that she didn't mind. She was in a pouty sort of pink dress with her hair in sleek finger waves – forties' style. Behind her, I noticed, the estate agents had left their desks and come to the window the better to scrutinize proceedings.

Nathalie waved me around the other side of the car. 'No, it's fine,' she said, 'I came all the way down here – you have a go. Madeleine and I will hang out in the back together.'

We ensconced ourselves in the tan leather seats and, after a few moments of unendurably gravid silence, I delivered the much-anticipated question: 'I know you're desperate to tell us, Will, so go on: what is it?'

But it was Nathalie who answered, leaning forward between us into the front seats as I attempted to click my safety belt into place, her voice a passable impression of William's: 'This, actually, is a converted Facel Mark Two, hand-built by the great – and oft overlooked – Facel-Vega car company in 1963. The marque is French, of course, but we have a very serious Chrysler V8 American engine under the bonnet. An odd collaboration, I always think, America and France – however, back in the early sixties, when life was truly worth living, I should say that – for a while – this was definitely *the* car to have. Stirling Moss drove one and, it is widely believed, grew his moustache to do so. They cruise easily at 110 mph. But, sadly, there are now only about fifty of the Facel Twos still running – and only two or three convertibles – all of them, like this, custom-made.'

'Couldn't have put it better myself.' William adjusted his gloves and let off the handbrake.

We looped the Paddington basin and soared up on to the Westway, heading out of town beneath cobalt skies and a heavy July sun, that lolled and slacked on the white ropes of the aeroplane trails. To the right, the thirsty concrete high-rise sagged. To the left, the cracked brick terrace rows slumped. All street life seemed to slouch as if desperate to escape the sullen heat and lie down somewhere quiet in the shade. High summer was falling across beautiful London like a late afternoon swoon.

The dashboard looked like the instrument panel of a light aircraft – gauges and levers and metal disguised as varnished wood. The tarmac baked and sweltered ahead of us and, as we sped up, the wind whipped and roared and flapped in our ears and an importunate smell of leather and motor oil came and went and came again. All the senses were absorbed in the single concentrated experience of automotion. With every mile, my mood grew lighter.

'How far is Isleworth?' Madeleine asked, inclining forward as we came to a stop at the lights on Chiswick High Road.

'Only about another couple of miles further. Around the next bend in the river,' William replied.

'And who exactly goes to this sort of thing? It's been ages since I went to a ball. I can't even remember the last. College probably. I'm very excited. I'm glad you thought of getting us tickets.' There was no sarcasm in her voice.

'It was Jasper's idea, actually.' William waved back at some children who were pressed up against the rear window of the four by four in front. 'There's a fair few tennis players – obviously – and their various hangers-on. And there are some umpires and such like. Then there's some of the more upmarket fashion crowd and the usual minor celebrity contingent –'

'I love tennis players,' Madeleine asserted.

'– and, as for the rest, the sycophantic magazines like to think of them as society but they are mainly the grand-children of boot polish millionaires or baked bean barons or photocopying tycoons.'

'Or arms dealers,' I added.

'Sounds great,' Madeleine said.

The lights changed. 'The trick is to try to have fun despite them. Or at their expense. Avoid photographers. Pretend to be in drainage if anyone asks. And feign absolute ignorance on all other matters. Thankfully, there is usually a huge amount to drink, although I – alas – will have to stay sober since vintage wine and vintage cars do not mix.'

'Do you go every year?'

William engaged first gear. 'Oh yes. Jasper and I make a point of it. It is one of the easiest places in the world to pick up idiotic débutantes. Or their vapid mothers. Or their vapid mothers' idiotic friends. Very easy indeed, actually.'

'William leads a different life from the rest of us,' said Nathalie, joining in from the back and addressing Madeleine. 'Ignore him – that's what the rest of the world does.'

'Anyway, it's not true,' I shook my head. 'We don't go every year.'

Putting the hood up on the car took the best part of twenty minutes – fastening down, press-studding, clamping over, hefting, heaving, tweaking and twisting – but finally we were done. Madeleine and Nathalie had gone on ahead and so, after William had taken us through the locking and alarming procedure (twice), we made our way round to the front of the building on our own.

At a guess, I would have said that the house was relatively recent – built some time in the latter half of the nineteenth century at the height of the gothic revival. The entrance hall certainly pointed in that direction – a black and white tiled floor, the inevitable wooden panels and, directly opposite the entrance, a double staircase that curved right and left up to a three-sided gallery.

After handing over our invitations, we were directed towards two glasses of not terrible champagne en route to the main hall. The noise of three hundred and fifty merry-makers in animated conversation rose to greet us as we walked through. We stood together for a few minutes on the threshold of the ballroom – on the first of the three wide steps that fanned down on to the polished parquet floor – sipping our drinks tentatively, looking around and hoping to catch sight of Nathalie or Madeleine.

The room was undeniably impressive and must surely have measured the depth of the building. And it was alive and humming with people: some already seated at their tables, some milling in clusters of conversation, others standing in twos and threes, laughing or exchanging hellos. Women of all ages swished this way and that – excited, lips glossed, seeing friends across the room, checking the seating plan, still sober and self-conscious with co-ordinated clutch purses; the men too seemed to be feeling more manly in their dinner suits – speaking in deeper voices, affecting elegant gestures, laughing in concert, offering chairs. Waiters wandered with much-welcomed wine. Glasses clinked and chinked and tinkled. At the far end of the hall, beyond the thirty or so circular dining tables, there was a low stage on which several unattended instruments were carefully placed beside empty chairs awaiting musicians. A single microphone stand stood in the centre, ominously suggestive of speeches before song.

Three girls came towards us up the stairs on the way back towards the reception champagne – students no doubt still intoxicated by the prospect of free alcohol. Involuntarily, I smiled and received a pout, a frown and a smirk in return. Pointedly, they carried on with their conversation as they passed.

William looked over. 'Well, this is going to be a very weird evening, Jackson – a bit of a first actually – you and I at a party and hoping to avoid talking to anyone attractive just in case disaster strikes and it starts to go well. Bloody strange this partner business, if you ask me. Hard to believe some people make a habit of it. Must have balls of steel.'

'I know,' I shook my head sadly. 'I think they call it growing up.' An old man wandered past with an attractively large young woman; he was struggling desperately to be likewise blithe and gay and to keep his wandering eyes from the tempting valley of her glorious bosom. 'Or the beginning of the end.'

'It's the same thing.'

Act One (the reception) gave smooth place to Act Two (the dining). Likewise Act Three (a few speeches and the presentation of some trophies) slipped happily into Act Four (that brief but charming time when the tables have dispersed and the formal dancing is well under way, and before the distance between those who are drunk and those who are not becomes too wide a gap to jump). But after that . . .

After that, things took a serious turn for the worse. I should have been on my guard, of course; I had been to enough events like this to know that Act Five (the tears, the confessionals, the crazed guzzling of half-empty glasses, the ugly, lurching strangers who sit down uninvited and brandish the truth) usually ends in a blood-bath. But then again, I had absolutely no idea that it was going to go on for so long or get so *personal*.

I was minding my own business, sitting agreeably becalmed at our table. The band were playing a song that I recognized as one of Madeleine's favourites: Nina Simone: 'My baby don't care for shows . . . My baby don't care for clothes . . .' Madeleine herself had disappeared with Nathalie – to dance maybe. The most idle part of my consciousness was eyeing the quasi-formal hand in which the place-names had been written and thinking that whoever was responsible should be taken outside and quietly bayoneted. Another part (and gradually gaining the ascendancy) was wondering whether I might yet be drunk enough to risk a dance. Another part again was considering going to the cocktail lounge and putting the bar staff through their paces. And yet another part was listening to the rare and pleasing sound of William being almost serious for once in order to wind up a certain Neil Bentink, a sweaty, red-faced, spiky-haired man, who had been placed on our table 'by mistake' (so he claimed) and who (so he insisted) wrote opinion pieces for political magazines – to my mind a secondary crime after his decision to wear a shimmering sequinned waistcoat.

'Oh no no no,' William demurred, 'you've got the wrong end of the stick; I *do* stand for things. I believe passionately in every side of every argument; in fact that is precisely why stasis sets in. I believe in the copious availability of interesting wine and unseasonable fruit for all; and I believe in fewer delivery lorries on the road. I believe in travel and discovery and years out for everyone; and I believe in fewer runways and green belts and the reduction of noise pollution; I believe in the absolute sanctity of life *and* the absolute right to decide, in less taxation *and* better services; and when I'm stuck in a traffic jam with the putative nippers on the way to recycling my putative newspapers, I also like to recycle the air so that I don't have to breathe the fumes of all the other cars. Don't look so offended. That is more or less exactly your position and the position of most people under forty. I'm afraid we're all suffering from chronic intellectual hypocrisy – a hitherto unimagined double-think – and it's people like you who –'

But much as I was enjoying William's uncharacteristically forthright denunciation, I never heard the final accusation because – just at that moment – the room was filled with a terrible whining, screaming hiss, like the sound of a giant rabbit dying in leg-ripped and gum-lacerated agony.

All around us, people broke off from talking and looked over towards the stage in horror, scowling or cringing or with fingers to their ears.

A well-groomed but shortish man in his early forties stood behind the shrieking, howling microphone holding his arms up unnecessarily for quiet. On the dance floor, the dancers shuffled in semi-suspended animation. The ball juddered to a halt. For the moment at least, the man had everybody's attention.

Though perceptibly swaying, he succeeded at last in judging the appropriate distance and the feedback subsided. He began to speak – his voice thick and clogged with too much alcohol taken in and too many emotions trying to get out.

'Sorry . . . Ladies and Gentlemen . . . sorry; sorry to interrupt.' He stood to one side, imitating a stance he must have seen on television. 'Ladies and gentlemen, I won't keep you long: I hope you are enjoying the . . . er . . . the piss-up!' He held up his thumb. 'Er . . . my name, as many of you know, is Steven Brooks and, as many of you also know, my company, Brooks Bailey and Forshaw are proud to be one of tonight's big backers. Long live lawn tennis!'

An uneasy chunter passed through the room.

'Anyway, the reason I am standing up here is that I have er . . . a little announcement to make.' His grin tightened to a grimace. 'The first thing – the first announcement – is to say thank you all for coming and may I add my own personal note of congratulations to Chad and Tanya who are deserving winners of the men's and the women's.' He broke off. 'Singles. In that order!'

Uncertain whether they were witnessing stand-up comedy or prostrate confession, three hundred and fifty people found themselves snagged between two reactions. Some half clapped. Others half didn't. That this unscheduled interruption from a peripheral sponsor was profoundly unwelcome was evidenced by the officials pushing their way towards the stage.

But Brooks carried on undeterred: 'Er . . . the second thing is that I have just found out tonight – after ten – no *eleven* years of marriage to my beautiful wife, Selina, that . . . SHE IS A FUCKING BITCH AND A CHEATING SLAG.'

Now, verily, the Devil rode in on a crescendo of appalled murmurs, suppressed gasps and dismayed profanity; he swirled his cloak about him and, with a derisory laugh, filled the hall with chaos and malediction.

Oh, I used to think that I had lived through some bad nights, I used to think that I had toughed it out through one or two personal lows – the self-loathing, the disorientation, the gagging at your own words, the swatting at your own head – but no. Oh no. Those other, seemingly embarrassing moments in my life, those other awkward, squirm-filled evenings, they were (it turns out) only polite dress rehearsals, warm-ups, jaunty misunderstandings, merely rueful, silly, *funny* by comparison . . . the Real Thing, now that was a whole different order of experience. The Real Thing was just getting started.

I realized more or less straightaway the significance of what I had just heard, but there was little time to think clearly. And I could not immediately see how the developing situation would affect me. Steven Brooks stepped down, assisted by two or three of the officials. The band resumed.

Someone else retrieved the singer from the back of the stage where she had been cowering in mortification since giving up the microphone. Dancers reformed, obscuring my view. People passed by, swearing or drunk or both. Two minutes must have elapsed – no more – and the emotional cordite was still hanging pungent in the air when I heard her voice at my shoulder.

'So, JJ, what an unexpected pleasure. Do you mind if I sit down? Well, anyway I already have. Hello, so sorry to interrupt.' Taking Madeleine's seat, she leant over, placing one hand forcibly – violently – into my lap for balance while offering the other first to Neil and then to William. 'Hi, I am Selina Brooks – one of Jasper's discarded lovers – isn't that right, Jasper? I am the famous bitch slag.'

Selina was slaughtered.

'Hello,' said Neil, blushing.

William, his face a picture of understanding, shook her hand wordlessly.

Selina sat back and looked fixedly at me. The would-be superior smile of a woman who does not think she is drunk wedged itself tightly into the corners of her mouth. Her head rocked slightly as she spoke and to counter the wine-slur she sometimes over-enunciated. 'And so, yes, anyway, Jasper, I just wanted to know – I mean I just wanted to ask – *why did you have to tell my fucking husband*?'

Even my DNA was wincing.

'I mean, use me for sex – that's fine – I was using you too – that's pretty much what it was all about, wasn't it?' Silence hurried to the tables around us. 'But I so totally fail to see, Jasper, why you have to tell my fucking husband and wreck my fucking marriage.'

More heads turned. A couple stalled as they blustered ungainly past. Selina fumbled in front of her to open Madeleine's foreign packet of cigarettes. She looked round. 'Does anybody at this table have a fucking light?'

William leant forward and offered his.

'Thank you.' She took the deep, stagy drag of a non-smoker, then addressed her gathering audience more widely. 'And does anybody understand why this man...' – she pointed with the cigarette – '... should want to wreck my marriage and ruin my children's lives? No? Oh, come on, Jasper. We do all *so* want to know. Why did you tell him? I know he's a wanker but I didn't realize that you were such a cheap fucking bastard too.'

I sensed Madeleine hovering behind me. How long had she been back? I didn't dare look around in case Selina guessed that she was the woman I was with and then turned on her. Everyone and everything within twenty feet was now staring at us. The situation was appalling. I had to take Selina elsewhere. I started to get up just as Madeleine slipped quietly into Nathalie's chair, next to William.

'Where the fuck do you think you're going?' Selina raised a white knuckle rapidly to her eyes, though there was no suggestion of tears. 'Oh, it's all very easy for you. Fuck me for a while and then when you get bored fuck off and who cares about the woman with a sad marriage and a stupid fucking wanker for a husband – I SAID SIT DOWN, I'M TALKING TO YOU.'

'Selina, I'm not –'

'Oh, fuck off then.' Selina jammed the barely smoked cigarette into the ashtray, rose swiftly but unsteadily to her feet and picked up the nearest glass. I was still only half standing. We faced each other for a sad, stuck moment – two stunt planes stalled at the top of their climbing arc. Then she let me have the wine full in the face.

As she removed my jacket and I took off my shirt, Madeleine said, 'Well well, that was all a bit smart-girls-carry-Cosmo – you're lucky it was only white. She works in advertising, you said.'

Wine in the face is seldom what you want. But all the same, while not exactly going brilliantly, the evening wasn't yet beyond all hope. Much to my surprise, Madeleine was still with me – and being uncommonly pleasant; plus we were in the Ladies – always more recuperative than the Gents'.

'Obviously, I didn't tell her husband,' I said, feeling – a little madly perhaps – that this was the most single important thing to get across. 'Selina's husband, I mean, I didn't –'

'I know you didn't. You're way too good for that. I think they just had a falling-out tonight is all. She probably told him herself.' Madeleine picked up a towel before running the tap and beginning carefully to dab at my lapels. Not once did she glance at herself in the mirror. 'And – you know – she must have fucked you back, right? Nobody forced anybody to do anything.'

'No.'

'And you know what else? Now that you have been very publicly revealed as the sort of man that no woman could ever really trust, like or live with, you have become significantly more desirable. You're the sexiest man at the ball. Such is the fucked-up nature of femininity. Enjoy.'

She handed me back my jacket and ran the collar of my shirt under the tap. Two women came in and eyed me with a mixture of disapproval and amusement. Madeleine shot them an explanatory glance. Simultaneously, they raised their eyes to heaven. Women need no words.

'You think we should stay then?' I asked.

'I think you should stay very close to me and I'll look after you.' She banged on the hand dryer and held the collar in the hot air. 'This place is far too dangerous for you to be wandering about on your own.'

I stood bare-chested in my dinner jacket, feeling like a male stripper in a television documentary about the highs and lows of the job, and assessed my situation. Indubitably, my main self still felt pure and intense embarrassment. And my next self still felt residually wet. But – encouragingly – selves three and four – the devious twins – who had been busy running calculations, evaluating the effect developments might have had on Madeleine, were now reporting back with some unexpectedly favourable results. Self five – oddly narcissistic even in a crisis – felt obscurely flattered. Self six, the quiet but tenacious intellectual obsessive, who was forever wrestling with life's myriad Gordian knots, was wondering how Selina had come to be betrayed and how, in turn, she had come to the conclusion that I was responsible. Self seven marvelled at the capacity for so fractured a self. Meanwhile, self eight, who couldn't stand any of the above, wanted to have a large fucking drink.

So, to kick things off, much to Madeleine's amusement and every other cocktail bar-queuing person's annoyance, I chased a Talisker with a Moscow Mule. Such a thing is very wrong and insulting and disrespectful for many reasons – I doubt even a mulish Muscovite holidaying on the Isle of Skye would be so base – but when it comes to drinking, I am a commitment kind of a guy. Cocaine, Ecstasy, weed, even cigarettes – I can take them or leave them – a few one-night stands here or there, a fling, an affair, a dalliance . . . nothing serious. But with drinking it is love: it's for richer, for poorer, in sickness and in health, till death us do part.

And a guy who starts out with a Talisker followed by a Moscow Mule may have been around the block a few times, but at least he knows the first kiss still matters.

And I swear, I felt 100 per cent finer than fine afterwards. Delicious. (Anyway Madeleine was rather gleefully paying.) So next I went for a hot-me-up Kir Royal (not my style but Madeleine's suggestion since she was having one too) followed by a cool-me-down Tom Collins. Which, with a random vodka and lime to go, finally unlocked the doors of perception.

'You wanna dance?' Madeleine asked.

'Let's dance.'

She offered me her hand and led me out of the bar. I followed her back into the main hall – the immortal god of rhythm, moving through the multicoloured women and the black and white men. The oak walls scorned me and the chandeliers leered but they didn't have a chance: I was all groove. We swung low by our table sweet chariot big grins all round and maybe hung a friendly arm around Will, who seemed to be sitting silently alone. And a cutchy-coo. Except – miraculously – it wasn't Will, for Will had gone. As had Neil. And there was no sign of Nathalie either. The man sitting in what I thought was Will's chair, the chair of Will, turned out to be someone who didn't really look like Will at all. A total non-Will. An anti-Will.

'Hello, hello,' I said, very friendly all the same. 'Are you lonely? Cheer up. Why not go dancing. That's what we're going to do. It's very good for you.' 'Because,' he said, 'I am waiting for my wife. We're getting a divorce.' Well, OK then, I thought, and 'I'm sorry,' said Madeleine, taking me by the arm. 'I'm afraid my boyfriend is trying to kill himself. Please don't pay any attention. Come on, Jasper, you promised to dance. Come *on*.'

That's right, I thought, I promised to dance. And dance I fucking well will.

But it should be recorded that Steven Brooks, though irrefutably short and indifferent to the question of the divided dramatic self in the poetry of John Donne, didn't waste time when it came to dealing with the guy who liked to sleep with his wife: the first punch connected somewhere in the solar plexus and the next crunched awkwardly into the side of my nose.

I fell, delirious, into my sweetheart's arms.

After that, things took a serious turn for the worse. When I came round, there was less immediate intoxication but much, much more pain – oh yes – much more pain ... In fact, pain, I discovered, really enjoyed hanging out with me, slaloming back and forth across my ribs, doing fancy stunts on the bridge of my nose, skidding to a halt in my eyeballs. When I came round, there was also plenty of blood on my shirt; there was the distant noise of the ball still going on; there was the leather chair in which I was slumped; there was the strong impression that I was alone in a stranger's study; there was being drunk; there was wanting another drink of course; there was the taste of iron running thick through the valleys between my teeth; there was shame; there was no Madeleine, no William, no Nathalie, no friends and no family.

But there was Lucy.

She was sitting in the opposite chair in a purple ball gown, regarding me with the patient eyes of the ill-treated.

Some long moments seemed to doggy-paddle past, during which I remember I wanted to get up but feared that doing so might make me seem strong enough to withstand an attack. So I sat tight while the minute hand on the grandmother clock above the empty fireplace hauled itself upright to mark the hour.

Two o'clock. Seconds away. Were we two now going to fight? How, I thought, did a man defend himself against a woman who was trying to kill him? What were the rules? What was the protocol? Restraint obviously, but what if she was really death-threateningly violent? Nauseously, I realized that when it came right down to the bare-knuckle stuff a real man could never find it in himself to hit back. Perhaps then, if the moment arrived, I would just surrender.

Lucy blinked the blink of the steadily deranged, slow and deliberate as though counting blinks. Her stillness, I feared, contained a dozen maelstroms fighting with twenty angry hurricanes. The few remaining selves of mine who were not dead or wounded or too embarrassed to stand up huddled together in a bare corner of my wind-whipped soul. There was a poker and a brush and some coal tongs lying neatly in the grate by her feet. We were all very worried.

Lucy had also lost weight. She looked more austere, pale, spare – the lines of her cheekbones seemed sharper. And her hair had been scissored dramatically around the neck so that it arrived in two asymmetrical points below the jaw line. Her voice, too, seemed thinner than I remembered.

'I wanted you to know,' she said, at last, her mouth moving as if there was some kind of satellite delay, 'that I was here. I shouldn't be. But I am. I am here.'

I gathered my selves.

She smiled. 'Don't worry; I am not going to hit you or anything. I feel much better now than I thought I would. It's OK. I'm glad I came to see you.'

It was impossible to think anything clearly. I raised my hand to my face to assess the agony of what was once my nose. Some questions declared themselves out of the fog:

'How long have I been here? How long have you . . .' My
voice sounded strange to me, clogged and nasal as if in the
grip of some deathbed cold.

She ignored me. 'I knew you were here and I just wanted
to come and see that I was OK – you know – face to face. I
think I am – now. You look awful, by the way, Jasper. Your
nose has been bleeding. And you'll have a black eye too.'

Woozily, I sat up. The contents of the room swilled like
the dregs in a bum's bottle.

'I saw what happened before with Selina's – that's her
name isn't it? – with Selina's husband, I mean. You were
lucky – you were lucky that . . . that someone caught you
or you might have cracked your head on the table behind.
You could probably sue.' She smiled. 'But best not get me
to represent you.'

I shook my head.

She bit her lip and seemed suddenly to make up her
mind. 'You're OK. I'd better go.' She stood. 'I'm sorry about
phoning you. I won't do that – any more. I'm feeling a lot
better.' She hesitated. 'But if . . .' – she drew a heavy breath
– '. . . if – after – whenever – you ever want to call me, that's
OK.'

I got to my feet. Guilt was squatting on my heart like a
bloated toad.

'Lucy, listen, I am so sorry about what has happened,
what is happening.'

But she was already at the door. 'So am I.'

I remained as still as possible for a while. I was finding it
much harder than usual to stand. The room was spinning –
or rather sliding – away to the left of me. I tried imagining
sliding it back to the right, but it would not correct itself.
Staggeringly, I got the impression that what I actually wanted

most was a drink. The pain in my face and my stomach was extraordinary. I wondered how I was going to find the others and what to say. I ran my tongue across my upper lip. Dried blood. I wondered how I was going to find the others and what . . .

Madeleine came through the door in a hurry and seemed almost to rush towards me. She was frowning, her lips tight and set. She was carrying cotton wool and a wet flannel.

'Sit.'

She led me forcefully back to the chair and set me down. Firmly, but with care, she began wiping at my face – a Sister of Mercy with her most persistent sinner, her administrations busy, concentrated, effective.

'Head back,' she said.

The ink was running in my mind and I am not sure whether or not the words formed as I tried to speak: 'Where've you been?'

'To get these.' She indicated the cotton wool and the flannel.

'How long have I been here?'

She wasn't terse but neither was there any slack in her tone. 'Not long. Twenty minutes maximum. Shut your eyes. They were going to call an ambulance but there was a doctor who helped us carry you up and he said you would be OK. You're lucky. Your nose isn't bust and your teeth are fine and I stopped you smashing your head open.'

'Thank you for catching me.'

'It was a complete waste of time cleaning up your shirt earlier.'

I felt I had to tell her. 'Guess what?'

'Undo your collar. What?'

Honesty had me by the throat. 'One of my old girlfriends is here.'

Madeleine did not pause in her swabbing. 'I noticed,' she said.

'No, not Selina.'

'No?'

'No. Selina was never my girlfriend. I mean someone else. She just came in here but I dunno where she's gone now.'

Madeleine held off for a moment and looked into my eyes. Her beauty hurt my head. 'Really. And what did she have to say for herself?'

'She's a little bit weird actually.'

'So what did she say?'

'She said she wanted to come and see me and check that it was OK. That I was OK. That she was OK.'

'That's all?' I mistook her tone for curiosity.

'Yes. Pretty much. She said she saw Selina's husband hit me and that I should sue.'

'What else?'

'She wanted to . . . to kind of say that she was better and that she wouldn't silent call me.'

'Silent call you?'

'Ring me up and breathe down the phone.'

'That's all she said?'

'That's all.'

Madeleine looked at me again. She discarded the cotton wool and undid the cap on her bottle of water. 'Drink.'

I did as I was told.

'So what do you mean she's a little weird?' Madeleine took back the bottle and poured a drop of water on to the flannel.

'Ow, that hurts . . . Christ. Am I bleeding still?'

'Not much. What do you mean weird?'

'I don't know – you know, fragile or something. When we split up, she sort of . . . lost it, I think. Used to ring me up all the time and not say anything down the phone. She freaked.'

Madeleine stopped. 'You're done.'

'Thanks.'

'What did you do to her?'

'Nothing.'

'Come on, you must have done something. People don't just freak out.'

'She was pretty together when I first met her but –'

'So what happened?'

'Nothing.'

Madeleine pressed. 'Nothing? She just went whacko all of a sudden?'

'It's a long story.'

'Give me the short version.' A metallic note of coercion declared itself in her voice. I felt my remaining dignity veer away but there are no U-turns on the motorway of truth.

'Lucy thought that I had been with someone else when we were together and I think she was upset by it.'

'Were you?'

'What?'

'With someone else?'

'Yeah . . . Yes I was.'

Madeleine's face emptied and she looked at me for what felt like a long time. 'You know, Jasper, you should choose the people you plan to hurt even more carefully than the people you plan to love.'

21. Song

> Sweetest love, I do not go
>   For weariness of thee,
> Nor in hope the world can show
>   A fitter love for me;

I survived it, though, the ball of beatings and despair, of women and blood. And as far as Madeleine was concerned, there seemed to be nothing further for me to worry about *vis-à-vis* Selina, or Lucy, or anyone else. None of it was mentioned again. Nor did Madeleine alter in her attitude towards me. As far as my previous life went, she appeared relaxed. All that seemed to matter to her was how I behaved now, and that she was comfortable in my company and I in hers. As for me: increasingly, disconcertingly, I was finding it difficult – or too depressing – to imagine a time without her. I was aware, whenever I stopped to consider, that somewhere in the corridors of my mind a decision was forming.

A few days after the weekend of the ball, in August, she went away – back to Jordan to do some more research in Amman. Almost straight after that, she was off again, to America – something about a crayfish festival in Sacramento, she said, for the *Sunday Times*. We were together for just a single extended weekend between these trips – though still my memory of the summer seems like one long liaison punctuated only by the necessities of work and sleep. I find it hard to believe that we spent so much time apart.

I, too, worked hard during August – seven-day weeks, ten-hour days and longer, racing through 'The Curse', 'The Triple Fool', 'A Valediction Forbidding Mourning' and 'Twickenham Garden'. At last, I felt I was gaining a glimmer – distant, faint, infrequent – of what *The Songs and Sonnets* were really about.

My Bâtarde was also becoming quicker and more certain; however, as my confidence with the quills continued to grow, I began to find it necessary to take care not to stray too far from the slightly more stilted style of my work on the earlier poems. I hung 'The Indifferent' and 'Air and Angels' on the wall beside my board so that I could bear their overall composition in mind and ensure a better unity to the work as a whole. I was pretty sure that all thirty of the poems would be displayed in the same place and – despite everything – I remain committed to the principles of artistic coherence. Someone has to make a stand.

Madeleine never contacted me when she was abroad – after all, as she said, she was working, and nobody sends postcards home from the office. But that Thursday night in the middle of August, when she returned from the Middle East, she rang me as soon as her flight had landed and came straight round to Bristol Gardens from Heathrow with her undersized suitcase and her laptop.

The weather wasn't particularly summery – so we ignored London's muggy solicitations and declared an end to the discover-the-city regime of July. On Friday, she dashed home for a few hours to make some calls and catch up with the progress of her renovations while I did her washing and coaxed the launderette into a twenty-four-hour turnaround for her more sensitive fabrics. Saturday was a reprise of our most lazy July days. But in the evening I stirred myself and prepared an excellent monkfish with thyme while Madeleine had one of her epic baths. Then we sat down to watch the flickering horror of Saturday night TV.

Or rather tried to. Truly, seeing is believing: for twenty minutes we suffered the presence of some rictus-beaked, thirty-something TV-bubbly bottle-blonde – nose job, tit job, lips job, hair job, face job, feet job, all over body job and still looking like a sack of sickened shallots – who was conducting a disastrous interface between two contestants (dragged blinking and gurning and burping from the studio audience) as a prelude to . . . what? It was hard to tell. As a prelude to something like their winning a new home with round-the-clock garden makeovers thrown in and ongoing interior design rethinks and a famous chef who cooked boiled eggs in the kitchen step by step and new hair-dos every night for mum and the kids and live-in décor consultant and undercover neighbours who were really more TV celebrities and a permanent patio redesign expert and Christ . . . who knows whither the cathode ray will Pied-pipe us next?

By nine, we could take it no more. The wine was finished, and sensing the urgent need for a mood change, I suggested some cocktails.

'You want a pink gin?'

Lying with her head in my lap, she twisted round to look up: 'What's that?'

'Gin and Angostura bitters – more or less.'

'Sounds horrible. Let's give it a try. I always wondered what you used Angostura bitters for.'

'Oh, it's OK if you're in the right mood.' I tried to rise and go to the kitchen but she caught my legs between hers and dragged me back.

'You're trapped,' she said, pulling out the television

remote control from under her. 'Do you know where Angostura is?'

'No.' I thought a moment but no information came.
'Sounds like Tibet or Nepal or something. Somewhere where
they make wool or keep goats?'

'Loser. Wrong continent altogether: it's in Venezuela – on
the Orinoco river.' She released me. 'Get into the kitchen,
ignorant slave.'

When I returned, carrying the two glasses, she was standing by the open window playing with my mint plant. I passed
her a drink.

'So is there anywhere you haven't been?'

She looked at me reproachfully, as though to ask such a
question of a traveller was in some way to deny the vastness
of the globe and by implication the longevity of her career.

'Of course. Hundreds of places: the Ukraine, Azerbaijan,
Indonesia, Alaska, Uruguay . . . I mean, literally hundreds of
places. Afghanistan.'

'What about in Europe?'

'Again, yes. None of the Baltic States – Estonia and so on.
Not Poland. Not really Portugal, not Lisbon anyway. Not
Turkey or Cyprus or Sardinia or . . . lots of places – Rome in
fact, and Malta and Jesus – even Mon—'

'Rome. You haven't been to Rome?'

'No. Never.' She took a sip and sucked her teeth. 'Nice. I
like this drink.' She licked her lips. 'Is this the window where
you used to spy on me?'

'No. I used to do that from my studio.'

She nodded, slowly. 'It's very romantic.' Her tone was
only half joking. 'My fingers smell of your mint.' She offered
me her hand, which I kissed. 'But of course it's all the wrong
way around.'

'What do you mean?'

She studied my face a moment. 'You writing love poems at your window while I bask in the garden below.'

'How so – the wrong way around?'

'Well, I should be up at the window and you should be down in the garden walking melancholically – is that a word? – walking melancholically back and forth beneath my window as you write. Like a true Renaissance man.'

'Oh, I get you.' I crossed to find some music. 'Except that I can't write sonnets very well and we don't live four hundred years ago and anyway, they're not exactly love poems.'

She slurped her drink childishly. 'Christ, Jasper, you've come over very grounded all of a sudden. What's happened?'

I crouched down to look at the covers of my discs. 'I'm sorry. I'm changing uncontrollably. My inner Don Quixote is slowly passing away. I think it's the male menopause. Although Roy Junior reckons it's to do with eating too many fish. It's making me more normal . . . nicer apparently.' I rocked on my haunches. 'I've started regretting sleeping with other people's wives and I'm even considering arranging my music alphabetically – or maybe by date of purchase – or composition.'

'You are right, though.' She came over and stood directly behind me, pressing alternate knees lightly into my back.

'I know,' I sighed. 'About what?'

'They are not really love poems. I'm catching up with you there. I read the copy you gave me, by the way, when I was in Amman, when I got back to my hotel. Quite a few times, actually. They are so . . . so dense – like puzzles. But better than going to get hit on by horrible fat guys in the bar. Although now I feel strangely like I've been hit on by Donne. Which is weird. He wasn't a horrible old fat guy, was he?'

I began the process of putting all the discs back in their cases – a task which Madeleine seemed congenitally incapable of performing. 'No. Not as far as I know. He was a thin guy. Normal build. But very popular with the ladies.' I took Schubert from the cradle and replaced him with Madeleine's Billie Holiday. 'Maybe later, after he got himself snookered by his marriage and his kids and religion and all the rest – when he was Dean of St Paul's – maybe then he started putting on weight. People do that when their circumstances get the better of them – it's a way of cancelling themselves out sexually. But I don't know. Maybe he was lean all the way through. He certainly never gave up taking the fight to God or being fucked off with his fellow man.'

'I think he stayed thin.' A change of knee. 'So what are they about, Jasper? Now we've agreed it's not love?' She gave the word a heavily sardonic inflection, which nevertheless failed to deflect the sincerity of her enquiry.

I stood up and faced her. 'Honestly – I still don't know. It's not exactly *not* love either. The problem with Donne is that everything is about everything all the time. Or rather, everything is inside everything else: faithfulness, unfaithfulness, faithfulness, unfaithfulness; truth, falsity, truth, falsity . . . there's what he might call "a plaguey subtlety" about everything that he writes.'

She mocked me: 'A "plaguey subtlety"?'

I ignored her. 'It's from one of his poems. He's talking to himself, as usual: "But thou which lov'st to be / Subtle to plague thyself / Alas –"'

'So what's his problem?' she interrupted. 'Women?'

'Not women specifically – although nobody is underestimating the amount of trouble women can bring to any situation. More, I think, his problem – if that's what you want to call it – is something to do with "possession".'

She collapsed over the end of the sofa, holding up her drink to prevent it from spilling before settling properly, fold-

ing her legs under her as she had done the first time she
came round.

I sat down beside her and put my feet up on the little
table. 'Once something is apprehended, possessed intellectually, then it's no longer vitalizing for him. And that goes as
much for, say, religion or travelling to a foreign country as
it does for women. Most of all it goes for the experience of
writing the poems themselves. Sometimes you can feel him
not engaging so much with their endings because once he'd
got enough of them down on paper, that's them had. It's a
possession aversion.'

'Is it? I didn't read them – or, I should say – I didn't
experience them as being about possession.'

I considered. 'No, in a way you are right: that's not what
they are about. That's more what they – I don't know – what
they enact. What they are about is . . . something to do with
vicissitude, mutability. You might say that what really animated Donne more than anything else was inconsistency: in
the world about him, in the women he met and, most of all,
in himself. But there *is* a lot of straightforward love there too
– especially for his wife.'

'Who was she?'

'Ann. He married her in secret, thinking he'd get away with
it, but he misjudged the reaction of her father and totally
fucked up. She was out of his league – different social rank –
and he was fired when he came clean and they had to go and
live in penury in a damp little cottage miles away from London
. . . miles away from all the action for years. But when she died,
he wrote that he was *dolore infans* – by grief made wordless –'

'A sad thing for a poet to say. How old was he when he
got married?'

'Twenty-nine, I think, or thirty.'

I think more clearly during the night – perhaps because the darkness and the silence are closer to the true nature of the universe. The stars – our juvenile sun included – are all just local distractions of light, heat, noise, hardly worth counting against the vast spaces in between. But at night you can take communion with a deeper truth. You can make decisions.

The chronic inattention that so many people pay to life also strikes me most at night. As if the living of it could ever be enough. 'Oh,' they say, with that facile glibness of the self-appointed wise, 'but all the most important decisions are made for you.' And yet this is only another form of cowardice or evasion. Because, in truth, all the important decisions are yours and yours alone. There is no God, no justice, no externally verifiable right or wrong, and you cannot blame your parents. (They had no idea what they were letting themselves in for.) No – against the screaming chaos of all those hell-bent genes inherited from all those unknowable ancestors within, and against the vast and silent indifference of the universe without, you, and you alone – expecting no reward and certain only that death is coming – must choose your ridge and make your stand. The alternative is a wretched slavery: to be pushed and hustled and nudged and shuffled through muddy valleys into a series of positions that you did not mean to take by people whom you did not intend to love. To become, in effect, nothing more than the breathing aggregate of all your failed intentions and ducked decisions. At which point chronic inattention is the only recourse.

And if there was a single night, a moment of election, then it was that night in August. We stayed up late – talking, drinking, doing nothing. At three or four, I was still awake, lying beside her as she slept. I remember the weather was distracting, falling over and getting up again outside the window like a toddler given whisky as a joke. My decision wasn't loud or resounding – but rather cautious and mute – a change in the way I thought about her, a change in the way I thought about myself. But that, I think, is what love is: an unknowable risk taken in the darkness during unsettled weather. And anyway, I had been meaning to see grandmother for ages.

Of course, on the Sunday, when I awoke and there was light in the room, and she was turned the other way, her hair on the edge of my pillow, her shoulders small and almost frail, and outside I could hear the agonized whirr of a builder's stone cutter . . . of course, when I awoke there were other, more facetious voices: 'Oh pul—lease, Jackson. Will you leave it out with your dumb-ass questions? Surely we don't have time for that stuff any more? I mean come *on*. The human race is much too fast these days for such enquiries of the soul. Sure we can stop for inner calm work-outs with our New Age buddies if we really must; or, hey, who knows? – maybe a cup of self-conscious green tea twice a day just like they used to in ancient China. But as for the serious stuff – the nature of Love – or, for Christ's sake, any of the love poets – well, fuck that. Fuck them. No chance. Not *now*, Jackson. The rest of humanity is pumped up on steroids, pal, and on a special no-food diet and there is absolutely not time for you to be hanging around the side of the track asking bullshit questions like that. This is a race. Get set. Get involved. (And make some money, for fuck's sake.) 'In love': who on earth has any idea what that means?

'(A) As far as you can tell, do you sort-of like your partner enough to ignore the tiresome, underlying truth of his/her personality? (B) Can you remember thinking that he/she is sweet now and then – when he/she brings you presents, for example? (C) Is he/she more or less as nice/acceptable as anyone else you may have met or are likely to meet; and do you seriously doubt that other people would have the stamina to put up with your raging insecurity and ferocious ignorance? (D) Is the physical attraction marginally above the generic appeal that you feel towards members of the opposite or same sex? (E) Are you shit scared that you're not going to meet anyone else?

'OK. If you score more than a 50 per cent "yes" . . . then go for it! You are in love! So tell your parents (not that you have any): buy a house: get married: have kids: start the whole show again. Great.'

Thus spoke the morning.

But, as I say, the night voices come from deeper, clearer places. And so my decision stood. Even as she packed her bags for Sacramento and looked up ready to go – hands on hips at the end of my bed. Especially as she packed her bags for Sacramento and looked up hands on hips at the end of my bed. My decision stood.

'Thanks for washing my stuff,' she said. 'So, I'll see you in a couple of weeks, right?'

'Yep.' I got out of bed. 'Then I'm going to whisk you off somewhere very special. On a mini-break just like I know all the ladies love.'

She grinned. 'Especially travel writers.'

'It's somewhere you haven't been.'

'Tell me.'

'You have to wait 'til you get back.'

'Can I guess?'

'You can – but I won't tell you if you're right.' The taxi beeped on the street outside.

She kissed me. 'Right, I have to go. It takes fifty thousand hours to check in for American flights these days.' She gripped her bags and stood for a further moment. 'How does it go?'

'What? How does what go?'

'The – you know – the I-don't-go-because-I-am-weary-of-thee-or-whatever poem.'

'Oh that. It goes: "Sweetest love, I do not go / For weariness of thee, / Nor in hope the world can show / A fitter Love for me . . ."'

'That's it.' She smiled. 'That's what I'm doing. That's exactly how I'm not going – or whatever.'

I held her for a moment. 'You're not a very good student.'

'I'll read them more and argue with you better.'

For my money, 'Song' is surely the most beautiful poem of parting in the English language. But, as with 'The Dream', I am now struck as much by the disquiet on the way to the steadfast declaration of the final couplet as I am by the couplet itself.

> Let not thy divining heart,
>   Forethink me any ill,
> Destiny may take thy part,
>   And may thy fears fulfil;
>   But think that we
> Are but turned aside to sleep;
> They who one another keep
>   Alive, ne'er parted be.

22. The Ecstasy

> As 'twixt two equal armies, Fate
>   Suspends uncertain victory,
> Our souls, (which to advance their state,
>   Were gone out), hung 'twixt her, and me.

To Rome then. Eternal city of love and faith, of Venus and the Vatican, of sacrament and sacrilege. Where everything collides. And grandmothers live. To Rome.

Riding down the Viale di Trastevere, we stood close together by the doors, hanging on to the suspended straps and swaying along in that curiously unrhythmical dance that tram rides everywhere require of their passengers.

'Where do we get off?' Madeleine asked, deliberately swinging further than necessary after a minor change of direction so that her face was pressed up against mine. We were passing the elaborately porticoed façade of the Ministero Pubblica Istruzione.

'At the Piazza just before the river – it's only about another two stops,' I said.

'The river being the Tiber?'

'Yup – although they call it the Tevere; hence, I think, Trastevere.'

'So give me it in three sentences.'

'What?'

'The introduction to your piece: "Forty-eight hours in Trastevere."'

'Oh right . . . erm . . . something like . . . Trastevere is the closest Rome comes to a properly defined neighbourhood. In the best traditions of counter-culture, it is situated across the river from the main city, much like the Left Bank in Paris, and enjoys a similar reputation for bohemians and artisans.' I paused. 'Actually, that's probably bollocks. I think it just used to be the poor part of town – sort of slums and lacklustre artists – narrow lanes. Somewhere not to go after dark. But these days, because it's so well preserved, all the tourists come to wander around and – you know – it does look great – and it *is* kind of cool in its own way – distinct from the rest of Rome.'

'Not very pithy – as introductions go. But I get the picture.'

Our tram ran down its own empty lane in the centre of the road but on either side cars were horning and revving their way determinedly in and out of the city, while the scooters swarmed around them taking advantage of every fleeting gap. We came to a halt and everyone was thrown forward just far enough to cause universal loss of composure.

'One more stop,' I said.

The trip had been easy enough to arrange: I had called my grandmother and we had enjoyed our usual telephone marathon during which I explained that I was nearing illumination time on the Donne and that I felt like a break and wondered whether I could come and visit for a weekend . . . with a friend. (Oh the euphemisms of family life.) And, seeing as Grandmother knew the best examples in the world, I thought that maybe she could point me in the right direction and I could look in at the library to garner some ideas for versal design – if she could fix to get us in; and oh yes, I asked, did she know anywhere nice that we could stay – like the Vatican apartment she got me the last time – because, if so, I wouldn't need to bother her. I told her the prospective date and she said what a shame but that she was away in Orvieto (with Professor Williams) that weekend, until the Saturday afternoon, but it would be lovely to see me then – why not dinner all together on Saturday night? And of course she could find us somewhere to stay and arrange for one of her underlings at the library – perhaps Father Cedric would be so kind – to meet me on the Saturday and get me inside the Vatican because it would take for ever to get official access on my own. I said that this would be perfect and she promised to send me an e-mail with everything that I needed to know – where to collect the keys and so on, as well as some good references for the best Bâtarde – all on one condition: that I would bring with me copies of the work that I had completed so far so that she could have a look at them; and that I would definitely come for Christmas again, which was really two conditions, she knew, but once you pass seventy then really, Jasper, you can't be expected to observe the more pedestrian laws of life.

The third weekend in September duly arrived and Roy Junior drove us to the airport, taking so many short cuts that the route somehow felt much longer than it actually was.

Privately, I feared the usual fourteen-hour delays while they hastily air-fixed a plane together and we sat marooned in the corner of some powder-blue departure lounge looking on in dismay as our fellow countrymen – the world's most embarrassing travellers – treated all and sundry to an extended exhibition of our least attractive national characteristics. But there were no problems or delays. And in any case, I had not counted on how curiously calming an experience taking a trip with a professional would be – all the usual minor apprehensions disappeared; one felt sure that people, places and events would all be faced with patient equanimity and that reports of missed flights or cancellations would be shrugged off like news of an undone lace. After all, this was, as Madeleine pointed out, something like her thirtieth visit to an airport since the start of the year.

Having cleared security – where I couldn't help but admire the bulging scrapbook full of rainbow colours and unfamiliar alphabets that Madeleine so nonchalantly brandished as a passport (there were stamps in there from countries that did not even *exist* any more) – we took off on schedule and flew south across Europe, over the Alps and down the Italian coast, reaching Rome at six o'clock. Our first view of the city was from the air – of ochre buildings, bathed in the evening's light, nothing too tall or glinting, only churches, palaces and triumphant ruined gateways, and all looking as beautiful as only the Eternal City can look.

I was glad I had suggested we take the tram ride down the Viale di Trastevere once the airport train had dropped us at the eponymous *stazione*. It was a more intimate way to arrive than by taxi. In the same spirit, once we were set down on the pavement, I didn't take Madeleine directly to our rendezvous at the Piazza S. Egidio, but chose a route through a series of ramshackle back streets so that her first real hit of the city could be as captivating as possible.

We trundled along, suitcase wheels clicking behind us over the fanned cobbles, and I watched her absorbing the surroundings: on either side, the uneven old town houses crammed together in dilapidated terraces, but looking sexy and suntanned nonetheless in their various shades of brown – almond, amber, caramel, nut, tobacco, sienna or deep dark orange-yellows – with now and then just the occasional façade tricked out in a precocious pink. Here and there some of the buildings had been entirely renovated while others were swathed in scaffolding, but always the prevailing atmosphere was one of dishevelled style – wooden shutters that needed painting, terracotta tiles that had baked too long in the sun and cracked, and the elegant Italian arches – slightly chipped and worn. We swung by a couple of restaurants – chairs carefully positioned outside so as to maximize the possible number of tables, menus confidently displayed on their chalk boards, daring the passer-by to pass by. We admired the odd cascade of vine, the flower pots in the windows, the lines of washing hung high above our heads and I pointed out the fountains that ran with drinkable water night and day – to the great pride of every true Roman citizen. On the Via della Pelliccia, we stood aside to let a yellow taxi edge past and then watched as an old woman dressed in regulation black emerged and stood self-importantly aside while the driver unloaded her shopping. A young man came out of the launderette looking harassed with a mop.

'What's the name of the place where we're picking up the keys?' Madeleine asked.

'It's called Ombre Rosse. It's the best bar in Trastevere. My grandmother drinks there. We have to ask for Massimo. It's just up there. He will be expecting us.'

We entered the Piazza S. Egidio.

'OK – this is it.' I looked at my watch. 'Do you want to wait here with the bags and I'll go fetch the keys?'

'Sure,' she said, taking out a cigarette from her breast pocket. 'But what should I do if a handsome young Roman comes and sweeps me off my feet?'

'It won't happen. They've all got the Madonna complex. The better looking the woman, the less action she gets. Back in a minute.'

The apartment succeeded in giving the impression of being much bigger than it was by stubbornly remaining as one long room. There was a short run of kitchen units, a dining table and a living area and then, at the far end, a low futon bed, framed by identical dark camphor wardrobes. The floor was covered in brick red tiles; two tall windows looked on to the street on the right; and huge, thick oak beams ran along the ceiling. The whole was as cool and airy as marble. We didn't waste any time.

'Give me three minutes,' I said, 'and I'll have us something worth drinking.'

Snatching up the keys, I shot back out to Via della Scala and into the tiny wine shop, where I bought the only vintage Laurent Perrier they had and a hideously over-priced white burgundy, which was, at least, ready chilled. Madeleine, meanwhile, must have unzipped her case, fished out her favourite Oscar Peterson, found the stereo and worked it all out. Because when I got back she was already prancing around to the strains of 'Wine and Roses'. I found two glasses and, after she had taken a careful moment to restart the song, we stood barefoot on the bed, hooked through one another's arms and drained our drinks dry. This led inevitably to refills, which in turn seemed to require more joke jazz dancing, which likewise – by the time 'You Look Good To Me' had come on – somehow seemed to demand striptease.

At nine, I got up to check on the temperature of the Laurent Perrier.

'We've still got time to get ourselves up the hill behind to the Piazzale Garibaldi – if you want to see the city at dusk,' I said, wishing that the icebox wasn't so small. 'Our table is at ten-thirty and it's only thirty minutes walk to the restaurant – maximum.'

'What's the alternative?'

'Well . . . I could give Oscar an encore and we could just lie here until it's dark or this bottle gets cold enough to open. Whichever happens first.'

'Fuck Garibaldi.'

With the exception of a brief and aberrant moment of what I suppose I will have to characterize as jealousy on my part, that first night in Rome went OK. More than OK. The air was balmy and the street lanterns were lit on the Ponte Sisto when we stopped midway across to survey the view: up the river, the mad crenellations of the Castel San. Angelo and the squat shape of St Peter's, looking almost eerie in the strangely subdued spotlights which cast the dome in a shade approaching cardinal red; downriver, the old island hospital stranded and quarantined midstream. Beneath us, the scrawny Tiber seemed to be dawdling even more unhurriedly than usual; a wise old man forever passing through town whom nobody ever bothers to consult.

Back in London we had struck a wardrobe deal – modern life being such a turgid dress-down affair. We had agreed to dress up. So I was in my best dark-blue single-breasted suit, cut classically with vents (by a moonlighting Chinese tailor who works out of an attic on Carnaby Street) and teamed with my roster of non-negotiables: my New York shoes, a white shirt and a silk tie. Madeleine, though, was an ode to flirtatious cool: she wore a cerise Anna Molinari dress, which dipped to a draped 'Y' at the back (and seemed constantly to swish about her knees), with a pair of strappy sling-back shoes.

We hadn't managed to finish the Laurent Perrier and since it was far too pretty to leave oxidizing, we had brought it with us. I took a swig and passed it across to Madeleine and we set off the rest of the way across the bridge.

'I shall be falling over by the time we get there,' she said, as we waited for the lights to change on the far side.

'Does it matter?'

'No. But you mustn't take advantage of me.' She handed the bottle back and smiled warmly. 'Or I will have you beaten up next time we go to a ball.'

'I can think of worse things.'

We swung left down the Via Giulia where kindly Raphael had once lived, before taking a right on to the Via del Mascherone. Every twenty steps or so, the pools of light around the street lamps caused the buildings to glow more intensely and a wooden window frame would declare itself in great detail before the shadows deepened again and forms replaced features. A cat sidled out of a darkened doorway and Madeleine leant forward, pulling on my arm, to hiss at it. (Her dislike of cats was, I came to realize, surpassed only by her loathing of dogs – 'filthy disgusting animals'.) We stopped again to drink some more by the ancient fountain in the Piazza Farnese, which, except for the listless guards who stood smoking beneath the motionless French flag, was quiet.

'It's supposed to be the most beautiful of all the Renaissance palaces in Rome,' I said, looking up at the vast façade of the palazzo. 'The French rent it for a nominal fee in return for some place that the Italians get in Paris. I would love to see inside.'

'The Italian embassy in Paris is on the rue de Varenne,' she said, lighting a cigarette. 'But I would say that the French have the best deal – as usual.'

'Oh right. Have you been?'

'Yes. My father works in Paris and –'

'Oh yeah – you said.'

'– he used to take me to parties at the Hotel Gallifet –

where the Italians have their receptions – when I was on holiday from boarding school, so that I would look forward to seeing him.' She exhaled. 'Guilt.'

I had forgotten the French connection. 'You don't like him, do you?'

'No,' she shrugged. 'Well, yes, actually – sometimes. He's an eloquent, intelligent man. Used to get called brilliant. Double firsts all the way. But he's a complete waste of space, the worst kind of, like, hypocrite. Spends all day with his stiff-upper-lip friends talking about being awfully decent but he has actually behaved like a pathetic bastard all his life. Everything important he fucked up.'

'Did you know your mother?'

'Not really. She looked after me for a few months then she drank herself to death. That and the pills apparently. Impressive, huh?'

I nodded slowly.

There was silence, then she said: 'Don't you wonder about your parents?'

'Yes – of course. Sometimes. But – you know – you don't miss what you never had so I don't get down about it or whatever. People think orphans spend all their lives being sad and lonely but the no-parents thing gets to be normal if it has always been that way and you don't really notice what difference it makes. In fact, in a sense, it makes you much more relaxed than your peers – more resourceful anyway. And you get this excellent relationship with the over-sixties – like my grandmother and her pals – because you both think the generation in between are complete arseholes.'

Madeleine smiled. 'I can't wait to meet her.'

'You'll like her.'

We entered Campo dei Fiori, made our way through the musters of vociferously appreciative Italian men, crossed the

angry traffic on the Corso Vittorio Emanuele II, wandered
through the Piazza Navona and, having disposed of the last
of the wine, pressed the doorbell of Il Convivio.

The mâitre d' appeared first – a one-man morality tale
concerning the virtue of buffed nails and expensive moistur-
izer – and it was he who led us to our table, (a dapper parade
of linen and silver), whereupon he offered Madeleine an
ankle-height stand for her handbag. But it was the table
waiter who made the evening. A delicately moustached man,
he flourished the menus (on which only mine had the prices
displayed) as if they were the tablets of Moses, and then
proceeded to deliver such a richly animated, passionate and
labyrinthine discourse on the joys of the various fish, fowl
and fungi on offer – how they would be cooked, prepared
and served, as well as which member of the kitchen would
be responsible for doing so – that I began to fear there was
a danger that all three of us might be rendered insensible by
the sheer Epicurean drama of his descriptions. At the last,
Madeleine settled on the cuttlefish with rosemary and squid-
ink rice and I succumbed to a Spanish dried duck, served
with wild thyme, walnut and raspberries.

Did we talk further about our families during that dinner?
No. I am sure that we did not. I would remember. There was
a question about my grandmother – but only about where
we were going to meet up the next day. Certainly, I did not
ask Madeleine anything more – if only because talk of her
mother and father had seemed to unsettle and subdue her
and I had no wish to do that.

A little drunk and more than sated, sometime towards the
end of the midnight hour, we slipped across the wide Viale
di Trastevere into Big Mama's, a basement jazz bar – cavern-
ous and dark with no windows and sawdust and square

industrial pillars that obscured the view and fifties-style neon signs on the walls that blinked on and off. The Friday night crowd seemed mostly to comprise youngish Italians in just-so jeans and specially-set-aside-for-the-weekend long-sleeved shirts – all smoking Marlboro Lights – but there were one or two more serious-looking aficionados as well, sitting around the tables closer to the stage and taking care to smoke the real thing. We looked a little odd in our dining clothes. But cool as fuck too.

For half an hour, we stood together at the back, drinking Jack Daniels and Cokes – Bonnie and Clyde taking it easy before the next big heist – and listened to a guy with an untidy beard play the blues. He was good and his audience followed him closely. Indeed, we were both sorry that we had come in late because too soon he was closing his set (with 'Hey Joe'), though quite clearly neither he nor his band really wanted to stop. When, finally, the drummer hit the last cymbal, the whole room fell victim to that slightly displaced, end-of-the-movie feeling for a minute or two before the spell wore off and everybody filed back to the bar or regrouped around their tables to reassess the night.

I lost Madeleine just then – she went off to the cigarette machine – and I found myself leaning against a pillar and watching this baby-faced boy inch his arm around his date while simultaneously attempting to be fully involved in the general conversation of his peers. It was slow-motion agony, like the replay of a downhill skiing accident. She was young and darkly pretty and she let him get almost comfortable before lifting his hand from where it had come to rest on her waist and discreetly but decisively moving it off to more neutral territory. I caught her eye and she looked away in embarrassment.

When I saw her next, Madeleine was at the bar, talking

to the bass player from the band. He had long, light-coloured hair but he was good-looking in a sun-tanned, flamenco-dancing kind of a way. She was buying him a drink.

Jealousy came without warning and from nowhere. But there was no mistaking it: hot and stinging – the sudden piercing of the green-tipped dart, followed by the flood of poison. For some reason I delayed going over. I stood unseen and watched her. Now she was laughing at whatever he was saying. Now she had her arm draped over one of his shoulders. Now she was whispering her replies in his ear as if the background music made it impossible for her to be heard otherwise. She had only been gone ten minutes – or less.

I confess, the next few minutes were far worse than I previously pretended. They were piss-awful and disgusting and I hated myself throughout. But the surge of feelings took me by surprise: anxiety, panic, anger, indignation, vulnerability, insult, hurt, embarrassment, the sudden fear of loss – all felt simultaneously with good reason (just look at her) and without good reason (she was with me, we were in Rome, she was only playing, it was all OK). Yet that is what jealousy is really like, I thought: a toxic brew, made up of equal parts reason and unreason, and the true source of its power is that it destroys your sense of which is which – it makes you doubt your own judgement.

As I approached, she disconnected herself from his ear and raised her voice. 'Hey Jasper, this is Marco. I'm gonna sleep with him as well tonight. He says he's happy to take turns with you if you can handle it. He's very cute, don't you think? And he says he can fuck without strings. I think it will be good.'

I opened my mouth but there was no voice within me. I knew – though there had been nothing in her tone to suggest a joke, no sarcasm or slyness – I knew that I should laugh or at least say something that recognized her challenge for the brinkmanship that it was. But I could not. My sense of humour had vanished like water into desert sand. I understood that she meant nothing; and yet what she had said – it seemed to me – snagged by the moment – was an unprovoked act of pure psychological violence. My adrenalin rose.

Marco spoke – his English almost perfect but his accent more Swiss than Italian. 'Hi, how you doing? I gotta say, man, I like this idea *very* much.' He grinned in Madeleine's direction – he did not appear to think she was joking. 'I've never done with two people before – how about you?'

'Yes,' I said slowly, 'I have.' I caught the bartender's attention. 'But I'm afraid, Marco, nobody touches this woman except me.' The paralysis was passing. 'Sorry. But I own her and that's how it is. You could buy her for an hour – maybe – but it's a lot of fucking money and she's not very cooperative. In fact she's a bitch. Who wants a drink?'

'Same again for me,' Madeleine said, looking slightly taken aback but with a glint of entertainment in her eyes.

'You?' I looked at Marco.

'Sure,' Marco nodded, 'a beer would be cool.'

'OK then.'

I ordered and then turned back from the bar. Madeleine stood up off her stool to allow her dress to fall straight, then sat back down again, crossing her legs provocatively. Marco, meanwhile, had joined his hands in the prayerful gesture of an Italian football player, exasperated by a decision that had gone against him. 'Oh man. That's such a big shame. I thought maybe today was my lucky day. For four years, I play the blues in a band and nobody ever offers me sex after the show. Not even a blow-job. Not even in Hungary. I thought maybe today for once God was looking after me. It's a big shame.'

'For me too,' said Madeleine, looking forlorn but winking slyly at me. As I passed her another Jack Daniels and Coke, I felt her other hand on the back of my legs.

Almost as quickly as they had come, the feelings passed. But I was residually surprised at how shaken I had been over what was hardly anything. The experience had made its point: and once you're on jealousy's direct mailing list there's no getting off.

The rest of that night was too drunken and delirious to remember. At three, we staggered out into the street – arm in arm once more and beneath stars that flickered when we weren't looking and a moon that wobbled when we were – and we sluiced back across the Viale di Trastevere, taking care to avoid the jabbering of the junk-fried junkies outside the frazzled-food joints and keeping our ears open for the waspy buzz of the motorino boys, who swerved and banked and weaved across the Piazza as if in search of some spectacular collision that might just jolt everyone sober for long enough for us all to leave the childishness of the night behind and finally matriculate into the more serious business of tomorrow morning. We swayed down a side alley and fumbled and stumbled and groped our way along the warm stone walls – now whispering, now shouting, now giggling, now kissing – around a corner into the dimly lit Via del Moro, and on from there towards the blurred but stubborn sanctuary of Stardust, the last of the late-night retreats for all those who refuse to believe in the sun rising.

When they kicked us out, the air smelt fresh and the night was fading pale. We set off unsteadily home together, me trying to remember Italian swear-words to call her, and Madeleine giggling and walking backwards in front of me, pouting, pulling up the hem of her dress scornfully and deriding me. 'Are you enjoying your weekend, Jasper, are you enjoying me? Yes? Huh? Yes . . . oh I think you are. But it's so hard to tell with you, isn't it? That's right. Because you are a . . . a man. Oh so *serious*. A man! And real men never let you know what they are thinking, do they? No, they don't. But a woman can always guess; that's our great advantage. To a woman, the mind of a man is like a very boring game of noughts and crosses and the only thing that surprises us is that you keep asking for another round. There is nothing subtle or hard to figure in men. So come and get me then if that's what you want.'

I did and I did.

In the shuttered darkness she asked me if I was awake. Yes, I told her, and rose to fetch her some water. She sat up and gulped it down and I went to fetch her some more.

23. The Canonization

For God's sake hold your tongue, and let me love, ...

We can die by it, if not live by love,
 And if unfit for tombs and hearse
Our legend be, it will be fit for verse;
 And if no piece of chronicle we prove,
  We'll build in sonnets pretty rooms;
  As well a well wrought urn becomes
The greatest ashes, as half-acre tombs,
 And by these hymns, all shall approve
 Us canonized for love.

'For Christ's sake, Jasper, what time is it?' Madeleine raised herself briefly and looked down the room to where I had just succeeded in rather noisily steaming some milk.

'Nine.'

'Well, what the fuck are you doing?' She rolled over and buried her face in the pillow.

'I'm trying to make this coffee machine work.' The first burnt-treacle drips dropped into the white cup I had found. 'Ah ha – there she goes. Fantastic.'

'Can't you be just a bit quieter? Some of us have terrible hangovers.'

'It's not me. It's the machine.'

'What time do we have to meet your priest?'

'Not until half-past ten.' I took the quarter-full cup away and replaced it with another. 'Would you like a cappuccino?'

'Only if you promise to get the paracetamol out of my bag first and give me a glass of water.'

'Of course.' This meant that her coffee would probably

lose temperature so I quietly poured it back into my cup, making mine a double, before adding the milk and taking a hesitant sip. Not bad for the first time out with a new machine. I ran the tap cool, broke some ice into a glass, and took it over to her. 'Here you are. How bad is it?'

'Not that bad. I've had much worse. The tablets are in my washing bag. Bring the whole bag in here.'

The bathroom was little more than a small ancillary chamber – a walk-in cupboard, more or less. I switched on the light and went in.

'How come you're dressed?' she asked.

'I got up to go to the market to get a few things for our lunch. And the ingredients for a Bloody Mary in case you wanted one. Although even the English shop at Piazza S. Cosimato didn't have Worcester sauce, I'm afraid.' I stepped out again and handed her the bag.

She rummaged. 'Are we really having a picnic?'

'Not sure. But I thought we'd have nectarines for breakfast – with live yoghurt and some lovely honey that I found in the shop.' A moment of sudden misgiving for me, the after-shock from my former life. 'Unless there's something else you want.'

She took another gulp of her water, threw back her head, took the pills, and then threw back the covers. She swung her legs around so that she was sitting on the side of the bed – finger and thumb to her forehead. Wincing, she said, 'Your obsession with what to have for breakfast is fucked up, Jasper. I'll eat whatever. But first I'm going to have a shower so that Father whoever-his-name-is gets me fresh.'

There was no way around it – Father Cedric was a big guy. And what with the no-sex drill that goes with his line of work, I can't say I blamed him: were I forty-nine, forced into frocks twice a day and having to work Sundays, I'd take to my grub big-time too. Yeah, and the booze. In fact, I find it pretty hard to say what the upside of being a man of the cloth is these days. No one believes a word you say, the hours are unsocial and sporadic, the money is not what it used to be, and the chicks are more or less over their thing about dog collars or whatever it was. Plus most people think that you're an alcoholic or an undercover paedophile or both, which – whether true or not – must really put the brakes on things when it comes to socials with the flock. As for the so-called sacraments, well hardly anybody can keep a straight face anymore when you're up there on the altar mumbling away to yourself; and who among the congregation really wants forgiveness or penance or any of that crap? Nobody. They all want more sin, plenty of it and with a 'Pause' button if possible. About the only time you get so much as a word or two of genuine respect is when you're called out in the middle of the night to chuck eau de Cologne over dying octogenarian widows – who, tragically, are also about the only people left on the planet still interested in getting it on with you weekday afternoons. It can't be much of a life. But at least Father Cedric had somehow arranged his billet as close to the action as possible: if you're going to be a priest, then you might as well hang at Vatican City.

It must have been a few minutes after the anointed hour when I first saw him bustling in our direction. We were standing to attention in front of the Swiss Guard at the command post just off the Via di Porta Angelica, which runs north out of St Peter's Square itself. I was enjoying the pleasant sensations of a Bloody Mary (previously thought a little too fiery, but which was now delivering exact measures of peace and good will). Madeleine was powering her way through a second litre of mineral water. In what I took to be a send-up of my efforts to persuade her to dress conservatively, she was wearing her pumps, a white shirt, a camel pleated skirt, a printed headscarf and her tortoise-shell sunglasses. We had kept conversation to a minimum on account of our hangovers but I had tried to impress upon her the need for a compromise between modesty and lightness – a futile exercise, of course.

'Hello, hello, hello! You must be Jasper!' Father Cedric now stood before us, head to toe in bursting black cotton, rolls of fat piling up as if caught in some atrocious bottleneck above his belt, which was itself straining at the very end of its tether. Red-faced and bespectacled, with a rather self-conscious tonsure, there was, I thought, a faint Irish note to his voice. He had also acquired that curiously exaggerated lilt of a person used to talking to others in a second language, and he was hopelessly out of breath. 'Mrs Jackson told me to watch out for a young man with very black hair! How useless – to think – here in Rome! But I knew I knew I knew it must be you because you are with such a fine young lady!'

'This is Madeleine,' I said.

She took off her sunglasses and gave him a smile sure to plague his prayers forever more.

He took her hand in both of his. 'Oh yes! Mrs Jackson told me all about you both. Welcome, welcome, welcome.'

Liar, I thought.

'And has your stay with us thus far been a pleasant one?' he enquired, not looking at me.

'Wonderful, thank you,' said Madeleine, not looking at me either, 'Jasper and I have seen lots of churches.'

Surrounded by liars, and about to enter the inner sanctum. At least we'd all feel at home.

'Oh, how splendid!' Father Cedric clapped his hands together and wrung them from side to side as though celebrating some private triumph. 'But there are so many . . . so many beautiful churches in Rome. It's most difficult to say which one I like best of all. Most difficult.'

I stepped in quickly: 'Oh, we're both big fans of San Pietro in Vincoli – especially the Michelangelo.'

'Yes – it is beautiful. Very beautiful.' He pushed at the bridge of his glasses. 'Moses with horns: a mistranslation of the Hebrew, which actually means something like "ray of light", I think. But easily done. Even the great make mistakes – which is some comfort . . .'

'We have both remembered our passports,' I said, steering us away from further danger. 'And we wondered whether or not there was a chance of getting them stamped?'

'Oh yes: do you think the guards will stamp my passport?' The water must have drowned the pain because Madeleine was suddenly eager as a convent girl. 'Only I collect stamps and it would be great to have one from the Vatican.'

'Well, let's see, shall we. We can certainly ask. Follow me, follow me.'

Having surrendered passports and filled in all the necessary reams of paperwork (with many helpful intercessions from our guide and guarantor) we walked on either side of Father Cedric up the slight incline through the gardens underneath the arch of Pope Julius II and entered the vast Belvedere Courtyard. He raised his arm to point to the elevated passage that leads tourists to the Sistine Chapel – high up and to the left, an awful scaffolding construction that nobody seemingly could do anything about. And then beckoned us along: 'Now – Madeleine, Jasper – it is my privilege to take you inside. This way – here we are, here we are: the Biblioteca Apostolica Vaticana.'

Under Cedric's watchful eye, we signed in with the surly attendant, deposited our bags, picked up our passes from the vice-prefect and followed the priest's hulking figure into an elevator.

Olfactorily, the short ride was exquisitely unpleasant. But the library made it all worth it: pure celestial Renaissance beauty, long arcades through which pellucid light streamed (as if straight from heaven) to play upon the marble and alabaster and bring deeper colours to the master frescos on the vaulted ceilings. And the books . . . the open shelf books everywhere thrumming with learning and imagination and intelligence.

Father Cedric led us – dumbfounded, awestruck – into the manuscript room beyond. Though the reading bays were empty, he spoke in a hushed but clear voice, the trademark of the professional librarian: 'Here are the forms where you must fill in the titles of manuscripts that you wish to read. Give them to the man at the desk that we passed before – in the main room. No more than three at a time, I'm afraid. There are some others – over there – already on display and on the shelves – here – which may be of some use.' He indicated along a wall of shelves, then looked at me with a concerned frown. 'But I think, Jasper, that there are some things that you specifically want to see – so Mrs Jackson said?'

'Yes – I do. I have the catalogue numbers here in my notebook.'

'You are lucky that she has so detailed a memory. It will save you a lot of time searching.'

'I know.'

He touched the bridge of his glasses again. 'Mrs Jackson tells me that you are quite a calligrapher these days – a professional – working on John Donne for the Americans. The Holy Sonnets by any chance?'

'No. I'm doing the love stuff –'

'His family were famous Catholics, you know – steeped in the Faith.' His manner became even more confidential. 'And at a time when it cost you your life. His uncle was the leader of the secret Jesuit mission. And, of course, his brother died in prison where he had been sent' – Father Cedric allowed himself to dwell on the words – 'for sheltering priests.'

'Yes, I have been reading about –'

'Which is of course why he is – was – and shall forever be – so unhappy, so angry with himself, because he never really forgave himself for renouncing his beliefs and entering the Protestant Church, just to get on – to win position – eventually, of course, to become Dean of St Paul's. It must have been difficult. Very difficult.' He sighed lightly. 'I read a few lines when your grandmother told me you were coming . . . now, how does it go? ''Oh, to vex me, contraries meet in one: / Inconstancy hath unnaturally begot / A constant habit.''' He nodded wisely to himself. 'That's my favourite of the Holy Sonnets. And perhaps the key to it all . . . Well now, I shall leave you both here for half an hour – I'm afraid it will take at least that long for them to fetch your requests. Then I'll come back and see how you are getting on . . .' – he twinkled like a fairy godmother '. . . and if you would like, perhaps I could show Madeleine around a little . . . while you make your sketches and your notes, Jasper.'

'Oh, that would be so good,' Madeleine whispered too loudly. 'A private tour of the Vatican. Jasper said that they have all sorts of secret documents here – like Henry VIII's deathbed conversion and lots of torture things from the Inquisition.'

Father Cedric nodded chivalrously. 'Well, we can't go everywhere but I will do my best to show you some of our little treasures.'

'Thank you, Father,' I said. 'I won't need much more than an hour and a half – so we should be out of your hair by lunchtime.' I cleared my throat to distract from the infelicity of the phrase.

'It's no trouble at all.' He rubbed his hands vigorously and with a smile somehow both beaming and wistful, he took his leave.

I sat down at a desk to copy out the references I had made back in London on to the requisition slips. After I had handed them in, we wandered together around the library, looking at everything – books, the ceiling, the high clear windows, more manuscripts, illuminations, taking care not to talk too loudly. Though the story about having to come to Rome to look at manuscripts was in one sense a fabrication – the British Museum contains everything a calligrapher could ever want or ask for – I could not help now but be excited to be surrounded by so many great examples of my art. Whenever I see close-up – hold in my hands – the work of the true masters, hundreds and in some cases thousands of years old, I feel as though I can almost talk to them, as though the scribe has just put down his quill and popped next door for his bread and cheese and will be back any minute. All the intervening centuries just dissolve away. There's a quality in the movement of the ink – breathtakingly beautiful, yes, but effortlessly so when in the hands of men whose lifelong, day-to-day work it was and lacking the self-conscious cramp of all but a handful of modern artists – a quality which makes the words seem forever freshly written. More than in any other artistic form, I think, you can see and feel the intimate making of the constituent parts even as you behold the magnificent impact of the completed whole. The experience is both acutely humbling and at the same time uplifting.

'My God, what is that?' Madeleine was pointing at a single sheet, which was pressed and bound between two thin panes of plastic glass. 'Who could read that?'

I walked to where she was standing. 'That's called Ravenna Chancery script. I know, it looks like a spider crawled across the page.'

'When's it from?' She picked up the glass tablet with care. 'It looks very precious.'

'I don't know exactly – you'd have to ask Cedric. But it's called a sub-Roman hand because it is one of those that emerged with the new kingdoms after the Roman Empire began to fall apart. So my guess would be between 500 and 700 – or something like that.'

'Can you read it?'

'I can make out the words – yes. But my Latin isn't very –'

'What does it say?'

'I think it is some kind of list.' I pointed. 'You can see that the scribe is using loads of what we call abbreviation bars – those long thin swirls under the words. Something about a register of witnesses. I don't think the document itself is that special – what it actually records, I mean – but it's important as an example.'

'But why is it so hard to read?'

'It wasn't. Not to the people in the Ravenna Chancery because it's in their own particular hand – and they liked it that way, nice and distinctive and individual.'

'It looks mad.'

'It's meant to look idiosyncratic. Each place developed their own particular style and took great pride in it. They're like different dialects or different regional forms of architecture, all with their own oddities, although, of course, everybody travelled around and different features got mixed

up, so you do get lots of hybrids and cross-referencing and
variations and so on – like you get people speaking French
with a German accent in Alsace or whatever.'

I had started talking in the librarian's whisper. 'Ravenna
is famous because it's a very attenuated script – fine-
nibbed – as well as being full of contractions and abbrevi-
ations. It's really a development of an earlier cursive, more
Roman ha—'

'Cursive? What does that mean?'

'Cursive is what we call a script designed for speed – so
you'll get fewer pen lifts and more devices called ligatures
– joined letters like the 'A' and the 'E' there – and lots of
loops. And yet Ravenna is also very elegant and formalized
– like with the high 'L's, or that descender on the 'R', or the
way that all the line ends have flourishes. Which is what
makes it so distinctive – the combination of momentum with
sophistication.'

'Can you write like this?' She looked at me quizzically.

'No. Not straightaway. I've never learned Ravenna, but I
could – with practice and time. It's like studying a new piece
of music. You have to break it down and learn bit by bit and
it takes ages – but a sound underlying technique will be a
massive help.'

'Show me a script that you can do then.'

'Here –' I leant over a leather-bound book that was lying
open on the desk. 'This is a Book of Hours, a kind of prayer
guide, which a noblewoman might have owned – there are
lots of these – and this is called Carolingian Minuscule. It's
one of the first that professional calligraphers have to learn
because it became like a model hand. In the late 700s, from
Charlemagne onwards, it was the script that got disseminated
throughout Europe because – look, you can see – it was
a more disciplined and clearer alternative to all the others

that were flying about. You could say that it was an early effort at standardization – the answer to your problems with Ravenna, if you like.'

'It's beautiful. I can even read it a bit – "admirabile est nomen". And look at these pictures.' She ran her finger gently over the vellum. 'They're still so bright – they must have taken weeks to do.'

'They used proper colours for their illuminations in those days. That blue is made from ground lapis lazuli – they had to hike it in from Persia – the most prized pigment of all: the colour of heaven and the Virgin's clothes. And yes – it takes a long time to do. But illumination was a separate job back then.'

'Have you got to illuminate all the poems?'

'No,' I smiled. 'Not anything like this. I'm just going to style and flourish the initials of the first verses. Illumination would probably take me another two years at least – if I were going to do all thirty poems. Anyway, it wouldn't look right on Donne. He needs to be spare and black and white and stark and unwavering. But the last thing I did was a single sonnet – Shakespeare – and that was fully illustrated – cupids and everything.'

'And what's the script that you're doing at the moment? Bastard Gothic or something, you said?'

'Bâtarde. It's called Bâtarde.' I walked along a shelf and pulled down some of the books. This was a calligrapher's paradise: Rustic Roman Capitals, Half Uncial, Cursive Half Uncial, New Roman Cursive; something that looked like Ravenna again – maybe a Merovingian Chancery; some crazy stuff I had never even seen before; lots of Littera Documentaria Pontificalis; and so on and so on. 'I can't see any Bâtarde,' I said, after a while. 'But I'm going to order some up anyway. So I'll show you when you come back, if Father

Cedric doesn't kidnap you and lock you in a cell somewhere for his eternal pleasure. Or worse, make you confess.'

Later, sometime after two, as we joined the surprisingly short queue to enter the Coliseum – or rather, as I stood in line while Madeleine went off to fetch some more bottles of water (a task which somehow managed to take her the precise number of minutes it took me to reach the kiosk), I asked her idly what Cedric and she had talked about.

'It's getting even hotter,' she said, ignoring my question as I handed over the entrance fee.

'We'll catch a taxi up one of the hills after this,' I suggested, 'and do nothing all afternoon.'

'What about Moses with Horns?' She asked, adjusting her headscarf. 'I want to see him now he's become such a talking point.'

'OK, we'll say hello to Moses. He's only just up the road. Then we can relax.'

We walked together beneath the imposing entrance, imagining, on Madeleine's suggestion, that we had come to see a gang of Christians die. A few steps beneath the arch and we stood on the threshold of the arena and the great tiers of grey- and sand-coloured travertine stone rose up on all sides to greet us – grimy, ruined, but still mighty – with the blue sky framed through each of the uppermost arches. We stood by the rail at the edge of the great oval and looked down at the deep and narrow maze of passageways where the animals and slaves had been kept beneath a wooden floor.

'We talked about all sorts,' Madeleine said, lighting a cigarette. 'Actually Father Cedric told me quite a bit about you and your grandmother.'

'He doesn't know anything about me.'

'He knows what your grandmother has told him.'

'Which I doubt is very much.'

'They see each other every day. And apparently they worked together before – in Oxford. He did some sort of librarian's exams there one summer.'

'Did he?'

'He knows, for instance, that you used to do portraits of people.'

'I was never any good.'

'That's not what Cedric seemed to think. He said that you used to sit in libraries and draw pencil sketches and that you won some kind of competition.'

I looked sideways at her. 'Really not. I won this minor thing advertised in the local newspaper when I was six.'

'And another prize when you were at Cambridge – a scholarship to be funded for a year and –'

'Jesus Christ. Again, minor. Madeleine – seriously – there were fewer than twenty entries. It was a university scam they ran for the poor students who were on full grants.'

'Yeah – but you entered, right? And you won?'

She stood back from the railings and we filed along until we reached the gangplank that ran the length of the arena to the glorious gate of death on the far side. We stopped as near as we could judge to the centre and spun ourselves around three hundred and sixty degrees, looking up.

When we were back to back, she said: 'And he told me about your mother.'

'What about my mother?'

'That she was an actress. That you have copies of her films but you never watch them. Is that why you don't have a video recorder, so you –'

'No. It's not. And how the fuck would Cedric know whether or not I watched my mother's films?'

'She was going to be quite a star, wasn't she – just before she died?'

'Yes. She was.'

In silence, we followed a thousand American sports shoes up the interior stairs that led to the gallery and emerged into the hot sun, halfway up the steep terraced sides. We circled halfway around, found an empty ruined-stone alcove and sat down with our backs to the iron railings. I opened up my bag and handed out the sandwiches, provisions from the morning's foray: fresh bread, tomatoes from the vine, fresh basil and chopped olives, and the sacred *prosciutto di montagna*. We sat and ate for a while, trying to imagine watching death live. The distance from our seat to the sandy floor of the arena seemed much further looking down than it had when looking up from below.

'To unknown mothers,' she said.

I touched my water bottle with hers. 'To unknown mothers.'

My grandmother's latest local was a low-key, family run, gingham-clothed restaurant, occupying one side of a small piazza near the Teatro Marcello. Twin rosemary bushes squatted in huge pots on either side of the entrance and every table leg was bedevilled by Italian cobbles. Although it was only around the corner from her apartment, and although we were exactly on time, there was no sign of Grandmother or Professor Williams when we arrived.

I said my grandmother's name to the woman who came out and she smiled broadly as though I were telling her a funny joke that she did not quite understand. Mrs Jackson, she declared, always has the table on the corner, nearest to the fountain.

We sat down and she brought bread, olives and a plate

of pickled chillies. Madeleine set about the chillies as though they were the most delicious things she had ever tasted, while I picked up the handwritten wine list and tried to remember which was my grandmother's favourite.

'Do you think there are as many types of olives as there are grapes?' she asked.

'Without a doubt.'

She picked up another chilli and began to more or less drink it. 'Do you ever think about coming to live here instead of London?'

'All the time.'

'How old is your grandmother?'

'Seventy-eight. Go on, have the last one – they'll bring us some more.'

Ever since we had set off from Trastevere, Madeleine had been unusually chatty, noticing the names of streets, talking about what she called 'my music and your music' and pulling me into shops to look at shoes or clothes that she was never going to buy. Perhaps it was my imagination, but I sensed that she was nervous. And perhaps I too was apprehensive.

'Let's have white wine while we wait,' I said, 'I fancy something really light and –'

'Hello there!' A reedy voice hailed us from the fountain steps. 'Sorry I'm late. Hello. Oh wonderful – wonderful, the best table.' Grandmother was coming across the square at double speed. Along with her pair of rather stylish charcoal-coloured cashmere trousers, she sported brand-new whiter-than-white trainers and what looked like a woollen cloche hat. 'Sorry we're late. There was a terrible incident outside my flat – two men bickering about a parking place and the whole square gathered around to watch. We couldn't get through. It's the bloody *bella figura* is what it is.'

I stood and hugged her. She felt light and small, but

irreducible. Her eyes were alight and alive with obvious delight. And it struck me then that in all her life she had never before used the first person plural when talking to me, despite the fact that good old Professor Williams had been her 'brave escort' for at least twenty-five years.

The man himself had caught up and was standing right beside her, beaming away and waiting patiently for us to finish our embrace.

'Hello, Jasper,' he said, clasping my hand warmly, 'it's been a year or two – Grace tells me that you're flourishing.'

I laughed. A bad calligraphy joke. But the professor's good nature was irresistible.

Madeleine was also standing. I turned.

'Grandma, Professor Williams, this is Madeleine, she's –'

'Hello, Madeleine, how nice to meet you at last.' My grandmother leaned over and kissed her three times, Italian style. 'I'm afraid Jasper has been keeping you a secret but I'm glad he's letting us share you now – if only for tonight. Us oldies like to be reminded of how good we looked when we were your age.'

Madeleine actually blushed. 'It's very nice to meet you too – Jasper has told me all about you.'

This was not strictly correct. Neither had been told all that much about the other. But I noticed how it was my grandmother and not Madeleine who found a way to make the truth – my silence – eloquent.

Professor Williams offered his hand. 'Call me Fergus,' he said.

Another shock. In all the time I had known the professor, I had not once heard him volunteer his Christian name before.

Amidst further small talk and pleasantries, and with that contained excitement and sense of well-being that comes with long anticipated meetings and the prospect of eating outside, we all sat down and Grandmother ordered our first bottle of wine.

'So, have you both been enjoying yourselves? I hope Jasper has been a dutiful guide?' Grandmother addressed Madeleine as she took off her hat; she had cut her hair short and she looked younger – or rather she looked ageless, like one of the senior goddesses in those old Hollywood films about Mount Olympus.

'Oh yes. He's been taking me everywhere. Today we've been to the Vatican and the Coliseum and the Moses statue – I can't remember what the church is called. And Father Cedric was great.' Madeleine was recovering her self-assurance. 'I felt like I should have thanked him more. He was so knowledgeable and enthusiastic. Apart from explaining all the pictures properly, which nobody *ever* does, he told me the complete list of cardinal virtues and which of the English kings were secretly Catholic. I was hoping he would take me to see the Pope but apparently he's more or less dead.'

'Madeleine pumped him for all the information she could get,' I said, sounding slightly aggrieved.

'No I didn't, Jasper,' Madeleine interposed. 'He only told me about your art competitions because we were looking at so many pictures ourselves. It's true we did make some comparisons at one stage but in the end we decided that – of the two of you – Caravaggio was the more interesting man.'

Grandmother chuckled. 'What's the flat like?'

'It's perfect,' I said.

'Absolutely perfect,' Madeleine added. 'I'm starting to wish we were here for longer. I guess I'm just going to have to come back.'

'You must.' My grandmother smiled.

'A-ha. Here is the wine,' said Professor Williams, eyeing each glass as it travelled from tray to table.

The woman who had greeted us poured a little for Grandmother by way of inviting her to taste; but Grandmother was having none of it and waved her to carry on.

Some moments passed as we each made friends with the Orvieto. Then Professor Williams broke the silence: 'Grace mentioned that you travel a lot, Madeleine?'

'Yes – it's mainly for my work. I've just been in America.'

'Oh and how is New York?'

'It's very odd – a different feel to before. More together. Everyone is very conscious of being a "New Yorker". It's much nearer the surface.' Madeleine spoke quickly. 'But I was only in town for an overnight flight swap this time. So I didn't really get a chance to hang out . . . Then I was straight down to Sacramento. And believe me, nothing much happens down there. Except for the crayfish.'

'Yes,' Professor Williams said, affecting world-weariness. 'I have been to Sacramento. On a lecture tour. It's not exactly an exciting place, is it? Where's the festival?'

'Oh, it's in a small town about seventy miles north. And before that I was in Amman in Jordan for my work.'

'You're writing a book?' Grandmother interrupted.

Genuine modesty as always from Madeleine on this subject: 'Hardly a book really – more a sort of literate travel guide. Or I hope it is.'

Madeleine eyed a second bowl of chillies that had arrived.

'It's going to be promoted, though,' I said. 'The publishers care about it being a success. They rate you.'

Madeleine crossed her fingers.

'Where is it set? – if that's the right word – I get confused.' Grandmother frowned as though dismissing a lifetime spent with the awkwardness of language.

'Syria mostly – but Jordan as well. A kind of woman's tour guide.'

Professor Williams interjected: 'Why a woman's tour guide, if I may ask?'

Grandmother replied for Madeleine. 'Because men aren't worth writing for, Fergus. They think they know everything already.'

Madeleine grinned. 'Lots of reasons. Mainly because the bookshops are crawling with normal guides so there's no way a publisher would buy another one. Also because people think that these countries are tricky for women and that bothers me. I want to open places up a little – or at least say that, hey, it's OK, everything you need is there if you know where to find it.' She went for a chilli. 'But most of all because there *is* something about writing for women which I like – I think women pay more attention.'

'Come on,' I said, taking a sip of wine, 'you can't say that, men pay just as –'

Madeleine interrupted. 'No, they don't. Men have to concentrate hard to detect the feel of what is being said beneath the exact sense – but women pick it up more easily. Really. Women just – you know – get it.' She turned and smiled at me. 'Anyway, how would you know? You only read books written by other men hundreds of years ago and you said yourself that you have no idea about travel writing. You're not even interested in travel – or not anything that isn't European anyway. Portugal is an adventure for you.'

Grandmother and Professor Williams laughed. I held up my hands. 'I know nothing. It's true,' I said. I had been humbled.

'Never mind,' said Grandmother with pretend sympathy. 'You have plenty of time to start learning.'

As the fountain ran, so the conversation took its easy course and I watched and I listened but there was nothing but good humour and congeniality in all eyes. And though I make no claim to understand the mind of my grandmother – much less Madeleine's – it seemed to me as though they were getting on. (I must have been a fool, I thought, to have ever imagined otherwise.) At Madeleine's suggestion, my grandmother ordered for everyone and it was nearing midnight before we faced the happy herbal madness of our Averne – the liqueur to end all liqueurs.

Just as we were leaving, Grandmother asked: 'And your friend William – how is he?'

'Oh God, I forgot to say: he's getting married.'

We walked around the corner to my grandmother's flat on Via Gustiniani, a dimly lit street that must have looked more or less the same for four hundred years. We were a close-knit ensemble, I thought, as we stopped together outside the huge front door with its heavy iron hinges and rows of metal studs braced in the wood. Grandmother took out her key, which was comically large (as though fit for some medieval treasury), and inserted it into the lock.

'It's a knack,' she said quietly, 'you have to pull it out two millimetres and then tilt it to the left.'

She jiggled a moment. The smaller door, which had been cut into the larger, opened smoothly and we stepped inside one by one. The air smelt different – of older stone and of the cypress tree in the courtyard ahead. We fumbled along in the dark a little way until Grandmother hit the light and then we began climbing the groaning wooden stairs that led up on our left.

'I'm afraid Jasper and I have always lived on top floors,' Grandmother said to Madeleine as we paused to gather breath on one of the landings. 'I have no idea why it has turned out that way. It's a real pain. Especially at my age. But at least it means that only people who really like us ever come to visit. Isn't that right, Fergus?'

The timer lights went off and I heard Professor Williams click them on again behind me. 'That's right,' he said, out of breath. 'Absolutely right.'

By average Roman standards, Grandmother's flat is luxuriously big. Even so, the piles of books and manuscripts were encroaching – forsaking the huge dining table (never once used for dining), running past all her book shelves (stacked and banked with a librarian's ruthlessness), collecting in heaps and rolls beneath her favourite wall map ('Europe: 1492'), gathering here and there in string-drawn bundles around her leather reading chair, taking over the room in a slow but inexorable tide – and this despite her also having a separate study and a master bedroom, likewise overrun. And the books were not the only things taking up space.

'What are all these statues doing?' I asked.

'And how did you get them up here?' Madeleine added.

Professor Williams cleared his throat eloquently.

Lined up against the wall just inside the door, a collection of five shoulder-high white stone statues stood unselfconsciously on random pages of *Stampa*. Round about them on the floor, also on newspaper, lay a number of extra fragments – an arm, a head, a thigh, an ear.

'Oh – I'm guarding them for someone,' Grandmother said, as she switched on various sidelights. 'Don't worry, they aren't Roman or anything, and I promise I haven't stolen them – they're only late sixteenth century – second rate. Now, I shall make the coffee and then we –'

'Madeleine,' Professor Williams broke in, 'I'm going to take my pipe on the terrace. Would you care to join me?

Grace won't allow smoking in here, I'm afraid. Upsets the manuscripts – apparently. But out there we can do what we like. We'll smoke enough for the next hour and I'll point out some views.'

'That would be great,' Madeleine said, meaning it.

They opened the terrace doors at the far end of the room and the city raised its voice for a moment as they stepped out. Then all was quiet again.

I followed Grandmother into her kitchen, where I watched her going through the cupboard in which her coffee beans were kept. 'Do you want me to do this?' I asked.

'No – no. Of course I don't. Now what do you think? Kibo-Chagga or San Agustin? What kind of a girl is Madeleine?'

'She'll like anything you make.'

'I realize that, Jasper. I'm just wondering what would be – you know – optimum.'

'Kibo-Chagga.'

'OK.' Grandmother selected a packet, unpegged it and began pouring the beans into the electric grinder. 'Kibo-Chagga it is.'

A high-pitched whirr filled the kitchen. Grandmother shook the grinder then ground again. She turned to face me, waving the coffee under her nose. 'And don't ask me what I think about her, Jasper, because it's not a fair question.'

'What do you think about her?'

She smiled. 'I don't think anything.'

'Yes, you do, you always think things.'

'Don't be silly and don't be facetious.'

'Sorry. But anyway: what do you think?'

She reached down her espresso cups and shrugged. 'What do you want me to say? For ten years you maintain absolute silence about your relationships – you take care to keep your private life private – for which I am grateful – then one day you turn up . . . with someone. Obviously, you feel strongly. More than that. Obviously you feel very strongly.' She turned on the espresso machine. 'I for one am not going to question your judgement. I trust what you think because I know . . . I know you wouldn't think anything unthoughtful.'

'Come on, Grandma, stop talking in riddles. What's that supposed to mean?'

'Exactly what I say.' She placed the cups on top of the Brasilia to heat. 'Honestly, Jasper, *you* come on. I have known Madeleine for less than five hours.' She tested the steamer. 'Had I better froth some milk?'

'Not necessary,' I said.

'Good.'

'I wasn't asking you to be profound, Grandma. Just: do you like her?'

'And I'm saying, Jasper, that my opinion doesn't matter. I will be dead –'

'Grandma!'

'I will be dead soon enough. You will still be living with the consequences of whatever you decide. So the most important opinion is your own. And the fact is' – she locked in the metal barrel and pressed the magic button that sent the pressurized steam surging through the powdered beans – 'the fact is that I know you have made up your mind. I can see it in the way you are with her. So I am happy for you.'

Her insight was so clean and clear that I felt compelled to deny its truth. 'I have not made up my mind about anything.'

She looked me in the eye before returning to her ministrations. 'Yes, you have. You have definitely made up your mind. Or you wouldn't be standing here asking me what I think. You only ever ask me what I think when you already know what *you* think. So don't lie – and if you must, then please lie a little better.'

'I forbid you to say ever again that you are going to die soon. It's –'

'True. It's true.' She smiled – without her usual impishness but tenderly instead. 'Jasper, you have got to stop being such a romantic. Listen to me.' She turned to face me directly. 'Of course I like her very much. Yes, yes – I do. I think she is intelligent and you will never be bored. I think you will always find her attractive, which is important. I think that she is capable of dealing with you and you with her. I think she's . . . well, for want of a better word . . . I think she's your match. At my age you have an instinct for what people are really like – because you have seen it all before. And, yes, she is your equal in many ways.'

'But what?'

She sighed. 'There really is no hiding from you, is there?'

'But *what*?'

'But I think that you may not necessarily be very . . . very content.'

'What's that supposed to mean? Grandma, you can't just say that and not –'

'Jasper, don't be cross, I –'

'I'm not being cross. I just . . . I just want to know what you really think because . . . because it's important for me to know what you think. I want to – you know – I –'

'OK, OK. Dear, oh dear, oh dearie me.' The cups were full with their shots but she let them be. 'If you really want to know,' she shook her head, 'I think that Madeleine is unhappy inside of herself and that she is using you as a way of working out her upset – which, by the way, she will never admit to. Probably parents. Probably a great deal of unhappiness. I don't know. She's still young and most people's parents impair the first forty years of their lives whatever they do. In the meantime, I think that she might begin to torment you instead – to give herself some time off from tormenting herself if you like. Therefore, the only question you have to ask yourself is – simply – can you cope with it? And if so, for how long? For a year? Ten years? The rest of your life? Because it seems to me that you are going to have to be quite strong and ready for a lot of ... turbulence.' Grandmother took a long breath. 'I imagine that she never really lets her hair down emotionally – right? She never tells you that she likes you or even that she is interested in you; you spend a lot of time guessing her feelings?' I nodded slowly. Grandmother continued: 'Which can be tough going – especially for men. I'm sure that you will have your moments – everyone does – but most of the time she'll be as distant as the horizon. There could be whole years when you'll have to be prepared to care for her even though she doesn't seem to care for you.'

She let her words have a moment to themselves then allowed her eyes to flicker a second with gentle sarcasm. 'On the other hand, she may well be just the answer to whatever you yourself have been – shall we say – *looking* for. Someone to take your mind away from itself, once and for all. You probably need that. And – you know – it's not just the worst but also the best marriages – relationships, partnerships, call them what you will – that are founded on mutual need and dependency. Some turn out to be all fighting. Others turn out to be all bliss. But with her, I think you can be sure that it is never going to be one of those everyday happy-as-we-go things.' She held up her finger to stop me interrupting. 'Yes, I know you think happy-as-you-go is too dull to bear and you would rather die than be run-of-the-mill or incurious or mediocre – that's my fault, I brought you up to think that way – but now I feel slightly differently. I feel that there is a lot to be said for ease and contentment and fulfilment – there's a certain dogged grace in everydayness which is not given the credit it deserves. You can get things done, for one thing. You can make progress in other areas of life. Think about that. Anyway, they're coming back in. That's all I am saying. You'll have to fly back here and visit me again if you want to hear any more. Henceforward my lips are sealed.'

'Thank you,' I said and put my arm around her. 'I'll take those through.'

'No, you won't. They've cooled. I'll make fresh,' she said. 'And I haven't forgotten by the way: tomorrow I want to look at your work.'

We went to a nightclub after that – until four or later – somewhere in Testaccio. On the way back, I got us a little lost and we entered Trastevere by way of the market in S. Cosimato. The stalls were already setting up – a woman unloading figs from her van and the flower seller arranging his lilies. Arm in arm and gladly tired, we walked past. In the Piazza S. Maria, it started to rain.

Part Five

24. Farewell to Love

> Whilst yet to prove,
> I thought there was some deity in love
>   So did I reverence, and gave
> Worship, as atheists at their dying hour
> Call, what they cannot name, an unknown power,
>   As ignorantly did I crave:

The way she did it wasn't even cruel. A quiet assassin on a routine evening job at the kasbah: the swish of the light-weight cloak, the intimate glint of the sliver-thin knife, the first incision, the smothering hand to the mouth, a flick left, a slit right, a little exertion for the final upward stroke that splits the ribs and touches the heart; her victim slumps, but already the assassin is fading into the crowd and away with the dusk.

She must have arrived at Bristol Gardens around seven. Definitely, she was a little early, because I was still in the bath (with the door to my bedroom propped open so that I could listen to Bach's D Major suite) when the buzzer sounded. Without rancour, I stood up, dried hastily and made for the hall. The lock popped smoothly below. I went down to wait for her at the bottom of my stairs.

It was the last Friday in September. A week after we had returned from Rome. We were going to a firework display together. Not going all that far. Just down to the garden in fact, for the residents' association bonfire. (This event is staged annually, in the last week of September. According to the literature that we had both been sent, the purported purpose of this ongoing calendar shift is to assist the local fire service in its aim to 'spread fire risks traditionally associated with November 5th over the whole year and thus help to ensure a more cost-effective and tailored service for individual fire risk scenarios'.) And yes, I know, I know, I know: the prospect of residents' associations, of fireworks, of bonfires, of sparklers, of holding hands beneath an amorous garland of stars should have been the cue for frantic bouts of reversed peristalsis all round. But the devil love is a sick little son of a bitch and his last waltz is always the schmaltziest.

I opened my front door in my towel. She smiled and I kissed her. She was, I noticed, dressed more soberly than usual: dark trousers, black lightweight canvas training shoes, a merino wool turtle-neck and a leather jacket that I had not seen before. The weather had relapsed into its customary madness and we had suffered an unusually cold day. I remember the pleasant thought occurred to me that a whole winter of taking even more of her clothes off lay ahead.

'Sorry,' I said, stepping back to let her past, 'I'm still in the bath, but I won't be long. There's wine open on the table.' I pushed the door shut and followed her up the stairs.

'It's OK, there's no massive rush,' she said over her shoulder. 'They only just lit the fire. I saw them carrying the paraffin cans from my window.'

'That means they'll be getting going with the food and things soon, though. I'll get a move on.' But I lingered, watching her from the threshold of my bedroom, stupefied anew by the disregard that beauty pays itself.

She helped herself to a glass from the cupboard and said: 'The cleaner was early, so I was done by five. I thought I might as well come straight over.'

'You have a cleaner now?'

'No, it was just a one-off. A nice guy from this new student company. He did a neat job.'

She came towards me and placed her hand on my chest, fingers spread and tensed so that I could feel her nails. But she kissed me softly.

'I think I'll wear my emerald sarong tonight; what do you reckon?'

'No. Not right at all.'

I considered. 'You think mauve?'

'Or something black.' She left me and went in search of the bottle.

I turned, but just as I got back into the bathroom, the telephone rang.

Madeleine answered it.

She stuck her head through the door: 'It's Roy Junior.'

I frowned. Roy only ever called when an order was ready to be collected and I had ordered nothing. 'What does he want?'

She shrugged.

'Tell him I'll call him back.'

I pulled the plug out of the bath and ran the shower to speed things up.

Bach's harpsichord walked a slow and stately march behind his grief-stricken violin.

We squeezed through the crush of off-road vehicles (mostly parked off the road and on the pavement) and made our way towards the main garden gate. An improvised walkway had been created between the backs of two wooden benches and people had formed a short queue. When we arrived at the front, we handed our red residents' tickets to the elderly man in charge of admissions. He nodded and looked up. I returned his smile and carelessly allowed my arm to rest lightly around Madeleine's waist.

The garden had been divided into three. Most people were gathered just beyond the entrance where a number of makeshift tables had been set up. Hot punch, hot potatoes, hot sausage sandwiches, mulled wine and what looked suspiciously like parkin were being dispensed.

Further up was the bonfire itself – actually quite small – and beyond that a roped-off (or, rather, stringed-off) area, which was strictly out of bounds for all but the industrious and responsible few, whose job it was to bustle about in pastel-coloured fleeces and administer the fireworks.

There was quite a crowd, maybe one hundred and fifty people all told. The infants were up on their fathers' shoulders around the bonfire, or held askew against their attractive mothers' sides while clutching soggy pieces of cake in their tiny hands. The older children, meanwhile, ran this way and that, threatening to knock over the tables or collide with the elderly or trip on over-lengthy shoelaces headlong into the flames. And, as usual, it was impossible for anyone to tell exactly how old the teenagers were and so a rather arbitrary system of age-assessment seemed to be in operation at the mulled wine table where two jowly fathers in their fifties dispensed plastic cups to the accompaniment of various embarrassing observations or rebuffs: 'Take it easy, son, that's your third'; or 'Oh 'ello 'ello Jonathan, back again, are we? It affects your performance, you know'; or 'Well, go on then, Louise, but please don't tell your mother'; or 'You'll have to make do with the fruit punch for another couple of years yet Stacey, I'm afraid, there's plenty of time for alcohol later on.'

It was completely dark now and above us the cranes of the Paddington basin developments loured against the sky like the gruesome overlords of a science-fiction comic. Every few minutes another train could be heard moaning and heaving its way out of the station.

For the first hour or so, we stood around, sampling the fare, exchanging pleasantries, joining in. Madeleine drank both her mulled wine and mine and mine again and some more of hers (I can't stand the wretched stuff) and I ate an unreflecting jacket potato and a piece of the parkin.

A little while later, we stood by the fire, swapping crabbed sentences with a rueful couple in their early thirties. (Not-so-newly-weds: together for ever but discretely mourning the passing away of their sexiness nevertheless.) Then the word went around that the display was starting and, taking advantage of the diversion, we slipped away to join the people pushing into position for the best view.

There were hisses and bangs and banshee screeches and those quick-fire rat-a-tat explosions that sound so like the gunfire you hear on the news. Showers of light illuminated the inky night – first a bluish glare, then carmine red, next a soft potassium silver, then a hard magnesium white, perse, verdigris, cadmium yellow . . . Everybody whispered and gasped and pointed, partly for the benefit of the children, but partly because, despite themselves, they were still prone to awe in the presence of what would have once been regarded as magic. (The sharp intake of breath at the wizard's sparking wand, the sudden quickening of the heart at the sizzle and flash of the weird sisters' pot as they cast in the lizard's teeth, the pigeon gizzard . . .) We stood side-by-side in the small crowd, staring upwards in that wide-eyed, open-mouthed way that the entire human race must forever watch fireworks regardless of age, sex, creed or circumstance.

What kind of mood was I in? Aside from my potato and the colours, I cannot recall much about the first part of the evening. I guess that for once I was not thinking forwards or backwards or even side to side; rather I was living in the moment, enjoying myself. Doubtless, I was looking forward to going to bed. But even in this I was no longer feeling the ache of round-the-clock necessity; Madeleine and I had been together for a good few months by then, and the emotional weather had shifted a few points on the barometer, bringing less fervid seas and a calmer, deeper swell. If I were to go out on a recollective limb, I would say that I was ... well, content. I do remember that I had the idea to take Madeleine to Italy for Christmas – after I had finished the last of the poems.

What kind of mood was she in? Well now, that is the question. What kind of mood was Madeleine Belmont in? I can tell you what kind of mood she *seemed* to be in: wound down, comfortable, cosy, calm, at ease. I would even go so far as friendly. And I swear she squeezed my hand before she asked if I would come across the lawn with her.

A sidelight cast a sepulchral glow through the lily-white curtains that hung at her new patio doors. I breathed the smoky night air. She took out her keys and turned the locks one by one: click, click, click.

My initial thought was that she must have planned on returning to her flat all along so that we could sleep there for the first time – we never had – a kind of sacramental act. Though still without books or any real evidence of her person, the main room looked as though it was finished. Where previously there had been only twisted or severed wires, now there were brass plugs and dimmer switches, and where I remembered plaster and holes, the walls were now painted in pale cream against the dark stained wood of the sanded and polished floorboards, which, when I took off my shoes, felt smooth and slippery beneath my socks. An artist's drawing of the lost New York skyline hung near the table.

'Sit down, Jasper,' she said, indicating an unashamedly new, calico-covered futon that faced her windows. I did as I was told, taking her serious tone for play. She crossed over towards her kitchen area.

'Where did you get this?'

'Online. Would you like a drink?'

'What are you having?'

'I'm having water.'

'OK. That's fine.' I sat back. 'Hey, you know, as futons go, this is really quite comfortable. I can never work out how to make them flat.'

She didn't answer. Still I thought that she was building up to some minor surprise – new clothes, a present, the new bed. I looked over to where she was standing with her back to me, cracking ice cubes. The clock on her oven said ten thirty-five.

She came back with the two glasses of water and set them down without looking at me.

'Thanks,' I said. 'The flat looks amazing. I can't believe the difference.'

'You haven't been here for a while, that's all.' She left her drink and walked behind me, towards the hall. 'It's finished.'

I heard the sound of running taps in the bathroom. I sipped my water. She had put a slice of lime in with the ice, just as I liked. I thought about putting some music on and looked around for her little portable disc-player. No sign.

When, a minute or two later, she returned, I was mildly surprised that she hadn't changed. She threw a coat over the back of one of her dining chairs and moved another one round so that she could sit opposite me. Her back was to the side-lamp. She reached across for the ashtray on the dining table and placed it on the floor in front of her. Her expression was impassive. But her skin had a sort of lustre. She had, I realized, just washed her face.

She said nothing for a long time but looked at me instead with an eerie blankness – eyes still, mouth tight shut, running her tongue back and forth over her teeth. At first I too sat still. But after a while, I reached forward to touch the side of her face and ask her what was wrong. Calmly, she took hold of my wrist and moved my hand away.

And then, in a measured voice, she began. 'Jasper, I want to talk to you about Lucy.'

'Lucy?'

'Yes. Lucy.'

'Lucy who?'

'The Lucy you were with before me, Jasper. The Lucy who came to find you at the ball – when I was getting stuff to clean you up. Lucy Giddings.'

'Lucy who I used to go out with?'

'Lucy who you said you were going to marry.'

'I never said . . .' And now, at last, I saw it.

Madeleine spoke quietly: 'Lucy is my sister.'

25. The Curse

The venom of all stepdames, gamesters' gall,
What tyrants, and their subjects interwish,
What plants, mines, beasts, fowl, fish,
Can contribute, all ill which all
Prophets, or poets spake; and all which shall
Be annexed in schedules unto this by me,
Fall on that man; for if it be a she
Nature beforehand hath out-cursed me.

My head felt like it was swelling, overheated, humming with cross-wired currents of panic and anger and confusion and guilt; the sudden shame-fever of a child who has been caught in some terrible act.

'Jasper, listen, we don't have long. I probably should have left more time . . .' She sat forward, her elbows on her knees, shoulders slightly hunched and her hands loosely joined.

My voice was thin and sounded strange even to my own ears: 'Your sister? I don't understand.'

'Same father,' Madeleine said, softly. She lit a cigarette and dropped the match into the ashtray. 'There's no good way of doing this. So I'm just going to give it you straight: Lucy and I planned everything, Jasper, even down to the number of lunchtimes I made you wait at Danilo's. Shepherd's Bush, that fucked-up dinner party with those two idiots I conjured up – Christ that was boring, and you have no *idea* how rude I have had to be to get them out my life – the sunbathing, that sun dress, which days I went out there' – she jerked her thumb to indicate the garden behind her – 'and for how long. We planned everything. We knew that you would see me from your studio. We knew that you wouldn't be able to help yourself. We knew you would take the bait.' She half-smiled. 'We even guessed where you'd take me for dinner. The only thing that surprised us was how careful you were, how long you took ... Anyhow, the point is: we planned everything – or nearly everything. The umbrella wasn't our idea.' She stuck out her lower lip and blew her smoke up towards the ceiling away from me. 'Sorry. But you deserved it.'

Now she hesitated, as if waiting for me to speak, but a cold was crawling in the marrow of my bones and I was paralysed and dumb.

So she went on. 'I lied about my name. Nobody who actually knows me calls me Madeleine. Everybody calls me Bella. It's from my middle name. I think I've been Bella ever since my mother died ... so, obviously, it was me living with Lucy when you were ... when you were with her. I was her flatmate. I am Bella.' She looked at me steadily. 'Lucy calls me Bella like everyone else. I use my real name for the newspapers and my book, but only my father calls me Madeleine to my face. And now you.'

Again she hesitated.

'You realize ... you understand that Lucy has been very ill? Because of you. Directly because of your behaviour.' Her anger surged suddenly – as if the fearsome amount of energy required to withhold her real feelings for so long was now coursing violently into their expression. 'You damaged her way more than you could ever even guess. She found out about Selina of course and she was already forgiving you for that; but it was all the others. Christ, you must have thought she was an idiot. And then – when she's already in pieces – you go and write her a letter, *boasting* about how you've been fucking around.'

'I know.' My throat was dry. 'I know it –'

'No. You. Don't. Know.' She leant forward towards me – close – and I thought she was going to strike me or push her cigarette into my face. 'When I came back, the day after you helped her move, she was a mess. She wouldn't go to work. She could barely talk. Then you inform her not to worry because – oh – actually it is *much* worse than she thought and –'

'I wish that –'

'Let me finish. As a direct result of what happened . . . of what you *inflicted*, my sister had a breakdown. You fucked her up. You did that to her. She wasn't stupid or overly possessive or ruining your life or anything, she wasn't asking you to go out of your way for her. She might even have been OK if you'd just told her the truth. But instead you treated her like she was – like she was nothing. Like a piece of shit that you just had to *manage*. Jasper, she cared about you. She would have done anything for you. Nobody deserves to be treated so badly. No woman. No human being.'

Guilt ground in my stomach like blood and broken teeth.

She dropped her eyes from mine, then glanced at the oven clock. Her voice regained its self-control. 'Lucy told me all about you. In fact, she talked about you a lot. She was – I suppose this is true – she was in love with you. And not stupidly or blindly or girlishly or whatever . . . she thought you were going to marry her.'

'I never ever said that.'

Madeleine ignored me. 'We had the idea when she was in for treatment. I suppose it started out as a sort of therapy for her. I didn't know you and I hated you anyway.

'I don't understand.' Through the shock, I could feel my own anger surfacing. There were questions. 'You mean, you bought this flat just to—'

'No, of course not. I bought this flat because it was a good place to buy: cheap for where it is and fixable for a profit. But, obviously, Lucy was the one who told me about it in the flist place. She nearly bought it herself. I hadn't been able to look because I had been in the States. I needed somewhere fast and I took her word for it. No point scouring London since she'd already done the job for me. You can usually trust a sister's judgement.' Her matter-of-fact tone was just as hostile as her raw anger – the poison starting its work on the blood just as the fangs withdraw. 'But then, naturally, when the sale went through . . . well, it just seemed like too good an opportunity to miss. I kind of owed Lucy for saving me from getting married to that arsehole in Buenos Aires when I was younger. I had a few months set aside to do this place up . . . and, you know, we were just going to see how far we could go, to get at you, to make you suffer. It was a summer project. And I guess I kind of liked the idea of fucking you up. It's true – we were worried because Lucy had told you quite a lot about me – working for the newspapers and all that – but you never figured it out. Even at that ball, when she insisted on coming to see you after that guy hit you – that was a mistake, by the way.'

I'd had enough. 'You're saying that all of this . . .' I got up. And suddenly I was leaning over her and shouting. 'You're saying that all of this has been about some kind of private game between you and her. You were sleeping with me out of some kind of *revenge*?'

For a second I saw the flicker of fear in her eyes but she kept quite still and countered my aggression with quiet, baiting sarcasm. 'Yes. A game if you like. Revenge makes it all sound so histrionic, Jasper, but yeah – I guess that kind of covers it.' She looked up at me. 'I needed somewhere to stay while the work was being done. Once you passed up on me after dinner – well then, I thought, OK – so, right, I'm gonna really enjoy myself here, have some fun.'

I was shaking.

There was silence.

'Jasper: it was meant to be a lot quicker – a sort of joke – it wasn't meant to go on like this.' She bent to poke out her cigarette. 'Now it's nearly October and the estate agents on your street have got my flat rented out from next week and here we are and I have to go. I've left it way too late as it is.' She stood up. 'I have a plane to catch.'

Now we faced each other in bitter mimicry of two people about to kiss. Her self-control was killing me. I wanted to hit her. 'Where are you going?'

She stood her ground. 'I'm going to New York.'

'On a trip? Right now?' So complete was the devastation of her ambush, that it had not entered my mind that there might be worse to come. 'You're going on another trip and you decided to tell me all this shit in two fucking minutes?'

She met my anger with more stillness but there was resolve in her voice. 'Not on a trip. No, Jasper. Actually the truth is . . . the real truth is that I'm going to get married.'

I laughed in her face. 'To get *married*?'

'Yes. I am going to get married.'

But for the first time in all the time I had known her, her face was nothing but sincere.

Her buzzer sounded.

'*Shit*. That's my cab.' She ducked away, crossing the room to pick up her entryphone. 'You're a bit early, can you give me five minutes?'

She was putting on her coat. 'Jasper, there's no time for me to explain any more of this. I've been engaged for a long while. My wedding is in March – in a few months. I'm packed. I'm leaving tonight. The flat is finished. It's all done.

It's being rented out on Monday. I'm just not going to be here any more.' She shrugged. 'I'm sorry. But now, please, Jasper, you have to go.'

My anger turned to panic. I was no longer thinking. Whatever came to my lips, I said. 'I'm not going.'

'Jasper, you must leave.'

'Change your mind.'

'No.'

'Change your mind.'

'No.'

I went over and took hold of her. 'Maddy, change your mind. Don't go. What about everything we did, what about –'

'No. I know what you think. But you're wrong. I have made my decision. I . . . It has been fun. But I won't change my mind. I can't change my mind. I'm going to get married.' At last there was a catch in her voice. 'Oh God, maybe I should just have gone to the airport without trying to . . . I'm sorry, Jasper.'

I held her shoulders in my hands. From somewhere far away, my tears were coming and no matter how I blinked I could not stop them.

She was speaking softly now and her eyes sought mine. 'I didn't mean to do this so . . . so quickly. But it's better if I just go. For everyone. Really, Jasper, I am sorry. You know that I am. I wish . . . I wish that I hadn't been so . . . I don't know what. I'm sorry.'

She stepped away, out of my reach and gathered herself with a conscious breath. 'I don't think we should see each other again. I mean it. Once I am gone, please do not try to get into contact with me. If you do find out my address or telephone number, I will not open your letters and I will not return your calls. If you send anything to my computer, I will delete it. If you bother me or pester me in any way, then

I will contact the police. I will, Jasper. You know I will. Please, I mean it: don't come looking for me.' She emphasized her words. 'I do not want to see you again, Jasper.'

The buzzer hummed low.

'*Fucking* cab drivers.'

'Madeleine, this is insane. I –'

She spoke into the entryphone. 'Yes, I know. Just give me two minutes. I'll be out at eleven.'

'This is so fucked up.'

'Jasper, I've got to lock everything.'

'Change your mind.'

'Jasper, please.' She came over and physically tried to turn me towards the patio doors. 'Please.'

'This is not the end.'

'Go.'

'Madeleine.'

'Go.'

I picked up my shoes and went out into the garden where the last of the bonfire cackled and spat.

26. Twickenham Garden

Blasted with sighs, and surrounded with tears,
    Hither I come to seek the spring,
    And at mine eyes, and at mine ears,
Receive such balms, as else cure everything;
    But O, self traitor, I do bring
The spider love, which transubstantiates all,
    And can convert manna to gall,
And that this place may thoroughly be thought
    True paradise, I have the serpent brought.

'Twere wholsomer for me, that winter did
    Benight the glory of this place,
    And that a grave frost did forbid
These trees to laugh, and mock me to my face;
    But that I may not this disgrace
Endure, nor yet leave loving, Love, let me
    Some senseless piece of this place be;
Make me a mandrake, so I may groan here,
    Or a stone weeping out my year.

Hither with crystal vials, lovers come,
    And take my tears, which are love's wine,
And try your mistress' tears at home,
For all are false, that taste not just like mine;
    Alas, hearts do not in eyes shine,
Nor can you more judge woman's thoughts by tears,
    Than by her shadow, what she wears.
O perverse sex, where none is true but she,
    Who's therefore true, because her truth kills me.

27. The Broken Heart

> Ah, what a trifle is a heart,
>> If once into Love's hands it come!
> All other griefs allow a part
>> To other griefs, and ask themselves but some . . .

A scruffy, hand-delivered envelope had been placed on the flimsy wicker post-table in the communal entrance hall. The scrawl was childish – the Js of my name like meat hooks. I read the note.

> Jazz – give me a bell at the shop tomorrow. It's about yr bird. She's pissing u about mate. Video evidence. Thought u should know. Roy.

The sudden warmth of being inside was melting my eyes. I tore up the cheap paper and dropped it into the recycle bin. Then for no reason I ran up the stairs, taking them two or three at a time.

But with key still in the lock, I stopped cold. The television was on in my flat. I shut the door loudly behind me. Abruptly, the sound died. I stood still. Someone was coming to the head of my little staircase.

'Jasper?'

I walked up.

William looked at me steadily but he said nothing.

I went straight past him into my studio and crossed to the window. Her lights were still off. Her flat was in total darkness. I stood, looking down into the garden.

William spoke in a low voice from the lighted doorway: 'I've just seen Lucy. She called me. She told me everything. I came straight over. I let myself in with the spares you gave –'

'I don't believe it, Will. I just don't believe her. I can't believe she's done this. She *can't* have left it this late. She must be staying somewhere else in town. There's no way she would –'

'Her flight took off five minutes ago. She's already in the air. She's gone.'

'How do you know?'

'Lucy said.' He grimaced but his voice remained even and measured: 'Lucy wasn't sure if Madel— Lucy wasn't sure if *Bella* was even going to tell you. I mean – Lucy thought she might just disappear off and not say anything or make up some bullshit story and I think Lucy wanted . . . I think Lucy thought it would be better coming from me once she'd gone.'

'What time is it?'

'One.' He paused. 'Where have you been?'

'Sitting on a bench out there.' I turned from the window. 'There was no need for Lucy to be so concerned. The bitch made everything very clear.'

'I think actually that was what Lucy was really worried about. That Madeleine would tell you.'

'Oh Jesus, Will, she's been lying to everybody for months. Me. Him. You. For Christ's sake, she's absolutely fucking insane. But – you know what? – I think she means it: I think she's actually going to marry this guy. I shouldn't have left. I should have stayed with her. I should have . . . I should have got in the fucking cab with her.'

'I know.' William shifted in the doorway. 'I mean – I know about the other guy. I know she means it. Lucy told me everything.'

'Who is he? *Who the fuck is he?*' I met William's eye directly. 'How long . . . did Lucy say?'

He gave me the truth without looking away or changing the evenness of his voice. 'According to Lucy: three years.'

'Christ.'

'They met at some work thing apparently. Lucy wouldn't say any more. She said it wasn't important. She said what her sister wanted to tell you about her American life was up to her.' William became brisk. 'Listen, Jasper, anyway, I was meant to be going home tonight – home home, I mean – to Norfolk. I'm supposed to be picking up a car. Come with me. Come up and stay for a few days or a week or whatever – there's plenty of room and my parents are in London anyway – you can have a whole fucking wing if you need. It's not exactly cramped. Bring your calligraphy stuff. Seriously. I am in one of the tramp carriers – it's just outside. We can put everything in the back – there's room for a whole orchestra's worth of bin lids in there, we must be able to fit your board in – and whatever else you need. We can load it up right now and fuck off. I'll help. Tell me what stuff you want me to take. Pack some clothes. Get out of London. Finish your work. Think straight. Clear head. That sort of thing.'

I should have gone back to her.

But in the garden, I hesitated. I turned and turned again. I felt wrenchingly, acidly sick in the centre of my stomach. I thought that I might vomit. I rushed as far as the big gate – swallowing gulps of air and thinking that I must get home – but on the pavement outside I span around once more and, ignoring the spasms, I half-ran, half-pushed my way back inside.

People were leaving past me – teenagers, couples, young families. I barged through, scaring mothers, angering fathers, but paying no attention to their protests.

Ahead, two men were spraying the trees nearer the fire with water from a hose.

I rattled at her locks and rapped on her windows but the lights were out. She had gone. I knew it was hopeless but I carried on – banging, knocking, shaking – until, eventually, an old man with a torch came and shone his beam upon me.

I muttered excuses and made to leave. But I could not bring myself to go home and I could not imagine what I would do when I got there. So I sat on the bench and waited while they turned the hoses on the bonfire itself. By midnight the garden was empty.

The Transit van was noisy and slow. But the roads were quiet. And we were out of London quickly, driving east through the ghosted city before turning north for Cambridge. The engine was low geared and even fourth took us no faster than sixty-five. The heater clattered and whirred and the steering wheel juddered in William's hands. Now and then a car would blaze in the rearview mirror and William would pull back into the crawler lane until it had passed.

For almost two hours, neither of us spoke. I sat, watching tail-lights fade or staring into the blackness just above the feeble limit of the van's illumination. The windscreen wipers interfered with the radio's reception. So we turned it off.

The motorway gave way to a main road but after another half-hour, we struck off, due east, heading out across the fens. The drizzle stopped and it began to feel colder.

'You know I think there are some tramp smokes in the glove compartment,' William said, looking across, 'if you want one.'

'No – fuck it. Anything to drink?'

'Doubt it – the boys never leave their booze behind. Not the trampish way, I'm afraid.'

'Should have brought some. I wasn't thinking.' I looked out of the side window. A three-quarter moon rode out through a gap in the clouds, lighting their edges in armoured silver for a moment before being obscured once more. I wondered when it would turn light. It was freezing cold. There were shrouds of fog floating over the fens to our left. I sat on my hands.

Suddenly, William swore. 'Fuck. I just remembered there might be some miniatures in my bag actually. I was given them on the plane – last week. They'll be in the end pocket – the hand luggage bag – I don't think I took them out. Can you climb back or shall I stop?'

I had already unbuckled my seatbelt and was clambering over the passenger bench into the back. I found William's bag and called forward, steadying myself against the roll of a corner. 'Two miniature vodkas, a gin and a brandy. Is four right?'

'Think so.'

I dropped back into the front.

'I'd start with the vodka if I were you. Then the brandy.' William changed gear. 'That way you won't be able to taste the gin when you get to it.'

'Good thinking.'

We hadn't seen any other cars for a while. We came to a stop and turned sharp left on to a minor road. There was a humpbacked bridge. William crunched up through the gear box. On the far side, we entered the first wreaths of the fog.

Soon enough, it had closed in around us – dense and wet and eerie.

'Thirty more miles of this shit, I'm afraid,' William said, driving much more slowly and staring ahead. 'We're crossing the Wensum marshes. At least the road is straight and we're not going to meet anyone coming the other way. Let's just hope the bloody van doesn't give up on us. Look at it out there. I don't fancy walking. Believe me, this stuff gets into your bones.'

I opened the vodka and tasted it. 'What sort of a state was Lucy in?'

William kept his eyes fixed ahead. 'She was OK – together, I mean. She was in a funk about you and what was going on – but she wasn't foaming at the mouth or hallucinating or slitting her wrists. Just anxious that I go round and find you. I called from hers around nine. But you didn't answer your phone so I just came over straight away. I was watching those bloody fireworks actually, and I was rather shitting myself that you would come back with Madeleine – I can't call her Bella, it's ridiculous – and that you would be none the wiser. Christ knows what I would have said then.'

'Lucy said about her name?'

'Yes. I thought it might be something to do with her surname – Belmont – but it's not. Her middle name is Isabella. And everyone calls her B —'

'I know.'

'Lucy told me the whole fucked-up jamboree of their family's history.'

I took a proper swig. 'She tell you how come they are sisters?'

'Same father.' The road was dead straight and William risked a bit more speed. The fog swirled – there was no other word for it.

'That's what Madeleine said.' I finished the first miniature. 'But I've met Lucy's father – David. He's called David. He can't possibly . . . He's nothing to do with Madeleine. He's –

'Not her real father, Jackson. It all goes back to the real father. Lucy's real father is none other than Mr Foreign Office himself. Madeleine's father. She told you about him, didn't she?'

'Oh Jesus.' I let out a low whistle.

'Quite so. Julian Belmont is his name –' He glanced over. 'He's number three in Paris now – so Donald tells me. Used to fuck everything that moved. Still something of a rake.'

I looked over sharply. 'You asked Don to find out about Madeleine's dad?'

'No. I did not. Donald e-mailed me about something else. I'm going to New York next month to oversee the opening of our Christmas concert special – and he mentioned it in passing. That was all.'

I cracked my second vodka. 'I don't understand. How is this Julian guy Lucy's father?'

'OK,' William slowed again and wiped at the windscreen with his sleeve. The fog was seeping in. He cranked up the heater to four and raised his voice against the racket. 'Way back in the deep fried days of the early seventies, Julian Belmont married Madeleine's mother – also called Magdalena, in case you didn't know, and also, according to Lucy, suffering far more than her fair share of the affliction otherwise known as feminine beauty. Anyway, the young and happy couple are living together in London for no longer than a year before Mrs Belmont finds herself in the family way with your . . . with sweet little Madeleine Isabella.

'Soon enough – true to previous form and despite the fact that his wife looks like a latter-day Helen of Troy – Mr B. starts playing the field again. And guess who one of his very next conquests turns out to be? Lucy's mother. Who is, unfortunately, I might add, already married to someone else – the nice man whom Lucy refers to as Dad.'

'David.'

'David. That's what Lucy calls him too, isn't it? David? Always suspicious when a child calls a parent by a Christian name actually –'

A rabbit bolted across the road in front of us. William braked and my board and boxes all slid forward in the back. The frantic creature ran wildly along the verge – darting and bobbing, desperate to get out of the headlights. Then, just as quickly, it was gone.

'Sorry. Is your stuff OK?'

'Don't worry – the important things are in the hard cases. Go on.'

'So, anyway, Madeleine is conceived, Lucy is conceived: different mothers, same father. London is busy letting its hair down but all is obviously not well *chez* Belmont. Magdalena suspects her husband of doing the dirty and is drinking hard trying to prove it. Meanwhile, Lucy's mum –'

'Veronica.'

'Lucy's mum, Veronica, is going up the wall with her secret love for the dashing Mr B.'

'Jesus.'

'And so, one dark and baleful night, she – Veronica – comes looking for the man himself and is more than a little surprised when his darling wife answers the door.'

'What a fucking mess.'

'Quite so. Mr B. returns from a hard day shuffling paper to find not one but two unhappy pregnant women waiting for him. An unholy alliance. And the shit, as they say, has hit the fan.'

I winced. But I was enjoying the vodka at last.

William continued. 'Again, this is according to Lucy: David and Veronica were – are – unable to have children, and so Veronica decides to confess to David what has been going on. This confession goes down badly. But anyway, having left her husband chucking glasses at the wall, Veronica's first plan is actually to see how lover boy Julian feels about her leaving poor old David altogether and the two of them – Veronica and Julian – taking off into the sunset. However, as she now discovers, Julian is already married – and the main issue turns out to be not what Mr B. thinks about it all, but what his beautiful half-Italian alcoholic nutcase of a wife has to say.'

'Half-Italian?'

'Seemingly so. A Roman. In any case, the upshot is that Magdalena goes into permanent rage – refuses to talk to her husband or leave the house in his company – very bad news at Foreign Office bashes. And worse, she takes to drinking even more seriously – new-born baby or not – until eventually, ten months down the line, she decides to wash her evening case of grappa down with a box of pills chaser. Dead.'

'Poor woman.'

'Meanwhile, on the other side, Lucy's mother, who has seen Julian for what he is and detests both him and the very earth he walks upon, has started to suffer from post-natal depression and almost goes off the deep end too. See how the sins of the mothers are visited upon the daughters.' William shook his head. 'In fact, the only person to come out of the whole sorry show with any credit is Mr David Giddings, who somehow finds it within himself to forgive his wife so that Lucy can be brought up as if she were his own daughter – albeit with a generous input of cash for school fees, birthdays and so on from the real culprit.

'Age thirteen the girls – Lucy and Madeleine – are sent

to the same boarding school – guilt-wracked Julian footing
the bill from Paris. Lucy's mother accepts the money but
insists that Lucy is told the truth now that she's growing up.
Plus – so Lucy reckons – Veronica thought it would be a good
idea for Lucy to know that she had a sister in the same school
in case she became lonely or homesick or whatever – because
she didn't want Lucy to be trailing home back to London the
minute she got upset. Anyway, it worked. Lucy and Madeleine become best friends for life. The two of them united by
rock-bottom opinions of their mothers, a deep distrust of
their father and, I suspect, grave but undiagnosed problems
resulting in full-blown psychosis on the subject of young
men. Enter J. Jackson Esq.'

I switched to the brandy.

At some murky place that looked indistinguishable from
any other that we had passed, William clicked the indicator
on. 'People don't realize that, in certain circumstances, it is
still possible to indicate ironically,' he said. 'Now please –
please let me finish that brandy, Jasper, I can't stand it any
more.' He turned hard left. 'The next twelve miles are private
and if any fucker wants to stop me drinking, they can take
it up with Edward II.'

I handed him what was left.

28. A Nocturnal upon St Lucy's Day

Study me then, you who shall lovers be
At the next world, that is, at the next spring:
    For I am every dead thing,
     In whom love wrought new alchemy.
       For his art did express
A quintessence even from nothingness,
From dull privations, and lean emptiness
He ruined me, and I am re-begot
Of absence, darkness, death; things which are not.

For two weeks, I have been working with my crow quills –
slowly, patiently, applying the fine filigree detail to the versals,
moving through the whole sequence of poems for the second
time. There can be no mistakes in this – the smallest slip will
mean starting an entire poem again. But my concentration is
unwavering and the care I take in every consideration exact.

Outside, the tall poplar trees are bent and tugged about
by an October wind and there is a morning mist that drifts
and straggles across the lawns. The Norfolk sky is the colour
of watered-down ink run thin to almost nothing; but when
the morning clears and the autumn sun climbs, I will be able
to see for miles – out past the rhododendron trees, across
the river, over the fens and towards the sea.

It is quite early still, and cold. When we arrived, William
suggested I light the fire – set and ready in the grate – but I
was worried about the smoke affecting the vellum. So he
found me some old oil heaters and I have turned them all
on. They are lethally hot to the touch and yet somehow I
can't help but feel they are making the room colder. Perhaps
it is something to do with convection and high ceilings.

Perhaps it is because I have foolishly set up my board in this draught-beset bay window. But the light is irresistible and I have found a pair of fingerless gloves.

This morning, I am flourishing the last poem: 'Woman's Constancy'. Although my deadline is 25th October, I want to give myself a week with my magnifying glass back in London. Also, I would like to deliver them early to Gruber and Gruber, the framers, so as to allow as much time as possible in case the wood has to be ordered. Today is Saturday and I should be finished in an hour or two.

The first few days here passed slowly. Insisting that I must stay, William returned to London on the Monday for his business. And I made friends with Ellie, the Laceys' house-keeper, and her husband, Jim. When I wasn't working, I ate Welsh rarebit on my lap by an open fire and went through William's father's record library. I read without concentration and turned films off whenever the romantic interest declared itself. I walked around the lake into the village and talked marine disasters with a barman who used to live in Talla-hassee. Now and then I considered stealing the keys to one of the cars and driving all the way to Rome – sleeping with every woman that I met on the way.

My thoughts gathered painfully, limping in from across the filthy battlefield, one by one, under cover of darkness – wounded, bedraggled, dismembered. But soon they had mustered in such numbers as to require ordering.

I tried to be methodical, mainly to avoid sending myself mad as I lay awake watching the shadows of the trees, but also because I wanted to establish whether there was any chance that my mind might agree with my heart on the abysmal subject of what to do next – or whether I was just going to have to act regardless.

Initially, I'm not sure whether it was the coolness or the sheer scale of Madeleine's deceit that appalled me – that *frightened* me – the most. Whether planned or spontaneous, her capacity for falsehood was breathtaking. Everything that had happened I now looked back on with suspicious eyes. She must have known, I thought, that it was Lucy who was calling me that night, when she stood listening as I pretended to talk to William – hence her yanking the phone from its socket to remove any further threat until such time as she could deal with her sister in person. (The *bitch*. And what a fool I must have seemed to her as I garbled inanities into the receiver.) Then, of course, there were the trips abroad, which, I now saw, she had probably fabricated: Amman was likely to be true but the Philadelphia fat wars? The crayfish festival? They were surely lies; on both occasions, she was probably with him. I recalled how she had directed the conversation away from details when Professor Williams had showed an interest in Sacramento. She was only ever visiting him.

Did he come to London? He must have done. For one thing, I thought, he must have been to see her flat on the day that she left. That must have been when Roy caught them with his video camera. Nauseously, I recalled that the night before the bonfire Madeleine had gone 'to stay at her father's'. How many other times had this happened? How many other times had Madeleine gone to visit her 'father'? I couldn't be sure. (Did her father even have a place in London? Why should he? He lived in Paris.) I became convinced: whenever she was not with me – she was with *him*. How many nights were they together? How many nights did they spend just across the garden, sleeping in her assassin's camp bed? I didn't know. Surely it was too great a risk even for her. But such a possibility wasn't beyond her audacity and I couldn't quite see into her flat from mine.

I realized, of course, how much contempt there was for me in her composure. During the months we were together, the only time she had looked even vaguely unsettled was soon after we first 'met', when I asked her what people called her – that time when we were coming back from Camden on the barge and I was trying to find out about her boyfriend. (The harsh hysterical laughter of hindsight: I knew ... in my veins, I knew.)

Worst of all was the psychological torture that she must have enjoyed – *relished* – administering. Her little flirtation in Rome seemed inconsequential by comparison with the schedule of cruelties she had dealt out. Then there was all that 'so what did you do to her' questioning at that bastard ball ... The ball. Here my thoughts turned from anger and humiliation to something else ... not hope exactly but something less sickening than the rest.

My guess (so many guesses) was that Lucy and Madeleine had fought that night. Perhaps Madeleine's crossness when she came into the room had not, after all, been directed at me. Perhaps their quarrel was caused as much by Lucy's anger with her sister (when confronted with the evidence of how far Madeleine had let things drift) as it was by Madeleine's anger at Lucy for wanting to be alone with me after I had been hit.

Jesus Christ. Did they plan to have me hit? Or was that a bonus? They could not have known that Selina was going to be there. Could they? Could they actually have *arranged* it? Or did she just turn up and Lucy somehow knew. If so, how? Had Lucy seen me with Selina? How? Again there was no way of knowing. Unless she had followed me before ... or seen me out with Selina somewhere or ... what? The paranoia surged.

The real question, I told myself, was this: was their inten-

tion really for Madeleine to sleep with me at all? No. I did
not think so. Do half-sisters really accept (with a laugh and
a joke) the physical actuality of sexual revenge? Does one
sit happily back while (with a nudge and a wink) the other
makes love to the same man (so recently the treacherous
breaker of hearts) by way of getting even? Of course, venge-
ful conquests of men take place all the time – the I'll-show-
the-bastard-that-two-can-play-at-that-little-game one-night
stand with a hapless stranger at a random party, the just-you-
wait-to-hear-whether-I-am-over-it holiday romance . . . But,
in most instances, there is only one woman and two men –
the man she wants to hurt and the man she'll do the hurting
with. Rarely does it turn out the other way around. Rarely
are there two women and one man. And rarely are they
sisters.

OK, so let's grant them a special closeness, a real soul-
matey whoop-de-doop sorority. Let's grant inseparable sib-
lings against the world. Let's say two broken-home girls grow
up nursing an evil pair of grievances. What, then, do these
two do when they come across the epitome of all they most
dislike, distrust and disdain? Inflict agony upon the cheating,
lying bastard – yes. Cross, double-cross and triple-cross him;
tie ribbons with his nerves – yes. Lead him on, put him off,
lead him on, put him off, twist him around and around in
circles – yes and yes again. But get into bed and make love
to him over and over *until he's hardly able to walk*? What kind
of a punishment is that?

No. Madeleine was never meant to sleep with me at all.
She did so because – almost on the spur of the moment –
she decided she wanted to. Then she told Lucy that it was
only once or twice. But as our relationship deepened – or
carried on at least – she found that she had to go on lying
to her sister – about how often she was staying at my flat,

about how she was feeling, about what was really going on, about more or less everything. She found herself stranded in London for longer than she had anticipated; and she quite enjoyed the company while she had to wait. (Did she really have to wait? Was her flat really being worked on the whole time?) And somewhere in the middle of it all and quite by accident, she forgot to carry on hating me until, finally, the hour grew so late for her leaving that she could not put it off a minute longer.

And now, as well as everybody else, she was also lying to herself.

Or maybe not. Maybe I was wrong. Hecate has a heart of frozen venom and even were there man alive to melt it, he would be sure to die from the poison vapours. And perhaps unflinching intimacy was merely Madeleine's way of getting a good psychological run up for the final kick. In those parting moments, there was remorse in her eyes but not love. Or was there?

And round went my thoughts again. In the darkness.

Now, outside the window, the view is declaring itself. Most of the mist has returned to the river. And the oil heaters are at last doing their job; they gargle to themselves as if engaged in some weird alien conversation. In the stronger light, I return to 'Woman's Constancy'.

I don't like the letter 'N' as a rule – something to do with its austerity, I think, or its negative attitude: 'M's bony and resentful little brother. But I am proud of the work I have done to make this one sing:

> Now thou hast loved me one whole day,
> Tomorrow when thou leav'st, what wilt thou say?

I dread the thought that Madeleine has left belongings behind – in the bathroom, in the kitchen, in the bedroom. I fear the studio view. And I pray that my flat is not going to join the renegade troops of my memory.

If a woman says she doesn't want to see you again, do you take her at her word? Or do you dare to presume to know her better than she knows herself? Do you dare to claim to know what's best for both of you? And what, if anything, do you prove by crawling after her: that you love her, or that you're too weak and helpless and abject to deserve her love? And for whose benefit and happiness are you on your knees? Hers? Surely not. Truly love is three parts selfishness to every one part superstition.

But brave men and fools always go. Perhaps, we think, there is something sublime that we might say, some grand gesture that we might make, something that will cast everything in a new and clearer light, something that will change her mind . . .

As with all the versals, the design for the 'N' is entirely my own. I have three more strokes to make but I will have to wait a moment. If there is one thing a calligrapher needs above all else, it is a steady hand.

Then the work will be done.

I will check with the magnifying glass next week but I think I have managed: thirty poems and not a single mistake. There's something about 'Woman's Constancy', though.

29. A Valediction, Forbidding Mourning

Our two souls therefore, which are one,
Though I must go, endure not yet
A breach, but an expansion,
Like gold to airy thinness beat.

If they be two, they are two so
As stiff twin compasses are two,
Thy soul the fixed foot, makes no show
To move, but doth, if th' other do.

And though it in the centre sit,
Yet when the other far doth roam,
It leans and hearkens after it
And grows erect, as that comes home.

Such wilt thou be to me, who must
Like th'other foot, obliquely run;
Thy firmness makes my circle just,
And makes me end, where I begun.

I am returned to my lair and the good news is that my decisions have all been made for me. Not yet six in the morning and I am drinking tea and listening to the Mozart Missae Breves. There were no letters. And my telephone has been as silent as the rest of my furniture. Indeed, my flat isn't behaving as badly as I thought it might. And I am careful to cross over to the other side of the road when I see my memory heading my way. Also, it is impossible to feel bad in the company of Mozart.

Following my sojourn at William's, I newly discover myself a creature of the dawn. I go to bed at nine-thirty with John Donne and wake at five with my fellow London non-believers – the ironic joggers, the smirking, rough-gloved bin men and the calloused vegetable stallers, who shake their heads in incredulity and mutter at satirical parsnips. Dawn is promised. But we're not so easily persuaded: we will believe it when we see it. Cold, wet, bleak and dark: life, it seems, is one long satire on itself. *Gulliver's Travels* without the readership. Tomorrow is November and already the grim slouch towards Christmas has begun. Fat Mammon has kissed the runway tarmac and they've checked all the bulbs in the red streetlights.

But me, I'm going to New York. I am going to New York. Tomorrow.

I had no choice. I called Saul as soon as I got back and that was it.

'Where have you *been*, Jasper?' he said, asthmatic panic wheezing at the back of his voice. 'The whole of New York is sick with worry and anticipation. We thought you might have had an artistic tantrum or something. Disappeared to Tangiers in a fit of pique.'

'Anticipation?'

'For the opening.'

'The opening?'

'Oh Jasper Jasper Jasper *Jasper* – if only we could all communicate with you. If only, for heaven's sake, you would answer the phone or address yourself to the issue of voice mail. *Anything*.'

'I'm sorry, Saul, I've been out of London for a couple of weeks or so – finishing off. What do you mean, the –'

He interrupted. 'Well well, Jasper, then it falls to me to

tell you.' He paused for a moment; benign satisfaction hummed like background radiation in the receiver. 'The charming Mr Wesley, your client and mine, is throwing a very big and *very* exclusive party – for you and your work. A one-off opening night, a showing, an exhibition, an extravaganza – call it what you will. A happening. On November 1st. At none other than the Ruby Gallery in our very own East Village.'

'That sounds –'

'Cognoscenti, literati and intelligentsia expected in their droves. In their *droves*. A guest list that reads like the Who's Who of cultural America. Champagne in the glasses, glitter on the cheek and your work upon the wall. My dear boy, the whole thing will be one long and irresistible selling spree. You walk in an artist; you walk out a millionaire. Clients will be *queuing* all the way over to Fifth Avenue.'

'I'm not sure I –'

'You know what it's like here, Jasper, once a thing has been tagged as collectable, once an artist has been *recognized*, then every aspiring intellectual has got to have one of their works. They're chronically vulnerable to each other's opinions. Not an independent thought for three thousand miles. And right now if Gus Wesley says that callig—' Saul became suddenly and chillingly silent. 'You have finished, haven't you? There isn't a delay?'

I let it hang for a second just to enjoy the drama. 'Yes, of course. That's mainly what I was calling about.'

Pure relief flooded undiluted across the raging Atlantic. 'Oh, good man. Good man. Thank God for that. Thank God. And I wager they look absolutely fantastic. Really, I can't wait to see them.' He dropped a decibel or two. 'The thing is, Jasper, between you, me and the gatepost, I had lunch with Gus last week and I rather assured him that . . . Well, actually, I may have rather planted the exhibition idea – just a touch – and it would have been rather tricky to have to tell him that I –'

'Saul,' it was my turn to interrupt, 'I thought the work was a private gift – not for an exhibition or whatever?'

'Oh yes yes yes. That too. The whole thing is an exhibition cum birthday bash cum party cum presentation – but the point is that if Gus Wesley is there, then *everybody* is there. Obviously he pays all the important journalists' wages so coverage and photographs are guaranteed – but more than that, he knows all the right people. And I am sure that your work will look magnificent at the Ruby. I am already getting commissions for you merely on the strength of the rumours. How do you feel about the Sermon on the Mount? No – don't answer that – let's discuss. When do you expect the finished articles will be here?'

'Well, I'm seeing Gruber and Gruber tom—'

'Ah, they're the framers we used last time?'

'Yes. They're the best. I am seeing them tomorrow. It shouldn't take them more than two weeks. Then I guess they'll send them special courier. Wesley is OK with the framing and delivery tab – you cleared it with him?'

'Of course of course. Oh it's *so* exciting.' Saul had enough enthusiasm to power New York's electricity needs for a year. 'Oh, and Gus has asked me to promise that you will call him on his private line so that he can arrange your flight.'

'Well, I suppose that's it then.' The decision was made.

'You don't sound too thrilled.'

'Oh no no. I am.' I wrenched myself back to the conversation in hand. 'Honestly, I'm just worried about the work getting there OK and not being damaged and so on.'

'Mmm. I do know what you mean.'

'In fact, Saul, I want to wait until I am sure that you have them delivered safely. I don't really want to leave London until I am certain that they are with you. It's too risky with the party stuff going on. I'd feel a right fool if I got there and the poems didn't. In an emergency, I can always take them on the plane myself. I trust the Grubers but I don't trust couriers.'

'Wise. Very wise. I'm sure Gus will appreciate your concern.' Something like a diary was flicked open. 'Now you are also set to have lunch on the same day with me, and I take it you won't mind if I organize for some journalist friends to come with us. Nothing formal. But you know that a journalist can never resist a free lunch . . . Also, I would definitely make sure that you stay at least a week because Gus is in town and he will certainly want to see you personally – he'll cover the hotel, don't worry about that. And I sense, dear boy, that he may be good for more work, especially if he can hold up any of his friends' commissions by going straight to the head of the queue – I've promised him that – OK with you?'

'It's all OK with me, Saul. More than OK. And thanks for all of this. I really mean it.'

Saul chuckled. 'Least I can do for you, my boy, the very least. And can I also suggest you ring Grace – she's a little anxious about Christmas.'

'I will.'

But I cannot bring myself to ring my grandmother. So I am going to write her a letter from New York.

The framing, as it turned out, was a close call. I had to wait until yesterday – until I knew for sure that Donne had made it across the Atlantic. Which means that I have left it very late. I leave London tomorrow, early in the morning, and arrive in New York also in the morning, but the exhibition party – tomorrow night – will not begin until gone midnight by my body's clock. It will be a long day.

Oh yes: and I have an address.

Nathalie. Nathalie got it for me. She worked her magic on Lucy. More dishonesty, I'm afraid. (We are all of us, poor humankind, trapped in this double helix of deceit.) But at least Nathalie is cheery about it.

Since Saul called, therefore, I have written five separate letters. Two long, one short, one short with a two-page postscript, and one so long and wretched that even I couldn't read it.

My letters looked beautiful, no doubt, but writing when you're upset is like writing when you are drunk: it feels great at the time (profound even) and yet when you read it back in the morning – *my God*. Even at the most sober of times, words are hardly to be trusted – put two or three of them together and they immediately start revolting, conspiring unintended meanings here, fermenting duplicitous nuances there, and firing off in the wrong directions as and when they please. Of course, what I really would have liked to do was write her something so true, so moving, so elegant, so witty, so insightful, so fine, so direct and so oblique that she could not help but surrender – a poem, perhaps, or a whole cycle entitled 'Songs and Sonnets'. In the end, though, I found that I could not rely on words at all beyond carrying out their most basic tasks. So I settled for three lines – the postscript from my first effort:

Madeleine,

I am coming to New York for work. I'll be at William's opening night at the Carnegie on November 6th. Please come. I would like – at least – to talk.

Jasper.

Still I hated it. But I could not go on revising forever. And when, beneath filthy skies, I went into the shop to confiscate the video, I made Roy Junior write her address on my chosen envelope, that way, I reasoned, she wouldn't be able to recognize my hand and destroy my hard-fought efforts before she read them. She lives – *they* live? – on the Upper East side.

I didn't watch the video. I put it in the bottle bank on the way home before I could think, ensuring that it was impossible to retrieve. (Not that I have a video. Oh no, I have a DVD.) In any case, Roy Junior said that there was nothing to see except 'Just, like, you know, a bit of messing about.' His defence: that he too was 'just messing about' in the garden and saw them through her patio window 'totally by accident' and thought he had better get evidence because otherwise I wouldn't believe him. Which, in a way, was true: I would not have believed him. But, despite his voyeurism, I bear Roy Junior no ill-will: he will turn into his father soon enough. And you can't blame a guy for getting his kicks before that happens.

Lucy, I will not call. Not yet. Nathalie tells me she is back at work and has a new boyfriend ... I'll write to her from Rome over Christmas, I think, when I'm all straightened out. Then maybe we can see each other in the New Year. More than anything, I hope she is OK. I still feel the guilt, of course. (Of all the emotions guilt surely has the longest half-life. Except maybe love – but we'll see about that.) And I have not forgotten her kindness that night when the world was spinning: call me when it's over, she said. I will.

Now I detect that the light is thinning and here comes another Agnus Dei. I have switched off the side-lamp so that I can watch the dawn enter the garden. And sure enough, if I lean out and look further along the ledge, the leaves of my mint plant are slowly turning a silvery grey and there is a pale scar along the edges of the sky. Nothing is moving. But sooner or later a cat is bound to slip across the wet grass in the garden. And with just a little whispering, I can hear winter ushering itself into the orchestra pit. By this time tomorrow I will be on my way. To test a woman's constancy.

30. Woman's Constancy

Now thou hast loved me one whole day,
Tomorrow when thou leav'st, what wilt thou say?
Wilt thou then antedate some new made vow?
      Or say that now
We are not just those persons, which we were?
Or, that oaths made in reverential fear
Of love, and his wrath, any may forswear?
Or, as true deaths, true marriages untie,
So lovers' contracts, images of those,
Bind but till sleep, death's image, them unloose?
      Or, your own end to justify,
For having purposed change, and falsehood, you
Can have no way but falsehood to be true?
Vain lunatic, against these 'scapes I could
      Dispute, and conquer, if I would,
      Which I abstain to do,
For by tomorrow, I may think so too.

I took New York off of the 'red-eye' through JFK and a yellow cab driven by a Moroccan guy who wanted to know what the fuck the Chinese were doing when the Bible was written. I couldn't help him on that. But my question right back to him – had I been prescient enough to ask – would have been this: how the fuck does somewhere on the coast get so little fresh air? New York must be the only seaside town on earth that can be freezing cold and *still* feel grimy, fetid, dusty.

And man, could this city use some curves. Enough already with the intersections, the right angles, the blocks. How about some real corners and vistas and roads that wind. Enough function. Let's have some form around here. After lunch

with Saul and the journalists, I had to make my excuses and
go down to Chinatown *tout seul* – just because they have a
street down there which bends a little.

Today is November 2nd and I am staying in a minimalist
hotel off Times Square, somewhere up in the high forties
and around Eighth Avenue. Despite what the staff and the
other guests think, it's not cool at all – just minimal. Minimal
space. Minimal comfort.

Today I am the talk of the town. Or rather, I am mentioned
in a few gossip columns. And you're right: I'm feeling better.
A whole lot better. It's eleven-thirty and I have just enjoyed
a welcome breakfast of two sunnies with a side of tomatoes.
They still don't seem to have discovered baths here in Man-
hattan – so it will have to be a shower. After which I intend
to locate a writing desk and pen a letter to my grandmother.
I have a very happy surprise for her. And I'm sure she won't
mind if I practise my *Anglicana Formata*.

I guess there must have been about four hundred people in
the Ruby Gallery last night – something like that. The joke
(if that is the right word) is that the gallery is situated on
Avenue B – hence 'Rue B'. (I know, I know.) In fact, the
place was a converted warehouse, entered through a typically
nondescript New York door, which you might have passed
a thousand times with never so much as a squeak from your
East Village sneakers. My cab driver – not, I sensed, a loquaci-
ous man – had never heard of it and didn't give a fuck that
he hadn't. But, he suggested over his shoulder, 'There's a
whole bunch of people in coats just gotten out over the street,
dude. So I guess you should maybe follow them.'

Inside, there were two levels, both abounding in stripped
wooden floors and neutral walls. (Is it possible, I wonder, to
hold an exhibition consisting entirely of art gallery interiors

through the ages?) As far as spaces went – I was several times informed – the Ruby Gallery was as prime as anywhere in the world. If ever walls could become desirable, then these were they.

I tried, hopelessly, to forget about the Carnegie – whether or not she would come – and what I would do if she didn't. Instead, whenever I was introduced to anyone, I talked with proper attention and concentrated on what Saul had called the important business of winning business without being businesslike.

'Occasions like this,' he had said, 'you never know when you could be chatting to your livelihood. So it's better to assume that everybody you meet is a cheque book waiting to be opened.'

Around nine, those whom Saul had billed as the East Coast's most assiduous chatterati (and few people billed them more often than Saul) began to gather in the main room – a long gallery with a high-girdered ceiling and a smallish balcony at one end. They were waiting to hear whatever it was that their host, Gus Wesley, the billion-dollar man himself, had to say.

Saul had lied, of course: the exhibition was not just of my work – thank Christ. There were four of us. And the whole idea was that we were contemporary artists who declined to pander to the fashions of contemporary art. The other three – Candy, Ezra and Fred Donohue (he refused to be anything less) – were also standing in the long gallery, awkwardly corralled at the far end with me, and just off to one side of our host.

Wesley, meanwhile, was engrossed with one of his flunkeys, asking about champagne ('Make sure you got it ready to go, Henry') and the fire escapes ('It only opens inside out, Henry, so you gotta wedge it when you go out, right?') and how many place reservations have been made on his table for afterwards ('Gotta be more than twenty, Henry, I had already invited twenty, don't tell me it's any less, Henry, don't tell me that . . .')

I watched a lower level flunkey unfold a portable lectern. Then I let my eyes take in the room again. Donne was hanging along both of the long walls. People were still standing in attentive knots around them. The poems felt oddly distant and removed – no longer mine. But there was no denying it, they looked impressive: the austere starkness of the raven ink on the off-white parchment, the blood-red versals, the narrow rosewood frames. Also, for the first time, I saw that there was an unexpected drama in having them hung one after another: unlike reading them singly or even on consecutive pages of a book, they assumed a narrative on the wall that was more powerful, more lordly, more affecting, more resonant, more *abiding* than I had hitherto understood. Something, I thought, not unlike the Stations of the Cross.

Still, I felt vaguely specious to be standing up at the front with the other three. They each had their own exhibition room upstairs. And their work was art in its truest sense – paint and canvas. Plus it was for sale. Though flattered to be included, I was privately struggling to understand how Wesley might incorporate four-hundred-year-old poems written in a seven-hundred-year-old hand within even the broadest definition of contemporary art.

A third, middle-ranking, mop-haired flunkey tested the microphone. Then a woman, one of the gallery staff, stepped up from a group of people close by and stood behind the lectern. She tapped the microphone a second time. The room stilled.

Wesley left his arrangements man whispering into a

mobile phone by the fire exit behind us and took a moment
to summon his public persona.

The buzz turned itself down to a hum and the woman
spoke. 'Ladies and gentlemen – I guess we're all just about
in here now – I can see a few people still drifting in on the
balcony up there' – she raised her arm – 'so come on in,
come on in folks ... OK. So, I'll get right to it. He doesn't
really need any introduction from me, but anyway, it's my
job to introduce to you all our favourite benefactor ... and
tonight's host – Gus Wesley.'

There was a robust and professional round of applause.
Wesley gave one last grin in our direction on his way past.
Then he crossed to the lectern and began:

'Ladies and gentlemen, first off, thanks to you all for
coming in here tonight. Right now, I see a lot of familiar
faces and it's good to see 'em. Most of you I know and love
as friends ... and the rest of you I recognize and accept as
colleagues!'

Laughter – mostly, I suspected, from the colleague contingent.

'I wanna keep tonight relaxed and let people enjoy ...
This is a party after all. But first I do wanna talk just a little
about art, since that's one of the reasons we're all here.' He
paused, assuredly, and adjusted his stance to convey just a
little more gravitas and aggression.

'Ladies and gentlemen, I feel that the time has come for
us to reclaim serious art work – serious works of art – reclaim
them for mainstream culture.'

There was some clapping – less professional but more
spontaneous. Wesley continued with even more confidence:
'I, for one, am through with the concept. I'm through with
gesture. It's no longer thought-provoking and thought-
provoking is no longer good enough. Provocation is a poor

second to engagement.' He paused again. 'You know . . . in my humble opinion, the twentieth century was fatally attracted to horseshit. But that fatal attraction is now over.'

The crowd put down their drinks and began to clap whole-heartedly, partly because we were (in the main) gathered-together my-fellow-Americans, partly because Wesley paid our bills, but also partly because people felt the guy had a point.

Wesley, however, was just warming up. He nodded. 'I say again: we have for too long been fatally attracted to horseshit . . . in our politics, in our social programmes and – yeah – most of all in our art. But I also say the twenty-first century is gonna be different. From now on we're going to pay atten-tion to people who can actually do a thing like it's supposed to be done.'

Now there were whoops and cheers, especially from the journalists at the front, most of whom worked on his news-papers or thought or hoped or certainly didn't discount the idea that one day they might. Even the people on the balcony at the back joined in. I caught William's eye. He was leaning casually over the rails beside Nathalie. He gave me a royal wave.

Gus Wesley allowed himself a smile. 'So that is why I wanted to bring together four artists, all of whom, in different ways, represent what I like to call New Contemporary Art. Four artists whose work you have all seen tonight. And each of whom, in my humble opinion, is gifted and talented in real and measurable and endurable ways. Let me introduce them. First of all,' – he extended an arm in our direction – 'Candy Bukowski, whose portraits, I know, have already all sold tonight. There's not a single one left. You couldn't buy a Bukowski now, even if you had all the money in the world!'

There was more applause, some hooting and a few cries of 'Yeah – go Candy!'

Candy, who was standing next to me, blushed deeply – or rather, her freckles joined up.

Gus Wesley looked over again – a chat-show host with his special (but sensitive) guests: 'Candy, as you know, I love your work – we all do – but I just had to ask – why babies and old men side by side for this collection?'

Candy started to speak. But without the microphone, her voice sounded quiet and insignificant.

Wesley invited her up to the lectern. Bashfully, she went over.

I let my eyes drift again. Saul and his wife were right up at the front and they nodded and raised their glasses a fraction. I also recognized some of the journalists from lunch. Nathalie had her arm around William and I saw that Don had arrived with Cal.

My jet-lag came in waves. It occurred to me that there was no natural light or fresh air in the gallery, except for the unexpected and freezing draught that blew in from behind me whenever the fire exit door was momentarily opened by Wesley's assistant.

It was Ezra's turn to speak. He was from Belgrade. Nothing scared him. My mind drifted out of the gallery surrounds altogether and fell to fighting with itself somewhere far away.

Gus Wesley was speaking to me, or about me, or at me, or with me, or towards me, or maybe even through me . . .

'. . . And last of all, but by no means least – a personal indulgence which I wanted to include on the bill tonight. The man responsible for the beautiful manuscript copies of the work of John Donne, the great Renna-sonts poet, you have all seen and admired on these walls around you. Ladies and gentlemen, all the way from London, England – Jasper Jackson!'

Like the jet-lag, the applause also came in waves and I now found myself standing alone on a narrow isthmus out where the two tides met.

Wesley grinned. 'Jasper, there are so many questions that we all want to ask you, but right off I gotta say: where did you learn so beautiful a hand? I think that's the right word – "hand" – yeah?'

Fred Donohue backed out of the way and I took my cue, standing next to Wesley himself at the lectern. Unlike a lot of people you see in the papers or on television, he was still good-looking close up. Clean cut, fair-haired, he had the bearing of a famous actor cast as a charismatic politician. And there was no doubt from his manner that even at forty-two, he continued to consider himself an *enfant terrible*. But now I could also see where the perspiration was softening his collar, I could smell his aftershave turning thin and thread-bare in the over-used air, and I felt somehow immune to his spell.

The mop-headed flunkey popped up before us and swiv-elled the microphone towards me. I spoke automatically at first. 'Yes, that's the right word.' I looked out over the gath-ered heads. 'To be honest, I am just very lucky – I was taught by my grandmother . . . she's a keeper of medieval manu-scripts in Rome now. And she has always worked in the field. She tutored me. Right from when I was very young.' Slowly, I was waking up. 'But mostly it's about copying the masters over and over until you can do it on your own. Most of calligraphy is copying.'

The microphone was swivelled. Wesley addressed the room again: 'Well, I think they are truly beautiful works of art. And, you know, it's so rare for people whose day-to-day

life is words – like so many of us here – to actually get the
time or the opportunity to read and consider poetry – and
you have really brought these *Songs and Sonnets* to life for all
of us. I can only imagine how many hours you must have
lived them. And my second question is really to do with
that.' He looked over. 'What – with the benefit of the time
you have spent working on John Donne – what, in your
opinion, do you think the poems are about? What's the one
thing you learned?'

I thought for a moment. 'Well . . . I have to say that one
of the things that I have learnt is that Donne's work resolutely
resists simplistic –'

Wesley interrupted, catching the mop-head off-guard.
'Hey, come on – you gotta have a view. You English guys
you're always' – now the microphone was turned his way
and his voice was suddenly amplified again – 'hiding behind
ambiguity. Come on. Level with us.' Wesley grinned. 'Right
now – just today – what do you think – what do you *feel*
these poems are all about? We won't hold you to it.'

Laughter in the crowd. There was something combative
in Wesley's tone that pulled me up, out of the last of my
jet-lag. Loitering behind all the money and generosity was a
neighbourhood bully. At my back, the freezing air was blow-
ing again. I wished that Wesley's assistant would just keep
the bloody door shut instead of going in and out all the time.
I leant forward and fixed my eyes on the middle distance.
So let him have his answer, I thought.

'Well, Gus,' – using his first name somehow reduced him
– 'like everybody, I suppose, I came to the poems in ignorance. And I definitely believed they were love poems at first.'
I paused. 'But then . . . then I thought they were all about
the disappearance of God from human affairs; then I thought
they were about the collision of the mind and body; then I

thought they were all about the male psyche; then I thought they were about the hopeless divide of sex – both in the gender sense and in the sense of intercourse.' There was a low hum of amusement. 'And *then* I thought they were about all of those things at the same time – which they are.' I took a quiet breath. 'However – just a few weeks ago – when I was completing the work I had the opportunity to go through all the poems again for a final time. And I made an interesting discovery.'

Now I had the attention of the room. After Wesley's brash Chicago drawl, my voice sounded somehow soothing: 'When I re-read one of the early poems that I had begun with – a poem called "Confined Love" – it's over there' – I pointed – 'I came across a word that I did not understand. That word was "jointures".'

I quoted the lines from memory:

> Beasts do no jointures lose
> Though they new lovers choose . . .

I glanced up towards the balcony. 'On the face of it, Gus, "Confined Love" appears to be about a man complaining about not being allowed to be unfaithful. A man feeling trapped – confined – by the woman in his life – or by women more generally.' There were more murmurs of amusement, and a few counter-murmurs of light-hearted opposition. 'In any case, that's definitely what I took it to mean when I worked on the poem the first time. But I wasn't reading hard enough and I didn't know what "jointures" meant. So I looked it up in an old dictionary and discovered that it referred to' – I did a dictionary definitions voice – 'the estate settled to the wife for the period she survives her husband.'

I paused. 'This was quite a breakthrough for me. Because

understanding what "jointures" meant reversed the polarity of the whole poem. Instead of it being a poem about a *man* complaining about not being allowed to be unfaithful, it meant that the poem had to be delivered – narrated – by a woman. It meant that what the poem was really about was a *woman* complaining about not being able to be unfaithful. Because, in Elizabethan England, as part of an argument for greater – shall we say sexual flexibility? – only a woman would, or could, make the point that beasts do not lose their "jointures" if they choose new lovers. It would make no sense for a man to say that – to use that particular word.'

Some people at the front laughed. Saul was wide-eyed. I continued: 'Though written by Donne, the speaker of the poem, I realized, *had to be a woman.*' My hands felt hot but I was totally relaxed. 'So, anyway, once I realized that Donne's last trick – and, Gus, there are so many tricks in Donne – once I realized that Donne's final trick was that some of his poems were actually written as if spoken by a woman, I went through the whole lot again with an eagle eye ... which brought me to the last poem of the sequence that I completed for you. The poem over there at the back.'

I pointed. Heads turned. 'It's a poem called "Woman's Constancy". It's often thought of as something of a signature poem for Donne. And I do think that it gives us one of the best clues as to what his work is about.

'Again, on the first reading, "Woman's Constancy" looks like a piece of pure misogyny – a sarcastic title followed by seventeen lines of caustic grievance, delivered by a man with a cynical heart.'

I recited the first few lines:

Now that thou hast loved me one whole day,
Tomorrow when thou leav'st, what will thou say?
Wilt thou then antedate some new made vow?
        Or say that now
We are not just those persons, which we were?

I waited a moment. 'But hear what happens when you assume the narrator's voice to be a woman's.'

I spoke the lines again.

Now that thou hast loved me one whole day,
Tomorrow when thou leav'st, what will thou say?
Wilt thou then antedate some new made vow?
        Or say that now
We are not just those persons, which we were?

I was enjoying myself. '"Woman's Constancy" still makes perfect sense, of course. But now, delivered by a woman, the meaning is reversed entirely. Much in the same way as I discovered in "Confined Love". Now, instead of being a derisive poem about the transience of female fidelity, the work actually turns out to be an *assertion* of female constancy – and, in fact, the true target of the attack becomes men. In other words, the poem turns out to be precisely the opposite of what it first appears.'

I smiled. 'Amazingly, the poem works perfectly well in either voice – male or female – as I am sure Donne intended. But it is only with the lines newly illuminated by our female narrator that we can see into the very heart of *The Songs and Sonnets*. Yes indeed, "Woman's Constancy" *is* a signature poem, because here – more than anywhere else – constancy and inconstancy directly dispute. Not only that but they also depart, change sex and dispute again the other way round.

And I really think that no subject is more vitalizing to Donne. You can feel it: it is inconstancy that animates his soul.' I drew breath. 'And so, to answer your question, Gus, right now the subject that I think is at the heart of Donne's *Songs and Sonnets* is inconstancy. Inconstancy as animus. The inconstancy of women yes, but also, and at a deeper level, the inconstancy of men.' I stood back.

The applause was loud and rang hotly in my ears. I'm sure that they clapped because there was nothing else to do. But I felt applauded all the same.

Half a minute passed before Wesley could cut it short: 'Well . . . now . . . well now: there's my answer.' He held up his hand, palms out to the audience. 'Well now. Thank you so much for that. The inconstancy of men. Well, *there's* a thing.' He glanced over my shoulder towards his principal assistant and smiled. 'Thank you for that, Jasper.'

I stood away to let him have the lectern.

'Well folks, we learn something every day. But right now, there is just one more thing. I said earlier that Jasper's work has been a little indulgence of mine. And that's certainly true. I love John Donne and I have always wanted a collection. But there is another sense in which the poems are an indulgence. One of the reasons – and some of you know this – one of the reasons that I first commissioned these thirty beautiful works of art was because I kinda wanted to make a special gift of them to someone who is, in turn, very special to me. Someone who has – in the last few years – totally changed my life.

'I gotta confess. I got you here on a false pretence. Because, in fact, tonight is not just an art thing. Tonight is not just about hanging out. Tonight is also a surprise birthday party for the best and most beautiful woman in the world. All right! And we got champagne. And we got music. And we got more champagne!' Again, he glanced around past me; and this time he grinned.

'She came in a few moments ago, but ladies and gentlemen she didn't realize these were for her' – he indicated the poems – 'and I know' – now he had to raise his voice over the cheering and the applause – 'I know that you will all join me in wishing my future wife a very happy birthday.'

I turned.

Madeleine was looking right at me. Her eyes were wide with shock and something else I had not seen before. She bit her lip. The green sign above her head said 'Emergency Exit'.

Acknowledgements

My thanks go to Professor John Carey for a couple of richly informative Oxford afternoons. All the John Donne quotations I have used are taken from his excellent edition. Interested readers may like to know of his biography: *John Donne: Life, Mind and Art* – still, to my mind, the last word.

A cordial thanks also to Tony Curtis, Fellow of the Society of Scribes & Illuminators, for his kindness and assiduousness in helping me ensure that, for once, I knew what I was talking about.

I owe a tremendous debt to Bill Hamilton, my agent, for his belief and for his wise counsel over these past few years. And likewise to my editors: Christopher Potter for his acuity and well-judged suggestions with the early drafts; Catherine Blyth for her unbelievable concentration and formidable acumen when it came to the manuscript crunch.

I must also acknowledge the assistance and support of my sisters, Charlotte, Claudia and Adelaide, each of whom helped me in different ways at different stages in the writing.

I am grateful to Sophie for taking the trouble (all that time ago) and to Lucy for her candour. And here a deep and heartfelt thanks to Sue Ellis – surely the most intelligent and perceptive reader any writer could ever wish for.

A mention too for the unaccountably galvanizing spirit of the glorious M's: Antipodes, Wellington, Mr Pitt, Louis and even Lestopher – in such eloquent antipathy lies an important truth. Thanks as well to my friends in Rome: Daniel (the partisanship), Anthony (the knowledge), Gareth (the comedy) and Elizabeth (the insight). I am indebted to Lara for the fashion. Richard for his faith (and because there is always a way). Perry for the pies and sanctuary. And finally, to J.S. and B.D. – without whom nothing.